A Few Good Acres

A Few Good Acres

The Odyssey of Thomas Beaty and His Descendants in America

MARVIN T. BEATTY

iUniverse, Inc.
New York   Bloomington

iUniverse books may be ordered through booksellers or by contacting:

iUniverse
1663 Liberty Drive
Bloomington, IN 47403
www.iuniverse.com
1-800-Authors (1-800-288-4677)

Because of the dynamic nature of the Internet, any Web addresses or links contained in this book may have changed since publication and may no longer be valid. The views expressed in this work are solely those of the author and do not necessarily reflect the views of the publisher, and the publisher hereby disclaims any responsibility for them.

ISBN: 978-1-4401-4451-6 (sc)
ISBN: 978-1-4401-4452-3 (ebook)
ISBN: 978-1-4401-4453-0 (dj)

Printed in the United States of America

iUniverse rev. date: 6/10/2009

Cover photograph courtesy of The Wisconsin Historical Society.
All other photographs are by the author.
The author gratefully acknowledges these works of history:
Alfred Creigh, History of Washington County from Its First Settlement to the Present Time. Harrisburg, Pennsylvania: B. Singerly, 1871.
Boyd Crumrine, History of Washington County, Pennsylvania. Philadelphia: L. H. Everts & Co., 1882. The reference to Thomas Beatty is on page 475.
C. R. Harrington, editor, The Year without a Summer?: World Climate in 1816. Ottawa: Canadian Museum of Nature, 1992.
Malcolm J. Rohrbough, Days of Gold: The California Gold Rush and the American Nation. Berkeley: University of California Press, 1997.

Also by Marvin T. Beatty

Planning the Uses and Management of Land, editor, with Gary W. Petersen and Leslie D. Swindale

Soil Science at the University of Wisconsin–Madison: A History of the Department 1889–1989

To my hardy and intrepid ancestors: their struggles and accomplishments laid the foundation for this fictional story.

Contents

Acknowledgments

My sincere thanks to Laurel Yourke and members of the UW–Madison Division of Continuing Studies Advanced Writing Seminar. They guided and inspired me as I worked to create an interesting story from a few snippets of history. Equal thanks go to family members. Ellouise Beatty, my wife, was always available, always vigilant as she read copy, and always encouraging as she helped me create this story. Jenny Beatty, my daughter, did the hard work of helping to prepare the manuscript for publication. Colleen Pierce, my cousin, turned the motley array of pictures I gave her into images suitable for publication.

Chapter 1
Landing, Getting a Toehold

Thomas Beatty(sic) was a native of Ireland who emigrated (sic) to this country

—Boyd Crumrine, History of Washington County, Pennsylvania

The two Irish brothers sneaked up on deck at sunrise and studied the shores as the ship sailed up the Delaware River toward Philadelphia on a following wind. The morning sun created a vivid contrast between the smooth water of the broad river and the sunlit green trees on the banks. Occasional clearings with log buildings punctuated the line of trees; white smoke drifted up from the stone chimneys of a few. After months of seeing nothing but water, Tom and Will rejoiced at the sight of land and habitation.

"Don't that look beautiful, Will? All that land with them big trees. I can't wait to own some of it." Tom waved his arm toward the far shore. A broad smile lit his freckled face as the sunlight highlighted his mop of red hair. For the first time in three months, he was not seasick, and he felt wonderful.

"You can have your land. What I want is some friendly lasses. Especially one who'll have a penniless Irishman." Will, twenty-

1

two and fueled by testosterone, beamed as he thought about the possibility.

A flock of geese winged its way upriver, and Tom imagined how the land and water would look from their vantage point.

The brothers' reverie ended when the first mate burst out onto the deck and shouted, "Get yer sorry selves down below and swab out them cabins 'fore we dock, or ye'll get the lash instead of yer pay!" Tom and Will stole a last glance at the shore and hustled to work below.

As he wrung dirty water from a piece of rag and began to mop dried tobacco juice off the floor of a tiny cabin, Tom thought about how good it would feel to be on solid ground again. "Do ya suppose Ireland ever had trees like what we just saw? This has got to be good ground, to grow trees that big."

Will moved to clean a different section of floor and shook his head. "Dunno. Maybe there was trees back home a long time ago. But even if there was, they're gone, an' now the damn peat's coverin' everything." He rinsed the rag he was using. "'Tis a shame Pa an' Ma and our sisters had to stay behind in that miserable old place with the rent goin' up every year and the damned English shuttin' down the weavin'."

Tom looked up but kept mopping. "Pa and Ma probably wouldn't'a stood the trip across. If they'd'a come with us, they'd'a died and we'd'a had to toss 'em over the side, like they did all those other folk." He sighed and moved to clean a new corner of the cabin. "But we gotta send 'em some money, soon as we get a little ahead." They moved to the next cabin and surveyed its littered and dirty floor, then knelt to clean it. The ship was tied up at the dock in Philadelphia, the cultural and intellectual capital of the American colonies, when the first mate pronounced their work good enough to suit him. Tom was sure he had reached heaven when he and Will walked along the deck. He turned to his brother as they reached the gangplank.

"'Tis a miracle, Will, that we got on as cabin boys and that we're here at all. I was sure all of us'd be under the waves when them big storms hit this worn-out old tub last month." Will nodded a vigorous assent and stepped in behind Tom as they started down toward the dock.

As they disembarked, Tom staggered so close to the edges of the gangplank that Will grabbed his collar to keep him from falling into the moss-green water among the belly-up fish and horse manure. When he reached the dock, Tom knelt at the edge of the rough planking and kissed the hard-packed dirt. As he stood up, a dockhand glided down the plank, his right arm over his left shoulder, meaty fingers around the handle of a broad trunk that rode his sloping back like a bird riding a branch.

"How was the crossing, boy? Get used to them waves?"

"Tolerable, sir, except for them big storms out of Belfast. My brother and I sure prayed a lot then."

"That so? I'd'a guessed it was rough for you all the way. You look awful green and peaked." He slid the trunk to the planks in a motion as fluid as water. "Well, you'll soon feel better, now that you're in William Penn's city. So you come from Belfast?" Tom nodded. "Lotta folks coming from there lately. Got any friends or relations here?"

"Just my brother." Tom pointed at Will, the brawny red-haired and freckled young man who looked like his larger twin. "We aim to get land hereabouts and start farms, like the one our pa had once in County Fermanagh, but lots bigger."

"Then don't waste time stayin' 'round here. Go out to the frontier, where land's cheap. Lotsa yer Scotch-Irish kinfolk out there. All you need is a sharp ax, a musket, a strong back, a good wife, and luck." He spun on his heel and loped up the steep plank.

Tom ran his hand through his red hair, watching the sailor, and then searched for their tiny trunk in the field of humpbacked containers growing on the dock. When he found it, he lifted one end and tried to pull it up on his back, the way he'd seen the dockhands do, but he couldn't get it off the plank.

"Three months on that stinkin' old tub sure left me weak. I won't be any good at cuttin' trees for a few days, but that idea of goin' out to the frontier sure sounds fine. Let's head that way soon as we can."

"Not me!" Will's heavy eyebrows accentuated his scowl. "Remember what the captain said on the way across. There's Indians out there, thick as flies on a manure pile. An' they hate all the new settlers with a passion. A man has to farm with a musket by his side all the time. I'm fer stayin' right near here."

"Yer doing what I say. Pa and Ma put me in charge, told me to look after you. If I say we're goin' to the frontier, that's where we're going."

"You'll have to try and make me, an' that won't be easy. I'm a lot stronger'n you now, 'cause I wasn't sick all the time. Bet I weigh half a stone more'n you."

Tom appraised Will and decided to compromise. "Maybe you're bigger'n me, but you still gotta listen to what I say. An' right now, I'm starvin'. Let's get us a place to stay and some vittles. Help me carry this trunk." Will stared hard at Tom and then very slowly picked up one end.

They joined the crowd of pedestrians as they walked along Market Street with the small trunk between them, two immigrant Irish boys gawking at everything. "Sure's not like Belfast. These buildings aren't all black with soot. An' not a beggar in sight." Will's voice carried a note of awe. None of the folks walking with them paid any attention to the new arrivals.

"Watch out! There's a wagon behind us!" Tom dropped his end of the trunk and jumped toward the edge of the street, out of the way of a trotting team pulling a wagon and almost into the path of a carriage coming the other way. "Let's set a minute and rest."

Will dragged the trunk to the edge of the street. They sat on it and took in the scene. "Look at those big buildings. You s'pose this town's maybe big as London? An' the women here are sure pretty." Will's appreciative gaze followed a pair of young women who were walking arm in arm down the street, avoiding the carriages, wagons, and horse manure.

"Yeah, and it's so busy. All these folks with parcels, bundles, and sacks. Mmmm, that last one smelled like fresh bread. Makes me hungry all over."

They began walking again, looking for a place to stay and eat. Finally Tom spotted a possibility. "Here's a sign says bunk and board." It hung from the fence in front of a large two-story log house. They knocked tentatively. A few minutes later, the owner, Mrs. Catherine McLeod, a black-haired, tall woman who appeared to be about fifty, had shown them to a narrow bunk along the back wall of a dark upstairs room. Trunks, satchels, and deerskin clothing were scattered on the floor near other bunks. Sounds of pots banging, doors opening and closing, talk among the waiting men and the kitchen workers—*Jes' put that kettle of water in the fireplace!*—floated up the steep, narrow stairway as Tom and Will opened their trunk. As they spread their meager wardrobe on the bed to dry, they were startled by the clang of an iron gong and Mrs. McLeod's voice shouting, "Come an' get it!" When Tom and Will reached the dining room, men surrounded the sturdy plank table and jostled for seats on the log benches. Tom and Will squeezed in at the ends, sitting half on wood, half on air.

The furniture was sturdy, because the horde of hungry men would destroy anything smaller than thick planks as they attacked the bowls and platters of steaming food. A tall, black man stood in the doorway to the kitchen, arms crossed on his chest, and watched the venison, boiled cabbage, baked squash, potatoes, gravy, turnips, beans, bread, molasses, and butter disappear. Tom and Will reached in front of the men next to them to fill their plates. The abundance of food began to fill the hollow in Tom's soul as it filled his stomach. He couldn't remember ever eating all he wanted before. Back home, the table would have been bare when he was about half full, even though five of his brothers and sisters had died over the years, leaving fewer mouths to feed. Aboard the ship, the food had been abysmal, and he had always been seasick.

As their appetites diminished, the men resumed half-finished conversations and arguments that had been suspended in the face of the opportunity for food. A tall, rangy fellow who looked to be about twenty took another piece of venison and picked up his argument. "Like I was tellin' you, Joe, I can't stand all these newcomers crowding up the place." He reached far to his left and speared a potato, then picked up a pewter bowl and poured gravy on the potato and the meat. "There's way too many o' them Scots and Irish, and the English themselves comin' over." He talked as he ate. "Another shipload came in just today." He looked toward the newcomers at the end of the table and pointed his meat-filled fork in their direction. "If they keep comin', I've a mind to either shove 'em off the pier or head west to the Susquehanna myself." Tom and Will ate with heads down, peeking furtively at their accuser.

"John, if I was goin' to pull up stakes from here, I'd go even farther west." Joe, the brown-haired man beside the immigrant-hater, leaned forward as he spoke. He fished a goose-quill toothpick out of his pocket, pointed it down the table, and continued. "They say there's good country openin' up way out west, around Fort Duquesne. Only one road to there yet, an' some Injun trails. But I might just go."

The short, blond man across the table from Joe and John wiped his mouth with his shirtsleeve and shot the two speakers a hard look.

"You fellers get itchy feet too quick. There's a lot of opportunities right here. All these new folks comin' over need stuff. An' you don't have to keep watchin' your backside fer fear of getting an arrow in it, like you would out there."

"You're way too set in yer ways, David. The future's on the frontier." John's curt reply and sneer made David look down at his plate.

A slender, black-haired man with a brogue weighed in. "When I go, I'll head south. A lotta me clan's gone from here ta Carolina—the part with mountains, like back in Scotland. They say them mountains got lots of deer and turkeys, an' that tobacco 'n' wheat 'n' beans grow real good. Soon's I get a few more pounds an' shillings ahead, I'm gonna buy me a musket and ax, marry me a wife, and light out for as far as our money an' legs'll take us."

Tom and Will sat uneasily at the far end of the table. The black man in the doorway looked at them and smiled, the first spontaneous welcoming gesture they'd received since landing. The brothers glanced at each other and then smiled back tentatively.

Will leaned across the table and broached his fear in a whisper. "I think we oughtn't stay here more'n one night. That John seems pretty mean."

Tom kept his voice low. "Reckon maybe you're right. We'll move on tomorrow. I'll tell Mrs. McLeod soon as dinner's over."

He and Will sought out the proprietress as she washed dishes in the kitchen right after dinner. "Here's the rest of what we owe for our victuals and bunk, Mrs. McLeod. We're much obliged to ya for puttin' us up, but some of your regulars don't much like us."

Mrs. McLeod sized up the two young newcomers and smiled a welcome as she asked, "Where you plannin' to go?"

"Well, ma'am, we don't exactly know. Will wants to settle

somewhere close around here. I want to go out to the west. You got any advice?" Tom shifted from foot to foot.

Mrs. McLeod put her hands on the table and spoke emphatically. "You lads don't have to leave on account of that John and his talk. He always carries on like that whenever somebody new comes. Don't give him no back talk, and he'll treat you just fine in a few days. You're just like a lotta others that come from the old country. Been told it's better here, but don't know sic 'em about what it's really like."

Mrs. McLeod smoothed her apron and smiled. "You got honest faces. Stay here with us, an' I'll put you to work cutting winter wood. Then you can get your land legs and a few facts, so's you don't jump off the deep end and do somethin' foolish. Grub, a bunk, and two shillings a week between ya. Angus'll learn you to use an ax an' saw right quick. Want ta do that?"

Tom and Will exchanged dubious looks. Mrs. McLeod dispelled them quickly. "I don't make this offer to just anybody that comes off the boats, but we need winter wood cut. You'll have to learn to handle an ax an' saw from somebody, and Angus McDonald is one of the best. He's been out on the frontier and can tell ya what it's like out there. Got a good head on 'im. Now you just go right back upstairs and settle in. I'll tell Angus to sharpen two more axes. Be back here real quick, ready to go to work." Mrs. McLeod shooed the brothers upstairs before they could say a word.

As soon as their backs were turned, she dried her hands and went out to the backyard with its clutter of buildings. The outhouse was closest to the back door. Beyond it, four horses stood in a wood-fenced pen that adjoined a log shed. She headed for a log workshop and the grating sound of a grindstone rubbing against steel. When the man inside sharpening an ax stopped and looked up, she said, "Angus, sharpen up two more axes. I've hired two Irish lads to help you cut wood. Think they'll be good'uns."

"All right, Catherine. But they better have some Presbyterian ancestors from Scotland, not those damned Catholics who've been in Ireland so long the peat has rotted their brains. That last one was dumb as a post." Angus snorted and ran a finger along the ax he had been sharpening, nodded, put it down, and picked up another.

Tom and Will put on their caps and threadbare jackets, then

went to the backyard and peeked in the doorway of the log building that held saws, axes, chains, hooks, and other tools. Angus sat at the grindstone, his big, rough hands gripping an ax. He lifted it off the rotating stone and stopped pushing the foot treadles that turned it. "Hold out yer hands." He put his muscled and leathery right hand beside the boys' appendages, then shook his head. "Don't know what's come over that Catherine anymore. Hirin' on boys with no muscles and calluses an' expectin' me to get enough wood for winter with suchlike fer help. You boys are gonna have blisters, and then blisters on the blisters. Ya ready for that?"

Tom and Will nodded, then exchanged worried glances as Angus turned back to the grindstone. Life in Ireland had been tough. They had always been hungry, but they had been among family and friends. Everyone here was making it clear that they were on the bottom of the heap and had only each other.

Angus was as good as his word. The next morning at sunup, he led Tom, Will, and two other men, each carrying an ax, to a wooded knoll west of town. He showed them how to size up what direction a tree was inclined to fall, how to cut a notch low on that side of the trunk, and then how to open a bigger cut a little farther up the trunk on the opposite side and watch warily as the tree began to lean. Then he showed them how to make a few last cuts and jump back while the tree crashed to the ground. They ate supper at dusk with hands so raw that they could hardly hold their forks, and they fell into bed bone-tired.

It was three weeks before calluses outnumbered blisters on their hands. But they were determined to cut as many trees as the rest of the crew, as they learned the rudiments of how to work in the woods and began to understand a little of how to get along in a new land.

Angus reluctantly gave them Christmas Day off. After breakfast, Tom thought of home and family. He imagined his parents and sisters sitting around a peat fire and eating a meager breakfast, and he wished they could be here with him and Will. He borrowed paper and a quill pen from Mrs. McLeod and got a fellow boarder to help him write a letter to his father and mother. Mrs. McLeod watched as Tom struggled to address it. When she was satisfied that the address was complete, she watched Tom wrap a half-pound note in the paper before he sealed it with hot candle wax. "Your folks'll like that a lot. It's good of ya to send somethin'. I hope they got money to pay the postage when it gets there. What was it like for ya back in the old country?"

Tom hesitated; nobody had ever asked him such a question before. "Well, we were real poor. An' Pa spent most of the money he got workin' for Lord Waverly on drink. When I was real little, Pa had a parcel of land of his own, an' we ate fairly good. But Pa got behind on his payments, an' that thievin' Lord Waverly took title to the land. 'Twas a cryin' shame what he done to us. Gave us a hovel to live in that was little more'n a cave, an' next to no peat to cook with. All we got was the nubbins of his potato crop, an' a few old turnips, an' cabbage that was mostly rotten. We like to've starved. An' my brothers an' sisters died—five of 'em in all. Only Will an' me an' two sisters was left." Tom wiped his eyes after the torrent of words.

"Over here, at least you can eat good ... an' send a little somethin' home. You've put on a lot of muscle since you got here." Mrs. McLeod smiled approvingly. "Has Angus told you much about things he saw when he was out in the west?"

"Enough to make me want to get out there quick as I can." Tom's voice regained its ring of determination. "I want to get there an' get a few good acres o' my own. But my brother kinda likes it here. He's more easygoin' than me."

Mrs. McLeod thought a minute. "Well, I'm all for families sticking together. You never know when you're gonna need each other. I'll talk to the both of you sometime an' see if I can be of any help."

Mrs. McLeod hurried to the kitchen to supervise the cook. Tom put aside the letter for mailing and then smeared goose grease on the seams of his boots to keep them from leaking. As he rubbed the grease into the leather, he thought about his life back in Ireland and how different it was from life here in Pennsylvania. The day off was nice, but Tom looked forward to the tough physical work of cutting trees, trimming off their limbs, and chopping the trunks into pieces that would fit Mrs. McLeod's fireplaces. The day passed quickly, as did those of the rest of the winter. Tom and Will got stronger and more adept with their axes, and they took pride in their developing skills as woodsmen.

* * *

On a sunny day in early spring, the brothers took a brief break from work. "We've been choppin' wood for Mrs. McLeod for quite a spell now, and it sure isn't getting us much nearer to getting our own land." Tom put his callused hands on the top of the ax handle, leaned down, and took a deep breath. "Someway we got to get ourselves out to the west and try our luck there. You ready to go with me?"

Will leaned his ax against a tree and sat down on a log. "I'm thinkin' we should stay here. We're eatin' real good, the work's not too bad, an' I've met a few nice, lively lasses. Maybe now that we're better at workin' in the woods, Mrs. McLeod would pay us more if we asked."

"Guess we could ask her." Tom picked up his ax and began chopping limbs off the tree he'd just cut down. Will nodded and followed his lead.

That evening, the brothers sought out Mrs. McLeod. "Ma'am, we'd like to talk to you, if you don't mind." Tom looked at Will and then turned back to Mrs. McLeod. "We like working for you, all right, but I'd like to get to the west an' get land. Will wants to stay here. Could you give us some advice?"

"Well, first thing you should know is not to split up. If somethin' happens, you'll need each other. So whatever you do, stick together."

Will looked Mrs. McLeod in the eye and smiled. "We're wonderin'—could you possibly pay us a little more, now that we're experienced in cuttin' trees an' can cut a lot more in a day?"

"I'd like to, but it's cheaper to hire new help and let them learn from Angus. There's a lot of 'em comin' off the boats for me to choose from." Tom's face fell, and Will shook his head in disgust and walked away. Mrs. McLeod, eager to end the encounter, stood up. "Well, I gotta make sure the dishes are all washed an' ready for breakfast. Remember, now—you two stick together, whatever you do."

Tom picked up a worn book and sat down by a candle, dreaming of the frontier as he practiced his reading. Will stalked down the street to a tavern, hoping to drown his disappointment and maybe meet a friendly barmaid.

Chapter 2
Toward the Frontier

As their second summer of working for Angus and Catherine progressed, Tom's restlessness to move west increased. On a hot day in early July, Angus walked into the woods where Tom and Will had been working, to see how much firewood they had cut and piled during the winter and spring. Tom mopped the sweat off his brow and asked Angus the best way to get to the west. Angus looked at the enormous pile of oak logs, all cut and trimmed to the same length, and spat some tobacco juice before he replied, "You two Irishmen are real good workers, and I'd hate to lose you, but if you're so all fired eager to get to the frontier, you should just walk to the mouth of the Susquehanna and hope you can get hired on, helpin' to pole a barge up the river. That way you'll get paid while you're getting farther west. Beyond the river, yer on your own." Tom was ready to go the next day; Will finally agreed, reluctantly, to go along.

Most roads across Pennsylvania to the western frontier ended at the Susquehanna River in the 1770s. To the west, the rows of valleys and ridges that curved like a series of green rainbows across the land were cut only by trails, originally made by the aboriginal residents and appropriated warily by the European settlers. Commerce flowed up and down the rivers, and settlements had developed on their banks. Gristmills and sawmills had sprouted where the river had enough drop to turn a water wheel. Small iron smelters, called forges, had been built near deposits of iron ore.

A fellow boarder helped Tom and Will write a letter to their parents. They enclosed a one-pound note with it. Then they traded their trunk and the rest of their money for an old musket, put their spare clothes in sacks, said good-bye to Mrs. McLeod and their fellow boarders, and set out on foot downriver along the northwest bank of the Delaware.

The road was just two parallel ruts, but the brothers made good time, except in muddy spots, always keeping a sharp lookout for animals and strangers who looked unfriendly. At midday, they stopped to eat part of the food that Mrs. McLeod had given them—loaves of bread and boiled venison. By nightfall, they had reached a roadhouse and talked the proprietor into letting them sleep on a pile of hay in the stable in exchange for loading horse manure onto a cart.

The second night found them fifty miles from Philadelphia in a wide plain where the Susquehanna emptied into Chesapeake Bay. Tom and Will walked among the barges tied up to the wharfs and the sailing ships docked nearby. They watched a ferry leave with travelers headed for Baltimore and points south. Everywhere they went, they asked for work.

After two days, a barge loaded with lumber came downriver near sunset and tied up to a wharf. A bearded, muscular man limped from the barge onto the shore and asked loudly, "Who's ready to bend his back and earn a few shillings unloadin' these boards?"

The two brothers maneuvered to the front of the group and yelled, "We are! And we'll work hard!"

The bearded man looked at their hands and faces closely. "Be here at sunup, ready to go to work. I'll pay ye each two shillins a day."

They slept on the ground near the wharf, ate the last of the bread and venison, and were in line before sunup to put planks on their shoulders and tote them to a pile that grew on the wharf. The barge captain stood by, overseeing. When the new recruits had nearly finished the transfer, he held up a large, hairy arm for attention and addressed the group.

"All right. I'll need 'bout six a ye ta help reload the barge with barrels o' salt, sugar, rum, and suchlike when the lumber's all on shore. An' if ye want, ye can stay on an' help pole the big, old beast up the river. I'm gonna pick the best workers from among ye." He walked in front of the sweating men, pointing to those he wanted. When he came to Tom, he pointed and said, "You!" He hesitated when he came to Will.

Tom spoke up. "We go together. Both or nothing." The captain still wasn't convinced.

"I'll make sure he does his part of the work." Tom's voice carried more assurance than he really felt.

"All right. Guess I'll take ye both." He moved on, selecting men to augment his crew.

The next morning, they started poling the barge upriver against the current. The cargo was loaded near the center of the deck, so that narrow walkways remained on each side. Two men went to the front corners of the barge, each carrying a long pole, poked them into the riverbed, and then heaved on them to start the barge upstream against the current. When the barge moved a little, they walked toward the back, pushing all the way. As soon as there was room, two other men stepped in behind them, planted their poles, and pushed. They worked like two lines of ants hauling leaf fragments to their nest. By the time the first two men got to the back, pulled out their poles, and walked forward to repeat the process, the rest of the crew was behind them, each straining on a pole as he walked.

The river was running nearly bank-full, sweeping along occasional trees and brush as it flowed though a gently rolling plain. That night, when they stopped and tied up to trees along the bank, Tom climbed out and walked around, looking at the land and asking locals how much it cost. When he returned to the barge, he told Will what he had learned.

"We got here too late to be able to buy any of this good ground. Wish we'd'a been born sooner an' come 'bout twenty years ago. Then we coulda maybe got some farms hereabouts."

"Don't worry 'bout it, Tom. There's more land for you out west." Will resumed the card game he and some other boatmen were playing in the twilight. By the time darkness fell, all of the boatmen were asleep on the deck.

As the crew struggled to pole the barge upstream, they kept

a sharp lookout for trees that were floating downstream or were underwater but still anchored to the bank. When they spotted one, the crew took care to maneuver around it. But on the third day out, at a bend of the river, a tall, floating maple they hadn't seen rolled onto the port side of the barge and threatened to capsize it.

"Everybody get ready to jump off and swim for shore if she tips any more!" The captain's command caught everyone's attention.

"But I can't swim!" Will shouted.

"Neither can I!" another man yelled.

The crew clung to the railing on the top edge of the tilting barge as the water swept them and the mostly submerged tree downstream. Tom let go of the railing, took his pole, and eased his way around their load of barrels and down the steeply inclined deck to its lower edge, where big tree limbs had caught and were pulling it under the water. With his pole, he gave the biggest limb a mighty shove and saw it slide a little toward the edge. He slipped, barely avoiding going overboard. Once back on his feet, he set his pole against the limb again and pushed with all his strength. It slid a few more inches. On the third push, it went back into the water, and the barge righted itself ever so slightly. By then, the rest of the crew had joined him and were pushing on several of the smaller limbs. Their combined efforts finally slid the tree off and into the water.

When the barge floated free and level in the middle of the river, moving downstream with the current, the captain and another crew member scrambled to the handles of the sweep oars fore and aft and rowed it toward the bank, where the river was shallow enough for the workers' poles to reach the bottom. When they were getting under way, the men congratulated Tom for his efforts as they resumed their routine of walking, front to back, along the edges of the deck, poles set against the bottom, pushing the barge upstream. The captain slipped a five-pound note into Tom's hand as they met.

"You done right good work, young fella. Saved us all from a swim and kept the cargo from goin' overboard."

"Thank you, sir. Anybody coulda done it."

They settled into a grueling routine of poling the barge from sunup to sundown and tying it up to a couple of trees along the riverbank overnight. Most evenings, they fell asleep on deck soon after eating the hearty supper the cook laid out. Will was too tired to spin any yarns of life in northern Ireland, even though his fellow crew members begged him to. Tom watched the land along the riverbanks as he worked, appraising its potential for farming as best he could. The level areas were already occupied and partly cleared of trees. When he learned of the cost of these farms, Tom resolved to get west to the real frontier as soon as he could.

"Not much farther. The captain says we're gonna land around the next bend at Harris's Ford." Will passed the word to Tom when they met, walking the deck.

"Can't be too soon for me! My hands an' arms have just about given out." Tom's words came in spurts as he heaved on the pole, then lifted it, walked forward, reset it on the riverbed, and pushed. "I could eat a horse, I'm so hungry."

"Same for me. Bet my muscles'll be sore till fall. An' I could sleep a week straight." Will took a deep breath and looked upriver as he walked forward with his pole, ready to set it again and push. "There's some buildings around the bend. Looks like a sawmill."

When the crew had poled the barge to the wharf, made it fast, and unloaded it, the brothers gathered their extra clothes and musket and went to the captain.

"You two done real good. 'Specially you." The muscular, swarthy man pointed to Tom as he spit a brown stream at a skinny dog that had come onto the wharf. "Git outta here. Now git, ye damn thievin' cur! Hear me?" He turned back to Will and Tom. "You're more'n welcome to crew back down with me if ye want to. I like men who know how to work and use their heads in a tight spot."

"We're much obliged, sir, but Will an' me plan to stay hereabouts. So just give us our pay. Know anybody who needs some hands?"

The captain augmented his cud of tobacco and thought a minute. "I'm takin' on another load o' lumber for a guy named John Rea. He might need men. Ever used an ax an' saw?"

"Yes, sir!" Tom's response came almost before the captain had finished the question. "We cut trees out of Philadelphia. Learned to use an ax an' a saw real good. That's what got us in shape to pole your big, old barge."

"Well, if yer sure that's what ye want, here's yer pay. Rea's that big man over beside that pile o' lumber. I'll vouch for ye both." The two brothers took the money and looked at each other, elated.

John Rea needed more men who knew how to work in the woods. He was selling as much lumber as his laborers could cut, saw, and get on the wharf. Some of it went to build Baltimore and Philadelphia; more of it went to Europe.

"John, I got a couple o' good, young lads here who say they know how to cut down trees. Ya want to hire 'em?" The captain pointed to Tom and Will and kicked at the stray dog as he spoke.

John Rea looked the two up and down. They were clearly brothers, even though one was larger and more muscular. "Ya ever done any work in the woods?"

"We cut trees for 'most two years for a woman who runs a boardin' house in Philadelphia, sir. We're real good workers."

The captain chimed in. "On the way up here, this smaller one saved the whole lot of us from capsizin' when a tree hit the barge. Got a good head on 'im, he has. T'other one's full of stories and yarns. He works hard too."

Rea nodded. "I'll give you each five shillings a week and keep. Take yer stuff to the bunkhouse, an' be ready to start workin' right after dinner." He pointed toward a long log building that stood back from the river a quarter mile.

Tom felt closer to his goal. He and Will learned to cut bigger trees and to get along with a new group of men. Harris's Ford, where they'd landed, wasn't exactly on the frontier anymore, but it was far from being a city. Now he had to figure out how to get some land and work for himself.

* * *

As they cut and sawed trees, Tom and Will learned, sometimes from personal experience, sometimes from the stories of tragedies that were told in the bunkhouse, how to avoid getting hurt. They learned more about how to predict which way a tree was inclined to fall, how to get out of the way when it did, and how to avoid cutting themselves as they worked. They grew more confident of their judgment year by year; perhaps they were too confident at times. In the middle of their second winter working for Rea, they were cutting trees in a stand of large white oaks when Tom surveyed a tree that Will was about to cut.

"Take a close look over your head before you cut the notch. One o' those limbs looks like it could be a widow-maker." Tom directed Will's gaze up the oak tree to a limb that was rotted near its middle. "A snag like that killed that German fella last year."

"It's fine, Tom. If I hear it crack, I'll step lively and get out of the way." Will drew back his ax and swung. He glanced up and then swung again and again. The notch deepened with each swing. "See, it's fine. Couple more swings, and I'll be done."

They heard the crack as the limb broke in the middle. Tom yelled and saw Will slip as he tried to jump sideways. Then the limb smacked Will's head. Blood spurted from his nose and temple as he crumpled into the snow.

"Will, Will! Oh, Will, don't die." Tom took his brother's limp hands and stared at the crimson stream as it advanced into the crystalline snow. "Will, can you hear me?" He ran his left hand under Will's bloody cap and put his fingertips on the remnant of curly, red hair that was diminishing ahead of the advancing front of blood. "Oh, Will, it's my fault. I promised Pa and Ma that I'd look out for you, and I didn't." Tom lifted his hand and stared at his bloody fingertips. Then he bent close to his brother's broken face and put his hand on Will's head.

Will's eyes fluttered open briefly, and he whispered, "Tom, it's up to you now." Tom held his brother in his arms until Will's breaths rattled to an uneven stop.

Tom felt numb and reacted entirely from instinct as he leaped to his feet and ran, yelling, toward the other men in the woods. Minutes later, he dashed back with three men behind him, put his hand on Will's wrist, and felt the chill. As the men helped to lift Will's limp body, one of them kicked the frozen ground and said, "It's gonna be real tough digging a grave."

They burned logs on the gravesite to thaw the soil. Even so, two of the strongest men on John Rea's crew had to use picks and shovels on the frozen ground all day before they got the hole deep enough. Tom asked Mr. Rea for boards to build the coffin. As he sawed and hammered the box for his brother, Tom's thoughts went back over their life together.

They'd been the first and third sons in a family of nine children, five of whom had died before age ten. When the chance to work for a few pence and passage to the colonies came, Tom had jumped at it. His father insisted that Will go with him, and it had finally been arranged, and Tom had welcomed the company of his jolly brother. The boys promised to send money back as soon as they got a little ahead, and they'd been true to their word. They'd even talked about buying passage for a sister. Now the dream was shattered, and Tom had to arrange to send home sad news. Will had always been his parents' favorite, the fun-loving child who could make them smile and laugh, even in grim circumstances. Tom hammered in a square nail so hard that he split the board and had to saw another. He'd never felt so alone and desolate.

***

The procession left the log church and moved toward the open grave a hundred yards away, next to the woods. Six men carried the coffin on their shoulders as they walked behind the preacher, with Tom walking numbly in a daze behind the pallbearers. Tom, the preacher, and a few other men stood in silence as the pallbearers set the coffin on three ropes, lowered it into the open hole, and pulled the ropes free.

The preacher stepped to the grave and raised his arm. "Man that is born of a woman hath but a short time to live and is full of misery. He cometh up and is cut down like a flower. He fleeth as it were a shadow and never continueth in one stay."

Tom had heard those words before. At services for his brothers and sisters back in County Fermanagh, their impact had been softened by the presence of his family. Now they hit him like a fist in the stomach. He stood rigid, blinked several times, and then shut his eyes. *I'm alone,* he thought. *O God, forgive me the bad stuff I did to Will.*

"For as much as it hath pleased almighty God of his great mercy to take unto himself the soul of our dear brother William Beaty, here departed, we therefore commit his body to the ground, earth

19

to earth, ashes to ashes, dust to dust, in sure and certain hope of the resurrection to eternal life, through our lord, Jesus Christ, who shall change our vile body that it may be like unto his glorious body, according to the mighty working, whereby he is able to subdue all things to himself. Amen."

Tom wiped his nose with his coat sleeve, snuffled and swallowed, and dabbed at his eyes. The preacher handed his bible to one of the pallbearers, picked up two frozen clods, and dropped them on the coffin. The thuds reverberated in the winter air. Then he looked at Tom, motioned toward a shovel, and stepped back from the graveside. The cold of the shovel handle raced through Tom's mittens, up his arms, and into his chest, but he pushed the shovel into the pile of clods, blinked back tears, and tipped its load onto the coffin. They sounded like rocks as they banged on the lid. John Rea and two other men picked up shovels and joined him. When they finished, the mound over the grave was above their knees. It wouldn't settle until the spring thaw.

"I'm mighty sorry, Tom." John Rea put a hand on Tom's shoulder. "Will was a good worker, and he really livened up the bunkhouse with his banter and stories. We'll all miss him. Anything I can do to help?"

Tom looked at his employer, wiped his nose, and said, "Well, Mr. Rea, there's one thing. I've got to let Pa and Ma know the bad news, but I can't write anything much but my name. You know anybody who could help me?"

John rubbed his beard. "Well, I'll bet Margaret could. She just come back from gettin' some schoolin' in Baltimore. Never thought it would be any use havin' a girl who could read 'n write, but it don't seem to hurt none, long as she don't forget how to spin an' sew an' cook. Come over to the house after a while."

"Thank you very much, sir. You've been very kind. I'll clean up a little and come by." Tom buttoned up his coat and walked slowly, head down, toward the bunkhouse. He walked even more slowly toward the Reas' house an hour later.

A plump, round-faced woman answered his hesitant knock. "Come right in. John said you'd probably be coming for some help." Elizabeth Rea smiled at the sturdy, somber, red-haired young man in the doorway. "Hang your coat and cap on that hook. I'll call Margaret. She was feelin' poorly this morning, but she said she'd be glad to help."

Tom stood by the fireplace and marveled at the size of the house and the abundance of its furnishings. He'd never been in a single-family home that had more than two rooms before, or one with anything but log tables and benches. This one had four rooms, furniture made from boards that had been planed and fitted, and white curtains at the windows. Mrs. Rea reappeared, followed by an open-faced, sturdily built young woman with lively hazel eyes, light brown hair, and a warm smile. "This is our daughter, Margaret, Mr. Beaty. She learned to read and write when she was with our kin back in Maryland. Margaret, this is Tom Beaty."

"I'm pleased to meet you, Mr. Beaty. And I'm very sorry about your brother." Margaret curtsied and smiled.

"I'm honored to meet you, Miss Rea." Tom bowed and tried to smile but couldn't. "It's mighty kind of you to help me. I need to let my family know what happened."

They sat a long time at the table near the fireplace, writing the letter. Margaret wanted to know about Tom's family, how he and Will had gotten to Pennsylvania, and what he would do now. When she had written Tom's bleak news, she gave the sheet to him and watched as he slowly inscribed the letters *T H O M A S* across the bottom. Then she watched him take a little lock of red hair and a five-pound note out of his pocket and fold the page around them. "Could I send some money too? Let me get it before you wax it shut, Tom. May I call you Tom?"

"Why, I guess so. Sure, Miss Rea ... Margaret. That'd really be a big help to my family. Thank you."

Margaret went to the back of the house, returned with a pound note, and put it alongside Tom's inside the letter. "You and Will must have worked a long time to save that much. I know Father doesn't pay his men a lot."

"We saved all our money an' sent some once before, to help Pa and Ma buy back some of the sheep they sold to pay part of Will's passage. We both earned the rest of our fares by working. The money'll help, but they'll be awful sad. Will was their favorite, always so jolly and carefree." Tom stood up and moved toward his coat and cap.

"Well, Margaret," he said, "I'm sure much obliged to you for the writin', and puttin' in your money for my family. Time for me to go back, I guess."

"It's near supper time, Tom. Why don't you stay and eat with us? You'll be awful sad back in the bunkhouse without Will. I'll tell Mother and my sisters to set another place." She smiled, and this time Tom came close to smiling back. Margaret had liked Tom as soon as they met. Perhaps it was his obvious deep grief for his brother's death, or perhaps it was because she sensed that she needed a husband after that lively night she'd spent with a black-haired man a week or so before in Baltimore.

As Margaret went to the kitchen, Tom's gaze took in her curved waist and lively step. *Sure would be nice to get to know her better,* he thought. *Wonder how?*

Margaret arranged to sit by Tom at dinner, and she drew him out with questions about his family back in Ireland, the trip to the colony of Pennsylvania, and his just-buried brother. Tom found her interest a welcome diversion from his grief. Even though he refused the glass of whiskey her father offered, he enthralled the whole Rea family with his responses to her questions. He told them of a dirt-poor life after his father lost their tiny farm and took to drink. They wiped away tears as he described the deaths of one sibling after another in the damp Irish winters, when they didn't have enough money for a peat fire to warm a corner of their house. And they rejoiced when he described his family's enthusiasm when a chance came for him and Will to sail as cabin boys on a rickety old ship from Belfast bound for Philadelphia.

When Tom finally left to return to the bunkhouse, his grief had been tempered a little by excitement. Margaret saw him to the door and kissed his cheek as he put on his coat. He was too shy and flustered to return the gesture, but as soon as he was out the door, he'd wished he'd done so. Did she like him, or was she just being friendly to her father's hired hand? He pondered the possibilities as he walked through the snow.

Chapter 3
Wife, Family, Feeling Restless

Tom and Margaret began to cross paths frequently in the days right after the funeral. Margaret made sure to be where she knew Tom would be walking, and she always smiled her best smile and greeted him warmly. If no one else was around, she'd give him a hug and tell him she hoped he was feeling better. Tom began to reciprocate her obvious interest in him, and very soon they were taking long walks together along the river. Soon those walks ended with a long kiss and a tight embrace.

On a mild Sunday morning in late winter, the tall, thin, blond preacher finished reading the Gospel, looked out at the congregation in the log church, and announced, "I publish the banns of marriage between Mr. Thomas Beaty and Miss Margaret Rea. If any of you know cause or just impediment why these two persons should not be joined together in holy matrimony, you are to declare it. This is the first time of asking."

The interval of silence seemed to last a lifetime. Tom, sitting next to Margaret with the Rea family, was terrified that someone would speak; Margaret knew that nobody would dare to. For Tom, it seemed like an eternity before the preacher resumed the service. The announcement was repeated the following week, and again Tom waited with dread for someone to speak up with an objection.

The following Sunday, the congregation was enlarged by most of

John Rea's crew of loggers and mill hands. They'd dressed in their best buckskin shirts and pants, and a few had washed their hair and trimmed their beards. For some, the inside of the log building was a new sight. They gawked at the pulpit, the altar, the communion rail, and the cross high on the front wall. The preacher pronounced the banns for the third time, and at the end of the service, he summoned Tom and Margaret to come forward. They stepped toward the preacher together, each feeling awkward in front of so many people and in their unaccustomed new clothes. Tom wore, for the first time in his life, a wool suit that John Rea had arranged to buy for him. Margaret wore the same white silk dress that her mother had been married in. Its fitted waist emphasized the curves of her young figure.

"Dearly beloved, we are gathered together here in the sight of God, and in the face of this congregation, to join together this man and this woman in holy matrimony, which is an honorable estate, instituted of God in the time of man's innocency, signifying unto us the mystical union that is betwixt Christ and his Church."

Margaret stole a glance at Tom, thinking, *Wonder if he's scared too? He kinda looks it.*

The preacher looked at Tom and Margaret sternly. "Marriage is commended of Christ and Saint Paul to be honorable among all men, and therefore is not by any to be enterprised nor taken to hand unadvisedly, lightly, or wantonly, to satisfy man's carnal lusts and appetites, but reverently, discreetly, advisedly, soberly, and in the fear of God, duly considering the causes for which matrimony was ordained. First, it was ordained for the procreation of children, to be brought up in the fear of the lord, and to the praise of his holy name."

As she stood beside Tom at the front of the church, Margaret remembered the queasiness she'd felt some recent mornings and knew that they'd meet that requirement.

"Secondly, it was ordained for a remedy against sin, and to avoid fornication, that such persons as have not the gift of continency might marry and keep themselves undefiled members of Christ's body."

Tom thought of the recent nights he and Margaret had bundled in the bed from which her sister had been displaced. *Good thing we're gettin' hitched. Maggie and I sure got on the same side of the bundling board right quick.*

"Thirdly, it was ordained for the mutual society, help, and comfort, that the one ought to have the other, both in prosperity and adversity. Into which holy estate these two persons present come now to be joined. Therefore, if any man can shew any just cause why they may not lawfully be joined together, let him now speak, or else hereafter forever hold his peace."

The preacher waited. Tom's heart pounded. Then he looked at Margaret and saw calmness in her eyes. His heartbeat subsided.

Finally the preacher turned to Tom and Margaret. "Wilt thou have this woman to thy wedded wife, to live together after God's ordinance in the holy estate of matrimony? Wilt thou love her, comfort her, honor and keep her, in sickness and in health, and, forsaking all others, keep thee only unto her, so long as ye both shall live?"

Tom's "I will" echoed off the walls and the low ceiling of the church. The two words surprised him.

"Wilt thou have this man to thy wedded husband, to live together after God's ordinance in the holy estate of matrimony? Wilt thou obey him and serve him, love, honor, and keep him, in sickness and in health, and, forsaking all others, keep thee only unto him, so long as ye both shall live?"

The preacher fixed Margaret with a severe scowl. It didn't deter her. Looking at Tom, not at the preacher, she announced, "I will!"

Tom fished a little gold ring from his pocket and handed it to the preacher, who blessed it and handed it back. Margaret lifted her hand, and Tom slid it on her finger, giving her hand a little squeeze as he did so.

"Forasmuch as Thomas and Margaret have consented together in holy wedlock, and have witnessed the same before God and this company, and thereto have pledged their troth each to the other, and have declared the same by giving and receiving of a ring, and by joining of hands, I pronounce that they be man and wife together, in the name of the Father, and of the Son, and of the Holy Ghost. Amen."

The preacher motioned for the couple to kneel, and he raised his right arm over them. "O merciful Lord and Heavenly Father, by whose gracious gift mankind is increased, we beseech thee, assist with thy blessing these two persons, that they may both be fruitful in procreation of children, and also live together so long in godly love and honesty, that they may see their children Christianly and virtuously brought up, to thy praise and honor, through Jesus Christ, our lord. Amen." Tom's body relaxed as the tension drained ever so slightly.

The pastor lowered his arm and motioned for Tom and Margaret to rise and face the congregation. They joined hands as they turned. Mr. and Mrs. Rea stepped forward to congratulate them, smiling.

"Welcome to the family, Tom. You won't be alone from now on." John Rea put out a muscular hand.

Tom put his callused one on John's and matched his new father-in-law's grip. "Thank you, sir. I'm proud to be a part of the Rea clan. Sure feels good to have family again. I'll try to do well by Maggie, sir, and make you both proud of me."

"You and Margaret will do just fine. She's kinda high-spirited, but I 'spect you'll learn to keep her on the straight and narrow."

"I'll surely try, sir." Tom looked at his new bride, who was laughing at something one of the mill hands had told her. "She's lively, like Will was. I'm gonna like that."

After the newlyweds had received the best wishes of the assembled men and women, Margaret touched Tom's arm. "Don't you think we ought to mosey on over to see our new cabin? Those men you been workin' with don't look like they'll wait too long before they surprise us with a housewarming." The two slipped out as the members of the congregation continued to visit. As the new couple began to settle into their new abode, a combination of excitement and apprehension fueled their minds and actions. They had barely changed from their wedding clothes into everyday apparel when visitors arrived and the clang of a stick of wood hitting a metal pan banished the silence of the night around the new cabin. The cacophony of a dozen more makeshift percussion instruments followed. Shouts filled the air as several hands banged on Tom and Margaret's door.

"Put out your latchstring. We want to come in!"

When Tom lifted the latch, a throng of people surged in. Those who weren't able to crowd in celebrated outside. Women, mostly young, had bowls of applesauce, blackberry preserves, peach preserves, and pitchers of cider. Three men each held a corncob-stoppered jug in a curled finger. As the calls of congratulations and friendly jibes echoed around Tom and Maggie and wooden bowls of venison and the fruit sauces were being set on the split-log table, the men with jugs eased themselves to a corner of the cabin. Once there, they pulled out the stoppers, lifted the jugs on the crooks of their arms, and let some of the contents flow into their mouths. Other men moved toward them like iron filings to a magnet. The drinkers passed the containers to the newcomers with admonitions to "go easy—leave some for the rest of us."

Tom thought of his father and gave the drinking men a disdainful look as he stepped outside to greet the well-wishers. When he'd gone, Margaret sidled slowly to the corner where the jugs were circulating.

"Have a little nip to wet your whistle, Maggie. It'll help you enjoy your wedding night." A tall man with a scar over his left eye proffered a jug.

Margaret glanced to see that Tom was outside. "Don't mind if I do, Zach. Make this yourself?" Margaret took the jug, tipped it quickly to her lips, took a couple swallows, wiped her lips with the back of her hand, and passed it back.

"Yes, ma'am. The best I've ever run off, if I say so myself. How's it taste to ya?" The scar curved upward as the man's face framed the question.

"Right good. Much obliged." She eased through the crowded room and out the door to join the group around Tom. One guest produced a harmonica, and another uncased a fiddle. The newlyweds and guests danced, laughed, talked, ate, and drank with abandon. But Tom made sure he drank soft cider and water, not whiskey.

The moon was far past its zenith when the last of the self-invited guests left and Tom and Maggie were free to slip under the new quilt her mother had given them. The late hour seemed to add zeal to their newly legitimized passion. Maggie gave a joyous yelp as she felt Tom enter, and she reached down to pull him in. "This sure beats havin' to be so quiet in my bedroom at home these last days," she said. Tom's thoughts seemed to dissolve into pure action.

Tom showed up for the tree-cutting crew the next morning after only two hours of sleep. His ax swings lacked oomph, as did those of some of his colleagues, but he worked until quitting time. He and Maggie thrilled as her profile began to thicken a few weeks after the wedding. Her pregnancy added to their enjoyment of each other's bodies when Tom came back from work in the woods. The spring and summer passed like magic for the newlyweds.

"It's a boy, Mr. Beaty. From the way he bawled when I washed him off, he'll be a sturdy'un. Maggie's holdin' 'im and helpin' 'im suck his first meal." Mary, the midwife, looked satisfied with herself as she stood in front of Tom, drying her hands on her apron.

"Good to hear they're both strong. Can I go in and see 'em?"

"If you're just dyin' to. I've still got a lot of cleanin' up to do. Since you're goin' in, bring that big pan of afterbirth when you come back out. I'm ready to sit down and have a pot o' tea." Mary tipped the kettle that hung on a swivel hook over the fire and poured steaming water into a pewter cup. "Where ya keep the tea?" Tom pointed to a wooden box on the mantel and went into the bedroom.

"Take a look at your new son, Tom. He sure came into the world with good lungs and a big thirst." Margaret pulled the newborn from her breast and lifted him toward Tom's outstretched hands. The black-haired baby with light almond skin began to cry as soon as Tom's big hands curved around him.

Tom looked intently at the boy and made shushing sounds. "We still gonna name him John, like we talked about?" The baby wailed louder, so Tom handed him back to Margaret, who helped him reattach his mouth to her nipple and resume his meal.

"I reckon that's just fine. It's a name's been in my family a long time. May as well keep it goin'."

Tom nodded his approval and glanced around the room until his gaze encountered the big, metal pan of afterbirth beside the bed. "How you feelin'? Things sure went a lot faster than I was expecting. I didn't even have time to tell your folks the baby was coming."

"Really pretty good. I was fearin' a long ordeal, but he just slid out a couple hours after Mary came to help. Reckon I'll be on my feet by noon. You go over and tell Pa and Ma, while Mary's still here to look after us." Maggie ran her right hand over the thick, black hair of her nursing son. Tom picked up the bloody pan, carried it to the hog pen, and tossed its contents over the fence to the knot of omnivorous pigs that were squealing on the other side. Then he walked jauntily along the path toward the Rea house near the sawmill.

"You've got a grandson, and he sure arrived with a thirst." Tom's news brought beams from John and Elizabeth.

Elizabeth's first concern was for her daughter. "How's Margaret doin'? Should I go and give her a hand right now?"

"She had a purty easy time. Says she'll be up by noon. Mary's gonna stay the day. So come and see young John and his ma when you're free."

Elizabeth brought a pot of tea and three cups, and sat down, smiling at Tom. "Has he got red hair like you?"

"No, he's real dark-complected. Lot of black hair. Doesn't look like me—or like Maggie, as far as I could tell."

Elizabeth and John Rea exchanged quick glances. "My father had sort of dark hair, before the damn Injuns cut it off along with his scalp. Back in '42, I think it was." John Rea's face clouded as he remembered his father's disfigured head with its welter of scars.

Elizabeth poured more tea for her husband and Tom, then put on her bonnet. "You men sit and talk. I'm goin' to see Maggie and my new grandson."

After she left, John Rea said, "Tom, I need to talk with you about the sawmill. Old Sam showed up drunk again yesterday and let one of the mill hands get hurt in a belt. He was pretty good as foreman when he was sober, but I had to tell him to move on. I'd be mighty pleased if you'd take over. It'd help us both. I'll run the mill today, but I've got to take care of the work in the woods and selling the lumber real soon."

Tom listened but didn't say anything. He liked working outdoors in the woods.

John continued, "A foreman earns about twice what I've been payin' you. You're a hard worker, and you know how we do things. It would be good for both of us if you'd take over the mill."

Tom's expression softened. "I figured the drink would get old Sam one of these days. I've got my heart set on gettin' some land o' my own and goin' farming soon's I can, but I'll take over the sawmill for now."

John looked relieved. "You can start tomorrow."

"I'll do that. And I'll try to do a good job." Tom finished his tea and walked home, whistling as he went. When he arrived, Maggie was cooking dinner and using one foot to rock the baby in the cradle Tom had built.

"Good news! I'm going to be in charge of the sawmill, starting tomorrow. No more cutting trees, at least for a while. I'll kinda miss that."

Margaret stopped stirring a pot of porridge and beamed. "That's great, Tom. I worry about you when you're out in the woods every day. That's how your brother got killed. An' there's been three more since him."

The next morning, Tom was at the sawmill before any of the other mill hands. They were wary of him at first, but over time, they came to like his leadership. They discovered that he was dependable and, unlike the previous foreman, worked alongside them wherever it helped most. When a piece of equipment broke, he did whatever it took to get things working smoothly again.

* * *

Almost before Tom realized it, two years had passed and another son arrived. This one had red hair and looked like Tom from day one. They named him Thomas Junior. James, their third son, arrived a year later. Two years after James's arrival, they had a daughter and named her Catherine. Young John doted on his new sister.

Margaret marveled at how different her oldest son was from his younger brothers and sister. John was dark, headstrong, and restless. His black eyebrows and hair and his almond skin reminded her of the black-haired man with the high cheekbones, heavy eyebrows, and charming manners with whom she'd shared a night in Baltimore just before she came home. Tom Jr., James, and Catherine resembled their father so much that she could look at their red hair and freckles and see her husband. They were as quiet and obedient as John was headstrong.

Year by year, Tom and Margaret had more children, and the cabin grew crowded. Tom, with help from some of John Rea's men, built on a room and then a second. The lumber business and sawmill grew and prospered as the war between England and her American colonies got under way.

But Tom was fascinated by stories that men returning from the west told of the expanding immigrant settlements there, as the Indians lost battles with the new settlers and with diseases they had never before encountered. The few survivors retreated westward. The stories of a big river that flowed west and south, away from the ocean he'd crossed, made the western country seem exotic. Travelers who made the long journey from the east brought word of war with the British and a declaration of independence by the Second Continental Congress.

As that war dragged on and more men joined the Pennsylvania militia, John Rea had trouble finding enough able-bodied men for his lumbering operation. He traveled east and south looking for workers, leaving Tom to keep things running in the woods and the sawmill. Tom managed both, even though he was more and more anxious to strike out on his own.

When the war ended and word came that the proprietors of the Commonwealth of Pennsylvania had lowered the selling price of their land, Tom made his decision, and he told Maggie at supper. "Alex Wiley and me are figurin' to go out west an' see about getting ourselves some land, now that the price's come way down." He watched her expression closely. She didn't stop rocking the cradle that held their second daughter, Elizabeth.

"I'm not surprised. You've been talking about it as long as I've known you, so just be sure we got plenty of firewood handy before you take off. If I need help, I'll ask my father. When you reckon you'll be leavin'?"

"Soon as we line up somebody to run the sawmill while I'm gone. Prob'ly in two, three days."

John Rea was furious when Tom told him of his plan. "You're plumb crazy to go chasin' off to the west like that, lookin' for land! All you need to do is stay here and keep runnin' the mill like you have, and I'll make you a partner. Don't throw that chance away."

"That's mighty nice of you, sir, but I came over to this country to get land o' my own, and I aim to go lookin' for some, now that the price is down an' I got a little money ahead."

John Rea looked his son-in-law right in the eye. "From what I hear, it's mighty chancy out on the frontier. There's lots more Injuns than we see around here, and some o' that country is claimed by Virginia. So maybe what they're sellin' as Pennsylvania land is really Virginia's. If that's true, an' you buy it, you'll be up the crick without a paddle."

Tom stared back and spoke without faltering. "I know it's risky, sir, but I'm gonna go take a look. I like bein' where everything's all new and growin'."

His father-in-law shook his head. "Have you thought how tough life will be for Margaret and the young'uns out there on the frontier?"

"Yes, sir. Maggie and I talked it over. She's ready to go with me if I can buy a few good acres." Tom's assertion conveyed more confidence than he actually felt.

"Well, go ahead, if you're both dead set on it. But remember, you're throwing away a good thing here for somethin' real chancy."

"I'll take that chance, sir, an' Margaret's ready to go with me."

Chapter 4
Claiming His Own Land

"Let's give it one more try before we give up." Tom flipped a pancake in the skillet he was holding over an open fire. "Old Man Patterson said that about three miles up along the middle fork of this crick, there's a big chunk of unclaimed land from the creek bottom all the way up the east side of the valley and over the ridge. If we're lucky, we can get pieces that join." Tom shivered a little in the crisp air, though he took heart from the sun shining through the red, yellow, and orange leaves of the trees around their campsite.

He and his friend Alex Wiley, a fellow employee of John Rea, were camped in the north end of the Appalachian Mountains about thirty miles southwest of Fort Duquesne. They'd slept just inside the rail fence surrounding Patterson's mill. As they ate pancakes and fried salt pork beside the open fire, moving from time to time to keep the smoke out of their eyes, one of Patterson's employees opened the gate to the water flume, and the repetitive clunk and splash of the waterwheel that powered the mill added a rhythmic note to their breakfast. Both men were tired after walking and looking for land for three weeks. Home was 250 miles away, over the mountains—at least a ten-day hike. Alex nodded his head, with its prematurely whitening hair, and began shifting his belongings into his pack.

The two friends walked along the trail beside the Middle Fork of Cross Creek up through an open valley between high, forested

33

ridges northeast of Patterson's gristmill. Dew glistened on the grass and wildflowers. It seemed to Tom that the goldenrod reflected every ray of the morning sun straight into his eyes. He knew he could walk forty miles on a day this nice. They crossed the creek by jumping from stone to stone. When they reached the low cutbank on the far side, Tom filled his hand with soil, ran it through his fingers, and smelled it. "This is good dirt, Alex. Oughta grow real good crops. A lot better'n all those places we looked at back east of the Monongahela."

Alex looked at the soil in Tom's hand and then at the woods on the long, steep slopes. "These trees are sure are big and healthy. Bigger than any we saw on all those places we looked at before. That's a good sign for sure." The aroma of wood smoke wafted toward them as they passed two log cabins in small clearings surrounded by split-rail fences. After they'd walked about two miles through the forest, they came to a larger homestead. The log cabin and barn sat beside a two-story log blockhouse large enough to shelter thirty or forty people.

"Well, look at that. Guess there really are Injuns round here." Tom's eyes widened as he looked at the tall structure with its rows of narrow slits from which defenders could shoot at anyone outside.

Then he remembered something they'd learned from the gristmill owner. "This must be Charlie Reynolds's place. Remember, Patterson said that's where they'd built a blockhouse where all the folks in the valley could come if the Indians started any trouble."

Alex gave the big building an appraising look. "A place like that'd be mighty handy if the Injuns do start any trouble."

A pair of hounds ran out, bellowing a cacophony of howls; the two men beat a retreat up along the creek. As they ran, Tom said, "If we move out here, we'll have to get on Reynolds's good side right off. Maggie'll feel better about comin' way out here if she knows there's a safe place to get away from the Injuns." They walked fast, keeping a sharp lookout.

"How much farther to that land, Tom?"

"I think it's right at the upper end of Reynolds's land. Should be just a few hundred yards or so up the creek."

The men put down their packs at the corner of Reynolds's pasture fence and, as Patterson had advised them, looked for a tree with a slice of bark slashed from the trunk about eye height, and found it on a young oak.

"Now we'll have to start lookin' for the next blaze, Alex. From what Patterson said, this unclaimed land goes straight up the hill, angles along the ridge, goes over the other side to a creek, and then comes back over the top again off to the north. Guess we'll just have to walk slow and keep our eyes peeled for more blazes like this one." Alex nodded, pulled a hand ax from his pack, and hung it from his belt. Tom pulled some jerky from his pack and picked up his musket. "Looks like climbing this young mountain and findin' all the corners may be a long job. Let's take somethin' besides tobacco to chaw on." He handed Alex a piece of jerky and kept one himself as they started up the hill through the woods, studying the trees for a hatchet blaze.

The line of marked trees led them southeast to the ridge top. Tom and Alex followed it down the other side to another small creek, where they discovered the ashes of a small campfire with a cluster of freshly worked flint flakes beside it. They loaded their muskets.

"Injuns! Not too long ago." Alex's whisper broke the silence. "Sure hope they're not watchin' us."

They stood a long time without moving, scanning every opening. Finally, satisfied that no Indians were there, they resumed their search for blazed trees. They found the irregular line that turned back up over the high ridge and meandered down the long slope to the Middle Fork of Cross Creek, upstream from where they'd left their packs.

"Looks like this chunk of forest's already marked out for us. Must be the only one around not claimed." Tom looked up and down the creek as he put down his musket.

"Reckon you're right. Wonder if somebody claimed it and then pulled up stakes and left? Didn't Patterson say somethin' about some folks bein' here years ago but then moving on?" Alex wiped his face with the broad sleeve of his buckskin shirt.

"If they were here, they sure didn't leave much trace. No trees cut. Just the blazes on the edges—no trail, no nothin'." Tom looked up the long, wooded slope and scratched his head. "It's steep. But most all the land we've looked at out here is steep. These oaks an' chestnuts are real big, so the ground under 'em must be strong—'specially down along the crick. Looks like it's all ours to claim and divide. What part would you take, Alex?"

"I liked the part from here to the ridge top." Alex pointed toward the top of the long, steep slope. "Would you want the other side?"

"No, I like this side best, too."

Steep cropland on the farm Thomas Beaty
purchased from the Proprietors of the
Commonwealth of Pennsylvania in 1795

After a moment, Alex picked up a smooth stone from the creek, scratched a cross on one side with his knife, and said, "Let's use this. I'll toss it, an' you pick the side you want."

Tom nodded. As the stone was spinning in the air, he said, "I'll take the cross."

They bent over the stone. It landed cross up. Tom smiled, and Alex said, "Looks like you won. Shall we divide it at the ridgeline, you on this side, me t'other?"

"Sounds good to me." Tom put out his hand, and Alex gave it a hearty squeeze. Tom looked down the narrow valley beside the creek.

"I'm sure Maggie'll like to be near that blockhouse." They lay down on the bank of the creek and slaked their thirst with cool water.

Tom wiped his chin. He felt like a king as he sat on the grassy bank and looked up and down the valley. "You know, Alex, I never thought I'd see this day. This here's a hundred times more land than my pa and ma ever dreamed a person like me could have. What they farmed was a few acres of rocks and turf somebody else owned. Nary a tree. Their little hovel was just stone and thatch. There's trees enough here, a body could build a thousand cabins and still have plenty left." He sat for a long time, looking at the creek and inhaling the smells from the trees and fall flowers. Finally he tossed a small stick into the stream and watched it turn this way and that as it began its journey. "Did you know, the water in this little creek don't wind up in the same ocean that we sailed on to get here from Ireland? They say it goes into a big river to the west of here, an' down that river to some Spanish city named New Awlins or somethin' like that." He watched the stick glide round the bend. "When I left Ireland, I sure never thought I'd wind up way out here. This is paradise."

Alex paced back and forth along the creek bank and finally said, "We better cut a few trees where we want to build our cabins. Then folks'll know somebody's claimed this ground. It'd be a shame to have some claim jumper come and take it while we're back gettin' our families." Tom nodded but didn't move. Alex stood, ax in hand. "We gotta get a move on if we're gonna leave today."

"Yep, you're right. I just have think back a little. Sure wish Will was alive to be here." Tom ran the back of his hand across his eyes as he picked up his ax.

Alex was already walking into the woods. "When we start back, we oughta leave word at Reynolds's and Patterson's that we aim to take up this land. That way they can head off anybody else who shows up lookin' to claim it."

Tom nodded and began to look for a cabin site. "I s'pose right over here would be where we oughta start cuttin'." He gave a maple a careful look to see which way it would fall, swung his ax, and cut chip after chip until a third of the trunk was cut away. Then he moved to the other side, opened a gash a few inches higher, and kept widening and deepening it until the tree fell into an opening between two oaks. Alex matched him swing for swing on an oak thirty feet away. After they'd felled eight trees and tugged four of them into a rough rectangle where the cabin would be, they walked over the ridge to a gentle slope beside a spring and cut several more for Alex Wiley's cabin site. When they'd lined out the framework for a cabin, they walked back over the ridge and started down along the creek as the sun moved toward the hill on the west side of the valley.

Tom spat tobacco juice as he walked. "Tomorrow, on our way back home, we gotta go to the county courthouse in Washington—see how soon we can get us land warrants."

Alex nodded. "Yep. Sure hope Pennsylvania and Virginia have quit fightin' over which state this land's in. An' I hope my moccasins hold out and I don't go lame. It's at least ten days hard walkin' back to home."

Tom looked down at his own deerskin moccasins and saw a tiny hole in the front of the left one. "Mine don't look too good either."

The next morning, after a ten-mile walk to the Washington County Courthouse, the two men discovered that it might be several years before they could get warrants and patents for the land, but they were delighted when the clerk suggested that they should occupy and start developing it as soon as they could, so they'd have priority claims.

"We'll be back to finish building cabins real early next spring." Tom's announcement defined their resolve. The clerk wished them well as they left.

* * *

Early the next summer, a team of oxen plodded up a rutted, narrow track along the Middle Fork of Cross Creek, straining as they pulled a canvas-topped wagon. A muscular, red-haired man wearing deerskin pants and shirt walked on their left, urging them along with prods from the pole he carried and guiding them with shouts of "Gee!" and "Haw!" A woman sat on a wooden bench at the front of the wagon, holding a baby. Two small boys and a girl wiggled beside her. Behind the wagon, a dark-complexioned boy rode a bay mare, driving a skinny black and red cow and four sheep: a ram and three ewes.

As the procession passed a log-rail fenced clearing that contained a house, a barn, and a two-story blockhouse, several children and two hounds burst out the door and ran to the fence, waving, barking, and shouting greetings. Tom was thrilled to be so near their destination, and he was heartened to see activity at the Reynolds homestead. He waved to Reynolds, who was splitting wood, and yelled, "Howdy, neighbors!" as his procession jounced up the rough, rutted track.

Reynolds waved and called a greeting, but Tom and his entourage were already bouncing on up the trail. They were almost at the end of their journey, and Tom felt like he was approaching the gates of heaven. When they had gone another half mile and their land came into view, he watched Margaret's face as she surveyed the small cabin of newly peeled logs. "Well, Maggie, what do ya think? Will it hold all of us?"

The cabin stood in a clearing on the east bank of the creek, amid a profusion of stumps and piles of brush. A small area enclosed by a split-rail fence showed the bluish-green of young cabbage, along with some small flax plants. Margaret's face betrayed only a fraction of her apprehension. Almost no land was cleared and planted. *What will we eat in the winter?* she thought. *Will the neighbors help us when we need it? What about a midwife?*

She put on a brave face and said, "Well, it's sure at the end of the road. Guess it's all ours to make into something we can live in. At least it's something we can call our own, or it will be when you pay for it and get the patent."

"Are there b'ars in the woods, Pa?" Seven-year-old John got off the horse and scanned the forest beyond the cabin as he walked around the wagon and moved close to his father. Tom Jr., Catherine, and James looked around timidly as they climbed down over the wagon wheel and ran to him.

"I reckon there may be, son. But we'll take care they don't hurt you or any of the family. I'll kill us some so's we can have their skins for the floor. We'll kill some wolves too."

"How 'bout Injuns? They hereabouts?" asked John as he looked over the tiny clearing.

"There's some, but they say there's not so many anymore. Remember that big blockhouse we just passed? We can go down there to be safe if we ever need to." Tom squeezed his son's shoulder. Then he leaned the guide pole on the yoke between the two panting oxen, as he always did when he wanted them to stay. It was hardly necessary. They had pulled the loaded wagon 250 miles over the mountains from Harris's Ford on the Susquehanna to Cross Creek over the past three weeks and had no inclination to move farther.

"Let's see what it looks like inside." John, feeling the need to lead, motioned his siblings to follow as he ran toward the new log house. The roots and rocks didn't even register on their callused bare feet—feet that had walked behind the wagon most of the way.

Margaret handed year-old Elizabeth to her husband, then climbed down and looked around. "Looks like we better get the boys pullin' weeds in that garden patch you planted before you came back to get us." She lifted the front of her skirt just enough for it to clear the ground and marched toward their new home. "John, Junior, James, get me some kindlin'. We need a fire."

The cabin was about sixteen by twenty-four feet, all one room, with a fireplace at one end that Tom had constructed from brown sandstone he'd dug out of the hill to the east. Pieces of flat sandstone formed a hearth. The rest of the floor was dirt. The door was in the middle of the west wall, to give easy access to the creek. The one window, a square opening in the logs that could be closed by a wood shutter, was opposite it. The cracks between the logs were not chinked.

Tom, Margaret, and the three older children all worked from daylight to dark after they arrived. A month later, the garden was weed-free and twice as large. Clumps of corn, beans, and squash peeked from between the roots and stumps. Green shoots of rye grew between other stumps. The cow and horse were tethered on long picket ropes as they grazed along the grassy creek bank. The sheep were inside a split-rail fence that enclosed an acre or so of ground on each side of the creek. Two hens, a rooster, and a bevy of chicks clucked and cheeped as they gathered insects around the yard. Four logs, notched and peeled, were laid out in a rectangle. They were surrounded by several dozen loose, freshly peeled logs and piles of bark and wood chips. The thunk of an ax striking wood reverberated down from the long slope to the east of the cabin. It was followed by the sound of a tree falling, then by Tom's voice guiding the ox team.

On the day of the barn raising, Tom had been up since before daylight, tending the animals and eating breakfast. "Get them axes and hooks, boys. Put 'em beside the logs for the barn. Then drive the ox team in from the pasture, so's I can yoke 'em up. The Wellses and the Wileys'll be here any time now to help us raise it, and I want us to be ready." John, Tom Jr., and James nodded and started on the tasks. By the time the oxen were yoked and the tools assembled, the neighbors began to arrive, bringing their own axes, augers, and adzes, and accompanied by their own dogs.

Beside the cabin, Margaret tended a fire under a large iron pot that hung from a short chain attached to the apex of a triangle formed by three stout, green poles. When the water in the pot boiled, she dropped in large pieces of buffalo meat from a young bull that Tom had shot. A Dutch oven sat warming in the edge of the fire to bake the cornbread she had prepared. Half a dozen dogs ran about, barking and exploring. The children played tag among them and the visitors.

The walls of the barn took shape as log after log was pulled up a pair of sloping poles by the oxen, then held by two men in the place it would occupy in the barn wall. Two other men measured and cut notches where the log would cross other logs at the corners of the emerging barn, then the four workers set the notched log into place. They'd done this before, so they used their adzes and broadaxes like scalpels. The three Beaty boys stood as close as they were allowed, watching the men work and imagining the day when they'd be big enough to join the team of artisans.

John interpreted what was happening for the benefit of his younger brothers. "They try real hard to get the logs all straight and level. See how Pa sorts over the logs in the pile and gets the right-sized one to pull up next? Then those fellas on the corners cut the notches in it so it fits flat to the log below. An' they put the big ends of the logs at opposite corners so the walls stay level." He and his brothers moved to a new vantage point to watch as the construction moved to a new part of the barn.

By noon, the walls were six feet high. A tall, blond man

straightened up from bending over the notch he had just crafted, took a deep breath, looked toward the kettle boiling over the fire, and said, "Tom, I'm hungry as a b'ar in spring. When we gonna stop an' eat? Whatever Maggie's cookin' smells so good, it's got me famished."

"Two more logs, everybody. We gotta get this side done before we quit." Tom ran his hand over his sweaty forehead, hooked the chain around another log, and started the ox team on the path that would pull the log up to the top of the wall. "Look sharp, boys. It's comin' up to ya."

Half an hour later, the men gathered around the steaming iron pot. Margaret ladled the meaty stew onto their plates; the men grabbed big pieces of cornbread, covered them with wild honey, and sat down on the ground or on logs to eat. Tom came last. He'd unyoked, fed, and watered the ox team before getting food for himself. They were vital to the farm's survival, and he treated them with great care. The yard full of resting and eating neighbors and frolicking dogs made him feel like they really would be ready for winter.

"Those walls are comin' good, Tom. We sure got great neighbors." Margaret looked up and smiled after filling his plate with one of the largest pieces of meat.

"Yeah, but I'd hoped we'd be further along by now. Not sure if we can finish by dark. We'll work as long as we can see. So don't get supper ready too early." Tom picked up a piece of cornbread, found an unoccupied log, and sat down to eat. Margaret walked among the men sprawled on the ground and joined their banter as she offered more stew and cornbread.

As soon as he'd finished eating Tom was on his feet, yoking the ox team. "Let's get them walls up, boys. If we bend our backs to it, we can get done by dark."

The relaxing men grumbled. Walter Wells spoke to no one in particular. "That Tom's a real slave driver. If it weren't for Maggie's good vittles, I'm not sure I'd trade work with 'im."

When the sun was setting behind the tall hill west of Cross Creek, they heaved the last piece of roof into place and pegged it down. As Tom drove the ox team to the creek for water, Walter Wells tipped back his leather hat, "Let's see if Maggie's got any more of that good buffalo stew. An' I brought a jug fer us. It's hid over behind that bush, where Tom won't see it. He's just dead set agin whiskey."

"Fetch it out here, Walt, before Tom comes back. I sure need to get the wood dust out of my whistle." Alex Wiley ran a rough hand through his white hair and looked at Wells with a smile of anticipation.

When the last neighbor left for home, the stew pot and the jug were empty and the new log barn gleamed in the moonlight. Tom looked at it and felt pride in every fiber of his tired body.

***

Two days later, he was at Wells's place, taking part in a similar barn raising. Late in the afternoon, Margaret heard Tom ride up at a gallop and looked out the door as he shouted, "Get the young'uns, Maggie! We got to hustle down to Reynolds's blockhouse!" His voice had an urgent edge as he tied up the horse and rushed inside. "There's a bunch of Delawares on a raid." He took a quick breath. "I just saw Patterson, and he said they could be bad ones. They killed Matt Parks and a family down by Studa. Scalped 'em all, burned their cabin, run off their stock."

Margaret hurried outside to gather the children. Shortly afterward, the Beatys were walking briskly along the trail to the blockhouse, with Margaret in the lead. She was carrying Samuel and holding Elizabeth by the hand. Young Tom and John each carried a knife, blankets, and a basket of food. James and Catherine had quilts and sacks of food. Tom walked close behind, musket loaded, his tomahawk hanging from his side. When they arrived at the blockhouse, dogs were running around and barking, and families who lived along Cross Creek were milling about, getting children settled and arranging robes, quilts, and food on the floor. Men were talking about what to do as they kept a lookout in all directions through the narrow slits in the walls of the blockhouse.

Tom sought out Charlie Reynolds. "If you've already got enough men to take care of things here, I'll go back home and keep an eye on things there."

Reynolds set down a bucket of water and stared at him, open-

43

mouthed. "We're strong enough here, but that's awful dangerous. If they come, you'll be a goner. Do you really want to take that chance, Tom?"

Tom looked him in the eye without blinking. "I've put my whole life into gettin' my land and building a place for Maggie and the young'uns. No damned savages are taking it away from me without a fight. If they try to run off the stock and burn the place, they're going to get filled full of lead." Tom looked hard at Reynolds as he picked up his musket. Then he kissed Margaret quickly, hugged all of their children, and started back toward the farmstead. Reynolds and the others watched and shook their heads.

Margaret spread her arms wide, and the children gathered around her to watch their father walk up the trail. "Can't Junior and I go with him? We could help him if the savages come." John's voice carried an aura of confidence that belied the fear he felt.

"If he'd wanted you boys, he'd have asked. So you stay and help with your brothers an' sisters. Now, you and Catherine go get the blankets spread out. Your pa knows how to take care of himself all right." Margaret hugged Elizabeth and Samuel into her skirt and held them there as she watched Tom disappear around the curve of the creek. She wondered if she would see him alive again. *Sure wish he'd not've gone*, she thought. *But land and a house are almost like family to 'im. Maybe the same as family.*

***

As night drew down, Tom milked the cow, penned the sheep, oxen, and horse in the barn with her, and fed them hay. Then he climbed to the barn loft, where he could see the new log house, the garden with its array of vegetables amid the stumps, the narrow road between the trees, and the creek. He was determined to keep awake and watch, but by midnight the darkness and the deep breathing of the animals below soothed him into a shallow sleep.

A pair of owls hooted close by. Tom jumped and felt his hands shaking. He reached for his musket and peeked out. The animals below were quiet. After a minute, his thoughts clarified. He thought, *They say a horse can smell Injuns a half mile away. Old Molly'll be my sentry.* The owls hooted again, farther away. Across the valley to the west, a whippoorwill called. Another answered. The horse didn't stir. Tom listened to its quiet breathing and felt relief. After a minute he put his musket down, but did not go back to sleep.

The next morning, he did the chores, always with his musket close by, and always keeping a lookout for any unusual movement around the periphery of the farmstead. When the animals were tended, he left them in the barn and napped in the loft above it.

He tried to stay awake the next night but dozed off toward morning. The snort of the horse in the pen below woke him with a start. He shivered, picked up his musket, and scanned the premises for any movement. A twig snapped near the barn. Tom focused on the spot where the sound originated. He saw a tiny movement and aimed his gun at the spot. Then a light flickered where his gaze was concentrated. Without being conscious of doing so, he squeezed the trigger. The flash and roar of the musket was followed by a yell of pain, a few words in a language he didn't understand, then rustling in the brush as the would-be arsonists ran off, dragging their wounded comrade.

Tom reloaded and shot again at the retreating Indians, but there was no outcry or other evidence that his second shot had hit its mark. His heart pounded, and it didn't slow down for a long time. After an extended interval of quiet, he climbed down and calmed and fed the frightened animals. At daybreak, he examined the trail of blood that led away from where he had shot. He concluded that the Indian he'd shot had been bleeding heavily and the wound would probably be lethal. Then he climbed into the loft and went to sleep, his musket by his side.

When Margaret and the family, along with the Wileys and the Buxtons, walked up the trail two days later, they found Tom in the loft, still keeping a lookout. When they told him that the marauders had been caught and killed by some Frontier Rangers as they were preparing a dead comrade for burial, Tom smiled knowingly. He told his secret only to Margaret. They both dreaded the possible return of more Indians bent on revenge, but they never let their children know of their fears.

Chapter 5
Battling Nature's Worst

The snow in February was four feet deep in the woods and mountains and the weather continued exceedingly cold for two months.

—*Alfred Creigh, History of Washington County*

In the late 1700s and 1800s, most settlers on the western frontier survived primarily by hunting and trapping, so winter could be deadly for all but the hardy and intrepid. They usually cleared small tracts of land on which they grew flax, corn, and grass that they harvested and dried as hay for their oxen, sheep, and a horse or two. But most of their efforts were directed to hunting and trapping wild game for food and for the cash they got for the pelts and hides. Tom Beaty was typical of frontier settlers in this regard.

Tom shivered by the fireplace as he pulled on pants, shirt, and boots while Margaret hung an iron kettle over the fire he had just rejuvenated. "We're snowed in for sure. Another two damn feet came down last night on top of what we had. It's up to my waist, maybe deeper. I've got to dig out some fodder for the stock right away, or they'll be goners. Then shovel down to the ice and chop a water hole, if I can find the creek."

"I'll come out to dig more firewood out of the woodpile in a few minutes. John and Junior can mind the babies." Margaret shivered and began to pull a hooded buckskin shirt over her head. It partly hid the prominent bulge in the front of her dress. Tom heaved his shoulder against the door and squeezed through the crack he managed to open, then wrenched a wooden shovel out of the white blanket and cleared a space for the door to swing wider to accommodate Margaret's thickened profile.

The snow was halfway up the walls of the cabin. The muffled bleats of the sheep inside the log barn urged him to hurry. The horse had his head out the barn door and was looking at him. The lean-to shelter over the dried cornstalks and grass that he'd cut to feed the animals for the winter was just a mound. The creek was a curved depression in the pervasive whiteness. The snow-laden trees added a third dimension to the white world.

After an hour's shoveling, Tom had carved trails through the snow to the woodpile and the barn, and from there to a log manger he'd filled with hay. He stopped and banged his mittened hands together to warm them as the animals pushed and shoved to get at the feed. It took him another hour to excavate a trail to the creek and chop a circular hole in the ice, where he filled two oak buckets and carried them, with their chips of floating ice, to the cabin. Then he filled a wooden barrel in the animals' pen with water. Finally he extracted a scant gallon of milk from the cow. Only then did he return, his hands and feet numb, to the warmth of the dim cabin for breakfast.

Margaret had already piled the woodbox full of logs she'd dug out of the snow and fed the children breakfast. He and Margaret looked at each other, grateful for what each of them had done so that the family and their stock could survive the storm.

"Pa, we're going out and play in the snow." Young Tom and John were pulling on boots and heavy coats as he sat down. Later they burst into the cabin, snowy to their waists.

"Pa, come quick." John said excitedly. "We've found a deer in snow so deep it can't hardly move. Bring a knife, and we can just cut its throat and drag it home on our sled."

"Can it move at all? I'd like to finish breakfast." Tom looked up from a bowl of steaming porridge.

"It's just standin' in the snow clear up to its belly. It floundered a little when we came on it, but it gave up an' just rolled its big eyes when we touched it." John's voice and manner conveyed total confidence. Tom got up slowly, leaving his bowl of porridge half eaten on the table, pulled on his heavy clothes again, and followed his sons. The deer had moved a few feet from where the boys had first seen it. As the three struggled through the deep snow toward it, pulling a hand sled, a wolf howled on the hillside above them.

"Sounds like we got here just in time, Pa." John's face was shining, his eyes wide.

The deer offered only feeble resistance as the man and boys maneuvered the sled beside it, pushed it down, sliced its throat, and tied it on. Tom and his sons had to stop every few yards to catch their breaths as they trekked back toward the cabin, dragging the loaded sled. Once there, they hung the deer head-down from a tree about fifty feet from the cabin door. When they'd finished dressing it out, Tom glanced up and glimpsed three wolves watching them warily from the woods beyond the edge of the clearing.

"Let's pull it way up high, boys, so's them wolves can't get to it. There ain't a lot of meat on it, but I sure don't aim to give any to them wolves. An' we'll put a wolf trap in the snow right under it. Maybe we can get ourselves a new wolf skin tonight."

As he and the boys placed and anchored the trap, Tom thought about food. *Everything's hungry, includin' us. Sure hope we can stretch the grub supply, an' nobody gets sick. Maybe if this snow crusts, I can walk on it enough to kill us another couple a deer.* He showed John how to fasten a chain to a stake he'd pounded deep into the ground and finish by sifting a thin coating of snow over the trap's open jaws, then they all wallowed toward the cabin and the smell of fresh-baked cornbread. In spite of the hearty breakfast they'd eaten earlier, all three were famished, just as the deer had been. They spent most of the rest of the day in the cabin.

As darkness fell, the wolves howled close around the cabin. Margaret reassured the younger children that the noisy hunters could not get into the cabin or barn. The howls continued to resonate after she and Tom had gone to bed.

"Those critters howling so close sure gives me the creeps," she said and snuggled close to Tom.

He put his arms around her and held her tight, enjoying her warmth and liking the bulge that their next child made in her belly. "I get chills from hearing 'em too. But we built everything good and strong, so there's no chance for us or any of our animals to get hurt." The day's exertions had left them deeply tired, and the ebb and flow of wolf howls soon ushered the couple into sleep.

They woke at daybreak to loud howls and whines. Tom loaded his musket and eased the door open. A frantic wolf tugged on the trap under the deer carcass. The chain from it to a long metal stake skidded back and forth across the snow as the wolf tried to get free. Tom steadied the barrel of the musket against the doorframe, took careful aim, and squeezed the trigger. Smoke billowed into the cabin, and all the children woke up terrified from the noise of the gun. The wolf dropped in its tracks. Margaret tried to quiet the wailing children and eventually succeeded by giving them breakfast. After he'd skinned the canine, Tom chopped off a piece of frozen deer meat and brought it to the cabin. Margaret put it on the hook in the fireplace to cook for dinner.

***

Long before the spring thaw began, they had eaten the entire deer, as well as another that Tom shot. They were also out of flour and cornmeal. "We'll be out of food by tonight, except for a few scraps of venison." Margaret sighed as she put the last pieces of bread and some strawberry jam she'd made the previous summer on the table and watched the children grab them.

"The snow's melted a little, but it's still awful deep. Maybe I can pack some of the skins we've accumulated on Old Molly and lead her down to Patterson's. Hope he's still got some flour left to trade."

"Pa, can I go too? I'm sure I can keep up." John looked at his father eagerly.

"Not this time, son. I need somebody to stay home and tend the stock. If I'm late gettin' back, be sure to feed and water the sheep and then milk Blackie. And watch out she doesn't kick you." John looked disappointed as he turned away.

Tom loaded the old bay mare with as many deerskins and wolf skins as he thought she could carry, and then he led her through the deep, wet snowdrifts to Patterson's mill, where he traded the skins for rye flour, cornmeal, and salt. He and the horse returned at sundown, both completely exhausted. Tom's deerskin pants were soaked to the hips, and he poured water out of his boots when he sat down. While Tom dried his clothes by the fireplace and shared the news that everyone else was struggling just like they were, Margaret baked six loaves of bread. They were gone in three days, as was the last of the venison.

***

Tom waded through the snow, going farther afield every day, hunting for game. But all of the deer yards were empty, except for a few skeletons, half hidden in snow. He'd stumble home empty-handed every night—cold, exhausted, and wet to the hips—to feed the livestock and tell Margaret that there was no new food for the family. He knew they would starve to death, or have to kill their milk cow and sheep for meat, if he couldn't kill some wild game soon. Finally, on a late March afternoon, he shot a bear that had just come out of hibernation. It was too heavy for him to drag home by himself, so he waded home through the snow as fast as he could.

"John, Junior, put on your boots and coats and come help me drag home the b'ar I shot, before the wolves get to it! I already hear them howling way up on the ridge."

The brothers stopped shaving kindling for the fireplace, put on their outdoor clothes, and followed their father through the snow. He was almost running in his haste. They arrived, sweating and panting, at where the bear's carcass lay below a rock outcrop on the hill about a quarter mile from the cabin, just as six wolves appeared from the ridge above them. Tom fired his musket and wounded the closest wolf. It limped off, trailing blood, but the other five circled the man and boys as they stood by the dead bear. John and Junior shivered as they watched the five pairs of yellow eyes surrounding them come closer and closer. Tom ignored the wolves and tied a rope around the bear's neck, then he and his sons started to drag the dead bruin down the hill toward the cabin.

It was brutal work. The bear's carcass sank deep in the melting snow, and the wolves became bolder with each passing minute. The trio tugged the carcass a few yards and then had to stop for breath. While they rested, Tom reloaded and shot one of the wolves dead. The others retreated a few feet. Tom and his sons dragged the dead bear forward another twenty yards. The four wolves closed in again. The three Beatys picked up the rope and strained to slide their food supply farther down the hill. One of the wolves dashed in and bit a piece off the bear's leg. The four hunters began a snarling quarrel over which one would get the morsel. While the wolves were fighting, Tom and the boys slid the bear farther down the hill and then stopped to rest and watch the fight. As they resumed their trek, the wolves, emboldened by the piece of stolen meat, returned for more.

"Get out of here, you dirty thieves! Hyah, get away!" Tom shouted as he pulled. The wolves stopped for a moment and then closed in again. Tom reloaded his musket, took good aim, and shot the largest remaining wolf dead. "That's my last shot. We got to get this bear to a tree real quick and pull him up."

They dragged the bear toward an oak with a strong horizontal branch about fifteen feet up. Tom managed to throw the rope over it, then he and his sons tried to pull the bear up out of reach of the wolves, but it outweighed them. "Junior, run as fast as you can and get your mother to help us. John and I'll try to hold 'em off while you're gone."

Junior rushed toward the cabin through the deep snow. Tom and John stood guard on each side of the bear, waiting for the wolves to close in. All they had for protection now was their courage and some limbs they'd pulled out of the snow. John's heart pounded as he watched the trio of canines circle closer and closer. He could see Junior and his mother hustling up the hill through the snow.

"Hyah, keep away, or I'll brain ya. Hyah! Hyah!" John swung his club above his head as he yelled. His father yelled behind him.

When Margaret and Junior arrived, the four of them grabbed the rope and pulled with all their strength. Slowly the carcass of the bear rose out of the snow and into the air. When it finally swung free of the ground, Tom looped the rope around the tree trunk and tied it fast.

He unsheathed his knife and said, "Stand close guard. When those wolves smell the guts, they'll go crazy." He turned his full attention to the bear, making a cut the length of the abdomen, then carefully cutting around the anus and knotting the large intestine so that its contents didn't spill out and touch the rest of the carcass. He cut out the musk glands and threw them as far as he could toward the three wolves. They pounced, snarling, on the morsels and devoured them, then came even closer. Tom wiped his hands and knife on the snow to remove the stench from the musk glands, and then he cut the tissue that held the lungs, stomach, and intestines in place. They dropped to the snow in a steaming heap.

Tom leaped to untie the rope and yelled for the family to help him lift the bear out of the wolves' reach. They stopped guarding and grabbed the rope. The bear was easier to lift now, and they pulled it as high as they could into the tree before tying the rope high around the trunk. One of the wolves darted in while they were pulling on the rope; it grabbed the bear's stomach and backed away about fifty feet, pulling it and all the other organs. The other two joined it, and they gorged on their free feast. The wolf that Tom had wounded limped up to join them, leaving a trail of blood in the snow behind it.

The Beatys stood for a moment and watched in wonder. Then Tom reached over his head with his knife, peeled back the skin, and sliced off three pieces of meat from the bear's hindquarter. While the wolves were still busy at their feast, Margaret and her two sons headed for the cabin, each carrying a piece of meat. Tom went back up the hill and skinned the two wolves he'd shot, and then he returned home, dragging the skins. That night, as the Beatys gathered at the table for a tasty supper of roast bear and cornbread, Tom looked at his gaunt, lean family and offered a heartfelt blessing.

"Father Almighty, we thank you for giving us this bear to eat. We came mighty close to starving, an' we're awful grateful to you for givin' us meat again. In Jesus' name we pray. Amen."

As soon as supper was over, Tom fell asleep, exhausted from the day's exertions. The bear's meat, lean after its winter hibernation, tided them over until the snow melted, and its pelt covered a corner of the cabin floor.

Everyone was profoundly relieved when winter finally gave way to spring. They'd had more than enough of being cold and hungry, of wading through deep snow and trying to stretch the food and forage supply to sustain their growing families and their livestock. Tom stripped a ring of bark from a host of trees to kill them, cut down thirty or so dead ones he'd girdled the year before, and planted rye, wheat, and corn among the stumps in the newly cleared ground and the ground he'd reclaimed in earlier years. That fall, they had more food in reserve, some to trade or sell, and a new mouth to feed. But every time he heard a wolf howl, Tom thought of the close encounter with them on the day when he and his family had retrieved the bear, and he shivered.

Chapter 6
Religion and Education on the Frontier

The Rev. James Power, from York County, Pennsylvania, visited this region and preached several sermons.

—Alfred Creigh, History of Washington County

Two years later, on a warm, humid afternoon in May after the crops were planted, Tom rode into the farmstead, tied the bay mare to a post near the barn, and shared his big news with Margaret and the children. "They say there's a real preacher coming to Vance's Fort on Sunday. Let's go and take the whole family." He picked up Alexander, his three-year-old son, and swung him around in a circle.

"Will lots of folks be there, Pa? I haven't seen the Wells girls since last fall." Catherine beamed at the prospect of seeing her friends.

"I reckon so. Most everybody's likely to be there." Tom beamed as he rubbed sweat off the horse's back.

"That'll be somethin', having a real preacher. Maybe you kids can all be baptized." Margaret's proud glance took in their eight children. "I'd been hoping a preacher'd come sometime so we could make you all real Presbyterians, like your pa and me."

"What's bein' baptized, Ma, and what's a Presterian?" James's questions carried the uncertainty that all of the older children shared.

"We'll tell you all about it at supper. Now all you kids need to run and take baths in the crick. A preacher sure won't baptize a bunch of kids who have dirt behind their ears, like you all do." Margaret's admonition sent the four oldest boys scampering toward the creek, while Catherine walked behind with her three youngest siblings.

***

Early on Sunday morning, the newly clean family started for Vance's Fort. Tom had a deerskin pack of food on his back and led the bay mare that carried Margaret, with year-old Joseph in her arms and three-year-old Alexander holding on behind her. The two-mile uphill walk to the scatter of cabins at the crest tired Samuel, so John and Junior took turns carrying him on their backs. When they reached the small settlement of Cross Creek, they joined other families in the downhill walk to the fort. The children mingled happily with friends, and the adults chatted about the impending community gathering and speculated about the visiting preacher and his message.

Colonel William Vance's fort was about a mile from Cross Creek. It consisted of a blockhouse, a log house, and some small log outbuildings next to a spring, all enclosed by a stockade of tall logs set on end in the ground. This morning, the gate to the stockade was wide open, and the grounds swarmed with people, horses, and several yoked pairs of oxen that had pulled wooden-wheeled carts and their owners to the gathering. Neighbors shared the latest news; children ran among the horses, trees, and buildings. Dogs barked and chased squirrels.

The Reverend James Power was easy to spot, as he stood alone at the edge of the grounds, observing the scene. His high-collared linen shirt and black wool suit contrasted with the knee-length deerskin shirts and deerskin pants of the men and the gray linsey-woolsey dresses of the women who'd gathered with their families to hear his message and to enjoy each other's company. Even if he'd been wearing leather, Reverend Power's empty right sleeve would have made him conspicuous. When he marched up to the platform of rough new wood under an oak tree, set his bible on the chest-high plank at its front, and raised his left hand, the conversations trailed off, and everyone sat down on the grass facing him. Mothers and older daughters held young children who were sweaty from running and jumping, and they shushed them quiet as Reverend Power motioned for silence.

His strong, resonant voice engulfed the gathering. "Brothers and sisters, I have come to bring you the Word of the Lord and to call you to abandon your sinful ways. Be not like the heathen who wallow in sin, and who will perish in the fires of hell. Repent of your evil doing, and prepare for that fearful Day of Judgment when every man, woman, and child must answer for their thoughts and deeds. Think well as to what you will have to answer for and how the Angel of Judgment will decide your eternal fate. Will he welcome you into eternal paradise with God the Father and the Lord Jesus Christ, or will he consign you to eternal damnation with Satan and his minions in the fires of hell?"

Young Tom whispered to his father, "He scares me. Are we all sinners?" His father put his finger to his lips in a shushing motion.

Reverend Power looked over the congregated families, picked up the bible with his left hand, and held it high. "The Good Book says in Exodus, chapter twenty, 'For I the Lord your God am a jealous God, visiting the iniquity of the father upon the children unto the third and fourth generation of them that hate me. And showing mercy to thousands of them that love me, and keep my commandments.' That is my text for today's message from the Lord." Reverend Power paused again to let words sink in.

James leaned over and whispered to John, "What's *iniquity*? Does Pa have it?"

"Don't know. An' be quiet, or he'll take a switch to us."

The Reverend Power lectured the assembled settlers for two hours on the perils of violating the Ten Commandments, and then he implored God at length to grant forgiveness to this assemblage of miserable sinners seated on the grass, placed his bible over his heart, and stepped off the platform.

The crowd erupted into a flurry of activity. Children who had chafed at being restrained leaped into motion with a cacophony of happy shouts. Conversations sprouted among the adults, one or two about the message they'd just heard, most about the here and now of life along Cross Creek—the weather, crop prospects, new arrivals from the East, births and deaths, problems with locusts, successes and failures in hunting game, depredations by wolves, and rumors of Indian attacks. Food and drink were unpacked and shared. When the preacher called the congregation back to hear his second sermon, it included a call for all who wished to be baptized and accepted into membership of the church to return on the following Sabbath.

As the Beatys started toward home at the end of the day, Tom said, "We're for sure coming back next Sunday so you kids can be baptized. I'd hoped the preacher would do it today, but next week will do. We need to talk to the Wileys about bein' your godparents."

John looked at his father and asked, "What's bein' baptized mean, Pa?"

"It's the first step in being a Christian and a Presbyterian. Remember how your ma read you the story in the bible about when Jesus was young and John the Baptist took him into the River Jordan and sprinkled water on him? Then God told the people that Jesus was his son. Everybody who wants to be a Christian has to be baptized. Otherwise you're like the heathen, who'll all go to hell when they die."

"Even if they never heard of Jesus?" James's questions caught Tom by surprise. Margaret came to his rescue.

"That's why the church has missionaries, son. They go all over the world and preach to the heathen. Those that get baptized get saved. The others go straight to hell when they die."

"Is Reverend Power a missionary to us, Ma?"

"Yes, I guess so. Even though your pa and I are Christians because we were baptized a long time ago, the preacher's here to save everybody he can, and to see if he can help us start a church."

"I sure hope I don't die before next Sunday." James shuddered a little. "I'm gonna be really careful till then."

"Me too," said Catherine. Her siblings nodded agreement.

John asked, "Do we have to take another bath next Saturday, Ma? That crick's awful cold."

"You certainly do, young man. Now, don't ask again."

A week later, the five older Beaty children stood with their parents amid the throng of other families before the Reverend Power. The preacher put on his most forbidding look and asked, "Hath any of these children already been baptized?" A murmur of noes floated back. "Hath each child presented for baptism three godparents, and hath each godparent assented to serve?" A chorus of yeses followed his question.

He continued in a stern voice, "Dearly beloved, forasmuch as all men are conceived and born in sin, and that our savior Christ saith none can enter the kingdom of God except he be regenerated and born anew of water and the Holy Ghost, I beseech you to call upon God the Father through our Lord Jesus Christ, that of his bounteous mercy he will grant to these children that thing which by nature they cannot have, that they may be baptized with water and the Holy Ghost and received into Christ's holy church and be made lively members of the same." Power then motioned to Colonel Vance, the host of the gathering, to take a bowl of water and follow him. He moved to one end of the semicircle of families.

While the preacher and Colonel Vance were getting ready, James whispered to John, "Do you think the kingdom of God has trees and bears and wolves?"

"Dunno. Reckon there's no wolves. After that tussle over the bear Pa shot, them varmints make my hair stand on end when they howl at night."

"Shush!" Margaret put her hand over her son's mouth and pinched his face.

Reverend Power faced the family at the end of the line, looked at them and the godparents standing behind them, and continued the ritual. "Dearly beloved, ye have brought these children here to be baptized, ye have prayed that our Lord and Savior Jesus Christ would vouchsafe to receive them, to release them from their sins, to sanctify them with the Holy Ghost to give them the kingdom of heaven and everlasting life. Ye have also heard that our Lord Jesus Christ hath promised to grant all these things ye have prayed for. Wherefore, after this promise made by Christ, these children must also faithfully, for their parts, promise by you, who are their sureties until they become of age, that they will renounce the devil and all of his works, constantly believe God's holy word, and obediently keep his commandments. I demand therefore, dost thou, in the name of these children, renounce the devil and all his works, the vain pomp and glory of the world, with all covetous desires of the same, and the carnal desires of the flesh, so that thou wilt not be led by them?"

After anxious glances to one another, the parents and godparents behind a group of children managed some "I wills", "I renounce them alls", and one faint yes. Reverend Power looked mildly displeased, but he motioned for Vance to bring the bowl of water.

"What is the Christian name of this child?"

"Samuel, sir." The father's voice was tentative.

Reverend Power dipped his hand in the bowl and put it on the boy's forehead. "Samuel, I baptize thee in the name of the Father, and of the Son, and of the Holy Ghost. Amen." Samuel burst into tears, and his parents hustled him away.

As the ceremony moved to the next child, young Tom whispered, "Pa, what are works of the devil, and what's carnal desire?"

"Be quiet and pay attention, or I'll take a switch to your bare hide when we get home."

Two bowls of water later, Reverend Power pronounced "Amen" over the last moist-faced child, and the assemblage dispersed toward their homes. As the Beatys crested the hill at the west end of the settlement of Cross Creek, Tom looked across it and said, "There was talk back at the baptism of buildin' a church hereabouts. Right here on the ridge top would be a good place to put it."

Margaret appraised the rounded divide. "Maybe with a church building, we could get a full-time preacher who could teach the kids to read and write on weekdays. I'd sure favor that. An' if they built it here, our boys could walk to school easy as pie. It's only about two miles."

John and Junior looked at each other furtively. They sensed changes coming. It made them apprehensive.

***

A year later, the rough essentials of a log schoolhouse and its furnishings were completed, and word spread of the impending enterprise. Tom advised his three oldest sons of new developments. "John, Junior, James, I hear the schoolhouse's almost ready. When school opens, you'll go, but there's a lot of work to finish before then."

Catherine asked, "What about me? I'm old enough too."

"It's just for boys, honey, not girls. They say women don't need to read or write to cook, sew, and raise kids. Maybe your mother can read the bible with you when you both have a minute from the housework, and you can learn to read a little that way."

"That's not fair. I want to read and write." Catherine put her head down and walked out the door.

Tom continued, "I need you boys to finish piling the brush that's scattered on the south hill so we can burn it, and then use the ox team to drag all the small logs down here near the cabin and cut 'em for firewood. You'll have to hustle to get it all done." His pronouncement brought Junior and John to their feet.

John spoke for them both. "Aw, Pa, why do we need to go sit in that darn school just because they're startin' it? You need us here, helpin' you to clear trees and grub out stumps so's you can have more ground to plant come spring. An' we've still got to get us another bear or two so's we have meat for winter."

Junior nodded assent. "Send Catherine instead. I'll bet she'd like to get out of helpin' Ma daylight to dark."

"Out here, school's just for boys. Even though your ma had some schooling, that was back in the East. There're not allowin' any girls, and you're both going to go. So's James, and that's final. I'll kill the bears." Tom's expression signaled his complete resolve; the two boys looked at each other, shrugged, and walked out to start work.

A week later, the two, with James between them, trudged up the hill toward the cluster of buildings that formed the settlement of Cross Creek and to the new log schoolhouse that stood on the hilltop beside the Presbyterian church. The trio joined two dozen others, all as uncertain of what to expect and as reluctant to be there as the three Beaty brothers.

The new log schoolhouse was rough and simple. Split-log benches formed three lines across the dirt floor, perpendicular to the doorway.

In the front, farthest from the door, was a rough wooden table about four feet long. A chair sat behind the table. It was made from a slab of wood, with hand-hewn legs and two hand-hewn sticks that extended above the seat at the rear and were joined near the top by a crosspiece. Openings for windows had been left in the two side walls. There was as yet nothing in either, and insects flew in and out at will. The left wall contained the beginning of a fireplace near the teacher's desk. The outside chimney was only a few stones high. A pile of flat sandstone pieces showed the town fathers' intent to finish it before winter.

Most of the boys wore shirts and pants of tanned deerskin. Some wore moccasins, and others wore handmade leather shoes. One boy stood out in homespun wool attire and black boots. Shortly after the three Beatys joined a game of tag with other prospective students, the schoolmaster, a tall, lean man with black hair and a narrow face, came down the road from the center of the village in his high-collared white shirt and black suit. He carried a book, some papers, and a cowbell in his right hand and a short stick in his left. He stood in the doorway and rang the bell vigorously. The boys stared, uncertain of what to do. He motioned for them to come in, then entered his new domain and stood behind the table. The prospective pupils surged through the door, laughing and joshing one another.

The schoolmaster slapped the desk smartly with his stick as they milled about, finding seats. He announced in a firm voice, "There will be absolute quiet when you enter my schoolroom. Is that clear?" The boys looked stunned. No one answered, but a few nodded. They sat, meek as mice, looking at him.

"I'm Mr. Shotwell. You will stand and give your full name so I can know you." He reprimanded those who did not begin by saying, "Sir, my name is." After the first two, all the boys complied with his demand, until it was John's turn.

He stood up slowly. "I'm John Beaty." Then, after a long pause, he added, "Sir."

Mr. Shotwell's eyes blazed as he glared at John. John glared back. They were two potential antagonists, taking each other's measure.

After what seemed like an eternity, Mr. Shotwell said, "John

Beaty, go sit in the corner! Now, who's next?" John walked to the corner and sat on the floor.

When they all had introduced themselves to the schoolmaster, Mr. Shotwell summoned John back to the group and announced, "First we will learn the alphabet." He held up a large card with the letters *A* and *a* printed in bold black. "Here's how the first letter of the alphabet is printed." Then he held up a second card with letters forming the words "In Adam's fall, sinned we all." He read it aloud, emphasizing the word "Adam's" and pointing to the *A* as he read. "Now, all say it together."

In response, a ragged array of voices intoned, "In Adam's fall, sinned we all," with three dissonant voices announcing, "In Adam's fall, we all sinned." Mr. Shotwell frowned and reread the words on the card, placing a finger under each as he spoke it.

"Again, everyone together."

"In Adam's fall, sinned we all." The hopeful boys' voices reverberated off the log walls. Mr. Shotwell looked pleased.

"Better. Now, again."

The drill continued; by noon they reached the letter *D*, when the pupils recited, "The Deluge drown'd, the Earth around" with a modicum of confidence while Mr. Shotwell held up the card with his finger under the letter *D*.

"What's a deluge?" John's question caught Mr. Shotwell off guard.

"You haven't heard of the deluge? That was when God sent rain for forty days and forty nights, and water covered all the Earth. Only Noah and his family escaped in the ark, along with the animals he had taken on board. Now, John, come here, so that I can teach you some respect with this switch."

John walked to the front of the room, bent over a desk, and never flinched when Mr. Shotwell gave him ten lashes with his stick. He smiled as he returned to the log bench, but he sat down gingerly.

"Next time any of you have a question, you are to raise your right hand and wait until I give you permission before speaking. Then address me as 'Mr. Shotwell, sir.' Is that clear?" The teacher scowled at John as he spoke. All the students nodded.

In the two months it took the pupils to learned the alphabet and repeat the rhyming sentences associated with each letter, fathers of some of the pupils completed the chimney, hauled a supply of logs for the fireplace, and covered the window holes with paper smeared with lard to make it translucent. On cold mornings, Mr. Shotwell came early to build the fire. The boys crowded close around the fireplace after walking to school, rubbing their hands and stamping their feet as they warmed up.

The schoolmaster procured a supply of paper, goose quills for pens, and homemade ink. By then, the boys were learning to form letters and words, along with learning to read and do sums. But they never lost their enthusiasm for the freedom of outdoor life.

***

On a spring afternoon, Margaret stood beside the cabin and watched her three oldest sons and their friends troop down the road after school, laughing as they ran. She smiled at their exuberance and thought about how her life had turned out. *What a great place for the kids to grow up. Been awful tough sometimes. But we've done all right.*

When warm weather arrived, the schoolmaster had a class of only ten. At the end of the week, he declared the session over. The three Beatys and their school companions reverted to life out of doors—cutting, burning, clearing, planting, hoeing, harvesting, and hunting. It was a life they relished all the more after having been confined in the school building six days a week for several months.

In spite of their protests, they went back the next fall and succeeding falls. John was eighteen when, in 1790, he convinced his parents that he'd had enough schooling. By then, his younger brothers Samuel, Alexander, and Joseph had joined Thomas, Jr. and James as pupils, and the school had been moved to a larger building. Catherine never got to join them in the schoolhouse.

Her brothers learned a lot about life from their schoolmates as well as from the teachers. Some of the older boys brought knives, small animal skins, and bottles of whiskey to school in their pockets. They shared this contraband with classmates—temporarily, in the case of knives and skins, permanently with the whiskey. John was big and tough enough to be the first in line to sample the illicit whiskey offered during recess.

Chapter 7
Liquor and Lawlessness

> In these western counties, a large proportion
> of the inhabitants were Scotch-Irish, or of that
> descent, a people whose earlier home had been ...
> in a land where whiskey was the national beverage,
> and where excise laws and excise officers were
> regarded as the most odious of all measures and
> minions of tyranny.

—Alfred Creigh, History of Washington County

John ran through the fallen leaves and into the cabin, breathing hard. "Pa, Ma! I just pulled this piece of paper off a tree by the road. Tom the Tinker's after us. He and his gang are gonna burn us out, like they did the Strahens, if we don't put a notice in the *Pittsburgh Gazette* sayin' we support him."

"Read us what it says, son." Margaret turned from the kettle hanging in the fireplace to face her black-haired, dark-complexioned son, now twenty-one and man-grown. But she kept a foot moving the rocker of the cradle that held baby William. Tom stopped carving the piece of leather that he was shaping into a boot sole. John moved the sheet until light from the door fell squarely on it.

"To Thomas Beaty," he read. "Sir, you must have this notice

printed in the Pittsburgh paper this week, or you may abide by the consequences. 'Poor Tom the Tinker takes this opportunity to inform his friends throughout all the country that he is obliged to take up his commission to fight the whiskey tax once more, though disagreeable to his inclinations.'"

John squinted at the sheet and then looked up. "There's a passel of big words on here, but I reckon it's just like the letter he nailed to Strahen's before they was burned out. Listen to the end."

He continued, "This is fair warning. Traitors! Take care, for my hammer is up and my ladle is hot. I cannot travel this country, fighting the government's whiskey tax, for nothing. From your old friend, Tom the Tinker."

Tom put down the knife and piece of leather as he looked about at the cabin and the two additional rooms he'd added. "Well, I hate to think how hard it would be to build another house that'd hold all fourteen of us before winter. He's burnt everybody who got one of those letters and didn't do what he says, whether they sell whiskey or not. But I'll be damned if I'm going to knuckle under to those cheating, whiskey-lovin' outlaws. Especially since I hate the drink like sin."

Margaret pushed the logs in the fireplace together with the poker and looked at her husband. "Well, I think the same as you—we ought to stand our ground. Somebody's got to. The tax sure ain't fair, given how far us folks have to haul our corn and wheat to sell it, but what this outlaw's doin' is worse. I've been talking to Eliza Marshall and Cora Reynolds, and they both think somebody's got to stand up to these fire-mongers or none of us will be safe. We got three boys almost man-grown. They can take turns standin' guard through the night, just like you did when the savages was scalpin' and burnin' years back. If we have to, I and the young 'uns can go down to Reynolds's blockhouse an' sleep, like we used to then."

"That's pretty risky, Ma. You and Pa've worked for 'most fifteen years gettin' this place built up. It'd be a shame to lose all the buildings and feed so late in the year. I'm thinkin' maybe we should go to Pittsburgh an' put that notice in the paper."

Margaret glared at her oldest son. "John Beaty, grow some backbone. If you're man enough to be courtin', be man enough to help us stand up to these scoundrels. If I have to, I'll take your turn at night guardin'." John looked unmoved by his mother's words. "I know you're thinkin' of the danger, but sometimes a family's just gotta take a stand. Your pa didn't come all the way from Ireland for some land because he was scairt of taking risks. Get on Baldy, an' ride over to Reynolds and Marshalls and Wells an' see if they'll join us and help put a stop to this Tom the Tinker's nonsense."

John looked at his father, who said, "Get goin' right now!" John hustled to get the horse.

The Beaty men took turns guarding the premises every night with a loaded musket. First John, then Junior, then James, and finally their father patrolled the periphery of the farmstead, listening for any unusual noises or movement. They heard the familiar night sounds: wolves howling on the hill, the call of nighthawks as they flew about hunting insects, the faint rustle of the farm animals, whippoorwills making their three-syllable call as they flew, and near morning the calls of a host of songbirds in the trees responding to the first evidence of daylight.

Late on the tenth night, Tom thought he sensed movement near the road. He aimed and froze. His heart pounded as he stared at the spot through the dimness of early dawn. When he saw the figure of a man with a torch emerge from behind a tree, he pulled the trigger.

The interloper screamed in pain. Then another voice yelled from behind the barn, "Run for your lives, they're onto us." Tom whirled, reloading the musket as fast as he could, and saw two other figures run from beside the barn; he fired at one of them. He heard a curse and saw the man stumble, then get up and run. Then he heard horses' hooves pounding along the road as the arsonists rode away. Only when he ran to see if they'd lit a fire did he realize that sweat was running down his chest and back.

The Beatys and their neighbors continued to keep a round-the-clock guard until the leaders of the rebellion lost their zeal for arson and rebellion. This change of heart was aided by President George Washington, who raised an army of about fifteen thousand men and, temporarily leaving governance of the young country to others, led the troops along the National Road toward southwestern Pennsylvania, the center of the resistance. Albert Gallatin, western Pennsylvania's representative in Congress, met with leaders of the rebellion and made the government's intentions very clear.

The rebellion's key leader, David Bradford, slipped out of town and down the Ohio and Mississippi Rivers to New Orleans, out of reach in the Spanish colony. When he learned of the collapse of the rebellion, President Washington suspended the campaign and returned to Philadelphia. But all the men over twenty-one who lived in the area were required to sign an oath of allegiance to the United States.

> **Signers of the Oath of Allegiance to the United States, Cross Creek, September 11, 1794. Thomas Beaty and John Beaty [among many others] signed in the presence of William Rea, Aaron Lyle, and Thomas Patterson, Commissioners**
>
> —*Alfred Creigh, History of Washington County*

The collapse of the whiskey rebellion made citizens of the frontier realize, many for the first time, that their young government meant to have its laws obeyed. But it didn't make those freedom-loving Scots-Irish immigrants like that prospect.

Chapter 8
Getting Title, Getting Crowded

"Victory"
Thos. Beaty.
300 Acres and All.
War. Oct. 25, 1787. Sur. Mar 21, 1788.
Pat. June 16, 1795. To Warrantee.

> —*Notations within a tract on a Plat Map of the*
> *original landowners in Cross Creek Township,*
> *Washington County, Pennsylvania, filed in the*
> *Washington County Law Library*

"Tom," said Judge Marshall, smiling kindly at him, "What do you want to name this parcel of three hundred acres we've just patented for you? Most folks are givin' a name to their land once they get title to it."

"Yes, sir! I want to call it Victory!" Thomas Beaty ran his hand through his red hair and looked up at Judge Marshall, smiling like a boy who has just received his first horse. Then he looked at Margaret, who stood beaming by his side.

"Victory? That's a new one. Why you want to call it that? Most folks name their land something like Buck Forest or Woody Plains—kind of descriptive names."

"Well, your honor, I've been dreaming of owning a few acres of good land ever since I was a wee lad back in Ireland." Tom shifted his feet and then elaborated. "My pa was one of them crofters. The owner he crofted for was a skinflint, right near the worst fer being tight with a shilling. We was always hungry, sometimes on the edge of starvin'. More'n half my sisters and brothers died. My favorite sister died one winter when we had nothing to eat but a few turnips and potatoes. This paper you're about to give me is a real victory to my way of thinkin'." Tom's voice cracked; he wiped his eyes and ran his sleeve over his flushed face. Margaret put her hand on his arm.

"Victory it'll be, Tom, just like you asked." The judge inked a quill and lettered the word on a map, then handed Tom the sheet of paper that gave him title to his farm.

"Thank you, your honor. I feel like I just got something real great." Tom laid the deed on the table, ran his hand over it gently, and passed it to Margaret. When she'd glanced at it, he folded it double and put it inside his buckskin shirt.

Judge Marshall noticed Tom's emotions. "I'm real glad for you, Tom. You folks have done a good job of clearin' that steep piece of ground and making a farm out of it."

Tom beamed and straightened his shirt before he responded. "Judge, it's been terrible hard gettin' the sixty dollars to pay for this title, what with twelve young'uns to keep fed, an' me not sellin' my corn to make whiskey the way most folks do. Had to skin a lotta varmints and dig a lotta ginseng roots to get money to do it. Now that some of the boys have got big enough that they can do a man's work, it's a mite easier. The Lord's given me the victory, just like the Good Book says."

Highlight of the Plat Map showing Thomas
Beaty's property called Victory (Courtesy of the
Washington County Law Library)

Tom and Margaret's appearance before Judge Marshall in the Washington County Courthouse culminated a series of actions that began when the proprietors of the Commonwealth of Pennsylvania settled their border dispute with the Commonwealth of Virginia and opened land in the southwest part of Pennsylvania to purchase. Settlers could buy 400-acre parcels at £10 per one hundred acres, roughly thirty-three cents per acre. Some settlers, predominantly Scots-Irish, took out warrants on land, but few could raise the money to buy at that price. In 1792, the Commonwealth reduced the parcel size to 300 acres and the price to about twenty cents per acre. Land sales increased rapidly as settlers, Tom Beaty among them, purchased patents to land for which they'd already received warrants.

Tom and Margaret left Judge Marshall's courtroom walking tall and stopped on the top step of the Washington County Courthouse where they could observe the dirt streets that ran down to the north, east, and south. People were walking on the new wooden sidewalks that bordered those streets, or standing and talking to friends. Horses, including theirs, were tied to rails set between posts at the edges of the walks. Other residents were driving light wagons and buggies along the hilly thoroughfares. Three yoke of oxen strained to pull a pair of loaded Conestoga wagons up the hill from the east; the wagons' bright blue beds contrasted with the muddy red wheels and gleaming white cloth coverings. As they crested the steep pitch directly in front of the courthouse, the driver yelled, "Whoa!" While the oxen stood, sides heaving and mouths drooling saliva, the driver chained the rear wheels of the back wagon to the wagon frame.

Tom stood absorbing the scene and recalled his first visit to the courthouse. "Sure a lot more goin' on here than when Alex Wiley an' I came through here the first time back in '78. We've worked hard since then, Maggie, but we've been real lucky too." He put his arm on her shoulder as they stood watching the activity.

Margaret moved close to Tom and asked, "Where you suppose those purty wagons are goin'?"

"I reckon across the Ohio River an' on to the west. Settlement's goin' way out beyond us these days."

The freighter finished chaining the wheels and started his ox teams. Tom and Margaret watched the small showers of sparks that flashed when the chained wheels scraped over rocks as the caravan descended the steep hill to the south and turned west again.

"We've come a fer piece from when we got here." She took his rough, scarred hand in her equally rough one and squeezed. Tom squeezed hers in return. Their neighbors, the Wellses, waved from the street.

Tom waved back enthusiastically as he replied, "We couldn't'a done it without each other, an' without good neighbors like them, Maggie."

Margaret sensed that Tom had never been so happy, and she felt her life was complete in his success. As they drove home, he whistled lively Irish tunes he'd learned as a boy.

* * *

Most of Tom's neighbors got title to their land at about the same time he did. With ownership of land came a sense of security, so the landowners invested more time and effort in improving the community. They widened trails into simple roads, built bridges over streams, and erected bigger schools and churches. The threat of Indian raids abated. Neighbors became close friends as they shared work, danger, hard times, and celebrations, and progressed from subsistence living to something still chancy but better than before. Tom was elected supervisor of the poor for Cross Creek Township a year after he received the patent for his farm. He added those official duties to the farmwork that kept him and his family busy from daylight to dark. But when they could, Tom and Maggie joined neighbors in fellowship and fun. Some of their neighbors noticed.

"Maggie, you and Tom were both real lively at that dance Saturday night. I swear I don't know how you do it with twelve kids. I only have seven, but I'm plumb tuckered out come night. How do you keep goin'?" Cora Wells looked at her longtime neighbor with a mix of awe and admiration.

Margaret kept on darning the hole in a sock draped over her left hand. "It ain't easy, Cora, Lord knows, but I just do what needs doin' every day, and he gives me strength when I get about worked out. Last few years, the girls have been a lot of help. I'm sure goin' to miss

Catherine when she gets married. Liza's real good about lookin' after the babies. This year she's getting handy at spinnin' and gardening, and Mary's comin' along."

"But how'd you do it until they got big enough to help out? All that cookin', the garden to plant and tend, wool to card and spin, meat to smoke, fruit to pick and dry, fires to stoke, all those clothes to make, an' sick kids to look after. It's enough to kill a body."

Cora watched Margaret's face, but Margaret's expression didn't change, so she continued. "And you're about the only woman on Cross Creek who ain't had to bury at least one baby. Now, I hear tell you were the one who put your menfolk up to standin' up to that Tom the Tinker. You must have some secret that you ain't told the rest of us."

Margaret smiled and leaned closer. "Well, Cora, if you promise never to tell a soul ... I do have a little helper. It's in a jug right there under a loose floorboard over in the corner. When all the menfolk are gone, I have a little sip of whiskey once in a while. It's amazin' how it calms me down when the kids get to yellin', and it gives me some spunk to tackle the next job. I'm gettin' to like it better 'n' better every year."

"I know Tom's death on whiskey, Maggie. Doesn't touch a drop. Aren't you afraid he'll smell it on your breath? You two must get pretty close at night, given the way you've had a baby 'most every year or two."

"I worried about that when I started liking what it does for me, so after I take a nip from the jug, I cut a little plug o' his tobacco and have a chaw. He never smells that whiskey a'tall. Got other things on his mind when we get close. If he ever stops chewin', though, I don't know what I'll do. So I never object to his chewin', like some women. I just don't let him spit on the floor."

"Maggie, you're a caution."

Margaret went to the corner, moved the wooden churn, lifted a short section of board, reached down, and pulled up a clay jug. "Well, thank you, Cora. Want a taste? I was just fixin' to have a sip when I saw you walking up. The menfolk won't be back for a while. They're cutting trees to put in some big gullies on the hill."

"You folks havin' trouble with them gullies too? Seems like just when we get things going our way, some new problem crops up. Last year it was the locusts. This year it's floods and gullies. I swear I don't know if there'll be any farm left, now that our boys are almost growed and ready for land of their own." Cora lifted the jug to her mouth and smacked her lips as she lowered it to the table. "Maggie, this whiskey is real good. I see why you like it." She tipped the jug again. Margaret nodded agreement, picked up the jug, took a drink, and then put the jug back under the floorboard.

"I been wonderin' the same thing, Cora. We got eight boys, and they'll all need land. It looks like Junior's gonna need some special help, since that tree fell on him last winter. An' I'm afraid this farm ain't gonna be big enough for John and his father much longer. They fight all the time like a cat an' a dog." Margaret sighed as she picked up another sock and started darning a hole in the heel.

"How's Junior doin' these days, anyway?" Cora's worried look matched her question.

Margaret sighed as she responded, "Oh, if somebody's with him all the time to look after him, he gets along. But we can't leave him by himself hardly at all."

Cora glanced at the sun and decided it was time for her to get back to work at home. Margaret saw her off, threw a log on the fire, stirred the stew in the kettle that hung over it, and returned to darning socks.

* * *

"John, you'll take a load of wheat down to Patterson's mill tomorrow. Have James help you load the wagon this afternoon, then get on the trail by daylight." Tom lifted his blue eyes and round, red-bearded face to look up at his tall, black-haired son as they finished dinner on a warm summer day.

"Pa, you given any thought to takin' it on down to the river at Wellsburg? I hear they pay better than ol' Patterson. Reckon he's been makin' money off all of us ever since he's had that mill. It's only another day's travel." John crossed his arms on his chest and looked straight at his father.

"No, sir! You ain't goin' to that den of iniquity at Wellsburg, even if they pay a few cents more. We been sellin' to Patterson ever since we came here, an' I aim to keep right on. Go find James and start loadin' that wagon."

John shrugged and walked out the door, biding his time. *Guess there's no use arguin' with him now,* he thought. *But with the crops doin' poorer every year, Pa oughta get the best price he can.*

As he and James and piled bags of wheat on the wagon, John's anger at his father subsided, but his resolve did not.

As the deep purple morning sky lightened, John guided the ox team to the front of the loaded wagon. James fastened the yoke across their necks while John hooked the pull-chain to the wagon tongue. "Don't wait on the hay-cuttin' for me, James. I know Pa figures I'll be back this afternoon, but I'm goin' right by Patterson's and down to Wellsburg. An' don't you dare tell him. When I come back tomorrow with a heap more money, he won't have cause to be mad for long." James made a choking sound deep in his throat as he looked at his brother. John picked up the prod pole and yelled, "Hike!" and the oxen and wagon moved out, leaving James watching, open-mouthed.

The team followed the rutted track without guidance from John. As he listened to the slow plop-plop of their feet on the hard dirt, he reveled in the morning. His eyes were drawn to the beads of dew on the clover and grass that arched, heavy with blossoms, over the edges of the road. He breathed deeper than he needed to and let the moist, musky aroma mingle with the smell of woodsmoke from his family's fireplace.

A fast thumping of hooves drew his eyes to the pasture across the creek. Four horses galloped to the fence rails, snorted, and nipped playfully at each other. He contemplated their antics and thought of his own journey. *They're kinda like me, feeling free and frisky. But they don't get two days to kick up their heels, like I will. 'Nother hour, and Reynolds will have them in the harness and be layin' the whip to 'em. Pretty much the way Pa treats me and James. Gotta make the most of what Wellsburg's got while I'm free. Can't wait to get to that tavern by the pier. Wonder if that black-haired gal with the big tits is still servin' drinks and goin' upstairs with a guy every once in a while?*

John's thoughts drifted further into the future as he walked beside the wagon. He felt like an outsider—the dark, black-haired stranger in a family of fair-skinned and freckled redheads. They didn't look like him or think like him, any of them, especially his father. He wanted to get away, be on his own. But how would it ever happen?

The off ox reached down for a bite of grass. John laid his pole across the back of the near ox and poked the laggard hard. "Hike, you lazy bastard! Git a move on." The ox stepped back into line beside his partner. The sun rose in the sky and passed its zenith as he and the ox team traveled past Patterson's mill and went on toward the Ohio River at Wellsburg.

***

"Where you reckon John is?" Tom stopped cutting hay, glanced at the late afternoon sun, and mopped his forehead. James swung his scythe an inch above the ground, saw the purple-blossomed clover and slender stems of timothy topple behind it, and took another measured scythe stroke.

"Dunno, Pa. Wagon musta broke down."

Tom stood his scythe on its handle and began to hone the blade with a whetstone. When he was done, he handed the stone to James and looked down the valley but saw no team and wagon.

***

When they sat down to supper, John was still absent. He missed the next morning's chores and breakfast and the work in the hayfield. It was dusk the next day when the rattle of a chain and a loud "Whoa!" signaled his arrival. Tom was out of the cabin like a flash. The rest of the family ran close behind.

"Where you been? You was supposed to be back here yesterday afternoon!"

"I've been getting us a decent price for our wheat fer once. Take a look at this." John extended a hand full of money. "Got half again as much in Wellsburg as Patterson offered. An' they did a better job o' grindin' us some flour, to boot."

Tom stepped to John's outstretched hand and took the money,

77

then sniffed. "Smells to me like you spent some of it on liquor. That right?"

"If I did or if I didn't, it's none o' yer business." John caught the hint of a smile on his mother's face.

Tom looked stunned, and then his face reddened clear to the roots of his red hair. "You did that, after I told you to stay away from that hellhole?"

"I did for sure. What you gonna do about it?"

Tom's fist came up. He stepped toward his oldest son and glared up into John's calm, defiant face.

John's fists were in front of his face, and his feet were set to throw a punch. "Think about it, Pa, before you start hittin'. I'm younger'n you an' a whole lot bigger an' stronger. I'd hate to break your face, but I will if I have to."

Tom stopped, fists up, and stood a moment. Then he stepped back, lowered his arms, and walked into the house. Margaret and the children noted the stoop in his shoulders.

* * *

As summer changed to fall, neighbors along Cross Creek began to hold husking bees to add sociability to the monotonous job of pulling the husks off dried corn so it could be used in their whiskey stills or ground into meal for food. John and three of his younger brothers were invited to a bee at the farm of Robert Walker, a new neighbor.

The next morning at breakfast, when their father inquired about the event, James announced, "John couldn't take his eyes off Polly, that oldest Walker girl. Him an' her looked at each other all the time we was there. After we got the corn shucked an' started dancin', they only danced with each other." John felt himself blushing under his beard as his other brothers added details to James's gleeful account. But secretly he felt proud of being the center of this conversation. His brother's retelling reminded him of how captivating he'd found Polly Walker the previous evening. She had joined her father in hosting the event in place of her recently buried mother, and she had carried out the role with spirit and charm.

Her welcoming smile, warm greeting as they arrived, striking auburn hair, robust feminine physique, and enthusiasm all swirled in his memory like a delicious dream.

He was snapped back to reality as his five-year-old brother, Jesse, waved his spoon and shouted, "John ha'n't et hardly any o' his mush yet," and everybody laughed. But after supper that evening, John went to the Walker farm for another visit. Those evening visits continued through the fall and winter.

The next spring, John told his family as they ate supper, "Polly Walker and I figure to get married come fall." His dinner-table announcement surprised no one.

Margaret spoke first. "I figured you'd wait till you got a cabin built. You got any idea where you're goin' to live?"

"Pa, if it's fine with you, we're figurin' we'd have a house-building party the day o' the wedding and put up a cabin alongside that spring up on the hillside." John looked to his father hopefully. "Otherwise, Polly's father says we can put one up on his place. But he don't own that land, and I hate to build on somebody else's ground."

Tom ran his big, callused hands over his red beard very slowly. "Been givin' it some thought, seein' that you been courtin' that Walker gal so hot and heavy. This place seemed awful big when I came here and claimed it, but with eight of you boys comin' to be men, it looks like it'll be way too small for all of us. I ain't exactly sure what we ought to do."

Everyone stared. Their father had always had answers before. Catherine broke the silence. "Maybe some of us oughta plan to move west 'cross the river. Hugh Roger says if Jefferson gets to be president, he's likely to open a lot of land west of the Ohio for settlers."

Young Tom, impaired since a tree limb fell on his head a year earlier, shot Catherine a scornful look. "Why w-w-would he go 'cross the river? He already owns more land'n Pa does. He's j-j-just tryin' to impress y-y-you so's you'll m-m-marry him an' he can s-s-s-start a new family. Tellin' you those b-b-big stories."

James weighed in with another opinion. "Way I figure, Pa oughta rent John a few acres round the spring fer a cabin, a cow, a horse, and a few crops. Then maybe we'll be shet of him and Pa jawin' at each other all the time."

Tom looked at Margaret, then at his older sons. "That sounds purty fair to me. John, if we set you and Polly up with some ground and help you build a cabin, you can have it fer a few years, but we'll likely need it for some o' your brothers when they get married. Then you'll have to find somethin' else. There's only one spring on the place, an' we don't have enough ground down here along the creek for more'n one or two other cabins."

John looked relieved. "That's fine with me, Pa. In a few years, we'll be on our own."

***

On a sunny day in late August, the log church at the top of the hill in Cross Creek was full of family and neighbors as Reverend Smith pronounced John Beaty and Mary Walker, known as Polly, husband and wife. In the grassy field around the church, horses were tied to wagon wheels or tethered to picket stakes by long ropes. Polly's father, Robert Walker, had butchered a steer the day before, and the meat was barbecuing in a pit at the edge of the meadow east of the church. As the service ended and people spilled out of the sanctuary, children joined the dogs that had waited outside and began to run among the wagons and horses and explore the woods nearby. The adults gathered near the barbecue. Walker and some helpers began to uncover the meat and slice it on wide planks set across two sawhorses; women set bowls of vegetables, pies, bread, and cakes on another plank table nearby.

The Reverend Smith stepped forward, raised his arm, and waited for everyone to stop talking, then began his blessing. "Almighty God, we, thy humble and obedient servants, come on this happy occasion to give thee thanks and praise. We thank thee for rain and sun that grow wheat for us and hay for our animals, and we hope for a good corn crop. We thank thee for our families and all the new children—also for the families who have moved here. We give thee special thanks for the new family that John Beaty and Mary Walker have formed by joining as man and wife. Bless this food and those who grew and cooked it, and all of us who will enjoy it. We pray in the name of our Lord and Savior Jesus Christ. Amen."

As amens resonated through the crowd, John and Polly were motioned to the head of the line in front of the food. Polly was first. She was a robust, big-boned eighteen, with wavy auburn hair highlighted by combs set into it above her ears. Her tanned skin and her sparkling, brown eyes contrasted with a red linen dress that was fitted snug at her waist. A full skirt brushed new leather shoes that buttoned across her insteps. John was a step behind, holding her left hand. He was tall and dark, with black hair and beard, a long narrow face, broad shoulders, and callused hands. He looked self-conscious but shyly proud of the attention. The buckskin shirt and breeches he normally wore had been replaced for the wedding by a borrowed broadcloth coat and pants and a high-collared linen shirt. His sturdy leather boots were not new, but they were clean. As he stood by Polly, he ran his left forefinger around the inside of his collar, where its novel presence chafed his neck.

Robert Walker waited, knife and serving fork in hand, behind big chunks of beef. Thomas and Margaret stood beside him, ready to serve. Someone shouted from the midst of a group of young men, "Drink to John and Polly. Give 'em lots of whiskey. Let 'em have lots of kids."

Voices responded, "Yes, yes. Lots of drinks. Lots of kids." And some young men in the group tipped the jugs they were carrying to their lips, each raising a bent arm. A lone voice shouted, "Too bad you can't have some now, John. Come see us later."

Polly and John stepped forward, and her father beamed as he forked a slab of beef onto each of their pewter plates. "May you always have meat for your table." Margaret waved a hand over bowls of potatoes and peas to scatter the flies, then spooned some of the vegetables on the newlyweds' plates before they moved on to receive more food and the good wishes that accompanied it from neighbors and friends.

"It's quite a celebration, John." Polly smiled at her new husband as he followed her along the line of well-wishers.

"Yes, love, an' you look right purty in that dress. But these clothes sure feel strange on me. Can't wait to get out of 'em and join the boys to work on our cabin."

"Will be far enough done for us to use tonight?"

"I'll make sure of that." John squeezed her waist with his left hand.

When the feasting was nearly over, John and the other young men walked down the hill to the site for the cabin. They left among an offering of friendly admonitions and advice. "Get the walls straight." "Make 'em a good bed." "Keep John away from the whiskey jug." "Come back for the dance."

The women and girls covered the food against the flies and bees and then congregated in the shade at the south end of the clearing. Margaret felt like the matriarch of Cross Creek as she and other women sat and talked while they knitted or darned holes in clothes. Even though he was headstrong and independent, she was proud of her eldest son, whose black hair and dark complexion stood out among his fair, red-haired siblings. She saw some of her own feistiness in his personality and wished him and his new bride well.

The men moved to some shade west of the church. Talk among them ranged widely as they sat, some chewing tobacco, others smoking clay or corncob pipes. A jug was passed; everyone drank from it but Tom.

Thomas Patterson told of digging in a rock shelter between his mill and the Ohio River. "I'd been hearin' of strange stuff in that cave, so one day when business was real slow, my mill hands and I went in there and dug around. Lotsa strange Injun things—arrowheads, spear tips, scrapers. Some of it's real purty, an' sharp as a razor. Not like the brown rock from around here." He stopped for a few draws on his pipe "We musta dug down three, four feet. Never came to the end of it. I got some of the stuff in sacks down at the mill, iffen you want to look at 'em sometime while I'm grindin' your grain." He stopped to smoke, found that his pipe had gone out, pounded the ashes and unburned tobacco out of the bowl, and refilled it.

Charlie Reynolds spat tobacco juice on a rock and said, "I'd like to see that stuff, but all I figure Injuns are good for is thievin', scalpin', and burnin'." Nods of assent came from around the group.

The talk flowed on to weather, roads and where they should be built, the tax on whiskey, and the lingering resentment against President Washington and his government in Philadelphia. The men had all signed the oath of allegiance to that government, but they had done so out of necessity. Several of the men lamented the progressive declines in yields of crops and the burgeoning problems with gullies in their fields and sediment in the creek. Remedies for the gullies were shared, none were pronounced wholly satisfactory, and several men voiced concern about the livelihood they or their sons could get from the land, as the wild game they'd hunted and the ginseng they'd dug and sold each fall got scarcer every year.

This led to talk about the pros and cons of pulling up stakes and claiming new land across the Ohio River. Three of the men had crossed the river and explored the hilly land to the west. Others shared reports they'd heard from different travelers. The prospects of new land, land that would produce like their farms had after the trees were first cleared twenty years ago, were weighed against the hardships and risks of relocating and reestablishing homes, clearing fields, and building roads.

A man who had crossed the river and walked over the hills on the other side chimed in with a new factor for the group to ponder. "Up in them hills, there's places where coal lies only two, three feet down in the ground. Easy to dig, and sure beats wood fer heatin'."

"I hear tell that some folks are fixin' to start diggin' coal on the Monongahela up above Fort Duquesne—what's the town's new name, Pittsburgh?—and float it down the river on barges." The tall, stooped man who shared this news coughed and spat his cud of tobacco on the ground.

"Maybe this whole country has coal under it if you dig far enough. Ever think of that?" Judge Marshall ventured.

The talk ebbed and flowed until nearly sunset, when the men who had gone to finish John and Polly's cabin returned. A tall man uncased his fiddle and began to play. A younger man with a mouth organ joined him. Some couples began to dance. When the fiddler stopped, an old man blew up the bag of his pipes, tuned them a little, and began to play the melancholy songs of Scotland as the women finished laying out the remaining food. Calls went out for Polly and John to go first. Polly stepped to the end of the table and looked for John. He left the group of young men who were passing a jug and walked unsteadily toward her.

"We shuposhed to lead agin, Polly?

"John Beaty, you're drunk! And on your wedding day." She took his hand and guided him along the tables of food, and then to a large tree where they could sit with John leaning against the trunk.

"I'm real sorry, Polly. The boys had some jugs down there, an' every time they put another log on the cabin, they made me take a drink. They worked like beavers, an' I had ta drink an awful lot. Maybe we should wait a bit ta start dancin'."

When the eating, talking, and dancing reached full swing, Judge Marshall motioned to Tom. "I need to talk to you about that place of yours, Tom. Let's take a walk so's we can be by ourselves."

Tom caught an undertone of concern in Judge Marshall's voice. "Whatever you want, judge." They walked behind the church and down the road to the north.

"I hate to tell you this, Tom, but those Stephenson folks I told you about maybe havin' a Virginia claim to part of your and Wiley's land sent me a letter sayin' they want to take it up. We'll have to deal with them somehow." He put his hand on Tom's shoulder.

"Ya mean I could lose my land only two years after I got the patent for it?" Tom's voice matched his look of incredulity.

"'Tis possible, Tom. So could Alex."

"Judge, I sure hope you'll help us. I've put my whole life an' soul into that land. An' just when I thought I'd made it, troubles came in bunches. Young Tom ain't been right in the head all the time since that tree limb fell on him last year. John's takin' too much of a likin' to the drink. Now maybe I'm gonna lose my land. It's not a pleasant situation fer a wedding, I'll tell you."

Judge Marshall nodded. "You and Alex come see me about the land. I'll do what I can for you, but I'm sure it will cost you some money. You better start savin' up all you can." He left Tom and walked back toward the dancers and onlookers.

Tom stood, shoulders slumped, then walked slowly into the woods behind the church. A whippoorwill called just above the trees, and another answered from down the hill. He listened to their calls and responses. *If my name was Will, they'd be singing about me,* he thought. *Worked my heart out ever since I come from the old country, and maybe I won't even have a farm. Lord, help me. S'pose I'll have to tell*

Maggie before she hears it from somebody else. He walked back toward the celebration with slow, heavy steps.

Chapter 9
Fighting for the Farm

One morning in October as he finished milking, Tom spied a tall stranger riding a big roan gelding on the road along the creek, and it made him apprehensive. The man rode easily, like he'd been born on a horse, but the roan's ears were moving back and forth, then all the way back, like he didn't want to be there. The man reined him to a stop at the fork in the road. Tom moved a few steps across the yard to see the rider better through the trees. He appeared to be about forty-five, tall and lean, with a thin weathered face and a black beard. The man pulled a map from his buckskin shirt and studied it. Tom saw him turn the map, then look to his right at the field the Beatys had cleared year by year, and he felt a chill run up and down his spine and mutterd to no one in particular.

"Damn! Do ya s'pose that's Stephenson come to look at the land he claims is his?"

The roan's ears were still back. The man patted his mount's neck with his right hand and reined the horse toward the right-hand fork that passed by the Beatys' farmstead. The roan bent his head left. The man reined him hard to the right and then kicked his ribs to start him on the road between the creek and the partly cleared hillside he'd been studying. Tom watched him approach and motioned for James and Samuel to stop stalking the squirrels in the oaks beside the cabin and join him. They came to his side and leaned their guns against a wagon wheel as the man rode up.

"Howdy, stranger. What brings you hereabouts?" Tom's question conveyed both his curiosity and his worry. Margaret heard the dogs bark and came to the cabin door. Several children peeked around her skirts. The man reined his horse to a stop.

"Just riding through. Fixin' to see some land up ahead a ways. Looks like you got a nice place started here. Ya had this land long?"

"Been living here 'bout twenty years. Got our patent back in '95. But some bastard from Kaintucky's tryin' to steal it out from under us. Name of Stephenson. If he shows up, we aim to run him off. Maybe ventilate his hide a little, just for good measure. Don't we, boys?" James and Samuel nodded and looked toward their guns. Tom spat a stream of tobacco juice. "Nice horse ya got there. Ain't never seen a roan like that before. You ain't from 'round here, are ya?"

"I come from the south, an' I got a far piece to go today. Guess I'll be movin' on. If I see anybody named Stephenson, I'll tell 'im to steer clear o' you, less'n he wants his hide ventilated."

He tipped his hat, reined the roan to the right, clucked "giddap," and pressed his legs and heels in hard. The roan broke into a gallop after a few strides. The rider looked back furtively as he sped up the road. The Beatys were watching him.

As horse and rider disappeared around a curve, Tom said, "I've got a funny feelin' 'bout that fella. Looked like he wanted to talk some more—then changed his mind and left awful fast." He shook his head, told his older sons what he wanted done in the fields and woods after they'd shot squirrels enough for dinner, and told Margaret that he was going over the hill to see Alex Wiley about their problem. She seemed pleased.

"Go do whatever ya like. If yer over at Wiley's, you won't be here yellin' at me an' the kids. You've been ornery as a she-bear with cubs since this land trouble came up." She sighed and went back into the cabin.

Tom walked up the hill without noticing the fall flowers or the cougar that crossed his path. At the top of the hill, he sat on a stump, put his head in his hands, and prayed briefly. Then he plodded toward the plume of smoke that rose from the Wileys' chimney down the slope.

Two black dogs announced his arrival. Alex looked out the door, scanned Tom's lined and haggard face, and said. "Howdy, Tom. You look awful. Somebody get kilt?"

"'Tain't that. I'm worried sick about what we kin do to save our land." Tom sat down heavily on a log.

Alex's news began to burst out before Tom could pull out his plug of tobacco. "Well, we got a whole lot to worry about. I was in Washington yesterday an' learnt what this Stephenson wants, and it's real bad. That scoundrel's been to Judge Marshall. Wants us off a lot of our land by next summer—your part along the creek, my land here by the spring. Right where our buildings are—three hundred acres in all. Claims his Virginia certificate beats our Pennsylvania patents 'cause his family got it earlier. It's terrible!"

Tom was on his feet in a flash. "That just can't be, Alex! He's nothin' but a thief, trying to steal our land. Let's just shoot him an' his kin if they come tryin' to take what's ours. That's what we done with the Injuns. An' they're just 'bout gone now." Tom's face was as red as his hair. He threw his hat on the ground and then spat tobacco juice on a cat that was sitting in the sun beside the cabin.

"You can't do that to white folk, Tom! We could both get strung up if they caught us. Besides, them Stephensons may have more men an' boys that can fight than we do, an' we'd be the ones that got shot. The judge said a passel o' them was in to see him, and that one was comin' up this way to see the land they claim to own. Said he rides a roan gelding."

Tom's jaw dropped. "That thievin' son of a bitch was just ridin' up the road! Talked to us a minute, then turned tail and ran. If I'd'a knowed fer sure it was him, I'd'a shot him ... an' his horse, to boot."

"Good thing you didn't, Tom. The judge said some folks have tried that, an' had to come to court to straighten out who got kilt, an' then come back again to settle the land fight. Seems there's been a passel of these title fights between folks with Virginia certificates an' folks like us with Pennsylvania patents. I reckon we oughta go back to Judge Marshall and see if he can help us work somethin' out to buy these Stephensons' claim."

Tom's face was red, and his response was emphatic. "Can't do that. I got next to no money. So I'm for waitin' an' shooting 'em if they come an' try to run us off. We're as good o' shots as them Kaintucks. An' we know the ground better'n them." Tom's face was still red as he picked up his hat and glanced around Wiley's farmstead, mentally selecting trees and buildings from which he could ambush the Stephensons should they appear.

"Why don't you do like I done, Tom? Clear some more ground, and grow more corn. Then get a still and sell whiskey. Makes me good money most years. I got near about three hundred dollars ahead that I could put toward clearin' title to my land if I hafta." Alex bit some tobacco off a plug and slid it into his left cheek as he watched Tom's face. "Seems like you may be out on your ear if you don't grow somethin' that makes you some money. This country's 'bout trapped out of beaver. Bear an' cougar's gettin' scarce too. Fella can't make much sellin' just furs and ginseng anymore."

Tom kicked at a small stick, then ran the toe of his right boot around and around aimlessly in the loose dirt. Finally he said, "It'd near about kill me to do that. When I was a lad back in County Fermanagh, my pappy let us kids go hungry lots of times so's he could buy a pint fer himself. I've been dead set agin liquor ever since. Now I gotta decide between my principles an' my land. The Almighty must have it in for me." He pulled on his hair with a callused hand and walked around aimlessly. "Let me talk to Maggie and the boys. I'll let you know." Tom walked slowly up the hill toward home, head down, deep in thought.

***

Alex got his answer two days later when the thunk of axes chopping trees across the ridge echoed down to his cabin. He heard it every day except Sundays after that. By the time heavy snow made it difficult to work in the woods, Tom and his sons had cut the trees on nearly fifteen acres and piled the brush and limbs around the tree trunks. Early the next spring, they lit the piles of brush and stoked the fires through the night to get the brush and limbs completely burned. Charred black tree trunks lay scattered on the hillside like partly burned corpses.

They planted corn where the trees had been cut, using a pointed hickory stick to make holes for the seeds and a boot heel to cover them. The corn grew prodigiously among the scattered tree trunks on the newly cleared ground. Week after week that fall, every member of the Beaty family except Margaret carried baskets of corn down the hill to the enlarged log corncrib beside the new still. As they were picking the last ears, John said, "Let's put out the word that next Saturday we'll have a niggerin' off to get all these charred logs piled, so's we can burn 'em before winter. They're dry enough now to burn real good if we pile 'em right."

The news spread, and a week later, neighbors from the village on the hill and the farms along Cross Creek began to arrive. John, James, and Samuel appointed themselves team captains and selected members for their teams. Alex Wiley and Tom Patterson assigned work areas and agreed to decide which team had piled the most logs. At Wiley's and Patterson's loud whistles, the older boys and young men, well supplied with whiskey and equipped with long-handled iron hooks, ran to the tree-strewn hillside and began to roll, pry, and lift the charred logs into piles that would sustain a hot fire. Team members urged each other on as they heaved and rolled the blackened tree trunks. Charcoal, soot, and ashes mingled with the sweat that ran down their faces and arms and gradually obliterated all differences in color among them. The thirty distinctive individuals who had run to the hillside quickly became three groups of frenzied black apparitions, distinguishable only by differences in stature.

They eyed the competing teams as they worked, and they stopped only to wipe the charcoal and ashes off their lips and refuel themselves with quick slugs of whiskey when they thought they were a few logs ahead of their competitors. Wiley and Patterson walked among them, counting the piled logs and admonishing the captains not to cheat by making their piles too small to burn fully. When they were satisfied that a pile of logs had been properly erected and accounted for, they set it on fire.

Tom walked slowly to the top of the field, found a stump with a view of the hill slope and his farmstead, and sat down. He shook his head as he looked at the burning log piles, the frenzy of black figures, and the miasma of soot and smoke in which they strained. He mused to no one in particular, "So this is what hell's like. I make a pact with the devil hisself, and he gives me a look at his kingdom. Maybe a little hotter and smokier there … otherwise not too much different. I'm maybe gonna lose Victory, but I've already lost the victory over demon rum, now that we're makin' it an' selling it." He turned away and wiped his eyes.

When the last log was piled and the blackened men straggled down to the farmyard to eat, drink, and learn which team had won, Tom was still sitting on a tree stump high on the hillside, mourning his loss.

Margaret, Polly, and the women of the neighborhood had cooked and laid out mountains of meats, fruits, and vegetables on a line of tables. Patterson and Wiley declared James's team the winner. The men on his team cheered, brushed the soot and ash off their hands, and rushed to the food as though they were afraid it was going to escape. While they grabbed the best that the women had laid out, some of the soot-encrusted men on the other teams went behind the barn, peeled off their buckskins, and jumped into the creek. Others crowded around jugs of whiskey beside the still. When they all had eaten and drunk their fill, someone asked, "Where's John?"

A young man from Cross Creek spoke up, "I saw him lyin' on some straw in the barn. Looked like he was dead drunk. He never does know when to stop."

* * *

After they'd sold their whiskey, Tom and Alex visited Judge Marshall's courtroom in Washington. They had $390 between them. The judge agreed to postpone the Stephensons' request that the contested land be vacated by summer, but he said that he had no legal basis to deny their claim altogether, since he had been adjudicating other disputed claims, upon payment of two to three dollars per acre, to the earliest claimant. He said he would try to get the Stephensons to agree to such a settlement.

"But judge, we ain't got the money to pay more than a dollar an' thirty an acre now. Could you try to get us some more time to raise the rest?" Tom looked imploringly at Judge Marshall. "Remember, I only just last year started makin' whiskey an' gettin' a little money ahead."

Alex added, "An' get us the best price you can from them thieves. I'd say two dollars an acre would be more'n fair, since they never done any clearin' or nothin'."

"Don't know about that, but I'll do what I can for you. Keep saving your money. And come back about the middle of December. I should know something by then." Judge Marshall stood up, and Tom and Alex shook his hand and left, still dejected.

Judge Marshall apparently did some hard bargaining on behalf of Alex and Tom, because when the pair returned with what money they had saved in December, the judge had prepared a document that gave them more time to raise money.

Witnesseth that the said John Stephenson for and in consideration of the sum of Three hundred and Ninety Dollars to be paid to the said John Stephenson in hand and the obligation of said Wiley and Beaty for the payment of Two hundred and Forty dollars which is the balance of the purchase money do oblige themselves their heirs executors and administrators to procure and deliver to the said Beatty and Wiley their heirs and assigns a good and sufficient deed in fee simple for the Three hundred Acres as soon as the said tract can be conveniently divided and the patent obtained therefor.

—*From a document dated December 16, 1803, filed in the Washington County Courthouse, Pennsylvania*

The Beatys and Wileys felt relieved when the land claim settlement was complete. But Tom never forgave himself for the bargain he'd made to save his farm.

Chapter 10
Northwest Territory

John felt suffocated, even though the weather was mild, as he stood beside his father, swinging the scythe and cradle in his father's wheat field.

"Pa, next year we oughta try a new kind of wheat, one that doesn't get the rust so bad."

"This one's good enough for me. Why buy seed when we can save our own? We been doin' that for years." Tom snorted, stopped cutting, and began to sharpen his scythe.

John let his scythe and cradle rest on the ground as he retorted, "This wheat's no good anymore, Pa. Down at Patterson's mill, they're sellin' wheat seed they say don't get this damned rust. We oughta buy some."

"You been ridin' me 'bout this till I'm sick o' hearin' it. Now shut your mouth, forget your high-falutin' ideas, an' sharpen your scythe so we can get this field cut." Tom thrust his whetstone at John and began to cut again. A cloud of red dust engulfed him.

John looked at James and Samuel and shrugged as he pushed the stone along the scythe edge. They shrugged back and began cutting the thin stand of wheat again. The red cloud of spores grew and enveloped them all.

For John, life here seemed a dead end. Every innovation he or his brothers proposed to make the farm produce more was anathema to their father. But Tom saw all the little things that John did wrong, and he told him about them at length.

The next day it rained, and they couldn't cut wheat. John walked a few miles to see his sister Catherine and her husband, Hugh Rogers. As they stood looking over Hugh's field of wheat, John broached his idea. "Your grain don't look too good this year, Hugh. What if we went together and got us some new land 'cross the Ohio? From what I hear, the government's about ready to put it up for sale."

Hugh took off his hat and ran his hand over his bald head. "Been hearin' the same thing. This land's sure not what it used to be. But they say that over there, a guy's gotta buy a whole section of ground or nothing. 'Bout 640 acres—a whole mile square. Not sure I can afford that much all by myself, even if I can sell this place." He sighed as he examined the broken, rust-infected wheat stems with shriveled heads.

"Maybe we can get some folks to go in with us. I'll bet James and Samuel would. They got a little money saved up, an' they can't stand Pa any more'n I can. An' maybe Will Wiley would come with us. Heard him an' his old man are fightin' a lot." He looked at Hugh, hoping to hear agreement with his proposal.

Hugh's response relieved John's worries. "Now, if the five of us got together, an' each put in some money, maybe we could swing something. Why don't you talk to 'em? It's near noon. Come eat dinner with us an' talk to Catherine before you go home."

Hugh and John told Catherine their idea of teaming up to buy some land in Ohio, and she gave it her enthusiastic endorsement. After dinner, John walked home in the light rain with a spring in his step that hadn't been there for a long time. Polly was excited by his plan. She dreaded the perpetual arguments between John and his father and feared they would come to blows.

On a morning when Tom was hunting squirrels near the top of the ridge, John and Polly and their children walked to his parents' home, where John shared his plan with Margaret, James, and Samuel. "Hugh an' I are thinking of getting a piece of government land over across the Ohio that's big enough for all of us. Maybe buying what they call a section, an' then dividing it so's we'd each have a farm of our own, but right next to each other." He watched his family's faces closely for their reaction. "That'd give us a chance to get started on our own, an' leave this place for Pa an' the younger boys to farm."

Polly interjected a supporting idea. "There's too many of us tryin' to live on this farm. We better make a move while we can. We're just lucky Hugh's willing to join us to do it."

Margaret looked pleased. "Sounds like a good idea, John. I'm all for it, even though it'd leave a big hole if you all pulled out at once. But maybe you could get land like Tom and I did years ago and live without us old folks interferin'. I'll talk to Tom 'bout it, soon as he comes back with some squirrels for dinner. Maybe he'll listen to me for once."

John put his arm around his mother's shoulder. "Thanks, Ma. I'm glad somebody here has some good sense."

As he and Polly gathered their children, who were playing in the yard, and walked up the hill toward home, John felt hopeful. Polly shared his feeling, even though she wished he'd stop drinking. When Margaret told Tom of their son's plans, he grudgingly agreed that they could move west.

* * *

As John Beaty and Hugh Rogers stepped off the ferry at Steubenville on the west side of the Ohio River, John remembered how hot he'd been on the day last summer when he and Hugh had first seen the settlement. Today they sensed something strange and different. Men, horses, oxen, and wagons crowded the dirt street between a jumble of new buildings, many of them unfinished. Then they spotted the crowd of men at the end of the street and hurried to join it.

"Open up. We're here to buy land." The big fellow who shouted expressed the frustrations of all the men milling in front of the new log building with LAND OFFICE painted above the door.

Hugh and John looked at each other and shared a sense of mutual recognition. The excitement and frustration that emanated from the crowd, along with the smells of stale sweat, woodsmoke, and wet leather, kindled memories for them both. This was like the mobs that had gathered when they were trying to get rid of the whiskey tax a few years back. They used their broad shoulders to push slowly into the crowd. John speculated to himself about the men and their frames of mind. *They've got no time to waste standin' in line in front of some government office. They'd all be out staking out a parcel fer themselves if they thought that was enough to keep it.*

A slight man with black hair and a droopy moustache opened the door and stepped back quickly to avoid being trampled. His partner, a tall, sad-faced man, looked out from behind a rough plank counter at the men spewing into the room. "All right, stand back! Don't push like a bunch of hogs at the trough. We'll take you one at a time. You there—yer first." He pointed to a short man who had been among the first to enter. "What section are you fixin' to buy?"

"Whaddaya mean, section? I'm aimin' to claim a piece of the bottom on Oak Crick."

"Can't do that over here. Everything's surveyed in sections, neat and square. Lines run straight, north and south. None of those crooked metes and bounds like back across the Ohio. Look at that map on the wall, an' tell me what ya want. An' don't be slow. There's lotsa men waitin'." The man made a quick decision, paid his money, and got his deed.

After a long wait, the clerk aimed a finger at John and Hugh as he said, "Next!"

Hugh responded, "I want section nineteen there on Short Creek. Accordin' to the map, that's township nine an' range four, whatever that means." He nodded toward John. "I an' my brother-in-law done seen the land an' know we want it."

"Ya got the $1,280 it'll cost ya?"

"Yessiree, right here." Hugh emptied the contents of a leather pouch on the counter. They watched the man intently as he counted. When the clerk nodded and picked up a sheet of paper with the word *Patent* across the top, they both relaxed but continued to watch as the man dipped a quill and inked the name *Hugh Rogers* after the word *To*, then the numbers *19, 9,* and *4* in the spaces after the words *section, township,* and *range*.

When the clerk handed him the completed document, Hugh pointed to the bottom line. "That really President Jefferson's signature?"

The harried clerk's answer was abrupt. "Yup. He signs 'em all, right by that big seal. Take good care of it. Next!"

As he and John pushed out through the crowd, Hugh thought about how fast things had changed. A dozen years ago, he and most of the men there had been rebelling against the government for taxing the whiskey they produced. Now they were jostling and elbowing one another to get some of the new land that same government was selling. And he was one of them. Back then, he'd been all broken up after Abigail and all their kids died the night the cabin burned when he was at a rally against the tax. Now he was married to Catherine Beaty, raising a new batch of kids, and buying land for three of her brothers, their neighbor, and himself. Things had really changed.

Rogers, Hugh, valuation $1261, tax $2.52 [This entry is lined through and followed by the notation "gon Linwell Petter in place"] Beaty, John, 2 horses 2 cows, valuation $98, tax $0.12 Beaty, James, 1 horse, valuation $40, tax $0.33

—County Tax Records for 1806 filed in the Washington County Courthouse, Pennsylvania

United States Government to Hugh Rogers, section 19, township 9, range 4, May 13 1806

—Land Patent filed in the Harrison County Courthouse, Ohio

As he prepared to move, John reflected on changes he'd seen as he grew up. His father and their early neighbors had been content to claim a tract of land, build a log cabin and barn, clear part of it to raise enough to subsist on, hunt and trap wild animals to get cash for their hides, and count themselves successes. But people coming from the east brought word of new machines that made farming easier, wood-burning stoves to replace fireplaces, and new kinds of crops and livestock. These were all things that he and his brothers wanted but that their father didn't. And they all cost money. He understood farming was changing, turning from subsistence to something different. And he was ready to compete in this changing rural society.

* * *

On moving day, John was so excited that he was up before first light. He fed and watered the animals, milked the two cows, and then tied them behind the loaded wagon. When John finished milking, Polly was making breakfast. She put most of the milk in the wooden churn that sat on top of their household goods, where the jostling and shaking of the moving wagon would churn the butter. Then she fed the chickens and shooed them into the wooden crate John had made. She poured fresh milk for the children and ladled out the porridge, and after they'd eaten, she washed the dishes at the spring and put them in a box in the wagon. James and Samuel arrived, driving Tom's yoke of oxen and leading a horse. Before the sun topped the long hill behind the cabin, they were ready to leave.

Polly wrapped a hot towel around a pan of bread starter to keep it warm and put it behind the wagon seat. Then she gathered the children and climbed into the front. As the oxen pulled the loaded wagon down the hill beside Tom and Maggie's large, two-story log home that stood beside the original log cabin, the rest of the family was waiting to see then off. Tom, Maggie, and three of their sons were standing next to the road. Maggie was holding Junior's hand to keep him from joining the procession. Two younger children waved from the door of the house.

Tom looked at his wife and said, "Well, Maggie, they're on their own now." He ran a hand across his face. Margaret patted his arm and dabbed at her eyes with her apron.

"We had quite a brood, Tom. Still have. Even without them two we buried on the hill four years ago." She took Tom's hand and stood linked with her husband and disabled son as the wagon with its trailing animals creaked and jolted in front of them. They raised linked hands. Margaret pulled Junior's hand as high as she could, and then he lifted his other hand and waved. Everyone in the wagon train except the baby waved back. Polly held her high for everyone to see one last time as good-byes and Godspeeds resonated in the morning air.

Tom blew his nose on his sleeve. "It's hard seeing so many of 'em pull out all at once. The boys an' I argued somethin' awful, but I'm gonna miss 'em."

Margaret lifted her apron and dabbed her eyes again. "It sure will seem quiet without 'em. But they're raring to strike out on their own. And the younger boys are big enough to do most of the farming now. Without those older three to boss around, you'll have more time to help Tom Patterson set up the township poor farm." When the little caravan rounded the corner behind some trees, she led her disabled son back into the house.

Tom stood by himself, looking down the road, long after the travelers were out of sight. He remembered how wild the country had been the first time he and Alex Wiley had walked along the creek on a narrow, tree-lined trail. Now his three oldest sons had just set off, along cultivated fields, for frontiers even farther west on the road that had replaced the forest trail he and Alex Wiley has used twenty five years earlier.

When John, Polly, James, Samuel, and their entourage arrived at Patterson's mill, Catherine and Hugh Rogers were waiting with their family and belongings. Hugh's wagon was bigger than the one that Tom's sons had borrowed from their father, and it had two yoke of oxen in front. The travelers rattled down the valley to Wellsburg amid children's laughter and excited talk among the adults. John arranged for the ferry to take them across into the young state of Ohio the next morning.

At the ferryboat landing on the broad Ohio River, Hugh Rogers's goad drew blood before his ox teams finally pulled his wagon up the ramp and onto the deck of the ferry, a rough-planked, flat boat with a low railing. As they were pulled on board, his horses fought against the ropes that tied them to the back of the wagon. James and Samuel helped John prod his father's ox team up the ramp behind Hugh's. The families followed, driving the cows and sheep on board, and the ferry operator cranked up the ramp until it cleared the ground, and then he closed the gate. Then he and his men began to pull on the cable that stretched across the river.

As the ferry left shore, Hugh Rogers's bay gelding jerked back, broke the rope that linked his halter to the wagon, and lunged for the back of the ferry, where Hugh and Catherine's oldest daughter was guarding the sheep. She grabbed the dangling end of the bay's broken halter rope. He snorted, swung his head over the railing, and flung her into the water.

Hugh was closest to the careening horse and grabbed its halter. John, just behind him, threw his hat on the deck and leaped over the railing in one fluid motion. He caught his niece by the hair as she went under a second time, managed to get a hand on a rope that hung over the back of the boat, and pulled her head out of the water. She grabbed his arm and wrapped her legs around one of his as she coughed for air. John lunged upward and got enough slack in the rope to wrap it around his hand. Above him, Catherine screamed as she looked down. Hugh and James appeared, and John saw a coil of rope in Hugh's arm.

"Quick, man, I can't hold on long." John's words were half water, half air.

Hugh tied the rope to the railing, and James lowered it as an ever-lengthening loop over John's head and body. John lifted one foot and pushed the rope down until the loop was directly under him.

"Hold tight," he said. "We're climbing on." He got his other foot in the loop of the rope and felt the lift as Hugh and James took the full weight of the wet twosome. He looked down at the girl's dripping face, felt her shiver.

"Keep hangin' on. We're gonna be all right." He felt his niece's grip on his leg loosen ever so slightly.

John did careful sidesteps as Hugh, Samuel, and James pulled them up; he moved his free hand up the rope in short grabs. Then he felt strong hands lift and pull them both over the railing as he passed out from exhaustion. James's voice, offering a prayer of thanks for the rescue, seemed to come from miles away. It wasn't until Polly knelt beside him and said, "I'm so proud of you," that he felt he was in the world again. After they'd reached the far shore and unloaded, John picked up a handful of soil and pressed it to his lips. Then, when no one was looking, he lifted a bottle from where he'd hidden it, drank half its contents, and then hid it again.

The evening of the following day, the Beaty and Rogers families rattled up the steep-sided valley to the south edge of their property, made camp, and began to unload.

Early the next morning, John looked around the large circle of family at breakfast. "Well, first we gotta divide this section of land up among us, so's we can start clearin' and building. Will Wiley ain't here yet, so we gotta be fair to him."

John continued, "Pa used to tell about how he and Will's father flipped a stone to decide who got which piece of ground when they took up land together back home. But that won't work for five of us. Maybe we can draw numbers from a hat." There were general nods of assent, and the brothers walked over the square mile to get an idea of what parts they would select. Polly and Catherine washed the utensils and kept an eye on the children and animals.

James drew number one and selected the northwest quarter section, the least steep and least wooded of any of the four. Hugh drew number two and picked the northeast quarter because it had some open land. Polly drew number three for Will Wiley, and they decided that he should get the southeast quarter. John and Samuel agreed to divide the steep southwest quarter in proportion to the money they could pay toward its cost.

With the land decision made, they cleared building sites and built cabins. Since they were single, James helped Hugh while Samuel helped John. They understood that when they married and were ready to build a house, they would be helped in return. When Will Wiley and his family arrived a month later, everybody pitched in to help them get settled and build a cabin. Then everyone cleared timber and planted a garden and as much rye, wheat, and corn as they could. It was not until the next year that they formalized the division of section on which they'd settled.

Hugh Rogers and Catherine, his wife, to John Beaty, southwest 1/4, section 19, township 9, range 4, March 27, 1807

Hugh Rogers and Catherine, his wife, to James Beaty, northwest 1/4, section 19, township 9, range 4, March 27, 1807

John Beaty and Mary, his wife, to Samuel Beaty, part of the southwest 1/4, section 19, township 9, range 4, March 27, 1807

Hugh Rogers and Catherine, his wife, to William Wiley, southeast 1/4, section 19, township 9, range 4, March 27, 1807

—Deeds filed in the Harrison County Courthouse, Ohio

* * *

In the fall of 1815, skies stayed gray week after week, with a circle of faint brightness on some days where the sun would normally be seen. Along Short Creek, the Beaty, Rogers, and Wiley families—which now included James's wife, Janey Randall, and Samuel's wife, Mary Stebbins—watched the winter coats grow longer than normal on their horses, oxen, and cows and understood that they should expect a long, cold winter. They dug more coal than usual, laid in extra-large supplies of wood, and stuffed more peat moss into the cracks between the logs of their houses.

The winter was everything they'd feared and more—bitter cold, deep snow, and biting wind, with none of the usual intervals of warm, sunny days. People in eastern Ohio attributed the unusual weather to many things: God's judgment, a prelude to the apocalypse, even Indian treachery. But the cold, cloudy weather had its origin half a world away in the East Indies, where a volcanic explosion had blown an entire island out of existence and filled the sky with debris that shut out much of the sun's warmth.

The next spring was worse. The gray skies, cold winds from the northwest, and freezing nights continued after the snow finally melted. Pastures and hay meadows were slow to turn green. Fields they had expected to plow and plant in late March or April didn't dry out until May. The first wheat and rye seeds they planted rotted in the cold, wet ground. Everyone had to deplete their food reserves to get seed to replant. As avidly as his father had years ago, John stalked game in the woods to feed his family. Polly and her older daughters dug roots and scoured the woods for wild berries when they finally appeared.

The year 1816 is called the year without a summer.

—*C. R. Harrington, editor, The Year without a Summer?*

As John, his son, Sam, and his daughter, Jane, were replanting potatoes after a freeze in early June, a visitor rode up on a bay mare. John was the first to see him. He recognized his brother Jesse at once, even though it had been a decade since they'd seen each other.

"Jesse, what brings you over here?" He turned to his children, "Look, everybody, it's your uncle Jesse from back in Cross Creek."

Jesse swung down, shook the cramps from his legs, and put out his hand. John clasped it eagerly. Jesse said softly, "I came to tell you Pa is awful low. Ma would like to have you and James and Catherine and Samuel come if you-all can get away. We doubt that he'll last more'n another few days. He ain't been eatin'—just lies and coughs. Says he feels cold. Seems like he just gave up on livin' since the crops keep freezin'."

John nodded. "I been havin' a bad feelin' about him an' this cold summer, 'specially after it froze a inch of ice the other mornin'. This weather's enough to take the heart out of most anybody." He paused. "Well, I'll leave the young'uns to take care of the planting an' go with you to tell Hugh and Catherine, an' Samuel and James. I can get loose an' go back with you. Reckon maybe they can too."

Jesse and his four siblings started for Cross Creek the next morning, driving a team of horses hitched to a light spring wagon. Hugh Rogers came later, riding Jesse's horse. The rough trail they'd followed up from the ferry at Wellsburg during the move west in 1807 had become a road, with bridges and corduroy pavements of logs in swampy stretches. By nightfall, they were at the Ohio River. The next morning, they took the first ferry, and they were near their old home by early afternoon.

There had been a lot of improvements. New houses and barns made from sawed lumber stood near the small log structures they remembered. Bridges had replaced the muddy fords where the road crossed the creek. Rocks and stumps that had once been in the roadway were mostly gone. The frost-killed crops formed a broad, tan swath in the valley.

"Sure been a lot of changes." John's observation brought nods of agreement.

James said, "Yeah. And I'm real anxious to see the new house Pa and Jesse built."

"Too bad we didn't have it when all twelve of us kids were crammed into the one by the creek. You guys never gave me any room in the bed. That's why I grew up short and have a crook in my back." Samuel gave his brothers a look of mock reproach. "I'd'a done better if I'd gone and slept with the girls in the other bed."

"We didn't want anybody else. Four of us in a bed was enough," Catherine responded with a laugh. "Besides, we didn't want your lice. We had plenty of our own."

As the long, west-facing slope of the home place came into view along Cross Creek, James looked at Jesse and said, "You and Pa seem to have done pretty well since we left. After we started makin' whiskey, I wasn't sure if Pa wanted to farm or not. Now you've even got a decent new house an' barn." Jesse looked pleased.

There were several horses tied to the fence by the barn when they arrived. John said, "Looks like everybody else's already here. Hope we're not too late."

A brown dog with one white ear barked a warning and then a welcome as he recognized Jesse. Margaret met them at the door. "You got here none too soon. He's been just holdin' on, waiting." She led them into a room in the back. The rest of the family was standing or sitting around the edges. Quiet greetings were mumbled or whispered. Tom lay in a featherbed, breathing with slow, labored wheezes. Margaret took his hand. "Tom, the rest of 'em are here. Can you open your eyes?"

She motioned for the new arrivals to come. As one by one they took their father's hand, he responded with a weak squeeze for each and a barely audible word. For an instant he opened his eyes.

"I'd like to say a prayer." James's quiet statement drew nods of assent, and the family joined hands.

"Almighty God and Father of Our Lord Jesus Christ, we your humble servants beseech you to care for our husband and father, Thomas, in his last hour. Be with him and accept his soul into your eternal kingdom, as you have foreordained from the beginning of the world. And be with all of us as we carry on in his bodily absence. We ask this in the name of our Lord and Savior Jesus Christ. Amen."

Quiet amens echoed. Thomas's weak and gurgling amen came last. Margaret spoke softly. "That was real nice, James. Ever since you were a boy bein' baptized, I knew that the spirit of the Lord was in you real strong." James nodded in appreciation.

As Thomas's breaths gradually slowed and became less regular, Jesse took his mother's hand and whispered, "It don't look like Pa's gonna last the night. Do you think a couple of us should go up to the graveyard an' start diggin'? Beside where Mary's buried, I guess."

"If you want to, Jesse. I s'pose there's plenty of us here to keep watch. An' if you can find him, tell Parson Marquis we'll likely be needin' him tomorrow afternoon if he's free, otherwise as soon as he can."

Jesse and Hugh went out, and the rest of the family waited, hearing Tom's breathing get less and less regular. When it stopped altogether, Catherine took her mother's hand and gave her a hug. "He was a real good man, Ma. Loved you, just like he loved this land an' all of us kids."

Margaret lifted the corner of her apron to her eyes as her children gathered around. After a few minutes, she let the apron drop and said, "Yesterday morning, when I was watching over him alone, your pa started talkin'. It didn't make much sense, but I remember it real clear. He said somethin' like this. 'Maggie, I see some land. Flat as a table. Grass everywhere. Taller'n me or you. An' the dirt's black as coal. Not a tree in sight. We oughta go there, you an' me.' Then he sorta trailed off an' slept for a while. Sure was a strange dream."

She stood looking at Thomas for a minute, then she said, "Well, I guess we better start gettin' him washed up for the funeral and make a coffin for him."

The following afternoon, a wagon with Thomas's body in a wooden coffin wound slowly up the hill from the farm to the Cross Creek Presbyterian Church. William drove the horses; Margaret rode beside him, holding a grandchild. The rest of the family and some neighbors walked behind.

John looked at the field of frozen corn beside the road, He said, "That field sure is a sad sight. You gonna replant some of it, Jesse?"

"Reckon we'll have to. There won't be 'nuff feed for the stock come winter if we don't. I'm glad Pa can't see this field the way it looks now. He was helpin' me replant after it froze the first time, when he got cold and wet. Then he got the ague an' chills that killed him." Jesse sighed and looked at the coffin on the wagon.

John put his right hand on his younger brother's shoulder. "It weren't your fault, Jesse. Pa would do anything for the land and the crops—includin' workin' our fingers to the bone, along with his own. But he done purty good. Come across from the old country with nothin', an' wound up with three hundred good acres, a strong wife, and twelve kids. Nine of us are still livin', an' we got more grandkids than could get in his house at one time. An' Ma said he has some cash that he's divvied up for us in his will."

James looked at the coffin and added, "The Good Lord was always on his side. He sometimes didn't remember that, but mostly he and Ma did. Without the Lord, we can toil all we want and we will come to naught. It is the Lord who gives the harvest."

Neighbors, friends, and Pastor Marquis were waiting when the family arrived. After the pastor concluded the service, Tom and Margaret's six remaining sons carried their father's body to the graveyard, maneuvered the coffin over the open grave, and lowered it with ropes. Then they each shoveled some moist earth around it and passed the shovels to the other men who had come to pay final respects to their friend and neighbor.

As the Beatys were hitching the horses to the wagon, Tom Patterson said, "Be sure to get old man Buxton to cut a good gravestone, an' be sure he spells the name right this time. Not the way he did young Tom's last spring. Thomas Beaty was a good man, an' he deserves a real good stone, so's people will know he was here amongst us early comers. I'll see to getting his will executed good an' proper."

John shook Patterson's hand. "Thank you, sir. That makes us'uns who've gone west to Ohio feel like things back home are in good hands."

Joseph Beaty, age 19, died November 19, 1802

Mary Beaty, age 18, died September 17, 1802

Thomas Beaty, age 69, died June 11, 1816

Thomas Batey, age 31, died March 14, 1816

—Gravestones in the old Cross Creek Cemetery,
Washington County, Pennsylvania

As the family members were driving back to Short Creek the next day, talk turned to how they would get by after the disastrously cold summer. Hugh was the most optimistic.

"If there's no potatoes an' wheat an' corn in the fall, I s'pose we'll eat more meat. We can butcher a steer and an extra pig or two. An' we can buy some flour from folks farther south, where it didn't freeze. I've got some gold stashed away."

"That's good, Hugh." James looked at his brother-in-law with approval. "You folks always seem to do real well. Reckon we'll get along 'bout the same way. How 'bout you, John? You got anything in reserve?" He gave his older brother a quick glance.

There was a long interval when the only sounds were the jingling of the harness and the crunch of the wagon wheels on the road. "I figure it'll be a tough winter'n more ways than one. Polly's gonna have another baby. An' she nags me worse'n usual when she's in a family way. We don't have any extra pigs or sheep to kill, an' I got next to nothin' to buy flour with. Guess I'll be huntin' for bear an' deer an' such to feed us. Maybe we can find some folks who'd take

Eleanor and Jane to work for room and board. They're big enough to do a woman's work."

After a while, James said, "Don't worry, John. We won't let you folks go hungry. It bothers me somethin' awful the way you've wasted your money on drink, but I'll see if we can have Eleanor, an' maybe Jane, come work for us in the winter. That way they'd be close to home to help Polly when the baby comes. An' I'll keep praying that you get the demon rum that Satan sent you off your back."

John didn't know whether to thank James or to hit him. They drove home in an uneasy silence.

John, Polly, and their family survived the next lean winter with some help from James, Samuel, Hugh, and their families. In late May of the following year, the weather turned hot and humid. On a particularly oppressive afternoon, John heard a roar in the distance, something he'd heard only heard once before. He looked west and saw the dark gray clouds gyrating like foam on boiling water and a dark funnel of cloud hanging below them. As he ran toward the cabin, the roar grew and deepened behind him. An unreal calm pervaded the farmstead.

He burst through the door and yelled, "Cyclone's a-comin'! Everybody run to the root cellar!" Then he grabbed the cradle and sleeping baby in both hands and ran toward the underground shelter, yelling for the children to follow him. Close behind, Polly and her oldest daughters, Eleanor and Jane, herded all the younger children toward the root cellar. When he'd counted all the kids, John handed the cradle to Polly and yanked the cellar door shut as the rain deluged the farmstead.

It was pitch dark inside, and the storm was upon them. Its roaring howl was punctuated by deafening cracks and thuds as trees fell, buildings were demolished, and farm implements were swept away. A pig screamed as though it were being scalded alive. Then a brief, unearthly quiet descended, punctuated only by rain pounding on the door and the whimpers of the younger children.

John pushed the cellar door open a crack and peeked out. Rain was falling so hard that he couldn't see twenty feet. Water splashed in his face. He stepped back and closed the door. The pig's terrified screams rang in his ears again, followed by the plaintive, fear-tinged mooing of their cows. All the younger children were crying as they held the skirts of their mother or older sisters.

Polly's voice came through the darkness. "Well, at least we're all alive, even if we've probably lost the crops and the buildings."

"Yeah, but I hate to think what it's like out there, an' what it'll be like startin' over." John's tone conveyed defeat.

When the rain let up, they climbed out into a devastated landscape. Most of the roof of the cabin was gone, their belongings were soaked, and water was ponded on the floor. The trees that had shaded the cabin were reduced to skeletal trunks that ended in twisted and splintered wood ten or twelve feet above the ground. Some had been uprooted. The rail fences were gone, and their animals were wandering aimlessly among the litter in the farmyard. The brood sow lay on the ground in a pool of blood with a piece of board through her neck. Her piglets were vainly trying to suckle milk from her dead carcass. In the debris-littered fields, the young crops were beaten flat. When they looked to the north and east, they saw that the tornado had hit a corner of Samuel's farm, opposite the buildings, and completely missed those of James, Will Wiley, and Hugh Rogers.

They stood dazed, wet, and shaking, not knowing where to begin cleaning up and repairing the devastation. Then James rode up at a gallop and counted the children. "Praised be God, you're all alive!" His heartfelt greeting dissipated a little of the shock for John, Polly, and their family.

Samuel arrived on an old horse, saw Polly shivering, and put his raincoat over her wet shoulders. "You take my horse and lead your kids to our place and dry out. Mary's there. She'll help you." He helped Polly onto his horse and handed her the baby. She set off through the mud and water, followed by her children.

The brothers first rounded up the dazed oxen, sheep, cows, and horses and penned them in what was left of the barn. The chickens had completely disappeared. Then they dragged the dead sow under the crossbeam of the roofless granary, extracted a block and tackle from under some boards, and hoisted her muddy carcass high enough so that they could eviscerate her.

James volunteered to finish the butchering. "I'll go home and get a team and wagon to haul her to my place so that we can scald her and cut her up her right quick, before the meat goes bad. And we can take her pigs and feed 'em milk till they get big enough to eat corn." He left on his horse at a brisk trot. John and Samuel fed the frightened animals some water-soaked hay that hadn't blown away, and they began to gather the fence rails, farm implements, clothing, and broken boards that formed a trail of litter across the field of wheat east of the farmstead.

Hugh Rogers ran up as they worked. "Anybody get kilt or get hurt?"

John shook his head. "Nope. We got to the root cellar just in the nick of time."

"That's good, but I'm mighty sorry that cyclone hit you folks, an' right after last year's frost wiped out most of our crops, too." Hugh picked up a torn, wet quilt. "Catherine says that some of you can stay at our place till we get your house back together an' your things dried out."

"Same for us, an' I'm sure James and Janey will sleep some of you." Samuel pulled a wooden churn out of a ditch and began to look for its lid.

John and Hugh found the ladder and examined the roofless house. John pushed on a top log. It didn't move. "These walls are still solid. Soon's we get a roof on it and it dries out, we can move back in. Wish I had money to buy boards. Guess we'll just have to saw our own."

When evening came, James returned with a team and wagon loaded with timbers and boards. As the men unloaded them beside the house, James said, "Janey and the kids are heating a barrel of water to scald that sow in. We'll butcher her soon as we get there."

John nodded his thanks. "I better stay here and look to the rest of the animals. They're all pretty scairt." James, Samuel, and Hugh drove off with the carcass of the sow, her piglets beside her in a makeshift pen. John remained behind to milk the cows and strengthen the makeshift fence they'd thrown together around the half-roofless barn.

As he rebuilt the rail fence, John's thoughts turned to the events of the afternoon. *God musta been lookin' after us for sure. Sent his punishment to me for drinkin' so much, but he spared Polly and the kids.*

Maybe this time, I can stop. He wrenched another fence rail out of the mud and set it into place, then found a bucket and milked the cows. In the dim light of late evening, he walked along the road toward James's house, carrying the bucket of milk and studying the devastation around him.

He returned long before sunrise. His brothers and Hugh Rogers arrived soon after. By day's end, they had fashioned a makeshift roof for the house from the timbers and boards James had brought and started to re-roof the barn. John and Polly's older children and their cousins combed the debris-strewn wheat field and dragged their finds to the farmstead. Polly and her two oldest daughters served fresh roast pork for supper. After they'd washed the dishes, they hung the hams, sides of bacon, and shoulders from their newly dead sow in the slightly askew smokehouse where John had started a smoldering, smoky fire of green hickory and alder logs.

Everyone worked until dark. Even though they were bone-tired, they had trouble sleeping. Polly woke up in a cold sweat at midnight, sure she heard another tornado coming. John tossed and turned all night. When two of their children came crying to their parents' makeshift bed, he comforted them until they went to sleep, then got up, walked back to his farm, and began work on a new roof for the granary.

They replanted the wheat and corn, then repaired buildings and cleaned up debris all summer. By fall, most of the buildings were as strong as before, but the crops in the deeply eroded fields were sparse, and John was far in debt. The steep, battered land never recovered, so, unlike his brothers, he had only a few bushels of wheat and corn to sell each succeeding year.

* * *

On a crisp fall morning in 1822, John stood in front of the cabin, looking at the scraggly corn on the gullied hillside to the west. He shrugged and looked north, where the siding boards of James's new two-story house shone bright in the sun. Polly stepped out the door and tossed a handful of table scraps to the chickens.

"We're gonna have another young'un." She sighed and ran her

hand across the worn apron that covered her abdomen. "Any way we can build a room onto the cabin? We're so crowded, I don't know where we'll put another kid."

"Sure wish I could build us a nice house like James and Janey have for their brood, but that damn cyclone set us way back. I still owe him for the boards and nails. An' I owe Samuel and Hugh for the sow an' sheep an' grain they sold us." John shrugged and looked at Polly with a mixture of frustration and resignation. "And besides, this hilly old place just don't produce like it used to before that cyclone near about washed everything away." He pointed to the gullied hillside. "This land's about played out. I'm thinking it's time to look for a new farm farther west."

"Maybe so. Ya think anybody'll be fool enough to buy this patch of hills and ditches?"

"Hope so. Maybe somebody'll come through from the east an' want it."

Polly rubbed her lower back with both hands. "Catch that young black rooster and wring its neck for me, will ya? Hope it's enough for dinner." She sighed and went back inside.

After he'd killed the rooster, scalded it, and pulled off the feathers, John walked up the hill among the corn. He pulled the ears off some cornstalks that had fallen into a particularly deep gully and cradled them in his left arm. Their puny size saddened him. The next morning, he put Eleanor, Sam, and Jane to work shoveling soil into the largest gullies and rode west to look for new land.

Ten days later, he returned and announced, "I made a deal to buy a farm out west of here about thirty-five, forty miles. It's 'bout the same size as what we got, but not near as hilly an' steep. An' it ain't all been cleared and farmed out. I didn't see no gullies or no hardpan."

Polly asked, "How soon you think we'll be able to sell this rundown place? An' can we get enough to pay for that new one?"

"Don't know, but I'll start gettin' word around first thing tomorrow."

It took all fall and winter to find a buyer, two brothers from the East who didn't really comprehend how eroded the farm was, and John worried that the deal he'd made to buy land farther west would fall through. But the seller kept his word and waited for his money until John sold his land.

March 10, 1823 John Beaty to Issac Warner and Thomas Warner … for the sum of One thousand Dollars … one hundred acres more or less …

Signed and sealed by John Beaty and Mary, her *X* mark, Beaty

—From a Deed filed in the Harrison County Courthouse, Ohio

As they left the Harrison County Courthouse in Cadiz and walked down the hill to the hitching rail, John handed Polly the sack of money. "Here, you keep this. Then I won't be tempted. It'll take all of it an' then some to pay what I owe my brothers an' buy the land out west."

Polly slid the sack into the bosom of her worn linsey-woolsey dress. "I sure hope we do better out west. It'll be hard leaving so much family behind, but we sure ain't made a go of it here like Samuel and James and the Rogers have. Eleanor and Jane are women grown and ain't found husbands. 'Bout all you can raise is a thirst, an' all I seem to raise is kids and a backache." Her dark eyes glared. "Your brothers gonna help us move?"

"They said they'd each send a team and wagon and prob'ly drive 'em themselves. I sure hope things'll be better for us out there."

Chapter 11
Aiming for Better Land

As the time for the move west approached, Polly's worries grew. "You think this move's a good idea, John? What if another cyclone hits us, or if you get hurt? There won't be no family 'round to help us out."

John stopped loading sacks of potatoes in the covered wagon. "Remember, our folks came 'cross the ocean an' way out to the mountains of Pennsylvany amongst the Indians and such, all on their own, an' done just fine. So did lotsa others. Reckon we can too." Polly glared at him, shrugged, and walked to the house to finish packing.

The dog's bark signaled the approach of James's wife, Janey, and her two oldest sons, Joseph and Tom. The trio arrived carrying pieces of smoked meat.

"We brought some grub fer you folks, Uncle John." Joseph swung a ham from his shoulder and struggled to hold it out to his uncle.

"Well, I'm much obliged to ya." John grasped the ham and set it on the wagon bed. "We can sure use the meat." He looked at Janey. "But are you folks sure you can spare all this?"

Janey smiled and held out two sides of bacon. "We'll get by fine. James has three, four more pigs and a steer he can butcher when we run low."

John set the bacon beside the hams. "That's mighty generous o' you folks. Polly an' I was wonderin' how we'd feed everybody till we got settled out west. We sure thank you."

"You're more'n welcome. James said to tell you he'd drive our wagon over this afternoon so's you can load it. Prob'ly Samuel will too." Janey moved toward the house to help Polly and her daughters finish packing sacks of potatoes, dried beans, and cornmeal for the trip.

The next morning, the rising sun of the spring equinox illuminated a bustle of activity along Short Creek. Three covered wagons, each with a yoke of oxen in front, stood beside John and Polly's farmstead. Polly hoisted the last box of pots and pans into the first wagon. John, with help from James and Hugh Rogers, herded a small band of sheep and lambs into a moving circle behind the third wagon, where John and Polly's daughters Eleanor, Lucinda, and Jane had been stationed to keep them confined. Their brother, Sam, drove the family's four cows, two calves, and a young bull into line behind the sheep.

Polly gathered her youngest sons, David and William, in her arms, sighed, and climbed to the seat of the first wagon. John strode to the front of the lead ox team and lifted the pole that leaned against the yoke. "We're on our way west. Thank ya all for everything. Giddup!" James and Samuel prodded their teams into motion, and, as the wagons began to move, John and Polly's children herded the loose livestock along behind. James's and Samuel's families, the Rogers and the Wileys, roughly thirty-five adults and children in all, waved and called Godspeed and good luck, then they said, "See you soon," as James and Samuel walked by beside their ox teams. They watched as the caravan rattled westward up the hill.

As the travelers neared the crest, Eleanor and Jane turned for a last look back at the home and relatives they'd left. "S'pose we'll ever see any of 'em again?"

"Don't reckon it's likely." Eleanor pushed her long, black hair from her face and turned west again. "They was sure good to us. 'Specially that winter we was so short of food. But maybe there'll be some nice, young bachelors where we're goin'." A ewe and her lamb bolted from the flock and raced back toward home. The two young women ran to head them off and drive them back into the flock.

"That's sort of what I feel like doin', too." Jane stopped for a long look back at the home in the valley.

At the front of the procession, Polly looked down at David and William, who were playing in an open space behind the seat, and then back at the farmstead they had just left for good. She remembered the huge assemblage of relatives and friends who'd given them food, helped her pack, and come before sunup to see them off. How would life be without them? *Gonna be lonesome livin' amongst all strangers,* she thought. *But maybe it'll be easier for John without his brothers always doin' better'n him. Maybe out there, he can stop drinkin'.* William began to cry, and she lifted him to nurse.

John's oxen settled into a steady, slow pace. He looked back one last time at the steep farm he'd finally managed to sell, then faced west again and admired the spring landscape illuminated by the early morning sunshine. Even though his left leg hurt once in a while from a bad fall he'd had years before, and he worried that a five-day walk would make it worse, he was excited to be moving toward the new land he'd bought.

In late afternoon, the expedition stopped by a small river near the trail, and the livestock were turned out to graze under the watch of the teenaged children. Polly and her daughters, Eleanor and Jane, cooked supper over an open fire. When everyone had eaten, they washed the wooden trenchers and iron kettles in the river. Their livestock seemed content to graze nearby. John said, "Let's all of us sing a few songs together, since James and Samuel won't be with us after the move's done."

Polly nodded as she took David and William toward blankets she'd spread on a tarp under the wagon. "Songs'll help 'em go to sleep. I'll come back soon's they drop off."

Samuel squeezed through the circle of seated family and threw two logs on the fire as John asked, "What'll we start with?"

James pulled out his harmonica and said, "Since we're alongside the river, how about 'Shall We Gather at the River'?" John nodded and spat some tobacco juice over his gray-flecked beard; then the sounds of the instrument and John's mellow baritone floated over the voices of the other travelers.

> Shall we gather at the river, the beautiful, the
> beautiful river, that flows by the throne of God?

> Let us gather at the river, the beautiful, the beautiful
> river, that flows by the throne of God ...

Samuel volunteered the next song. "We're in a new valley tonight. Let's sing about that." James blew the first chords of "Down in the Valley," and everyone joined him, with John and his plump, fair-skinned daughter Lucinda singing harmony.

They followed it with an old song from Scotland, "Coming through the Rye". As they sang the line "If a body meet a body, comin' through the rye, if a body kiss a body, need a body cry?" Eleanor whispered to Jane, "If a man kissed me, I sure wouldn't cry."

"Me neither," Jane whispered.

Polly slid into the circle next to her husband. "Let's do that new hymn 'Rock of Ages.' John, why don't you line it out for us?"

James blew a chord, and John lined out the words. "Rock of Ages, cleft for me. Let me hide myself in thee ..."

James paused, then started the tune again as everyone in the circle sang. When they'd finished the song, Polly put her arm on John's shoulder. "Thank you. I love that song. And I love the way you sing." He smiled shyly and patted her knee.

Just before dark, the men herded the animals into a triangular pen they'd made by tying ropes between the three wagons. John, James, and Samuel took turns guarding through the night to keep away wolves and bears, and to be sure that no livestock escaped. Everyone else crawled into blankets that had been spread on canvas under the wagons. At first light, John turned the livestock out to graze; Polly built the fire and began to cook breakfast. An hour later, the caravan was under way again.

In late afternoon of the fourth day, the party topped a hill that sloped down to a large, south-flowing creek. John, whose leg hurt more as they'd traveled, turned to Polly and said, "There's Killbuck Creek. An' that little settlement alongside is Millersburg. After we cross the creek, we'll only have about six miles more. You can almost see our new farm." He pointed northwest to a low, rolling landscape.

Her gaze followed his arm. "That's great, but I hope we're gonna camp near here for the night. Six more miles is quite a ways for the girls to walk, an' David and little William need a quiet place to nap right soon."

"There's some wide bottomland across the crick. Reckon we could camp there if nobody objects. Sure's gonna be nice movin' to a place where there's already some buildings and fences." He rubbed his left leg. "I'm not feeling as young as I did when we built the other two places from scratch."

Polly smiled at John and kept rocking William on her lap. "I'm not feelin' so young anymore either."

***

Families moving west came through the small village of Millersburg frequently, but the locals always noticed their passing. As the Beatys' wagons and livestock rattled down the steep dirt street, a young man working a forge in front of the blacksmith shop glanced at the travelers and said to his companion, "Look at them girls herdin' the sheep an' cows, Alex. Kind of purty, don' ya think?"

His partner stopped shaping a spoke for a wagon wheel with a plane and looked toward the road "Aye, yer right, John. Why don't we offer to help 'em drive their critters across the creek?" Without waiting for an answer, he laid down his plane and started toward the rutted street.

James's ox team was straining to pull his wagon up the steep creek bank, and Eleanor, Jane, Lucinda, and Sam were crowding the reluctant sheep and cows to the creek bank as Alex Mitchell and John Harden came down the street.

Sam was yelling, "Hyah, get across. Hyah, hyah! Get in there now." A cow broke from the herd on the run and started back up the street. Eleanor gave chase, but she was surprised to see two young men confront the escapee and turn her back toward the creek with shouts and waving arms.

"Thank you, sirs. You're real kind to help us out." She stepped aside, panting, to let the cow rejoin the herd.

"Not at all, miss. We help 'most anybody comin' through. But it's right nice to help such a purty lady." A deep blush crept up Eleanor's neck and across her face. She pushed her hair off her sweaty face, smiled, and curtsied to Alex and John.

"Why, thank you, sir. But I don't feel real pretty after bein' on the trail most of the week." She glanced down at her dusty bare feet and ankles.

Alex tried to brush the sawdust off his hands and arms. "Nor do I. Carpenterin's kinda hot and dirty too. Ye got far to go yet?"

"Not far at all. Papa's bought a farm 'bout six miles up the creek from here." Alex smiled and walked Eleanor back to the circle of family that was hazing the sheep and cows across Killbuck Creek.

Finally, one of the cows waded into the water and splashed across, and all of the other animals followed. Eleanor, Lucinda, and Jane waded in behind them, holding up their long skirts just enough to keep them dry. Once they were on the far bank, they and Sam turned and yelled, "Thank you for all the help!"

Alex and John waved back, and Alex shouted, "Glad we met you! Maybe we'll see you again."

When they returned to work, Alex said, "Workin' here don' pay too good, but we get to look over all the new girls comin' through. Glad that bunch is settling nearby." His partner nodded in agreement as he cranked the blower on the forge to reheat the piece of iron he'd been shaping.

As the Beatys approached their new farm the next afternoon, they were struck by the contrast with the steep one they'd left. The hundred acres John had bought was on a broad, gently sloping ridge. The previous owner had built a cabin, barn, chicken house, and woodshed just above a spring. The buildings sat at the edge of a level field near the upper end of a wooded drainage-way that formed the north part of the farm. Split-rail fences enclosed the pasture and extended around land to the south that had been cleared of trees. The western end of the farm was a maple woods.

Shocked grain on farm near Millersburg, Ohio,
owned by John Beatty 1824-1840

"Appears to be a nice piece of ground, John." Samuel nodded
approvingly at the new farm. "It'll sure be a lot easier to plow an'
plant than that place you left. And I like that grove of maples. You'll
sure have maple sugar to trade."

James eyed John's new purchase. "Looks real good. If I hadn't just
bought some more land back home, I'd be tempted to sell out and
come join you." John beamed.

As soon as the livestock had been turned into the pasture, the
family explored the cabin. Polly climbed down the ladder from
the sleeping loft, looked around the two rooms, and said, "It'll be
crowded, but we can get along until you build another room on the
back."

John set a wooden chest on the split-log floor. "We got to get the
crops in the ground first, but after that, if some neighbors'll help, we
prob'ly can."

The Beatys found their new neighbors friendly and helpful. When
they spread word that they needed volunteers to build an addition to

the cabin, several young men from the neighborhood, including Alex Mitchell and John Harden, arrived to help.

The kitchen was like a beehive. Eleanor stopped peeling potatoes momentarily. "Be sure to put lots of good meat in that stew. And make plenty. We sure don't want to run out."

Lucinda stopped cutting meat and frowned at Eleanor. "If you want to make the stew, I'll take your place peeling potatoes, Miss Bossy. I want to make a good impression just like you do."

"Now, girls, act your age. I won't stand for anymore such talk." Polly stamped her foot and then resumed chopping cabbage for coleslaw. Jane took six loaves of fresh bread out of the oven and peeked out the window.

"The men are already sawing rafters. Maybe they'll be done by nightfall. Wouldn't that be nice?" She put two sticks of oak in the cookstove.

At noon, the men washed the sawdust off their hands at the stock watering trough by the spring and slicked back their hair with their wet hands, then headed for the kitchen. Eleanor, Lucinda, and Jane stood beside the door to welcome them. After John had said the blessing, all hands began to heap their plates with boiled potatoes, beef stew, baked beans, coleslaw, and fresh bread. When the men had each eaten two or three helpings, the Beaty daughters brought out dried-apple pies for dessert.

When he'd finished his second slice, Alex Mitchell wiped his beard and smiled at Eleanor. "With this kind of grub, I'd work here any day o' the week—'ceptin', of course, Sunday." Eleanor tried to hide her smile; starting with Alex, she offered everyone more pie. After they'd each eaten a second piece of pie, the men left the kitchen reluctantly, finished the addition to the house, and walked home.

***

"There's going to be a box social at the Killbuck schoolhouse!" Jane's breathless announcement as she walked into the cabin made everyone turn.

Three or four voices spoke at once, saying, "When?"

"Saturday night. We've got just time to get something baked

for the auction. And I have to sew up my good dress. The hem's ripped."

"And if Sam's going, he's got to take a bath and trim his hair and beard. I don't want anybody getting the wrong idea about us." Eleanor eyed her husky, black-bearded brother in mock seriousness.

"Don't be so prim and prissy, Eleanooor." He drew out her name as though addressing royalty. "I'd been thinkin' a bath would be good sometime this month. Might as well do it before Saturday night, I guess. But you don't get to cut my hair. Last time you cut it, I looked worse'n a sheared sheep."

"Do what you like, Sam," Eleanor sniffed. "I'm glad to know there's something that'll make you take a bath. You smell as bad as a sheep."

"He smells worse most o' the time!" Lucinda wrinkled her nose and looked sideways at Sam. Even Polly laughed, lifting her tired face from kneading bread dough. Sam tried to look chagrined but wound up smiling.

"Well, I'll jump in the watering tub after we finish planting corn tomorrow. Any of you fussy wimmin gonna wash my clothes afterwards?"

"Maybe you should just use 'em to make a scarecrow for the cornfield." Eleanor touched Sam's shirtsleeve gingerly while holding her nose with her left fingers. "But if you won't, I'll wash 'em along with all the others." Everyone laughed, and Sam went out to plant corn.

***

A rising full moon lit the rutted road as Sam, Eleanor, Lucinda, Margaret, and Jane walked east about three miles to the Killbuck school on Saturday night. Sam's hair and beard were newly cut. His homespun shirt and pants had just been washed. In one hand he carried boots to put on his tanned and callused feet when he arrived at the schoolhouse. The other held a large basket with his sisters' kitchen creations.

His sisters wore homespun linen dresses. Lucinda's, Margaret's, and Jane's were set off by contrasting broadcloth collars. Eleanor's was plain, but she wore a red ribbon around her black hair. Each of the women had bathed, washed each other's hair, and rinsed it with vinegar water to take out the last of the homemade soap and make their tresses shine. Eleanor, Lucinda, and Margaret wore shoes that buttoned over the ankle; Jane was barefoot. They'd taken great care to make the currant rolls, dried-apple pies, and peach cobbler for the auction absolutely perfect. As they walked into the schoolyard and heard music coming from the log schoolhouse, Eleanor said, "I hope there are some single men who'll buy our food."

"Maybe they'll buy it once, but I bet they won't a second time." Sam grinned at his four sisters.

A group of men stood talking near the corner of the isolated rural schoolhouse as the five walked timidly to the open door. "Alex, there's them Beaty women an' their brother." John Harden motioned toward the newcomers.

Alex Mitchell turned to survey the new arrivals. "Aye, John. So they are. Maybe I'll try to buy the box that Eleanor brought if it ain't bid up too high."

"You Scotchmen are all the same, tight as bark on a tree." John gave Alex a friendly slap on the shoulder. "Maybe I'll bid on Lucinda's." They sauntered inside, where the fiddler was playing a reel.

The five Beatys were standing together in a corner of the crowded schoolhouse, uncertain what to do next. Alex and John sought them out, and after getting Sam to show them which boxes his sisters Eleanor and Lucinda had made, they invited the happy pair of girls to join them in the line of dancers. Sam put on his boots and took the basket of edibles to the cloakroom at the side of the school, then invited a blonde girl standing near the back of the room to dance. Jane and Margaret were invited to dance by shy, young men.

The moon was in the western sky when Sam and his sisters started home. "I'm real glad we moved. There's some nice folks hereabouts," Eleanor said. She untied the red ribbon and let her black hair fall around her shoulders.

"I'll bet you are!" Sam slapped her lightly on the back. "That Alex was as close to you as a leech after he bought your apple pie. An' his pal took a shine to Lucinda. But he warn't quite so forward."

"Alex couldn't be too close to suit me. I love his Scotch accent."

Eleanor's face glowed in the light of the western moon. "He's coming to call tomorrow after church." She tossed her head and danced a few steps along the road.

> **Paint Creek, March 24th, 1825. That Alexander Mitchell and Eleanor Beaty were this day according to law joined together with bonds of matrimony is certified by S. Irwin.**
>
> —*Marriage Record filed in the Holmes County Courthouse, Ohio*

> **The wild strawberries were plentiful … Also noticed a couple sporting under the Mulberry tree. A closer look showed them to be Alex Mitchell and Eleanor Beaty. It's disgusting— they've been married for almost two months now.**
>
> —*From a column by the Roving Reporter in the Holmes County Gazette, Millersburg, Ohio, May 16, 1825*

> **I hereby certify that on the fifth day of October Inst. I joined together in the holy state of matrimony John Harden and Lucinda Beaty of lawful age.**
>
> **Given under my hand and seal this 16th day of Oct. 1826 James Craig J.P.**
>
> —*Marriage Record filed in the Holmes County Courthouse, Ohio*

* * *

John and Polly's new farm was a big improvement over the one they had left on Short Creek, but John struggled anew with his old demon. At Polly's urging, he had talked over his addiction to whiskey with the Presbyterian preacher.

"The only way you're going to be able to beat this demon is to take it one day at a time and ask the Almighty to help you." John felt Pastor McLean's stern gaze burn right into his soul as he listened.

"You mean every day I gotta pray for help?"

"That's right. You haven't been able to get the demon rum off your back by yourself for how many years now?"

John thought back quickly to when he'd started drinking whiskey. "Nigh on to thirty-five years, I guess."

"If you're ever going to beat the devil who makes you want to drink, you need to pray every morning for God's help to get through one more day, and every night you need to thank him for helpin' you make it. And don't go anywhere near where there's any whiskey, so you don't smell it or see any friends who offer you some."

"Parson, that's gonna be awful hard to do, but I'll try. And I'm much obliged to you for your advice." John sighed as he put on his hat and left.

Every day was a battle, but John followed the preacher's admonition. And day by day, he succeeded, although the days he went to Millersburg to sell produce or buy supplies were agonizing. He usually took Polly with him to ensure that he went straight home and didn't stop at the tavern in the hotel.

Polly was elated by John's resolve. One midsummer day, as they were driving home from Millersburg and talking about his struggle, she hugged him and said, "I always knew you could do it, love. I'm so proud of you."

John looked pleased. "Well, it's mighty tough, but I'm makin' it day by day. You and Pastor McLean sure have been a big help. I couldn't'a made it so far without ya both."

* * *

The Beatys and their neighbors timed their periodic butcherings to avoid summer, when it was so hot that the meat would spoil before it could be preserved by smoking or salting. In the late-spring butchering of 1830, Polly cut her thumb as she was trimming fat off a hog carcass prior to rendering it into lard. She tied a rag around the cut and continued to work. Two days later, she walked unsteadily into the kitchen, where her twenty-year-old daughter Susan was cutting meat.

"Susan, cut me some salt pork to wrap on my thumb after I soak it in hot salt water. It just keeps swellin' up and hurtin' worse. Couldn't hardly sleep, it was throbbing so last night." She held her right hand stiffly in her left, with her right thumb upright. It resembled a slashed sausage—red, with skin stretched taut and lips of gray, open flesh showing near the tip. "Never had a cut that wouldn't heal before. Now I'm gettin' a funny red streak up my arm."

Susan stepped close. "Gee, Ma, that's a whole lot worse than yesterday. Looks kinda like the cut on old man Grizzard's leg two or three days before he died." She shuddered as she remembered the greenish wound that filled the air with a putrid stench.

Polly dipped her hand into a dish of hot salt water and muffled a scream as she pulled it out. Sweat beaded on her forehead. After a moment, she put her hand back in again. "Quick, bring me a chair. I gotta sit down 'fore I faint."

Susan dropped the slab of salt pork she had brought to put on Polly's wound and ran for a chair as she saw her mother steadying herself with her left hand on the kitchen table. "You better get back in bed soon's you can. I'll get Rachel to help me finish cuttin' meat." She ran outside, yelling, "Rachel, Rachel, come an' help us, quick!"

As Rachel approached on the run, Susan caught her arm and said, "Ma's lookin' real bad. Help me get her into bed, then run quick and get Papa from the back field!"

When Rachel returned with John, Polly lay in bed, moaning, as Susan put a hot cloth on her arm. Her thumb was encased in salt pork. John hurried to the bed. "I'm sorry, Polly. If I'd'a knowed you were so bad, I'd not've gone to plant corn." He took her left hand gently.

"That's all right. You an' Sam need to get the corn planted when the moon's right." Polly groaned softly and closed her eyes.

John saddled a horse and rode at a trot to get Dr. Alsop in Millersburg. The doctor arrived that afternoon, a couple hours after

John had returned. After examining Polly's thumb, he sliced the wound open wider and prescribed more hot compresses and salt pork to draw out the infection. As John paid the doctor, he asked, "Is Polly gonna make it or not?"

"Hate to tell you this, Mr. Beaty, but it doesn't look good. I'm sure sorry there's nothing more I can do. It's in God's hands now."

"Well, thanks for comin', doc. We'll take the best care of her we can, and pray for God's help." John looked away and ran his sleeve across his eyes.

The next afternoon, Polly's hand and arm were swollen to three times their normal size. The tight-stretched skin was dull red. The gray flesh along the cut smelled putrid and oozed pus. As Susan and Rachel were putting on more hot cloths, Polly roused and said, "I want you both to look after everybody when I'm gone. 'Specially William and David—they still need a lot of motherin'. Mary Ann and Robert won't need quite so much. Tell 'em I love them but I'm goin' up to heaven to be with the angels."

"We'll try, Ma." Susan and Rachel joined arms and brushed away tears. Rachel went out quickly; Susan turned away but stayed near the bed. In a few minutes, Rachel returned with the rest of the family.

John entered, holding William and David by the hand. Sam, Jane, Eliza, Robert, and Mary Ann walked behind them. David's mop of black hair hid his eyes. He was lean, bony, and tall for his age.

John wiped his eyes and spoke softly. "It's time for us all to say good-bye to your ma. God and Jesus are takin' her to heaven to live with them." He motioned for William to put his hand on his mother's face.

"Ooh, Mama's real hot." William jerked back his hand.

Mary Ann kissed her mother's cheek, then backed away quickly, her apron over her face.

Robert walked close and whispered, "Good-bye, Mama. We all love you," before he turned to be enfolded in John's arm.

David pushed back his hair, touched his mother's fiery cheek, and whispered, "I love you."

Polly opened her eyes for a moment and whispered, "I love you,

Son. Make me proud of you." David turned, knuckles in his eyes, and ran out.

The rest of the children took turns saying sad good-byes to their mother. When they were done, John knelt and took his wife's left hand. "Polly, you've been a fine wife. I've always loved you, even though I haven't always been too good of a husband. I'll see that everyone gets taken care of."

Polly squeezed his hand. "I love you, and I know you'll take good care of everybody. I'm so proud you stopped drinking."

The family sat or stood around Polly's bed as she slowly lost her battle for life. John comforted his children as best he could, reaching back for support to what he'd learned from Tom, Margaret, and the preachers he'd encountered.

They dug Polly's grave under a lone oak at the edge of the waterway. Sam made a coffin of maple, and Alex Mitchell carved a head marker from a hickory plank. Family, friends, and neighbors overflowed the house; those who couldn't get inside listened through the windows and door as Pastor McLean read the service and gave a eulogy. John, Sam, and sons-in-law John Harden and Alex Mitchell carried the coffin slowly to the open grave, lowered it on ropes, and threw on the first shovelfuls of earth. After the grave was filled and the head marker set in place, the Beatys and their neighbors shared a solemn potluck meal in the warm spring afternoon.

The need to be strong for his children as well as supervising the cooking, caring for their animals, and planting of crops muted John's grief intermittently. But alone, he was inconsolable.

He and his nine younger children carried on as best they could. Amid ongoing arguments, the five girls divided their mother's duties of cooking, gardening, washing, cleaning, and making clothes. Sam helped his father guide Robert, David, and William as they learned to do farm work. Neighbors helped, and when they could, Eleanor and Lucinda came to the farm to comfort their father and encourage their younger siblings. But anger and rivalry abounded.

"That's the wrong way to wash the clothes. Didn't you ever watch Mama do it?" Susan frowned and shouted at Rachel, who was rubbing a pair of her father's wet, sudsy pants back and forth on a washboard.

"Who made you the boss, Miss Know-it-All?" Rachel ignored her sister and kept rubbing the pants against the wood-framed rectangle of corrugated brass that sat at an angle in a tub of hot water.

"I'll tell Papa what a mess you're making of his clothes. Then you'll be sorry."

"Go ahead. I dare you!"

The kitchen door opened, and John walked in. "What's all this yellin' about? I'm tryin' to pray for strength, and all I can hear is you two jawin'. Can't you to do anything without hollerin' at each other?"

Susan grabbed the pair of needles beside her and resumed knitting a new pair of socks. Rachel remained bent over the washboard, rubbing the wet pants against its ridged surface, as she wiped her eyes with the back of a wet hand and glanced at her father. "I'm sorry, Papa. It's just so hard without Mama, and my sisters are always tellin' me I'm doin' things wrong."

"It's right tough for all of us, I know. But yellin' doesn't help any. I got enough troubles of my own, an' I don't want to hear any more of it! Understand?" He frowned and looked from Susan to Rachel. They looked down and nodded.

As he battled his craving for whiskey, John felt a huge void in his life without Polly. He'd talked to her almost every day about how much he wanted just one drink, and how hard he prayed for strength not to take it. She'd listened quietly, then told him how proud she was that he was trying so hard to stay sober, and succeeding. After she died, he prayed for strength while he was milking, planting, and harvesting crops, and late at night when the day's work was done.

* * *

In mid-summer 1833, John and his son David were at the mill on Killbuck Creek waiting to have a load of their newly harvested wheat ground for flour when a neighbor shared some news. "John, did you hear? Next week, Zeke Bennett's gonna show off some new machine that cuts standing grain while a team of horses pulls it across the field. Calls it a reaper. Says if you buy one, it'll put an' end to cradling for good."

"Can we go see it, Papa?" David, tall for a twelve-year-old and adventurous, pushed a mop of black hair off his forehead with a big hand and looked at his father, hoping for a yes.

John hesitated. "It'll depend on us getting all of the back field cut and hauled to the barn. That's real good oats, and I don't want any of it rained on, if we can help it."

"Please, I'll work real hard. Go back after supper if need be. I'm getting better at usin' the cradle, even if I'm not so good as Robert and Sam." David studied his father's face for some sign of hope.

"We'll see, Son." John loaded the last sack of wheat flour, after the miller had taken his tenth for the grinding, and motioned for David to climb up on the wagon.

The next morning, right after breakfast, the Beatys started harvesting oats. John and his sons Sam and Robert cut the ripe oats with cradles—scythes that had a series of curved wooden fins behind the sharp blade to gather the cut stalks into small, loose piles. All the other children except Jane, who stayed behind to cook, worked bent over behind them. They removed a few stalks from each pile and wrapped them around the remaining stalks about halfway between the ripe heads and the newly cut bases. Then they tucked the ends of the wrap around each other and pulled them tight to form a belt that converted the loose pile of oats into a firm bundle that could be lifted and moved. When they had tied seven or eight bundles, the children stood them upright, so that they leaned into each other for mutual support. Before moving on, they laid a bundle horizontally across the top of the shock as a rain cap.

David started out at a ferocious pace. "What's the big hurry, David? We got lots of work ahead of us. Don't try to do it all in an hour." Rachel set a bundle she'd just made against the shock David had started.

"Didn't Papa tell you? If we get all the oats in the barn real fast, maybe he'll take some of us to see a new machine called a reaper. They say it cuts the grain and puts it out in piles all by itself—no more cradling. If we had one, Papa, Robert, and Sam could help us bind and shock. Then we'd be done a lot faster. Wouldn't that be great?"

"That would sure be nice. Working bent double all day like this kills a body. Papa made me start when I was ten." Rachel wiped blood from a crack in her thumb and then started binding again. The others followed.

"My back hurts." William, ten and just starting to work in the field, looked toward his sisters. "And the oats cut my hands ... look!" He held out small hands that had spots of dried blood on the fingers and palms.

"It's real hard when you're new at it. My hands looked like that when I started. Yours will toughen up after a day or two." Susan took William's hands, moistened a corner of her apron with saliva, and rubbed off some of the caked blood. Then she kissed them and said, "Just keep workin', Willie. Don't worry if you can't go as fast as the rest of us." She put her own hands on her lower back and rubbed the muscles that ached from being stretched since sunup.

John and his older sons finished cutting the oats at noon the next day. After dinner, they hooked the bay geldings to the wagon, called for everyone else to climb aboard, and drove to the field of oats. His daughters and youngest sons resumed binding and shocking. John, Sam, and Robert loaded the wagon with bundles of oats and hauled them to the barn. The younger Beatys continued their slow, stooped-over progress across the field. They finished tying the last bundle just as the sun touched the western horizon. As they walked, stiff-backed, sore-handed, and bone-tired toward the house, David said, "I'll get the cows in for milking. That way, Papa, Robert, and Sam can keep hauling longer, maybe even finish."

"You sure do want Papa to take you to see that new contraption tomorrow, don't you?" Susan brushed sweaty hair from her face and gave her brother a tired smile.

"I've worked real hard. Sure hope he takes me too." William rubbed his cut and bloody hands together gingerly.

Rachel looked at her brothers. "Wish us girls could go, but I guess we'll be home washin' clothes, making peach preserves, and cookin' to make up what we missed doin' these last few days."

***

With the oats all safely in the barn, John, David, and William started for Millersburg early the next day with a fast team and light wagon.

John had set a case of eggs on some hay behind the seat and put a tub of butter and a bucket of cream beside it, next to a dull plow shear. In his pocket, he had a list of supplies to buy. They saw two other teams and wagons ahead on the road, and a neighbor passed them driving a fast team and buggy.

In town, they tied their team to the hitching rail beside the creamery and carried the produce inside, where John and the proprietor exchanged news and haggled good-naturedly over prices. With money from the sale, he bought salt, sugar, tea, half a bolt of blue gingham, and some thread at Maclendon's store.

Then they walked to the blacksmith shop, where John left the plowshare for the smith to sharpen in his forge. David and William stood, fascinated, at the entrance to the shop, near where a horse was being shod. The blacksmith's helper grabbed a hairy fetlock, lifted the huge foot, and cradled it between his legs as he trimmed away some hair, pared off excess hoof with a knife, and held a horseshoe to the newly shaped hoof.

William whispered, "Ain't that somethin'? I'd always wondered how they shoed horses. S'pose Papa'll stay till they nail the shoe on?"

David looked at William with friendly disdain. "Don't think so. They'll put the shoe in the forge, an' when it's red hot, they'll hammer it to the right shape, then throw it in that bucket of water over there. When it's cool, they'll set it on the hoof and drive the nails through from the bottom, cut the sharp ends off, and curl the rest right down on top of the hoof. I want to go see this reaper contraption. We'll see horseshoeing another time."

They walked back to their father, who was talking with the blacksmith and some neighbors, and urged him to get on to the demonstration site. He continued visiting with two or three men he hadn't seen all summer. Only when he felt he had all the news did he untie the team and drive up the hill east of the village. The boys fidgeted on the seat behind him and looked at the gravestones among the oaks in the cemetery along the road.

William whispered to David, "Why wasn't Mama buried in there with everybody else?"

David put his mouth close to William's ear and whispered back,

"Dunno. Guess Papa wanted her close by, maybe. Papa sure does miss her, same as you and me."

The rolling hills beyond the cemetery formed a mosaic of colors and textures—green pastures with horses, cows, and sheep grazing or standing in the shade of trees; pale, creamy grain fields, some with short and bristly stubble, others dense with standing oats; fields of tall, green flax; small plots of tobacco with a pungent miasma of nicotine that floated to the road; oaks, maples, and hickories on the steeper hills; and gardens of vegetables and blooming flowers beside each farmstead.

John studied it as they drove. "Sure has filled up with people since we come through here back in '24. David, you were only three. William, you were a tiny baby. Mostly woods then. This road was just a rough trace. Gettin' plumb crowded now." The boys looked at everything with wonder. It was the first time they'd been so far from home since they were old enough to remember.

As they drove down the hill toward the reaper demonstration, John and his sons saw men and boys in wagons and buggies and on horseback moving toward the site from the east, north, and south. When they got to the field, John unhitched the team, tied the horses to the side of the wagon, and gave them some hay. The horses bobbed their heads, fighting off nose flies, and began to eat. David and William were already halfway to the reaper.

The oats around the outside of the field had been cut and hauled away, leaving about forty feet of stubble on all sides for spectators to stand or walk in as they watched the new invention. Men were ten deep beside the reaper where it stood at the edge of the uncut oats on the corner of the field nearest the gate. David and William wormed their way between the adult onlookers, dodging random streams of tobacco juice as they went.

"That sure is something, ain't it, Willie?" David looked at his brother and was disappointed that William seemed not to understand the importance of what they were seeing.

"What's it gonna do?" William asked.

"They say it's going to cut them oats and tip 'em right onto that tin platform, where a man can rake them off in a pile, all ready to bind into a bundle. No more hard work swingin' a scythe with a cradle. That's why we came. To see it do that."

As they talked, a man driving a team of horses and a man in a white shirt and beaver hat walked into the field. The crowd eased back. The man in the white shirt stepped up on the platform of the machine and motioned for silence.

"Gentlemen, your full attention, please! Today you are going to witness something that will leave you amazed. This machine will revolutionize your farming. It will replace the labor of ten men, let you harvest your crop before wind and rain destroy it, and let you plant and raise more grain to feed your families and livestock and have plenty left over to sell. McCormick's reaper can make you rich." He paused for breath and looked behind him to see if his compatriot had finished hitching the horses to the reaper.

A red-faced man in the middle of the crowd shouted, "Let's see it work first, 'fore you brag it up so much."

The man tipped his hat to the skeptic and said, "Please be patient a moment, sir. We'll start as soon as the team is hitched." The teamster signaled that he was ready. A second man, holding a wide rake, stepped onto the metal platform. The speaker stepped down, turned to his two helpers and nodded. The teamster flicked the reins. "Giddup."

David and William walked forward in the surge of men and boys. The reaper moved into the standing grain, and as it went, it cut the oats about six inches above the ground with what the boys thought was the longest knife they'd ever seen. The cut oats were tipped onto the metal platform behind the long reciprocating knife by horizontal wood slats that turned like vanes of a windmill as the reaper moved. The man standing on the platform raked the cut oats to its edge and dropped them in a neat pile. As more oats fell onto the platform, the man raked off another pile. Two men bound the piles into bundles.

"Ain't that somethin'?" the red-faced man exclaimed. The machine did not stop. The man with the white shirt pulled his sleeves up under the arm-garters he wore just above his elbows as he strode alongside. John and the boys followed the lengthening row of cut oats that the reaper was leaving as it moved. Behind them, men began to gather bundles and set them upright in shocks.

After it had made three rounds, the man in the beaver hat motioned for the driver to stop so that everyone could take close look. A few onlookers began to drift back toward their horses and drive away, but most stayed to inspect the reaper's inner workings and question the man in charge. John started to talk to neighbors. David squeezed in beside some men studying the cutting mechanism. William stood at the back of the crowd with another boy about his size. John found him there. "Where's David? It's time for us to leave, so we can be home in time for milking."

"Right in front, Papa, He's squeezed himself right up to that machine."

John spotted David standing on the spokes of one of the wheels and peering into the machine's interior. "Son. Time to go!" He motioned for David to get down and come out of the crowd.

"Just let me look a minute more, Papa. Please, I want to see how this works, so I'll be able to fix it when we get one." He studied his father's face for a possible extension of time.

"No, come right now. I gotta get back to Millersburg." John started for the wagon.

As they drove up the road toward the village, David asked, "You think we can buy a reaper, Papa? It would sure save a heap of work."

"Don't think so. We don't have much extra money, an' they say that thing costs a whole lot."

"But we could hire out, cut other folk's grain after we'd done our own, an' pay for it that way."

"Who'd run it? I doubt I'd have time. Sam's probably goin' farming on his own soon. You're too young and small."

"I'm young, but I'm big. In a year or so, I could do it. I know I could. Maybe we could even get some more land."

John slapped the reins on the horses' backs, and they began to trot. David saw the obsessive and preoccupied look on his father's face and decided not to say any more.

When they reached the village, John reined in the team as they approached the hotel that faced the courthouse on the square. "I've got to stop here a few minutes. We'll tie up at the rail in back. You boys stay close by and watch the horses. I won't be long." He tied the team to the hitching rail and went into the hotel, walking fast.

"Why's he in such a hurry?" William asked.

"Dunno. Maybe he has to meet somebody." David shrugged. "Let's throw sticks for that spotted dog to chase."

The dog had long ago tired of retrieving sticks, and for more than two hours the boys had inspected much of the village when John emerged from the hotel. He walked unsteadily to the horses and wagon.

"David, untie 'em right now! We gotta get home to milk." He put his right foot on the wheel hub, grabbed the edge of the wagon, and started to pull himself up. But his foot slipped, and he held himself up by his hand as his chest hit the edge of the wagon bed. David untied the team and jumped up on the wagon, where William stood waiting. John rubbed his chest, tried again, and finally managed to climb up after David and William reached down and gave him a hand. He sat down heavily and massaged the spot where his chest had hit the wagon.

"I'll drive, Papa." David slapped the reins across the horses' backs.

"Make 'em move, Son. Gotta get home and milk."

"Milkin' time was more'n an hour ago. The women probably already finished. No need for us to hurry, so long as we get home before it's too dark."

John's sons watched their father sway and occasionally hiccup. Nobody spoke. David thought he had never smelled anything as repulsive as the stale whiskey on his father's breath.

Chapter 12
New Beginnings

His mouth tasted like rotten fish, and every pore and joint of his head ached. John opened one eye for an instant, saw that it was already daylight, and pulled the sheet over his head. As he made the slow, painful transition from sleep to consciousness, fragments of the long stop at the tavern in Millersburg and the jarring ride home slithered into his mind. He remembered the look of loathing he'd seen on David's face and cringed.

"That damn whiskey! Gotta find somebody to help me keep away from it for good." He lay still and tried to figure out how. When he struggled out of bed, he gulped all of the water in the pitcher on the nightstand. The rest of the family had long since finished the milking and eaten breakfast, and they were at work on the day's undertakings when John came out to eat breakfast. Rachel stopped washing dishes and took a plate of ham and eggs from the warming oven of the stove and put it on the table without saying a word.

As he ate, John's thoughts wandered over the landscape of his dilemma. He couldn't get drunk again, but he was sure he couldn't stay sober by himself. His shame wouldn't let him talk about his problem with Pastor McLean or any of his children.

Rachel finished washing dishes, dried her hands on her apron, and asked, "Papa, did you hear? Zach Hill got killed yesterday when his team ran away and the wagon tipped over."

John tried to think of who Zach Hill was. Then the fog in his brain lifted briefly, and he ate another bite of cold eggs. "Was he the fellow who was gonna marry Eliza Steel this fall?"

"That's the one. Nice fella. But a lot older'n her." Rachel sat down beside her father. "Can I get you some more ham or eggs?"

John shook his head. "This will be plenty. Thanks for saving me some breakfast." He finished the glass of milk beside his plate, then refilled the glass with water from the tin water bucket on the bench beside the back door and drank all of it. "Maybe we oughta go over to the Steels and tell 'em we're sorry about the accident."

"Why don't you go, Papa? The rest of us are all busy. I've gotta start cookin' dinner, an' all the boys are busy threshing oats. The girls are off pickin' blackberries." Rachel began washing the dishes that had held her father's breakfast, and her father stood up from his late breakfast and wondered how well his sons were managing the threshing.

John peeked into the barn, where Sam, David, and William were driving six horses around a circular track with a slotted floor. Some of the oats they'd cut earlier in the week were spread on that floor, and the horses' hooves knocked loose the grains of oats. The horses and drivers circled round and round, and with each pass, more oats fell through the slots and collected on the solid floor below.

He was pleased to see them working without his guidance. Rachel's information about the accident resonated in his mind, and after checking the cows and sheep in the pasture and finding them all healthy, he caught and saddled a horse and rode west and south about ten miles to the farm of Adam Steel. There were several horses tied to the barnyard fence when he arrived. He tied his beside them and knocked at the door.

Adam Steel answered his knock. He looked flustered by all the visitors but glad to see a neighbor. John took off his hat and said quietly, "Adam, I came to tell Eliza and all of you folks we're sorry to hear about Zach Hill's gettin' killed."

"Come on in, John. Nice of you to ride over. Eliza's in the parlor with the rest of the family an' a bunch of other folks." Adam led the way toward the sound of voices. John followed, carrying his hat in his hand and noticing the attractive furnishings as he passed.

Eliza Steel was sitting beside her mother as she greeted well-wishers. Both were wearing black. Her father moved through the crowded room, John in his wake. "Eliza, John Beaty's rode all the way over here to talk to you." He stepped aside.

John wasn't sure what to say as Eliza smiled and turned to face him. Finally he managed. "Miss Steel, all of us Beatys are sure sorry 'bout your intended gettin' killed. That's a real shame."

"Thank you for coming over, Mr. Beaty. You're real kind to come all that way." She dabbed at her eyes with a white handkerchief. John saw how pretty her blonde hair, pink skin, and plump figure were, accentuated by their contrast with her long, black dress. He bowed slightly and stepped back. Eliza smiled at him again.

John retreated to the edge of the crowd and struck up a conversation with Eliza's father. "How's your oat crop this year, Adam?"

"Pretty fair, but now we'll get behind cradlin' it, havin' to stop for the funeral and all. Zach Hill was helpin' us when he got kilt. So we'll be short a man."

"We got all of ours in the barn already. Maybe I could come help you out when you start cradlin' again." John was astounded to hear himself making this offer. Adam looked surprised, but he recovered quickly.

"That'd be a big help. Reckon we'll start again day after tomorrow if the weather's decent. Could you come then?"

Two days later, John was up before dawn and on his way to the Steels' farm soon after. He arrived in time for breakfast and then joined the crew of cradlers and bundlers as they resumed work on Adam Steel's oats. At about mid-morning, Eliza, two of her sisters, and her mother appeared in the field with cold water, fresh cold cider, and apple pie. The men devoured them all.

Eliza smiled at John as she handed him a second helping. "Have another piece of pie, Mr. Beaty. It was sure nice of you to come way over here to help us out."

"Thank you. Glad to help out. It's kinda lonely at my place since my wife died. An' you can just call me John."

"They say it's good to keep busy after you've lost someone you love. So I've been baking pies." Eliza brushed a strand of hair from her face.

"You sure do make good pie. May I call you Eliza?"

"Certainly. I'd like that. And I do like to cook." Eliza curtsied and smiled. John smiled back as he ran a hand over his sweaty brow, and then he took a big bite of pie.

After the Steels' oats were cut and hauled to the barn, John found other reasons to ride to their farm. His children speculated about the visits among themselves, but on the whole they were pleased by his initiative, since they'd sensed his loneliness after Polly died. John and Eliza wound up taking long walks together.

"Since Zach was killed you've come over pretty often, John. It sure brightens up my day when you do." She looked into John's eyes, he smiled back, and the pair stopped to watch some horses that were standing under an oak tree, fighting off flies.

"You brighten my day too. And if I come over here I don't have such a hankerin' to go to Millersburg to the tavern. I have a real problem knowin' when to stop if I take a drink. When Polly was livin', she helped me stay away from whiskey. But with her gone, I sometimes can't do that." John was startled that he'd been so frank. He looked at Eliza and then looked at the ground. "An' then I think you're awful nice, and a great cook."

"You're real nice too. Not like some of those young fellows, who seem to just want to get me in bed with 'em." Eliza blushed and started walking toward the corner of the pasture. John followed, a few steps behind at first. Then he caught up and took her hand.

Eventually they walked back to her parents' home. At Christmas time, they set a wedding date for the next spring and invited their immediate relatives.

In May, the families of the bride and groom filled a small room on the north side of the courthouse. Outside the window, an old burr oak with a scar on its trunk renewed itself, pale new leaf by pale new leaf. Beside it, the fertile blue blossoms of iris mirrored the cloudless sky. The lilacs at the corner of the courthouse perfumed the building's rooms and the entire grassy square in the center of Millersburg. The mood of those in the office of the justice of the peace matched the spring afternoon.

The early season tan that Eliza had acquired while searching the fields and woods for mushrooms accented her white linen dress. The brownish hue in her cheeks was highlighted by a flush of excitement. She stood with her father, her mother, three sisters, two brothers, their spouses, and their children on one side of Justice Armor.

John stood on the other side, surrounded by nine of his children, five sons-in-law, and a bevy of wiggling, squirming grandchildren. He wore a high-collared, white linen shirt and a brown wool suit that contrasted with his gray-flecked black hair and newly trimmed steel-gray beard and sideburns. His sinewy hands, tanned deep brown, were clasped in front of him.

He smiled at Eliza. She magnified it and returned it to him, and to all of his family. She hadn't seen all of them in one place before. They were almost a village in themselves. But they all seemed to like her, especially John's four youngest children. And John—she'd loved his deep-set brown eyes since the first time he'd come to call after her fiancé was killed. And he'd treated her with respect, right from that first visit—not like the younger men who'd courted her after that tragedy. All they seemed to want was a brood mare who could cook and spin. She deepened her smile as the justice cleared his throat.

"Dear friends, we have come together today to join this man and this woman …"

The words carried John's thoughts back to the day in Pennsylvania when he had married Polly. It had been a happy day like today, but different. Today there'd be no neighborhood feast, no cabin raising, no brown jugs of whiskey circulating. He'd only broken his vow of abstinence once since Polly died, and he'd vowed never to do so again. Now there were some days when he didn't crave whiskey, not like he did day and night in the months right after he'd stopped drinking. He sure wasn't going to risk starting again today by having a big shindig with lots of neighbors urging him to have one, just one, for old time's sake.

"Do you, John Beaty, take this woman to be your lawfully wedded wife?" The question snapped him back to today for the moment.

"I do. I certainly do." His voice, always resonant, had an extra measure of inflection.

"Do you, Eliza Steel, take this man to be your lawfully wedded husband?"

Eliza's confident "I do" filled a void he'd had in his heart since he dropped the first shovel-full of soil on Polly's coffin over four years ago. He took Eliza's extended left hand and slipped a plain gold ring on her finger.

"I now pronounce you man and wife." Justice Armor waited until Eliza had stepped out of John's embrace, and then he extended his hands to them both. "It's an honor to marry such fine folk. I hope you have a happy life together."

I do hereby certify that on the 22nd day of May 1834 by virtue of a license from the Clerk of the Court of Common Pleas of Holmes County John Beaty and Eliza Steel were legally united in marriage by me a Justice of the Peace in and for said county.

Given under my hand & seal this 25th day of May 1834.

John Armor J.P.

—From a Marriage Certificate filed in the Holmes County Courthouse, Ohio

The two families filed out and regrouped beside the oak and iris on the courthouse lawn. After everyone congratulated the newlyweds, the men and older boys began to discuss the weather, prices, and prospects for crops. The women and older girls shared recipes and talked about how easy it was to make dresses, shirts, and aprons from the factory-made cotton cloth that Maclendon's store across the street had started to stock. The two youngest Beatys, their nieces and nephews from the Mitchell clan, and some youngsters from the Steel family played tag and hide-and-seek among the trees and lilacs on the courthouse square.

David and William struck up a conversation with a red-haired Steel boy about their age.

"So you got a new ma. Hope you like her." The freckled young Steel flexed his biceps.

"Reckon she'll be fine." David studied the boy's arms and decided that he would be easy to whip in a fight. "How do you like my knife? Made the sheath myself." He pulled the implement and its cover from his pocket. The red-headed boy took it and ran a finger cautiously along the blade.

"Wow. That's a good'un. Wanna sell it?" He looked at David hopefully as he handed it back. "Give ya fifty cents fer it."

"Two dollars and it's yours, sheath and all." David held the knife and sheath in the palm of his open hand. He saw longing among the swath of freckles below the bush of red hair.

"Ain't got but a dollar an' two bits. Give ya that for 'em." The boy's voice had a pleading tone. David looked at William, at the bevies of conversing adults, and slowly back at the boy.

"Well, they're worth two dollars, but seein' as yer aunt's my new ma, it's a deal." He handed over the sheathed knife and took the money.

As they walked away, William said, "Why'd you sell him your good knife? You use it all the time."

"'Cause I can get another one for fifty cents an' make a sheath in no time at all. Guess he didn't know that."

"You sure do like to make deals."

"Yup, if I can come out ahead." David and William joined the rest of their family as they were climbing into buggies to leave.

***

John and Eliza stood beside the iris in the shade of the scarred oak and greeted every well-wisher who came by, until long after their families had left for home. When they were finally alone, Eliza said, "Shouldn't we be starting for the farm?"

John put his arm around her waist. "Not till tomorrow, or maybe the next day. I've got us the best room in the hotel tonight."

"How sweet of you. I'd been expecting to go right out to the farm, 'cause the rhubarb's waiting to be made into jam." She put her arm on his shoulder, and he leaned down and kissed her.

After supper, they walked west from the hotel toward the creek, the smooth skin of her hand nestled into the creased and callused skin of his. It was a mild evening with no wind. Sounds lingered as though they wanted to become eternal: the bleats of contented ewes and lambs, the languorous mellow chiming of a bell on a grazing cow, the rhythmic thumping of hooves of frolicking horses, and, as they neared the creek, the melodic drone of hundreds of spring peepers proclaiming their readiness for mates. John realized how much younger Eliza was and hoped she would adapt to being married to a much older man. Directly in front of them, a woodcock hurtled straight up into the purpling sky and broadcast his urgings to any female of his kind who might be in earshot. Mars and Venus brightened minute by minute just above the line of trees that flanked Killbuck Creek.

They followed the rutted road onto the bridge and leaned over the railing with their arms around each other's waist. The water was a dark, rippling ribbon unfurling with quiet murmurs toward the Muskingum, the Ohio, the Mississippi, and the Gulf of Mexico. It added a modulating bass note to the chorus of spring peepers and the more distant sounds of sheep, cows, horses, and people. John squeezed Eliza's waist and was surprised how soft and yielding it was—not like Polly's large-boned muscularity that he remembered from thirty-two years of marriage.

Eliza took a deep, slow breath. "Doesn't it smell nice? All those lilacs and honeysuckles in bloom. And the cherry blossoms. I hope there's a good crop of cherries this year so I can make lots of jelly. I think cherry jelly tastes the very best. Do you like it, John?"

"I can eat half a jarful at a sitting. Prob'ly a whole jarful of yours." He tightened his arm around her waist and pressed his fingers gently inward. She turned toward him, face tilted up, lips ready. When they'd ended the long kiss, he took her hand again. "Let's mosey back toward the hotel. The lilacs'll smell even better there."

He noticed that Eliza was a half-step ahead all the way, and he extended his game leg to the utmost, trying to keep up.

***

Just after eight o'clock the next morning, John limped into the livery stable.

A man carrying a pitchfork of hay looked his way and said, "You're here earlier than we thought. One of the guys bet you wouldn't be able to get here till noon, what with beddin' that young wife an' all." He snickered and yelled to someone in the back to bring John's team.

As the man was taking his pay for the horses' feed and lodging, he looked John in the eye and said, "Thanks. An' if ya need any help keepin' that young wife satisfied, just let me know."

John slammed his fist to the point of the man's chin so hard that his victim fell back hard against a manger. By the time the stablehand regained his breath and looked out the door, the team and buggy were halfway to the hotel. John, sitting straight and tall, looked back and waved. The man looked at the departing driver and team and rubbed his chin gingerly. "That old John Beaty's got a lot more left in him than I'd'a given him credit for."

After Eliza entered the family, Samuel and Susan both married and established their own households. Rachel hired out occasionally as a housekeeper for a nearby family, and eventually she married Andrew Gamble, a neighboring farmer. John depended on David and William to do most of the heavy work of farming. He joined them for lighter work and hoped for good prices for his wheat, corn, and livestock. He didn't touch a drop of whiskey, even though his friends urged him to join them in the tavern when he went to Millersburg.

Late in 1835, a neighbor told John that he had a letter waiting at the post office. He picked it up on his next trip to town, walked to a bench on the Courthouse Square, sat down in the sun of the Indian summer afternoon, and started to read. It was from Janey, his brother James's wife back in Harrison County.

Word by slow word, he absorbed her chronicle of unremitting loss. The devastation had started in September 1827 when her ten-year-old son David had taken sick and died. Then, year by year, death took her children: William, John, Mary Ann, Margaret, Thomas, and Joseph. Her husband, James, had shared her grief and comforted her through their losses; but then he and James Junior, twenty years old and full of promise, died a few months apart in 1834. Martha, the oldest daughter, married and mother of three young children, died the next spring. That left Janey, fifty-seven and once the mother of nine, a childless widow who went across the road each Sunday after church to the line of ten graves in Crabapple Cemetery to weep and scatter flowers.

John sat for a long time. People walking by spoke to him. He nodded to a few but ignored most. Late in the afternoon, he got his team and buggy. After they crossed Killbuck Creek and turned north, he wrapped the lines on the buggy rail and let the team go at their own pace. Corn shocks threw long shadows to the east. The season's last goldenrod blooms amplified the sunlight and enriched the aroma of fall.

These workings of God baffled him. When he'd learned of his mother's death ten years earlier, it had seemed reasonable. She'd lived a full life, raised twelve children, had more grandchildren than she could count, and died at age seventy-three with family around her. Polly's death had been a bitter blow, but it had been only her, not his whole family. But this—what was God thinking of, wiping out James's family one after another, ten in eight years? James had always been the steady, sober, successful one. He and Janey had worked hard, helped build the school, given generously to the Crabapple church, and helped all their neighbors. Why did God kill these kinds of folks before their time? And why leave Janey to mourn alone? Why had he taken Polly, when she still had young children? *Why not me*, he thought, *the black sheep?* This predestination business he'd heard of in church so many times didn't make much sense after Polly died; now it made no sense at all. John shook his head and sighed.

The team had taken the left-hand fork in the road and headed west. When they got to their own lane, they turned north. John unwrapped the reins and guided them toward the barn, even though they knew the way. He was very quiet as he unharnessed them, rubbed them down, and led them into the pasture at sunset. When he got to the house, Eliza was mending a shirt. He surprised her with a warm kiss and a hug. "I'm sure glad you decided to marry me. Bein' without a wife was real lonesome."

"Not having a husband was too. I'm awful glad you asked me to marry you."

* * *

As the months and years passed, several of John and Eliza's neighbors moved to new farms in Ohio, Indiana, or even Illinois. Most of those who'd moved west sent back word of the good soil they'd encountered at their new locations and of the bounteous crops they had grown after the move. These stories made John restless. He watched his yields of hay, wheat, corn, and oats go down nearly every year, and he began to feel as if it was time to move on. Even though Eliza enjoyed her new family, John began to feel restless and longed for a new farm.

Chapter 13
Restless to Move

In 1839, John's daughter Lucinda had moved west with her husband, John Harden, and their family, to Indiana. The next July, as John, David, and William, their clothes and faces red from the wheat rust, came in for dinner after hauling the last of a dismal wheat harvest to the barn, the family shared a letter from the Hardens that Eliza and Rachel had brought from Millersburg. In it, the Hardens raved about how tall the wheat and corn grew in the black soil of Indiana and urged others in their families to join them. Lucinda and John's letter magnified her father's frustration with his farm and with growing old.

"Why don't we sell out and go west like John and Lucinda did, Papa?" David, now nineteen, bearded, and six feet tall, looked at his father, expectation in his eyes.

"Well, I'd like to, but we'd have to study a lot about a big move like that. We couldn't just up and leave. I done it twice, and it's a lot of hard work." John looked around the table at Eliza, Rachel, and William, then at David. "But it's tempting to think about ownin' some land that produces good, like this place used to years ago."

"I like it right here, with all the relatives close by." Eliza smiled at John as she dished out pieces of raspberry pie.

Even though he knew of the work involved and of Eliza's wishes, the idea of new land kept resonating in John's head. He remembered his father's large farm on the long, west-facing slope back beside Cross Creek and how it had supported the big family; he recalled how well crops had grown at first on the steep land he and his brothers had cleared after they'd crossed the Ohio, then how the ground had washed away and the crop yields had gone down.

Now the same thing was happening here. The United States seemed to have pulled out of the big panic of a few years earlier, and prices were improving. Maybe it was time to think about moving west again. He shared his decision a few days later when the family had finished dinner and the boys had not yet gone back to the field.

"We've got the work all caught up, except for the last hoeing of the corn. David and Willie can do that without me. I'm goin' west for a few days to look around for some good land."

"You goin' all the way to Indiana or Illinois, Papa? A man down at the mill told me there's lots of good land out there." David's question was larded with hope.

"Not that far, probably. I'm too old to go way out to the frontier again. But I'd like to get a place with better ground. This old farm's 'bout worn out."

"Are you sure you'll be all right by yourself? I notice you're limping more these days." Eliza's concern was obvious in both her question and her face.

"I'll take good care, love. Besides, I'll be ridin', not walkin', so my leg shouldn't bother." Eliza shrugged and began to wash dishes.

The next morning, John saddled a horse and left early. As the family watched him head west across the rolling landscape, Eliza sighed, "I sure hope he'll be all right. His leg's been botherin' him a whole lot lately."

William looked toward Eliza. "An' have you noticed how every once in a while, his skin's kind of yellow?"

"I've thought I saw a little something. He says sometimes he feels kind of punk, but it doesn't stop him from working." As John rode out of sight, the family returned to their daily tasks, but Eliza worried about whether her husband would be all right. David hoped his father would come back with news of a big, new farm on the frontier.

* * *

Two weeks later, John rode down the lane at dusk and handed the horse's reins to William, who had just driven the cows into the pasture across the road. The rest of the family rushed out to meet him. His news was too good not to share. "We're gonna move. I've bought a new farm. It's got some good bottomland on it. Not like this worn-out hardpan ridge."

"Out in Indiana or Illinois?" David's deep voice surged through his black beard.

"Not near that far, son, only about thirty-five miles away, south of Mansfield. Pretty country. Got a house an' barn already built, an' creek along the north side. The bottomland grows real good corn from what I could see, even in dry years like this. Only been farmed a few years. But we'll have to sell this place so I have money for the new one. An' we'll have to see if any of the rest of the family wants to go with us."

He kissed Eliza, who was holding a metal dipper she'd filled from the water bucket. He drank it and then a second as well. "Ya got anything left to eat? I'm starved." Eliza and Rachel hustled to set out some food left over from supper, and the family chattered about the prospect of moving.

By early fall, John had located a buyer and agreed to sell the farm for a thousand dollars in cash and a promissory note for the rest.

John Beaty to Samuel Vorhes
100 acres: Lot 23, Sec. 2, Township 9, Range 7
for two thousand dollars in lawful money
September 25, 1840

—*Deed Records of Holmes County, Ohio, Vol. 7, Page*
168

Of John's seven grown children who lived near Millersburg, only Jane and her husband, Joseph Reed, decided to join John, Eliza, and John's sons David and William for the move. The two families set out in early October with three loaded wagons, three yoke of oxen, a team of horses, and a diverse collection of other livestock.

When they were about halfway to the new farm, the fall rains turned the roads to mud. They slogged along, double- and even triple-teaming the wagons to get up the biggest hills and across the flooding creeks. As they came in sight of their destination, they found Toby Creek, the stream that formed its northern boundary, surging bank-full. The buildings of their new farm stood near a spring at the base of the hill just a quarter mile beyond it.

Soybeans on bottomland of Toby Creek on farm owned by John Beaty and then David Beaty, south of Mansfield, Ohio, 1840-1860

The rain came down in sheets as John goaded the ox team on the lead wagon into the stream. In the middle of the creek, the left front wheel hit a submerged tree. The oxen were frantic to reach the far shore and lunged ahead. The upstream wheel rolled up onto the tree, and the wagon started to tip. John, William, and David leaped into the swirling water, grabbed the wagon bed as it was starting its upward arc, and pulled down with all their strength while trying to avoid being run over by the wagon wheels. Joseph Reed jumped in from the far bank, grabbed the tailgate, and pulled down. Ever so slowly, the wagon righted itself as the four drenched and shivering men held onto the wagon bed and struggled in the surging water while John guided the oxen up the bank.

"Thank God that wagon didn't tip over. If it had, we'd'a lost all of our stuff." John's exclamation, uttered between chattering teeth, expressed everyone's relief.

Eliza looked at John as he shivered in the rain. "Here, get those wet clothes off, and wrap up in this blanket before you catch the ague."

John brushed aside the blanket she extended. "Not till we get all the wagons and the stock across. I'll be all right as long as I keep moving. Drive this wagon on to the house, and start a fire." Eliza looked dubious but followed his command.

Two hours later, when he appeared at the three-room log house with David, William, and Joseph, John was shivering uncontrollably. Eliza offered him a mug of sassafras tea, but John's hands shook so much that he couldn't drink. William steadied it at his lips, and he managed a few sips. Eliza and David pulled off his wet clothes and wrapped him in wool blankets. As he tried to lie down beside the fire, he found that his arms and legs wouldn't bend. David and William lifted him, almost as stiff as a plank, and laid him beside the fire.

After an hour, he moaned, "Get me a drink of cold water, an' get these blankets off. I'm burnin' up."

As Eliza brought fresh water from the spring, she put her hand on his forehead. "You've got the ague for sure. Just lie quiet, and drink this." She touched his forehead again and shook her head. "Just keep drinking water while I make you some broth from that rabbit David killed on the trail yesterday."

It was three weeks before John's chills and fever subsided enough for him to help William and David with the work of settling in. Then the malady came back again. He found that he couldn't work more than an hour at a time. His eyes sometimes looked yellow, and he had a hard, dry cough that sometimes produced thick, yellowish phlegm.

Most devastating of all, the thousand dollars that Samuel Vorhes had promised to send as final payment for the farm at Millersburg didn't arrive. Instead, Vorhes sent a letter saying that it might be several years before he could pay. John had counted on that money to pay off the land contract he'd made with Luther Cook for the new farm.

* * *

On a morning when Eliza had driven the team and buggy to nearby Belleville, John called William and David in from the field and told them, "I'm in a right tough spot, and I want you to promise me somethin'." He stopped as a dry cough shook his chest. "This ague an' whatever else I got is really about to do me in. I know you both want to strike out on your own and get some land, but I need you to stay here and work this farm till we get it paid off. Otherwise that fellow Cook might just up and take it all back, leavin' us with nothing. So I want you to promise to take care of Eliza an' me until we get it all paid for. If you'll do that an' pay off Cook, even if I die, this farm'll be yours." He coughed hard and then put his head on the table for a minute.

William and David looked at each other, trying to comprehend the import of their father's words. When John lifted his head, David said, "That's fine by me, but I want to have a lawyer write it all down and have us to sign it."

John's eyebrows arched, and he looked stunned. "Why in perdition would we do that? I've got no truck with lawyers an' their fancy words. Isn't my word good enough for ya?"

"Sure it is, Papa, but if you're dead an' gone, it'll be our word against all the rest of the family when it comes to the land. If it's not in writing, it's no deal, far as I'm concerned." He looked straight into John's eyes and noticed how yellow they were.

William put his arm on his father's shoulder, "What you want us to do for you and Eliza is fine by me too. I'm not keen on lawyers either, but if David says we gotta hire one, I'll sign somethin'." He looked toward David, who nodded.

John shrugged, coughed again, and waved his hand. "Get your damn lawyer, but you've got to pay him. I'm not gonna waste my money on those cheats."

A week later, a young man in a suit drove a sleek horse pulling a shiny, black buggy up to the Beatys' new farm. David brought him into the house. "Papa, James Stewart the lawyer's here with an agreement for us to sign, if we like it." Then he went outside to call William.

John stood up slowly and shook Stewart's hand, noting how soft it was within his own muscular, callused one. "Ya got somethin' ready for us, huh? Have a seat, an' read it as soon as Willie gets here."

Stewart took the glass of water that Eliza offered and unrolled the papers as William stamped mud off his boots and came into the kitchen.

Then the well-dressed young man glanced around the bare room at his new acquaintances and said, "All right. Just let me know if you have any questions. Here's what I've got so far." He began to read aloud, slowly and earnestly.

> **Articles of agreement made and concluded this 30th day of October A.D. 1840 by and Between John Beaty of the County of Richland in the state of Ohio of the one part and William Beatty and David Beatty of the same County and State of the other part. Witnesseth That whereas the said John Beatty did by articles of agreement executed between him and one Luther Cook and bearing date the 11th day of August A.D. 1840 contract with and agree to purchase from said Cook the following tracts of land …**

> **In which said Articles of Agreement the said John Beatty bound himself to said Cook to pay him said Cook as a consideration and price of said land the sum of fourteen hundred and fifty dollars as follows viz Three hundred and fifty dollars by the first day of October inst. three hundred sixty six dollars and two thirds cent by the first day of April A.D. 1841 three hundred sixty six dollars and two thirds cent by the first day of April A.D. 1842 and three hundred sixty six dollars and two thirds cent by the first day of April A.D. 1843 in full**

> payment ... and is bound on and by said articles
> of agreement to convey to said John Beaty the
> said first described tracts of land in fee simple by
> cowarrantee deed: and to assign and transfer the
> whole right and title of the said Cook therein to
> the said John Beaty his heirs and assigns forever.

John interrupted Stewart's recitation. "Just a minute, young fella! Are you sure you understand all you've writ down for us? There's so many highfalutin' words on that page, it'd choke a horse!" Stewart squirmed and ran a finger around the inside of his shirt collar.

David rescued him. "That's the way lawyers write, Papa. What he's read us is just a description of the farm and of what you promised Cook when you signed the contract with him last summer. Let him go ahead."

"Get on with it." John waved his arm impatiently, and Steward resumed reading.

> And whereas the said John Beatty is now well
> advanced in years and by reason of his age and
> inability to undergo and sustain labor and it being
> his desire and intention to provide out of his own
> property for his support and maintenance for life
> for the like support and maintenance during his
> life of such family as he now has or such as he may
> in addition thereto hereafter acquire and being
> also minded to keep about him and receive the
> services of his two sons the said William Beatty
> and David Beatty who are now come to mens
> estate and with the view and intent to provide and
> secure to them as well a compensation for their
> time fidelity and labor during his life towards his
> support to be given as well as to provide some
> estate for them the said William and David
> after his decease. He doth for the considerations
> aforesaid of and on condition of the true and
> faithful performance of the agreements and

> stipulations hereinafter contained on their part
> and behalf to be performed and fulfilled covenant
> and agree to and with the said William Beatty
> and David Beatty their heirs expectatory and
> administratory that he will and truly pay off
> and discharge out of his own property the said
> installments to the said Cook his executors and
> administrators or assigns according to his said
> article of agreement with him and will procure
> from him the deed or deeds for said several tracts
> of land therein described. And that from and
> after this date the said William and David shall
> have full possession of all and singular the said
> several tracts of land with the improvements and
> appurtenances thereon any or either of them.

John hammered his fist on the table. "Enough of that whereas-y an' hereinafter-y stuff. Just read me the part about what Willie and David are goin' to do for the rest of us if they're to get the farm."

Stewart ran a finger around his collar again, drank some more water, and scanned the pages. "Here it is, Mr. Beaty."

> Also the said William Beatty and David Beatty
> on their part and on behalf of themselves their
> heirs executors and administrators covenant and
> agree to and with the said John Beatty his heirs
> executors and administrators that they will for
> the consideration of the foregoing covenants
> herein contained by and on their part of the said
> John Beatty will well and truly provide for and
> reasonably and decently and comfortable maintain
> and support said John Beatty and his present
> family and such as he shall or may hereafter have
> and contract or take and furnish him or them with
> such support and maintenance during the natural
> life of the said John but no longer. Provided the
> family hereafter to be acquired contracted or

**taken by the said John shall not be more than a
wife and such child or children as may be borne to
him by her. Provided also that when any member
or members of the said John's family marry off or
leave his family they or any such of them as shall
leave are no longer to be supported.**

Stewart looked at John, then at his sons. "Is that what you wanted
to hear, sir?"

David spoke the instant the lawyer's question ended. "It sounds
just fine to me. Real fine, Mr. Stewart. Everythin' we talked about."
William nodded twice.

John looked perplexed. "It's so full of big words, it's mostly beyond
my understandin'. But seein' as I'm old and ailin', guess I'll have to go
along with my boys." He reached for the quill pen Stewart had put
on the table beside a bottle of ink.

**In witness of all which the said parties have hereto
set their hands and seals this day first mentioned
above.**

**Witness John Beaty, James Stewart, Wm. Beaty,
David Beaty**

Because John's health made him unable to work outside, David and
William, with some guidance from Joseph Reed, took over the work
of the new farm. They cut wood for winter and stacked it near the
house, repaired the fence where the flood on Toby Creek had torn it
away, and plowed the field along the creek bottom in preparation for
early planting the following spring.

On a clear day in November, as David was plowing the upland
field along the west side of the farm, he heard a clatter of horse's
hooves running down the road that formed its western boundary. A
woman was screaming, "Whoa! Whoa! Whoa, Blackie!"

He set the prod pole between the oxen so they would stay in place
and raced toward the road. Then he saw a black horse come running
over the hill from the south, pulling a careening buggy. A tall,

black-haired young woman was tugging on the reins with no effect whatever. David jumped the fence and reached the road just before the runaway came by. With one deft move, he grabbed the bridle of the running horse and held on as it dragged him. The weight of the new burden on its mouth stopped the panicked animal after several yards, and it stood in the road, foaming, sweating, and trembling in its harness.

"Whoa, boy, whoa. Nothing's gonna get you. Easy now, easy. Just take it easy, Blackie. Easy does it." He spoke softly as he stroked the horse's moist, glistening neck with his left hand, all the while keeping a firm grip on the bridle with his right.

"Oh, thank you ever so much, sir! You probably saved my life."

David liked her voice and the lustrous, dark hair that extended below her bonnet. He lifted his hat a little with his left hand and said, "Just glad I was nearby and could help, miss. You had quite a runaway going there."

The driver managed a weak smile of gratitude. David returned to rubbing the horse's neck and withers gently and felt its fear diminish. "Reckon he'll be calmed down enough to drive again in a few minutes."

He glanced back at the young woman with a shy smile. "By the way, I'm David Beaty. Me and my family just moved to this place on Toby Creek last month."

"I'm pleased to make your acquaintance, Mr. Beaty. My name is Maria—Maria Ruth Gault. My family and I live up the road a couple of miles. Father asked me to drive the butter and eggs to Belleville today and sell 'em." She glanced down at the square wooden box set on straw behind the seat and saw egg yolk seeping out the bottom. "Looks like the eggs are mostly broke, so I'll just sell the butter. Oh, well. At least Blackie and the buggy and I are safe."

"Real pleased to meet you, Miss Gault." David gave her a shy nod and then spoke softly to the sweating horse. "You ready to walk now? Let's walk together a little bit, big fella." He motioned for Maria to hold the rein snug and began to walk, leading the horse by the bridle. They walked slowly along the road. At the base of the next hill, David let go of the bridle but kept his hand ready to grab it again. The black horse kept walking. "Whoa, Blackie." The horse stopped at David's command.

He turned to Maria, "Miss Gault, your horse seems to be calmed down again. Reckon I better get back to plowin'."

"Thank you ever so much, Mr. Beaty. I'll be just fine now. I'm good with horses, 'cept when they get spooked." Maria let the reins touch the horse's back as she said, "Giddup, Blackie." The black horse resumed walking. Maria turned to wave as she drove away.

David waved, and then he stood watching until they disappeared over the hill. He whistled as he resumed plowing, and he scanned the road for the black horse and its driver all afternoon as he guided the plow. As the oxen were turning the last furrow, he saw her come over the hill, driving at a trot. David lifted his hat, and Maria waved in return. As he drove the ox team to the farmstead, he hummed "Yankee Doodle."

* * *

The Beatys had a hard winter. They were short of feed for their livestock and scrambling to meet the next payment on the farm. John was sick often, and Eliza's tender care didn't help him much. David took a job driving freight wagons between Mansfield and Belleville. William trapped and hunted for whatever wild animals he could find in the woods and sold their pelts. Between them, they took care of the farm animals and helped Eliza care for their father.

In late March, John took a turn for the worse. David heard him coughing all night and got up to try to help. Eliza was sitting beside John's bed, putting warm, moist rags that smelled of camphor on his chest. "Anything I can do for you, Papa?"

John turned slowly and gave David a weak smile. "Just take care of everybody … after I'm gone … like you promised. And … save the farm … if you can." His voice was so weak that David had to bend close to hear the words.

"We will, Papa. You rest easy now." He put his hand on this father's forehead. It felt cold. He and Eliza exchanged worried looks, and David went to wake William to say a last good-bye to his father. John's wheezing breath slowed and stopped before daylight.

Two days later, the Beaty family and a handful of neighbors gathered for the funeral at the little log church on a hill about mile southeast of the farm. It was a sparse congregation, since most of John's and Eliza's families lived three days of hard traveling to the east, and the Beatys hadn't lived in the neighborhood long. When it came time to carry John's coffin from the church to the nearby grave on the hillside, there were only three men from the family to do so. Adam Gault saw the problem and joined David, William, and their brother-in-law, Joseph Reed, to carry a corner of the wooden box. When it was safely lowered in the grave and covered with earth, he turned to David.

"I'm Adam Gault, Maria's father. She told us how you saved her in that runaway last fall. Glad I could help you out today."

David smiled through his tears and shook Adam Gault's hand. He looked around for Maria but saw only middle-aged and old women in the congregation.

It was a somber widow and her two stepsons who returned from the graveyard. They'd just buried the family patriarch. The next payment on the farm was due in three days, and they didn't have enough money.

Chapter 14
Passing the Torch

"With what we borrowed from Joseph Reed, we're short about fifty dollars." David looked up from the pile of money he'd just counted. "We've got to sell somethin' real quick!"

"We've got next to nothing that anybody will pay cash for, except the horses. But we need them for farm work that we can't do with the ox team." William's voice sounded resigned to their impending loss.

Eliza came in from the kitchen, her eyes red. "I've got five dollars and nine cents I saved up from butter and egg money, an' we could sell my winter coat. It'd help a little."

David stood up with a shrug. "Keep your coat, Eliza. There'll be another winter soon enough. So I guess, bad as I hate to, we got to try to sell the horses. I'll take 'em to Belleville and see what I can do."

After he and William caught and curried the team of bay mares, frisky after a winter of little work, David left for Belleville, riding one and leading the other. William went to check his trap line, hoping for some recent catches before the winter season ended. He found one fox, skinned it, and added the pelt to the small pile in the shed.

Late that evening, David returned, riding a limping, sway-backed chestnut horse and leading a smaller black that looked equally old. William was surprised to see his brother arrive with two horses.

"I thought for sure you'd have to walk home. How'd you get these two?"

David slid off the old horse. "Had real good luck at the livery stable. There was a stranger there lookin' for a good, fresh team to pull his wagon on west. I traded with him and got one hundred dollars to boot. These two don't look like much, but they'll probably get us by for the season, if we treat 'em careful." He led his new purchases to the water tub and, after they'd drunk their fill, turned them loose in the enclosure beside the barn, where the manger was full of hay. As the team began to eat hay, the brothers stood watching them. David shook his legs to loosen his tired muscles and said, "We're fortunate to have even these two old nags now. But the hundred dollars I got will give us enough to save the farm."

William gave his brother a tight smile and replied, "You were always a shrewd trader. Good thing you went to Belleville 'stead of me.

* * *

Early on the first of April, David and William drove the slow, mismatched team and the farm wagon to Luther Cook's farm and paid the $366.66 due on the land their father had bought.

The two brothers, now twenty and eighteen, started field work with a strange sense of emptiness. They no longer had their father to tell them when and how to prepare the fields and plant the crops, and they were on a completely new farm. As soon as the grain and corn were in the ground, David resumed driving freight wagons for the drayage company in Belleville. He saved all his wages toward the next year's payment on the farm. William tended the livestock and crops and then worked for neighbors to earn more cash. They were determined not to come so close to losing the farm as they had after John died. Eliza raised a garden and kept house for her stepsons and sent occasional letters back to her family and friends in Millersburg.

Even without their father's guidance, the brothers' crops were bountiful. The corn grew so tall and thick in the bottomland along Toby Creek that they had to work late into November to get it all picked and in the crib. When they were ready to haul it to the mill in Belleville in December, they only filled the wagon half full. But their two old horses were scarcely able to pull it up the steepest hill. David and William got off and walked behind the wagon, pushing. As they and their worn-out team were straining to get the half-loaded wagon up the last hill, they heard the clatter of hooves and the jingle of harness metal behind them.

A young woman's voice called out, "Hello, neighbors. Looks like you need some help." They turned to see Maria Gault sitting in a buggy loaded with butter and eggs behind her sleek, black horse. "My father could maybe loan you a better team for hauling corn."

"Morning, Miss Gault. An' many thanks for the offer." David touched the brim of his cap but kept on pushing the wagon with his left hand. "We could sure use more horses. I'll walk over and talk to him 'bout it after we sell this load of corn in town."

Maria smiled and touched the reins to her horse's back. "You do that, and good luck on this hill." David watched the horse and buggy ascend the hill at a brisk walk as he and William pushed on the wagon. Maria's offer thrilled him. He'd wanted a reason to get to know her ever since he'd stopped her runaway horse and buggy the year before.

Late that afternoon, Adam Gault answered David's knock. "Beg pardon, Mr. Gault," David began, "but your daughter, Maria, said you might have a team of horses we could borrow for a few days. We've got a lot of corn to haul to the mill in Belleville."

"Come in, David. Meet my wife, Ruth, an' join us for a cup of tea. Maria said you needed better horses, an' I'd be glad to help you folks out. I've hauled all o' my corn already."

It was deep dusk and the moon was rising before David left, riding a frisky black gelding and leading its mate. Maria stood in the door of the house and waved as he rode away. The harness jingled in the crisp air. David whistled as he rode, feeling happy about the prospect of getting to know Maria even better.

The next day, he and William piled the wagon high with corn and drove to Belleville behind a four-horse team. The hills were no problem, and the price of corn had gone up a penny a bushel. When David returned the Gaults' team about two weeks later, after delivering another dozen loads to the mill, Maria and her parents invited him to join their family for supper. He was thrilled and, at Maria's invitation, lingered into the evening. And he returned for a lot more visits as winter turned to spring and summer, and during subsequent years, until they set the date for being married.

David Beaty and Maria Ruth Gault, married 11 March, 1844

—Marriage Records of Richland County, Ohio, Volume 004, Page 212

Maria moved into the Beatys' modest log house on the afternoon of the wedding. Eliza welcomed her warmly, and they learned to enjoy each other's company. But after a string of letters came from Millersburg in the subsequent months, Eliza announced that she was returning there to marry a recently widowed farmer she'd known from childhood. David, Maria, and William drove her to Mansfield and, brushing back a few tears, wished her well in her new life as she boarded the stagecoach taking her back to Millersburg.

As the threesome started home, William wiped his eyes and said, "I'll miss Eliza a lot. She's more a mother to me than my real mother. I was so small when Polly died." William's words brought back memories for David.

"I wasn't but two years older than you, so my big sisters, and then Eliza, were mother to me for a lot of my life too. She sure was good for Papa. So far as I know, he never drank whiskey after they got married."

Maria looked fondly at David as she spoke. "Eliza made me real welcome when I married into this family. Doesn't always happen that way, from what I hear. It woulda been nice if she'd stayed a while longer, until our little one got here." She put her hand on David's arm, and they smiled at each other. "But my folks are just a few miles up the road in case I need any help."

"Any ideas on what you'll name it?" William's question caught Maria and David by surprise.

"Not yet. We're just getting used to the idea that we're gonna have a baby. Give us a few more months." Maria snuggled a little closer to David.

By the time the baby arrived in December, they'd decided to name him Theodore. His brother, Guilon, arrived the next year. After a two-year interval, sister Annetta followed.

David and William paid off their father's debt to Luther Cook on time, farmed the eighty-six acres, and rented some nearby land when they could. William married Mary Ann Stone and built a house on the parcel of their father's land to the south in Knox County as David and Maria's house filled with children.

* * *

"Oyez. Oyez, oyez! The court will come to order."

David and William Beaty stood up as the clerk's words echoed around the high-ceilinged courtroom, and Judge Adams walked to the bench behind a large oak desk and sat down. He seemed to be in a hurry.

"Call the first case, Mr. Irvin."

Irvin looked at the two brothers standing, hats in hand, as he said, "Your honor, the first case is William Beaty and David Beaty, who are complainants against a passel of their brothers and sisters. The names of the seventeen defendants are on the papers on your bench. They live all over."

Judge Adams glanced at the sheets of paper, then at David and William. "Are these men the complainants?"

David faced the judge. "We are, your honor. I'm David Beaty. This is my brother, William." They both nodded toward Judge Adams.

"Remind me again what your complaint is against your brothers and sisters and their husbands." Judge Adams leaned back and eyed David intently.

"Your honor, back in October of 1840, our father, his second wife, the two of us, and my sister, Jane, and her husband had just moved here."

"Where'd you come here from?" The judge's question conveyed interest more than skepticism.

"Near Millersburg, your honor. Should I keep going?" The judge nodded. "Our father, John, had signed a three-year contract with Luther Cook to buy eighty-six acres of land in the south edge of the county and just across the line in Knox County. John took sick with the ague real bad right after we got here. He asked us to promise to look after him and his wife, who thought she was in a family way at the time, if he died before he paid off the land. We said we'd do that if we got the farm when we paid off the contract. We did all we promised. It's those eighty-six acres that William and I want clear title to." David shuffled his feet as he paused and glanced toward William, who nodded in assent.

"Did you men bring any proof of this, other than your own words?" Judge Adams looked doubtful as he leaned forward.

"Yes, your honor, right here." David unfolded a long sheet of paper and handed it to the clerk, who glanced at it quickly and handed it to the judge. "We had everything all written down and signed, even though our father was awful hard to convince about the need for that." He waited, fidgeting, while Judge Adams studied the words closely.

The judge glanced up. "I remember this now. Sit down, gentlemen. It will take me a few minutes to read all of this again." David and William melted into their chairs.

William leaned in close and whispered, "Sure was a good thing you didn't listen to me and Papa when we argued we didn't need anything in writin'." Irvin, the clerk, ran his hand back and forth along the quill of his pen, then recut the tip twice with his pocketknife.

After what seemed like an hour to David, Judge Adams looked up and wiped his nose. "Have any of the defendants responded to the summons this court issued last fall?"

Irvin stopped cutting on his quill and looked up. "I think only those two, sir. Mr. and Mrs. Reed." He glanced at Joseph and Jane, who had just walked into the courtroom and sat down in the back. "An' I have depositions from three sheriffs that they served your summonses to all the rest of the defendants, or tried to."

Judge Adams looked at the Reeds. "Rise and state your names and your case before the court."

The Reeds stood and faced the judge, and Jane began, "Your honor, we are Jane and Joseph Reed, and we moved out here from

Millersburg in 1840 because we thought my father, John Beaty, and his wife, needed more help than what William and David could give him. We loaned them two boys money so's they could make payments for the new farm on time, and Joseph helped them with the farming till they got the hang of it better. We think, since we done all that, we should get part of the farm too." Jane looked to Joseph for approval of her speech, and he nodded.

Judge Adams looked at the Reeds and asked, "Mr. and Mrs. Reed, did William and David Beaty pay back the money you loaned them?"

Joseph glanced at his brothers-in-law and responded, "Yes, they did, your honor. It took 'em three or four years, but they paid it all back, with some interest."

"And, Mr. Reed, how many years did you have to help them with their farm?"

"Just the first year, sir. After that, we traded work back an' forth sometimes, but they got the hang of farmin' out here pretty fast."

"Are there any other reasons you think you should get part of John Beaty's farm?"

Jane Reed glanced at Joseph and responded, "Well, John Beaty was my father, and I don't see why his farm should go to just those two boys. All his children had to work daylight to dark on the farm he sold back by Millersburg, an' some of us are older an' worked a lot more years that those two did."

Judge Adams glanced down at the paper on his desk. "And are you aware of the document John Beaty signed with his two sons way back in 1840, Mrs. Reed?"

"The one that gives the farm to William and David, your honor?"

"Mrs. Reed, William and David get the farm only if this court decides they carried out their part of the agreement they signed with their father. Do you think they supported John and his wife reasonably and paid off the loan on the farm?"

Jane and Joseph exchanged glances before Jane spoke. "Well, I suppose so, your honor. They never done anything real fancy for 'em, but far as I know, they kept food on the table, made a good coffin for John when he died, an' paid for the farm on time."

"The court has no further questions. Mr. and Mrs. Reed, you may sit down." Judge Adams motioned for his clerk, and the two conferred in whispers before Adams pronounced his decision.

"This court finds for the complainants, William and David Beaty, and decrees the conveyance to them of clear title to the lands described in the complaint." He rapped his gavel smartly on his desk and then looked at David and William. "The land is yours, free and clear. The court will provide you a title. You do know that you have to pay this court the cost of your suit, don't you?"

"Yes, your honor. We have the money right here to give to Mr. Irvin." David's voice carried a note of relief and gratitude.

William spoke for the first time. "We thank you, sir, for finally getting this land business straightened out."

And afterwards on the day and year above mentioned to wit on this 11th day of April A.D. 1849 this case came on to be heard on the Bill exhibits and testimony [illegible] and the defendants still failing to appear plead answer or demur to said Bill, It is ordered that the same and the matters therein contained as confessed. And the Court upon further consideration thereof do find that the agreement mentioned in said Bill of the date of Oct. 30, 1840 was duly entered into between the said correspondents and the said John Beatty and that the same have in all respects been complied with by the said correspondents. And that during the lifetime of the said John Beatty they decently, comfortably and to his entire satisfaction provided for supported and maintained him and his family in the manner and according to the terms of said contract and that they are therefore entitled to a conveyance of the said two tracts of land in the Bill mentioned. And the Court further finds that the said John Beatty died before he had acquired the legal title to said two tracts of land and before he was able to make

the conveyance to the complts. According to the
terms of said contract leaving the parties to this
Bill his legal representatives and heirs at law. It
is therefore ordered adjudged and decided by the
Court that the said defendants and each of them
within thirty days from the rising? (ruling) of this
Court execute and deliver to the complainants
a deed with suitable content conveying in fee
simple all their rights and interest in and to the
said two tracts of land in the Bill described to
the complainants their heirs and assigns and
in default thereof this DECREE operate to all
intents and purposes as such conveyance and it is
further ordered that complainants pay the cost of
this suit in thirty days or in default execution pay
at law.

—*From Chancery Court Proceedings, Richland
County, Ohio, April 11, 1849*

David and William divided the land, David taking the parcel
in Richland County and William the one in Knox County to the
south.

Even though he was now a landowner and the head of a growing
family, David was captivated by stories from men who had lived on the
western frontier and returned east briefly. Those stories resonated in
his mind with the stories his father had told him about his grandfather
Thomas's harrowing trip across the ocean from Ireland, the three-
hundred-acre farm in Pennsylvania that Thomas had bought and
cleared, and the fights with Indians and wild animals. These tales
made him dream of being a frontiersman and of having as much land
as his grandfather. But the prospects seemed remote. And that left
him restless.

Chapter 15
Quest for Gold

**On Monday, January 14, 1848, at about ten o'clock
in the morning, James W. Marshall, employed
by John Sutter to construct a sawmill on the
American River, picked some flakes of mineral out
of the tailrace. [He] immediately identified these
particles as gold ...**

—*Malcolm J. Rohrbough,* Days of Gold

Gold—they're shoveling it out of the rivers and creeks in California! The
news electrified the country as it spread. Some believed it; some did
not. President Polk's reference to it in his State of the Union message
in April 1849 convinced many who had doubts. Early believers and
many newly converted doubters started for the goldfields.

In Mansfield, the president's message spread through the stores,
livery stables, banks, and boarding houses like fire through dry grass.
Then it engulfed Belleville, where David Beaty heard it, talked to
some excited friends, and brought it home with a load of flour, wire,
and groceries behind his lathered and winded team. As soon as he'd
unhitched and curried the sweaty horses, and even before he unloaded
the wagon, he rushed into the house to tell Maria his plans.

"Heard some big news in town. President Polk says those stories about gold in California are true. It's in all the rivers. Men're just shoveling it out, washing it a little, and getting rich, quicker'n scat. Big, black headline in the *Shield and Banner.*"

Maria gave her husband a sharp look. She'd never seen him like this. He was always calm, but he was usually figuring out how to get ahead. "That so? Still sounds like a snake-oil pitch to me. Do you always believe the president? He got any facts to back up such a wild story?"

"It's true, all right. The paper says he's got a big gold nugget from out there right on his desk. So those stories we've been hearin' about men finding nuggets worth a thousand dollars just lying in the rivers were true. James Stewart's puttin' together a group to go out there and dig, an' I'm thinkin' of signin' on with 'em." David ran a hand through his black hair and watched Maria's face.

"You're gonna' do what? David Beaty, you're a fool, a greedy fool! You know we've been savin' our money to add onto the house. An' what if you get killed? Ya thought of that?" Maria's dark eyes flamed like coals under her heavy black brows as she turned from the cookstove and glared at her husband. Theodore, Guilon, and Annetta scuttled into the bedroom and listened from behind the door.

"Maria, listen a minute! I know you don't want me to go, but Stewart's got only one space left, and he's savin' it for me for a day or two. I'd rather sign on with him and guys I know to sail out of New Orlins than go cross-country with folks I don't know. Ain't never sailed, but I sure don't fancy walking all that ways with a bunch of strangers." David glared at Maria, who stood with arms crossed, holding a wooden spoon in her right hand; then he shifted backward ever so slightly.

"David Beaty, you don't have to go at all. We'll do fine if you stay here and farm. We got the twenty-four acres you bought from George Irwin, and part of the land you and William got from your father. Ain't that enough fer ya?" She pounded the table with the spoon.

"It's a chance I can't pass up, Maria. If I stay here, we'll never have as much land or as good a livin' as old Tom and Maggie did back in Pennsylvania. He came from Ireland with nothin' an' wound up with twelve kids and three hundred acres of good land, all free an' clear.

I aim to do as well as he did, and a lot better than my pa. We'll not do it if I just stay here an' farm. Crops are getting poorer. An' the bottomland's flooding more an' more." David pounded a fist on the table. His six-foot frame dominated the room. "I'm gonna go!"

Maria was not mollified, and she glared at her husband. "An' leave me here alone with three little kids? I guess I might as well be talkin' to the chickens as to you. I swear I don't know why you Beatys are always pullin' up stakes and goin' west every few years. How'm I s'posed to manage? Ya thought o' that?"

"Yup. I'll talk to William an' Mary Ann. They'll likely tend the crops an' help take care of you and the stock. An' I'm goin' to talk to Adam about loanin' me money for the trip. Things'll all work out." David backed out the door.

Maria slammed it hard behind him, picked up a small hammer with a ridged head, and began to pound a piece of beef that she'd put on the counter. When she finished, the meat was in shreds. She gathered them up and threw them into a skillet on the stove. After a few minutes, the bedroom door opened a crack, and Theodore and Guilon peeked out and then tiptoed into the kitchen.

David walked south over the hill to his brother William's house. Their black-and-white dog announced his arrival. When his sister-in-law Mary Ann opened the door, he asked, "Could I talk to you and William for a few minutes? It's something important."

"Sure, David, come on in. I'll get William. He's pitching hay to the horses." When the three of them had gathered around the kitchen table and Mary Ann had put three slices of dried-apple pie in front of them, David shared his news and his question.

"You know all this talk we been hearin' about gold in California? Well, the *Shield and Banner* has a big story today about President Polk sayin' it's true. An' so I'm planning to join James Stewart and some other men from Mansfield and Belleville and go out there. But I need to be sure you could help Maria with whatever she needs while I'm gone. I'd be obliged if you could do that. It'd be a lot of work."

William and Mary Ann looked at each other, surprise on their faces. David ate some pie and fingered the bill of the cap in his left hand until William said, "I know a lot of men and boys are goin', but I hadn't expected you to. But ..." He paused for what seemed like an eternity to David. "We've been helpin' each other back and forth all our lives, so I don't see why we couldn't do it again. What's Maria think of you goin'?"

"She's mad as a wet hen 'bout it. But I think she'll get over it in a few days." David's tone wasn't as confident as his words. "I've got to talk to her father and see if he'll support my goin', an' maybe loan me some money to travel. If he'll agree, then I think maybe Maria'll cool down a little. Sure hope so." David ate the last bites of his pie, put on his cap, and prepared to leave. "Many thanks to both of you. That takes a big load off my mind. Now I'll go talk to Maria's father."

Adam Gault answered David's knock. "Howdy, David. Come on in an' set a little. You musta walked fast—you look kinda winded." Adam, a head shorter than his son-in-law and gray around the temples, motioned David in and sat down in an upholstered armchair. He put his left leg on a footstool as soon as he could. "My bum leg hurts a lot today. Damn Santa Ana and his dirty Mexicans anyway." He rubbed his left calf gingerly, especially around the scar from the bullet he'd received in the Mexican War.

"Anything I can do to help out around the place while your leg bothers you so bad?" David smiled at the tough New Englander, admiring his fortitude.

"Thanks, but we'll get by fine. You were real good about lookin' after things while I was gone fighting Santa Ana. And doin' the plowing and planting right after I came limping back. The boys are older now, so I don't have to impose on you so much." Adam lifted his injured leg and flexed his foot.

David nodded. "That's what I come to talk to you about. There's real big news in town about those rumors of gold in California. The papers say they're true—men just shovelin' it out of the ground. I'm hopin' to go get some of it. But Maria's dead set against the idea. I'd like to tell her you think it's all right. An' I'd be much obliged if you could loan me some money for the trip out there." He paused and studied Adam's face.

The older man rubbed his leg again. The interval seemed like an hour to David. Finally Adam asked, "You sure this story's true? You know, the world's full of swindlers."

"Yup, real sure. The *Shield and Banner* had a story 'bout what

President Polk said about it all over the front page. I read it all the way through. An' I got a chance to go with a group o' men James Stewart's puttin' together, if I act real quick."

Adam's expression softened. "That's different. If President Polk says it's true, it's true! I went to fight those damn Mexicans because I believed him. An' even though I got this bad leg out of it, I think it was the right thing to do. If he hadn't sent the army after them thievin' banditos, we wouldn't even have California. An' they'd have all the gold." Adam's eyes shone as he remembered his years in the U.S. Army during the Mexican War.

"So maybe you were part of somethin' that'll let me go and get some gold to support Maria and the kids a lot better than if I farm here all my life?" David hoped his question would led Adam's thoughts toward the endorsement and loan he'd come for. They sat looking out the window at the tree limbs with their faint green hints of emerging leaves.

Adam shifted in his chair and moved his sore leg. "Maybe so, if you can get all the way out there before other guys hog all the gold. Won't be easy. I learned that in Mexico." He paused and looked out the window again. David guessed he was remembering the hardships of his own adventure. "Tell Maria you got my blessing an' a loan for gettin' yourself out there." Adam stood up slowly and extended his hand. David gripped it hard.

"Thank you, sir. I'll be real careful an' tend to business. An' pay you back when I get home again. Now I gotta talk to Maria. She's really mad about my goin'."

The family was eating dinner when David tiptoed in and sat down at the table. No one said a word. When the meal was over and the children had gone outside, Maria piled the dirty dishes in the dishpan of hot, soapy water, looked toward David, and asked, "What did my father think of your harebrained notion?"

"He's real keen about my goin'. Says it'll make his gettin' shot in the Mexican War worth it. An' William and Mary Ann will look after the crops and the livestock an' help take care of all of you. Just call on them whenever you need help. Besides, the boys are gettin' big enough to help you some. I reckon I can be back with some gold in two years, three at the most." David hoped the arrangements he'd made would soften Maria's opposition, but he was disappointed.

"Seems like there's nothin' I can say to change your cussed mind, David Beaty! I s'pose you'll still go even if I tell you I haven't had to wear the rag this month, an' we're gonna have a new mouth to feed by next winter." Maria surveyed her husband's face, hoping for a flicker of indecision, but she saw none.

"Maria, I really hate to leave, especially now I know you're in a family way, but that gold's just waitin'. Mary Ann's a fine midwife. She was real good when little Nettie came. An' the boys are big enough to go over there and fetch her or William whenever you need help. An' your folks are just a couple miles away. You're a strong woman, Maria. I know it'll be hard, but you'll do fine." He put his hand on her shoulder, but she yanked it off and started washing dishes. David stood for a moment, and then he put on his coat and cap.

"Stewart's crew's leavin' for New Orlins in ten days, so I better start cuttin' you a couple years' supply of wood." Maria's shoulders slumped as she let out a slow breath. Then her face regained its resolve.

"Seein' as how that's the way it'll be, I may as well get used to sleepin' alone. Startin' now, you can just sleep in the haymow till you go!" Maria kicked the door shut behind David. He picked up an ax and walked to the grindstone.

Gold became the talk of the country, and of the world. People who had always thought a farm of their own or a steady job was all they would ever want suddenly resolved to go to the goldfields to get rich overnight. Even though the journey was long and dangerous, thousands of people converged on California from America, Europe, Asia, and Australia. Richland County, Ohio, sent its share. Some formed groups and started west from the junction of the Platte and Missouri Rivers; others set sail from ports in the east or south. Of these, most sailed all the way around South America, but others only to Panama. There they undertook the daunting, disease-ridden trek over the mountains to the Pacific Ocean, where they competed for space on any ship that stopped for supplies and had space to cram on one more gold-seeker—space left vacant by a man who had died during the trip around Cape Horn.

After David left, the Beatys and Gaults adjusted to his absence by helping Maria whenever they could, awaiting word from him as he and his colleagues made the long journey. On a fall day, Adam Gault brought a letter from David to Maria on his way home from Mansfield and sat by the kitchen table while she opened it.

"Like to hear it?" Maria looked toward her father, who nodded as he sipped a glass of hot cider.

"Only the parts you want to read me."

She ran her tongue across her cracked lips and began.

August 20, 1849
rio janeiro
Dearest wife Maria,

I am sending an acount of some of my experiencs since leaving you all. Two whaleing ships are leaving for home and I will see that this letter is on one of them. Most of the men in our party are writing today for the same purpos. I have kept a jurnal of my experiencs to pass some of the time on board ship, but will only relate the main hapenings in this letter. When I come back from the gold fields I will carry my daily writings of the events of the jurney to you.

Our party has had tolorable good fortune thus far. Our trip down the rivers to new orlins went without incident. I was taken with that citys many different people and customs. The wharfs were full of people of many colors from many cuntries. I never imagined there could be so many slaves. Most are pitiable creatures with whip scars on their backs bent under heavy loads. the smells were as mixed and strong as the people. We had very good fortune in procuring space for our party and our goods on the ship North Star and sailed for california less than a week after we first came off the river.

Thank your father for loaning me the money to make the trip. Tell him that I will repay him with interest when I return. His trust and generosety allowed me to engage a tolorable space on board ship and a full set of tools for mining at prices that were much more faverable than those we are told we'd have to pay in california.

I am now more resigned to the rocking and pitching of the boat, but still spend time at the rail sending my supper to the fish when the seas are ruf. If I am not too ill I look at the herds of porpises and flying fish that often suround our ship. One bird is particulerly strange. With its wings spread to fly it is as wide as a cow is long. It rarely flaps those huge black wings, but sails like a kite hour after hour near our ship. The sailors call it an albatros.

Many of the men on board have fallen into sinful habits, especialy gambling, for want of something better to do. I avoid it entirely and occupy myself with reading the Bible you gave me, writing in my jurnal and watching the strange birds and animals of the sea. We have religious service every sabath. I have preached four times, as we have no real preacher on board.

We're now ancored in a world I never dremt existed. The town of rio janeiro in Brasil where we are takin' on fresh suplies and water. The big harbor is surrounded by tall mountains almost all around. And one of the mountains is called Suger Loaf because its shaped just like a loaf of suger. We went ashore and stayed in what pases for a hotel one night. It was dirty, smelled worse than our barn and was noisy as a herd of jackases all braying at once. The buildings are mostly stone with tile roofs. The cathedrals are covered with gold inside on all the walls. They should have used it insted to feed the pitiable begers who are everywhere asking for alms. The streets are dirty and full of black slaves hauling heavy loads on their heads. They wear only a scrap of cloth around their hips.

One day we hired a big buggy and rode out to the botanic gardens. I never imagined the world held so many butiful trees and flowers. They say the Emperer of Brasil dom Pedro Segundo had the garden made and brought plants from all around the world to fill it. The soil was red as bricks but the trees and flowers grow in it thick as hair on a dog. There were armys of ants walking in a line on the ground carying peces of leaf bigger than they were. Glad we don't have those in Ohio. The birds sang all day among the trees. The parots were all purple yellow green and blue.

I am enjoying the many kinds of fruit that grow here they taste delichus after only salt pork and sea biskits. We bougt them in a huge market that was tolorable clean. They sell fruit meats birds monkeys vegitables and hunderds of slaves all in a big open yard with buildings on all four sides. This voyage has taught me to despise the evil of slavery.

We plan to sale tomorrow for the dangerusest part of the trip. The captain wants to make it around the Horn as soon as the winter storms let up a little there. Other ships are wating. 2 left yestirday. Tell Guilon, Theodore and Nettie that I say they must obey you just as they would me, and that I love them.

If anything happens to me be of strong faith, and

remember that we shall be together by and by. But I expect to return to you all with gold in a couple of years at most. I remember you all in my prayers to Almighty God every day and feel that you do the same for me.

Your husband David Beaty

Maria put her arms around Theodore and Guilon, who had been standing beside her, listening, and jiggled two-year-old Nettie, who had climbed into her lap. "Seems like your father's havin' an interesting trip. Now you boys take Nettie an' run along and play while Grandpa Adam an' I talk." She set Nettie on the floor. Theodore and Guilon each tried to take her hands, but after a little pushing, they settled for sharing as they started toward the fireplace hearth.

Maria ran her hand over the large bulge under her apron. "Well, we should thank Almighty God he's alive … or was, a couple months ago. It's been awful hard not knowin'. The baby's kicking a whole lot now, an' that reminds me of him."

Her father glanced around the room. "Yes, we need to keep him in our prayers. What I can do to help out today?"

Maria looked grateful. "There's potatoes in the garden that need to go in the cellar. I dug 'em yesterday, an' the boys picked. But they put so many in the sacks, I can't lift 'em. An' the squash and punkins need bringin' in before we have a real heavy freeze." She brushed a strand of black hair that had escaped from her bun away from her thin face and hung it over her left ear. "Sure is a lot to do, what with my own work an' as much of David's as I can manage. We sure miss him. The boys ask about him a lot."

"Should I split more wood after I carry in the potatoes an' squash?"

Maria nodded and sighed. "Thank you, Father. That'll let me just set a bit. I need that. Need to think about his letter." She managed a tired smile.

A few months after she received David's letter, Maria sent one to him in San Francisco announcing that Melissa had arrived in the world during a cold spell on the third of January. In June, William brought another letter from David. Maria read it in stages as she nursed the baby, already nicknamed Mel.

san francisco california
december 1849
Dearest wife Maria

Since I last wrote there were many times when I never expected to write you again. It is only by Gods grace I can write you now. I have just about got over the smalpox. It come within an inch of killin me. It is very hard to write my fingers are so sore I have no fingernails anymore. They came out when I had the fevers that near about killed me. They may not gro back ever. My skin is full of pits all over. But I am of good hope and slowly getting my strength back. Severul of the men on the ship who got it are at the bottom of the osean now. I thot several times I would be there to.

Our trip around the Horn was somethin from Hell itself. They say Hells a hot place but I think thats rong. Its a place with ice and snow and rain and winds that could blow a barn away without half trying. And waves so high they washed three men right overbord quick as scat. I'd a been one of em but I seen it comin and managed to rap both arms an both legs around a railing and hold on for dear life. The water was six feet over my head for a minute. A lot of days the fog was so thik you couldnt see your hand in front of your face and the captin didnt kno where we was. Once a gale blowed us to about a quarter mile from some rocky cliffs and we thot we were all goners but all at once the wind switched and blew us out to sea. I'm sure God saved us. I thank Him every day for lookin out for me and my shipmates.

After we got out of there we stopped for water and
suplies at an iland called won furnandes and took on
three new pasengers to replace the men washed over
the side. One of them brot the smalpox with him
but we didnt know it for a few days.

Farther on north we ran out of wind and the ship
just sat and rocked for 10 days. That most drove us
mad. Wed been sailin for most 5 months and would
have given anything to get off that cramped litle
boat. Thats when the pox got me.

Ther were lots of fites. The captin had to tie 2 men
up with ropes until we landed to keep them from
killing each other. I was so sick I hardly noticed.

I looked for a letter from you when we landed but
ther wasnt one. I spose the baby has com and I pray
God to keep you well and strong. I hope William
and Adam are lookin after you all while Im gone.
Tel them I will repay them when I get home.
Write me and send it to the post office here in san
francisco. We plan to get to the Gold fields as fast as
we can to stake our claims and start diggin.

Your husband David Beaty

Maria folded the letter, put Melissa in her crib, and rocked it with
her foot as she kneaded the bread dough that had been rising on a
sunny window ledge. But her thoughts were about David. She was
thrilled to know he was alive, even if he'd had some close scrapes.
She hoped he'd gotten her letter. She lifted her apron hem with a
floury hand and wiped her eyes, then straightened her shoulders and
resumed kneading with her head high.

Melissa began to cry, and Maria called to Theodore, "Ted, come
get little Mel, and burp her. I've got to get this bread in the oven."

Theodore came in from the porch, put Melissa over his shoulder, and patted her back as he walked around the kitchen, humming.

"Your Uncle William brought a letter from your father. He's had the smallpox. So he won't look the same when he gets home. His face'll be all pitted an' pocked. Like those folks up the road toward Belleville."

Theodore looked at his mother with hope in his eyes. "Will he get home this summer?"

"Doesn't seem like it. I just hope he gets home safe, whenever it is, an' whatever he looks like."

Theodore put the baby in the cradle and covered her with a quilt. "I want him to come home now."

"So do I, Son." She put a floury hand and arm on his shoulder and gave him a hug. "It's real hard without him, isn't it?" Theodore nodded.

Maria got David's next letter early in 1851. She read it a page at a time between splitting wood, milking and feeding the cows, cooking, and taking care of the children. Mel was a particular care now, because she was fascinated by fire and wanted to crawl into the fireplace.

> calaveras california
> august 1850
> Dearest wife
>
> Joe Davenport brot your letter from the postoffice
> yestirday with a load of suplies. I rejoice that our
> daughter is well and growing. Melissa is a good
> name. I know you must be awful busy. Get all the
> help you can from the boys and William and Mary
> Ann and your father.
>
> We finaly got to the gold fields in januery. Everyting
> costs a fortune here. We paid $40 for a barel of
> flour and $100 to have a greesy mexican haul our
> grubstake from sacramento up here to where we are
> digin. We got here the day they hung 2 chinks. there

bodies was hanging from a tree when we showed
up. The other miners said they'd killed their partner.
Claimed he was stealin some of their gold dust. The
miners had sort of a trial before they hung em. took
10 minuts they said. Other miners didn't want their
claims. Said they woud be hanted. So we took em.
They aint near as good as we'd hoped. Mostly we
just make wages, 5 or 10 dolars each on good days.
All 5 of us live in a big tent under some trees about
a mile from our claims. The tent leeked purty bad
last winter but it aint rained for over 4 months now.
We take turns cooking. Evury day we work sunup
to dark, exceptin Sunday we get up an hour before
sunup and cook flapjacks and salt pork for breakfast,
rap up some mor of em for dinner, and walk to the
diggins.

We try to keep 2 sluces goin all day to wash the gold
out from the gravel and sand and rocks. We work in
cold water up to our nees diggin and carryin gravel
and sand to put in the sluces. My hands are craked
an raw all over from being wet all day. Toward night
whoever is cook leaves and goes to camp and makes
supper. The rest of us work till dark. After supper we
sit by the fire a while and talk about home. Joe and
Jess and George and James smoke there pipes. We
all turn in early.

We work evry day cept Sunday. That's when
we wash clothes. Then most of the men go into
calaveras and drink whiskey and gambel away the
gold dust they worked so hard all week for, and
some go to the hore houses or they bet on horse
races or fights. They even bet on a frog jumping
contest. The way to get rich here is to run a saloon
and gambeling den or a hore house. The men and
wimmen who do are agents of Satan even tho they

have mor gold dust than all the pore guys who muck
and strain all week in the cricks and then lose all the
gold dust they got in one night.

After we get our clothes washt a few of us have a
church servis under one of the big trees if its not
raining. We read the bible pray together sing some
of the old church songs from back home and then
somebody usualy preaches. Most of the men dont
want to preach so I do it pretty offen. I'm getting
beter at it. A methodist preacher comes around evry
so offen and preaches to.

Even tho we are geting som gold dust evrything
costs so much we arent geting ahead a lot. My
pardners are tired of it here and talking about
moving to new claims a ways off to the south. They
would get ahead more if they stayed out of the
saloons and didn't gambel. I plan to keep on diging
right here and saving all i can even if I have to hire a
chink or gresy mexican to work for me.

Ive got over the efects of the smal pox purty well
but I miss having fingernails and tonails. I hope this
letter finds you all well. Trust God and be of good
cheer until I get home.

Your husband David Beaty

Maria put a log on the fire and sighed, thinking, *Sure would be a lot
easier to be of good cheer if he'd said he was coming home ... and if I could
be sure he'd even get here. Guess I just got to trust the Lord on that.*

* * *

David heaved one last shovelful of gravel into the wooden sluice box
and straightened his back. He groaned as he felt his way, feet numb

in his gumboots, among the rocks under the torrent of water surging down Squaw Creek. He had braced against the racing stream since daybreak, and he knew that if he fell, it could roll him like a log.

Would there be any nuggets caught behind the wooden cross-cleats on the bottom of the sluice? He shoved boards into the slots at its upper end to block the water and then dipped a large spoon into the glistening accumulations of sand and gravel above each cleat. There were only a few flecks of gold among the grains of dark gray and black sand. It was not enough to buy much food in this goldfield, where flour was fifty cents a pound. He put the small leather bag into which he'd spooned the sand and gold in his back pocket and ran his lean and cracked hand across the hollow of his stomach. Then he edged toward the bank, using the shovel for support against the push of the water.

He was alone. Before noon, James Stewart, George Irwin, and Joe Davenport had finally quit in disgust, saying that they were going to move on to new diggings and he could have their shares of the claim. He was sad that they'd decided to leave—partly because they'd been together for over two years, partly because they'd helped each other over the vertical, chest-high bank of the creek. David pushed his shovel into the stream bed to give himself a few extra inches, stepped onto it, and heaved his chest and arms over the top, trying to reach far enough to grab a bush and pull himself up and over. The shovel tipped. He caught himself just before he fell into the water. The bank was higher upstream and downstream. He'd have to dig a ramp. It would be dark soon.

After fifteen minutes, he had carved a narrow slot in the bank and built a cone of debris below it. He climbed on the sediment from his cut and tried to scramble out. The footing gave way. He was back in the stream. It was getting hard to see where to point his shovel in the narrow opening, but he kept working. He leaned forward, shoveled overhead, then heaved it in and down as hard as he could, over and over and over. Gravel and sand rattled down the ramp; some fell into his boots. He didn't notice. He just had to get out by dark, or they'd find his body in the morning.

He chopped, shoulder high, with his shovel again. The impact felt strange, like stabbing a sack of wheat, maybe. He felt for the spot again with his shovel: gravel, sand, one big rock, and then something soft. He stepped on the cone of debris below the ramp, braced the shovel behind him, and jumped. The rocks and gravel in the slot gave way beneath his knees. He reached for a handhold, felt the object his shovel had touched, and grabbed it. It felt like leather. He gripped hard and pulled. It held. He crawled up out of the water, then all the way to the top of the stream bank.

In an instant, he was on his stomach, hand feeling for the foreign body. A chunk of leather? A piece of hide? His fingers pushed away the gravel and rocks. He felt an opening, tied with a leather thong. It was not a leather scrap or a piece of hide; it had to be a pouch or a sack. He raked and clawed and felt blood oozing from his fingers. When he'd forced aside enough sediment, he grasped the object and pulled. He jiggled the top of it back and forth as he lifted, just like he would pull carrots in the garden back home. It was nearly dark when the sack came free from its gritty prison.

David rolled on his side, sat up, and dropped the pouch between his boots. It was as big as a turnip and twenty times as heavy. The thong around the top was triple knotted. He felt for his knife with bloody fingers, worked it out of its scabbard, slit the binding, and peeked in. The light was so dim that he could barely make out a yellowish hue inside.

He caught his breath. *So those two chinks they'd hanged were right. The partner they'd knifed really had been stealing their dust. Too bad nobody believed 'em.*

Or maybe not. He retied the pouch, then sat and pondered what he should do. If he hurried, maybe he could catch his partners—but most likely, they had already pulled out. And anyway, they'd given him their shares of the claim. He sat for a long time. Finally, when it was dark, he put the sack back into the hole and reached for his shovel. There was no need to take his find back to camp until tomorrow—after his partners were gone. He'd be gone soon too, just not in the same direction.

Chapter 16
Ambition and Abolition

As the stagecoach lurched and bounced him closer to home, David fretted about how Maria would receive him. Would she still be as furious at him for going to California as she had been nearly three years ago, or had her feelings mellowed a little? In the nearly three years he'd been gone, he'd gotten only one terse letter announcing the birth of their daughter Melissa. He frowned with apprehension about his reception. *Sure hope she's not still mad.*

As he sat alongside the other stage passengers, he watched the familiar, snow-covered landscape of gently rolling hills and valleys south of Belleville glide by and thought of how different the trip home had been from the harrowing trip out. The voyage by ship from San Francisco to the isthmus had taken only two weeks. He remembered how reassuring the vibrations of the laboring steam engine below decks had been as it moved the ship along when the sails were slack in a dead calm, and how good it had been to have a cabin of his own. He remembered how lucky he'd felt to cross the mountains of the isthmus between the Pacific and the Caribbean without being robbed of the sack of gold wrapped around his waist or getting sick, and then to find a ship, also fitted with steam and sails and bound for New York, when they arrived at the water again. But the trip from New York to Mansfield had topped everything. He remembered his surprise when he inquired about stagecoach passage and learned that instead, he could take a train nearly to Buffalo, get on a ship there for a trip along Lake Erie's south shore to Sandusky, and take a train from there all the way to Mansfield. His time as a stagecoach passenger was going to be a few hours, not a few weeks. Coming home had taken less than three months. Next, they might have steam engines pulling plows in farmers' fields.

"Let me off at the bottom of this hill, Sam." David leaned out the window and pointed toward a road junction just beyond the bridge over Toby Creek. The bearded driver stopped the stage as it reached the flat where a little road came in from the east.

"You're lucky to be home, Mr. Beaty. A whole bunch of men from 'round here didn't live to make it back." He reached behind his seat for a small trunk among the array on top of the stage coach.

"Jest this one trunk? You sure didn't bring much back from such a long trip, 'cept those marks all over your face." Sam handed the trunk down to its owner. David thanked him, ran his hand over the pockmarks on his cheeks, smiled to himself as he centered the trunk on the angle of his back, and strode up the snowy road, bent forward at the waist. As the farmstead came into view, he wondered how much the children had grown, and he grew anxious about whether or not Maria would even let him see them.

Everything looked well kept and just as he remembered. Smoke spiraled lazily up from the chimney, the cows and sheep were lying in the barnyard, chewing their cuds, and the horses were eating hay from the manger beside the barn. He slid the trunk to the ground just as a black-and-white dog skidded around the corner, barking fierce defense of the premises.

"Shep, Shep, Shep, easy girl. Remember me?" He put out a hand and watched the dog's fierce demeanor morph into tail-wagging acceptance. As she came forward to lick a greeting, the door creaked open. Two boys and a girl peeked out.

"Ma, there's a man here." Flickers of doubt and recognition raced across Theodore's face, like clouds on a windy sky. "He kinda looks like Pa, but his beard's gray."

"Ted, Guy, Nettie, it's me, your pa!"

Theodore's look changed to all sunshine, and Guilon followed his brother's lead. Four-year-old Annetta grabbed the homespun skirt of

188

the thin, black-haired woman with heavy eyebrows who'd stepped into the doorway behind the children.

Maria's heart leaped. "Well, traveler, ya made it. Welcome home. An' on the day before Christmas. What a great present!" She put out her arms. David stepped into her embrace and kissed her. Then he knelt and took his three oldest children in his arms. Maria smiled as she watched the reunion.

"I'll bet you're hungry. We were just settin' down to dinner. Guy, you and Nettie wake up little Mel and bring her out to meet her father. Ted, you set another place."

"I'm famished, Maria. But before you put food on the table, let me show you what I brought us." David unbuttoned his shirt, untied the knot that held a tubular canvas sack around his waist, and pulled it out. He laid the heavy sack on the table, slit the threads that secured one end, and watched Maria's eyes widen as gold nuggets and dust cascaded onto a plate. "Maybe these will make a nice present for Christmas."

Theodore looked at the sediment on the plate. "What's that? It looks like sand, 'cepting it's yellow."

"That's gold, Son. It's what I went clear to California to get. Don't you think it's pretty?"

"Looks kinda funny. I like white sand better." He shrugged and went to the cupboard and took out a plate and a cup.

David spooned the gold back into the sack and dusted the plate with his sleeve. "It's a whole lot better than sand, Son!"

When everyone was at the table, Maria looked to David. "Would you return thanks to God for us? We've sure got a lot to be thankful for today." David looked at his family, grown more numerous and larger, all but baby Melissa with their heads bowed, and felt a wave of gratitude.

"Almighty God, our Father, we thank you … Maria, you better do the rest."

He took out his bandanna and wiped his eyes as Maria intoned the blessing she had spoken at each meal for almost three years, adding a new line at the end: "Father Almighty, we thank you for the safe return of David Beaty to his home and loved ones." David blew his nose twice before filling his plate with potatoes, ham, and cornbread.

The afternoon passed like a dream for David and Maria. Their children gradually overcame their shyness and crowded around their father, climbing on his lap, looking at his nailless fingers, showing him new objects they'd made, and telling him of new things they could do. Maria made a pudding for Christmas dinner and watched her husband and children with her heart brimming. There'd been so many times when she'd despaired of ever seeing David again that his return seemed unreal.

That evening, as they tiptoed from the children's bedroom and stood by the banked fire in the fireplace, David smiled at Maria and asked, "Where should I sleep? In the haymow, like I had to before I left?"

Maria smiled back through the wrinkles that three years of tiredness, loneliness, and worry had etched into her face. "I reckon that might be kinda cold. Why don't you come sleep in our bed? I've been savin' a place for you—every night praying you'd make it back. Now you're here, I'm ready to give you a real welcome." She stepped close and put her arms around David's neck and searched through his beard for his lips.

He took her hand as they walked toward the other bedroom. "I hope we haven't forgotten how."

"Don't know about you, but I think I can remember." She squeezed his hand, feeling the novelty of pits in the skin on his wrist with her fingertips.

As the intensity of their unaccustomed intimacy ebbed, Maria ran her hand slowly across David's pocked chest and asked, "What are you going to do, now that you have all that gold?"

He caressed her breasts as gently as he could with callused fingers. "Look around to see if there's any land nearabouts that might be for sale and buy it, I guess. I've always aimed to have as much land as old Thomas did back in Pennsylvania." He snuggled as close to Maria as he could, and they fell asleep.

* * *

On Christmas Day, David was up early. He lit a candle and started fires in the fireplace and the cookstove. Then, before anyone else began to stir, he opened his trunk and took out the presents he'd bought in New York and put them on chairs around the table: for Maria, a black velvet dress with red trim on the collar, and a gray wool coat with a fur collar; for Ted and Guy, wool jackets, leather boots, and wool socks. Nettie's presents were a yellow dress and a doll carved from ivory that he'd bought from a sailor. And for Melissa, he'd gotten a tiny blue dress and an ivory doll.

Then he took the milk pail from its hook and went to the barn. The cows were less skittish than they'd been the night before when he'd tried to get them into their stanchions, and they didn't kick when he sat down to milk, as they had then. His hands felt stiff at first, but after a few minutes, the squeeze-and-pull rhythm of milking seemed as normal as breathing. He put his face against the warm flank of the brindle cow as he milked and hummed softly. She turned her head to look but didn't kick or step away, and she kept munching the oats he'd fed her. Two cats—one orange and white, the other black with white paws—came down from the hayloft and stood beside the cows. He squeezed a stream of milk toward their open mouths but found that his aim was poor. Daylight was breaking by the time he'd finished milking, fed the horses, pigs, and sheep, broken the ice in their water tub, and refilled it from the well.

He returned to a hubbub in the house. Everyone but Melissa was up and milling about the table. Maria was trying to cook breakfast and monitor the trying on of new clothes and the admiring of ivory dolls. In an instant, the children were around him with thank-yous and hugs. He had to lift the bucket of milk quickly to keep them from spilling it.

* * *

The activities at the Beatys' were paralleled by those at Adam and Ruth Gault's, where preparations for a family Christmas dinner got under way before daybreak. Ruth, her plump form making bulges in her calico apron, was bustling about the kitchen, stuffing the wild turkey that William Beaty had shot. Before Adam had finished chores and come in for breakfast, she put mincemeat and pumpkin pies in the oven. After the dishes were washed, she dug the linen tablecloth that she'd inherited from her mother out of a trunk and spread it on the newly elongated table. Adam limped in with two split-log benches from the porch and put them beside the table to supplement their six chairs.

"Adam, do you think you should go over to Maria's and help her do chores and get all the children ready to come over for dinner? She looked tireder than usual the last time I saw her."

"I'm going to ride to church soon as I get things set up for you, but I'll offer to do her chores tonight when they go home. She's wearing down some." Ruth nodded vigorous agreement as she put plates around the table.

Buggies began to pull in, and the house filled with Adam and Ruth's children, grandchildren, and extended family. Smoke plumed from the chimney of the new house, built the previous summer. As another buggy rattled up the road, a horse whinnied, and William Beaty and Joe Kearn, the Gaults' son-in-law, came out the door.

"Looks like Maria and her kids are finally here." William shot a quick glance at Joe. "You're all dressed up. I'll go help her tie up the horse."

"Look again—I don't think you need to." Joe, tall and imposing in his banker's suit, pointed to the family in the approaching buggy. "That's a man driving?"

"Sure is. Is that David? Doesn't look quite like him. But it must be." William stared at his brother, trying to connect the pocked skin and gray beard to the black-haired brother he remembered. Joe and William waved, and the buggy riders waved back.

The welcome for David and his family was tumultuous, with handshakes and heartfelt words of welcome amid children scurrying around and looking at the dinner table. Ruth and her daughters quickly returned to work in the kitchen. When the platter of bronzed turkey was centered on the table, Ruth nodded to Adam, who quieted the hubbub. "All right, everybody. Sit down for the blessing, so we can eat before things get cold and Ruth gets cranky."

After Adam's prayer, the platters and bowls of turkey, venison, baked potatoes, sourdough biscuits, butter, blackberry jam, coleslaw, squash, and baked apples moved in a slow procession around the table. When everyone had eaten as many helpings as they wanted, Ruth brought out the pies. David looked around the table as he took one last bite of mincemeat pie and felt overwhelmed. How many times he had despaired of being able to feast in the friendship of family and the warmth of a comfortable, new house. He wiped his eyes, took Melissa on his lap, and slid back from the table. Maria looked at her husband and family and felt that God had blessed her beyond measure.

The adults sent the children out to play in the snow, and the women gathered around two dishpans of steaming water in the kitchen. The men pulled their chairs to the corner of the dining room nearest the fireplace. Adam studied David, noting his pocked skin, the gray hair around his temples, his graying beard, the wrinkles across his forehead, his fingers with no nails, and a frame so lean that he could have been a scarecrow. "Well, David, looks like you came back some the worse for wear. Do you feel as worn out as you look?"

David put a foot up on the fireplace hearth and thought a moment. "I've got some rheumatism in my left leg and foot. That's prob'ly from standing in cold water day after day for more'n a year. I miss my fingernails, that's for sure. But I can do all a farmer needs to do. An' Maria's cooking will fatten me up." Adam nodded and seemed satisfied.

Joe Kearn took a cigar from his vest, lit it, and pointed it toward David. "What I want to know is, did you bring back any gold?"

"I got lucky at the end and come back with some. You willing to keep it in your bank vault and pay me some interest?" Everyone sat up straight and stared at David.

William whistled in amazement. Joe blew a cloud of smoke toward the ceiling as he responded. "You don't say. Last you wrote, you an' the others were just gettin' by, an' they were getting ready to move to new diggings. I thought you'd all come home broke an' ask me to loan you money. If you got some gold, course I'll keep it safe for you."

"The other guys did get restless and move on. Gave me their shares of our claim when they left. It was right after that I got lucky, sold the claim, an' headed home."

William, who had sat quietly while Adam and Joe quizzed David, smiled at his older brother. "Maria read us the letters you wrote, but I want to hear some more about how it was out there. Does California look anything like Ohio?"

David tipped his chair back a little. "Not hardly a'tall. East of San Francisco, there's country flat as a pancake, where it never rains even once in the summer. An' on further east, the mountains are so tall, the snow never melts off the tops. Then there's the big trees. There was a lot of 'em near our diggins."

William looked skeptical. "Bigger'n the oaks down along Toby Creek?"

"Make those oaks look like saplings. One day we measured one. It took sixteen of us with our arms spread as wide as we could, an' our fingers touching, to reach around it. And I heard tell there was some even bigger. An' they're three, four times as tall as our oaks. First branches are prob'ly a hundred feet up."

William whistled. "Holy smoke. They'd be somethin' to see. Must be three days work to cut one down."

Adam put another log in the fireplace. "A tree that big would heat this house for forty years." David ate another roasted chestnut from a bowl on the hearth and talked of life and death on board ship and in the goldfields, and of how fast his trip home had been.

After the dishes were washed and dried, the women joined the men, and talk turned to local happenings. Adam asked David, "Anybody tell you Ohio has a new constitution, or about this dratted new law from Washington on runaway slaves? Them rich plantation owners in Kentucky an' Tennessee can send their trackers and bloodhounds right up across the river to nab a Negro who's tryin' to get to Canada." His voice rose as he spoke. "An' if we hide some poor slave, we can get throwed in jail ourselves. It's just flat wrong!" David nodded in agreement, but William and Joe looked angry.

"Adam, I know you feel strong against slavery, but if us folks up north meddle too much in southern folks' business, there's going to be real trouble. I say we mind our business, let them mind theirs." Joe blew a cloud of smoke toward the fire.

"One thing I learned for sure on my trip—slavery is just plain wrong, an' we ought to put an end to it." David's head bobbed, and his voice rose as he spoke. "Didn't used to think so, but what I saw in New Orleans an' Brazil sure changed my mind."

William, who had sat quietly most of the afternoon, pointed toward Adam and David. "I think Joe's got it figured just right. We ought to mind our own business and let sleeping dogs lie."

The debate went on until the afternoon sunlight began to dim and Maria reminded David that it was time to go home to milk, gather eggs, and feed the sheep. As they were leaving, Joe Kearn got David aside and said, "If you bring me the gold you got, I'll take good care of it for you, an' pay some interest too. Any ideas on what you going to do with it besides store it?"

"I'm thinkin' that buying more land would be a good idea, if the prices are right. Know of any?"

After a moment, Joe's face brightened. "You bet. I've got a mortgage on a piece right near you, an' it doesn't look like they're going to be able to pay. I hate to foreclose on 'em. Maybe they'd sell to you and help themselves an' us out."

"I'll come see you first thing next week." They shook hands, and David walked toward his family waiting at the buggy.

* * *

As the nation lurched toward the rupture that culminated in civil war, David found opportunities to invest in land, and he bought parcels of various sizes that were close to the farm that he and William had inherited in 1849. He also bought his brother's half-interest in that farm.

> **1852 To David Beaty from F. Dickerson, parcel in NW, 6 acres, $300**

> **1852 To David Beaty from W. S. Beaty, half interest in 86 acres, $2,000**

> **1855 To David Beaty from M. R., N. E. and Rachel Dickey, 125 acres, $1,950**

1855 To David Beaty from James E. Cox, 13.75 acres

1856 To David Beaty from Jarmen Reed, 5 acres, $250

1856 To David Beaty from Mcclintic, 40.5 acres, $1,800

1856 To David Beaty from Downs, 16.25 acres, $800

1858 To David Beaty from L. Carey, 8 acres, $320

1860 To David Beaty from John Booth, 25 acres, $1,700

—Deeds recorded in the Richland County Courthouse, Ohio

As David and Maria were leaving the courthouse after closing a land deal, David said, "I've got a surprise for you. Let's go to the hatmaker's shop down the street and get her to make you a hat to go with your new coat."

Maria looked pleased. "Thanks, that's real nice. I'd been thinking a new hat would set that coat off better'n the old one. I've had it since before we were married."

They walked along the plank walk by various shops and stores until they came to a small shop with a sign in the window that read MISS NANCY STEWART, MILLINER. As they entered, a brown-haired woman of about thirty looked up from a hat she was trimming and smiled. "Hello. How can I help you?"

Maria smiled back. "I'd like to get a hat to go with this coat, if you please. Something practical, not too fancy." She turned around so Miss Stewart could see the coat from all sides. They began to discuss details of what Miss Stewart would create and how much it would cost. David gave the small shop and its owner a quick appraisal.

Everything was neat and orderly. And Miss Stewart was kind of pretty, and bosomy enough for two women.

As Maria and David left the hat shop, David spotted a small sign in the window of a nearby shop that said PORTRAITS PAINTED. He pointed to it as they walked past.

"When you come to pick up your hat, why don't you get your portrait painted? We could hang it right over the fireplace."

Maria's cheeks reddened. "Oh, that's awful extravagant, David. Besides, I'm not that pretty. Never was, really. My eyebrows are too big. Do you really want me to?"

"You're pretty enough so I want to have a picture of you. If I hadn't thought you were pretty, I wouldn't'a married you. Why don't you do it before the new baby comes?" Maria didn't say anything, but David could see that she was pleased. The next time he was in Mansfield, he stopped at the portrait studio and paid for a sitting for Maria. He hung the picture and admired the likeness of his wife on the day Maria was in bed, bringing a tiny baby they named Alice into the family, a month earlier than expected.

Alice started out small but grew quickly and fit right into the lively family. Maria and David's next child, a boy, arrived more than two years later.

When the midwife invited David into the bedroom to see his new son, Maria asked, "What'll we name him?"

David thought for a minute as he held the newborn. "What about namin' him Walker, for my mother? Her name was Polly Walker before she married my father."

"That sounds good to me. I'd been expectin' another girl, so I didn't have a boy's name in mind."

David beamed as he handed his new son back to Maria. "All right, Walker, you settle down beside your ma and drink a good fill of milk."

* * *

As David and Maria's family and their land holdings grew, the Fugitive Slave Law that incensed Adam Gault, his daughter, Maria, and David Beaty became more and more widely despised and ignored. Ohio's location between slave states south of the Ohio River and Canada to the north made it a natural route for escaping slaves attempting to reach that haven of freedom. Federal marshals attempted to arrest and imprison Ohioans who aided them.

On a summer day, as he went to do chores just before sunup, David noticed that the horses seemed edgy and the sheep were all bunched at one end of their pen. He went around the barn to see if a neighbor's dog was after the sheep and thought he saw someone duck behind a stack of hay. He stepped back into the barn and waited. In a few minutes, a thin black woman carrying a small child stepped around the haystack and moved furtively toward the chicken house. He peeked out the window and watched her set the child on the ground, ease the door of the henhouse open, enter, and moments later return with two eggs in her hand. As she picked up her child and started back toward the haystack, he stepped out into her view.

"You look mighty hungry. Come in, an' we'll cook those eggs for you." The woman froze in her tracks.

"Oh, massa. I wa'n't stealin', really. Jes' we're so hungry. Don' send us back. Please don' send us back."

"We'd never do that. You go in the barn out of sight. I'll go tell Maria to make more breakfast. Then you come in an' eat while we figure out how to help you get north."

"Oh, thank you, massa. I'se so afeered them men an' dogs'll ketch us. Heard 'em barkin' all last evenin'. Ah been a walkin' all night." She had a line of dried blood and a cut on her left foot. Her thin skirt was ripped over her left knee.

The boy's eyes looked as big as saucers as his mother followed Walker and tiptoed into the house with him on her hip. He whimpered softly.

"You jes' hesh now. These nice folk are 'bout to give us some victuals."

The boy was quiet, but his terrified eyes darted from face to face as the Beaty children stared at him and his mother.

As Maria dished up side pork, eggs, and cornbread for everyone, David said, "Let's let her and the boy sleep in the haymow today. Then if anybody comes snoopin' around, they can crawl under out of sight. Tomorrow morning, I'll throw a load of hay on the wagon and take 'em to that underground station up west of Mansfield." The woman kept her eyes on her plate and ate ravenously, feeding her boy pieces of food from her hand. Maria fried more pork and eggs.

When she'd finished a second helping, the fugitive raised her eyes and whispered, "Beggin' yo pardon, massa, but dem men got bloodhounds dat'll smell us right under the hay in yo barn."

Maria looked at her and smiled. "Then David should drive you to Mansfield today. That way, you won't leave any scent for their hounds." She turned to David and asked, "Can you do that?"

He nodded and got up. "I'll harness the horses and hook them to the wagon right away."

An hour later, the woman and boy, wearing clothes Maria had given them and holding a jug of milk and a sack of food, were on the wagon, huddled under a tarp that was covered with hay. As David reached the main road and turned north toward Mansfield, he heard hounds baying off to the south. He whipped the horses' backs with the ends of the reins until they began to trot. Whenever they reverted to walking, the reins stung their backs.

* * *

He and the very tired team returned with the empty wagon just before dark. Maria met him by the barn. As they each brushed down one of the horses, she exploded. "That was a real close call. Three men and a pack o' hounds showed up about an hour after you left, just after I finished burnin' that woman's clothes. Said they had a hot trail of a slave woman right up to our barn. I told 'em there hadn't been no strangers around here, but they snooped through all the buildings an' the cellar before they left. All the time, I was hopin' the kids wouldn't say anything and praying God not to strike me dead for lyin'. Those yappin' hounds scared us half to death and stirred the cows up so bad, they gave next to no milk tonight." She finished grooming the horse and threw her brush at the barn wall. "I'd'a liked to throwed that brush at one of them scoundrels."

David put his hand on her arm. "That poor woman was scared out of her wits. Nobody should be treated like that. And her little boy was just as scared. We were lucky to get them farther along the way toward Canada and not get caught ourselves. Now we've got to get this abomination she was runnin' from out of our country." Maria nodded as she picked up the brush.

As they bought land with the gold David had brought home, they became vocal advocates for abolition and invested time and effort in bolstering the abolitionist cause. Memories of the close call they'd had helping the fleeing slave woman persisted for David and Maria as tensions in the country over slavery rose year by year.

Maria enjoyed watching her children grow and her husband invest his gold in nearby land. But in the spring of 1856, she had a persistent cough, and one morning, she spit up some blood. She didn't tell anyone, but she worried about its ominous implications.

Chapter 17
Life Without Maria

As warm weather greened the landscape, Maria stayed thin and occasionally coughed up blood. When she realized she was pregnant, she asked her sister, Sarah Gault, to come live with them and help out. Even with Sarah's aid, Maria found that she was unable to get back to her full vigor. Being pregnant didn't help. The summer and fall dragged by for her as her pregnancy and illness sapped her energy.

A baby boy was delivered on December 7; they named him David Junior. He was healthy and vigorous, but Maria was not. Her chest and abdomen hurt, and she spit up blood every time a coughing spasm racked her thin body. Her appetite and energy faded. By Christmas, she could not get out of bed and stand without help. It was a bleak holiday, even though David and Maria's family tried to make it special for the children.

David summoned the doctor from Mansfield. He examined Maria, shook his head, and whispered to David, "Consumption all through her body. I can't do anything for her."

David stood stunned. He had known that Maria was very sick, but he'd clung to the hope that she'd recover. He thanked the doctor for coming to the farm and stood vacantly at the window, watching the snow fall; then he walked out to the barn and climbed to the hayloft, where he cried until there were no more tears. Finally he prayed for strength, stood up, squared his shoulders, and went back to the house. After he'd kissed Maria and told Sarah Gault the prognosis for her sister, he gathered the older children in the kitchen.

"I've got something real important to tell you. The doctor says your mother's got consumption real bad. She won't be alive with us too much longer. We need to do all we can to keep her comfortable and to help each other."

Ted and Guy linked arms and looked stunned. Nettie and her younger sisters held each other and began to cry. Walker, too young to understand, sat on his father's lap and pulled at David's watch chain, until Ted lifted him into his arms. David rocked the cradle that held his three-week-old son and namesake and wiped his eyes. David wondered how the children would cope and how he would manage alone. The baby kept crying.

"Guess we've got to get you fed, young man." David searched through the cupboard for a bottle and nipple that they had used to feed orphan lambs, poured some fresh cow's milk into it, and warmed the bottle in a pan of water. Then he coaxed the baby, who was by now fussing and crying constantly, to drink a little. The baby quit crying and fell asleep. After their initial shock had diminished, the older children tried intermittently to help with Walker and the baby. David and Sarah, with help from Maria's parents, did whatever they could to console the older children, care for the newborn, and keep Maria comfortable.

She died on January 8. David and his children held hands as they stood around the bed and wept when she breathed her last. After he'd cried all he could, David gently turned the blanket up so that it covered Maria's face. Then he went out to the shed that held tools and lumber and selected some straight, knot-free boards for her coffin.

Adam and Ruth drove to the Beatys' as soon as they heard the news. "How can we help you the most, David?" Adam Gault's question, as he stroked the horse hitched to the sleigh, was a touch of healing to his son-in-law. David, who was working just inside the open door where the sun provided good light, stopped planing a board for the coffin, blew his nose, and wiped his eyes.

"I want Maria to have a church funeral, not the kind my mother had on the farm. But what with trying to feed the baby and take care of all the older kids, I don't have time to go see the preacher and make arrangements today."

Ruth craved activity to help her deal with her grief. "We're on our way to Mansfield, and we'll be glad to start making the arrangements for you. Amanda and Joe live close to the church. They can take care of details. We'll even go by and tell the folks at the newspaper, so they can print a notice about Maria."

David looked relieved. "That'd be an awful big help. I need to stay here with the children. They're real upset, even though I've told them their mother's gone to heaven and they'll see her there someday. When he came to see her the day before she died, I told Pastor Blackwell to expect us for a funeral soon."

"I'll go in and hug the kids, give 'em the cookies I baked, and an' talk to them a few minutes." Ruth unwrapped the blanket around her legs and got out of the sleigh.

"I'll go hug 'em too." Adam tied the horse to the fence. David mumbled a thank-you, wiped his eyes, and resumed work on the coffin.

OBITUARY

DIED—In Madison township, Richland county, On the 8th inst. of Consumption, MARIA R. BEATTY, aged 38 years, 4 months and 17 days.

Her kind, intelligent and consistent deportment was such as to embalm her memory in the hearts of all who enjoyed her acquaintance. Her illness was of short duration; and when dying, she remarked she "had no fears of death—that she reposed her trust in the Savior"—She leaves a husband and seven children to mourn her loss.

—*Richland Times and Banner, January 14, 1857*

The family and other mourners filled nearly all of the pews in the Presbyterian church in downtown Mansfield. David and his older children were comforted by the presence of so many family members and friends at a service to honor Maria.

The stove in the center of the sanctuary created a small circle of warm air, and those sitting near it unbuttoned their heavy coats. The rest of the people, including David, his family, and Maria's family, sat wrapped to their chins. After Pastor Blackwell's solemn opening and prayer, he lined out Maria's favorite hymn, "All Hail the Power of Jesus' Name." The mourners in the coldest corners of the room sang with extra gusto.

In his eulogy, Pastor Blackwell extolled Maria's steady and sincere faith with moving words that praised her life. He closed the service with a prayer of hope.

"I sure hope he's right and we get to see Mama again in heaven." Nettie whispered to Melissa. She wiped her eyes as she accompanied her sister, brothers, and father out of the church behind the coffin.

"We will." Ted turned to assure her as he shifted two-year-old Walker from his arms to those of his brother Guy. The family held hands as the procession reached the open grave.

The pallbearers, six male neighbors of the Beatys, struggled to maneuver the coffin over the mound of dirt alongside the grave. Two of them stumbled on frozen clods, and the coffin slid off the ropes and fell into the grave with a dull thud. Everyone gasped. Nettie and her sisters began to cry. David stood with his arms around his children, his face as grim and gray as the winter sky, as Pastor Blackwell gave a hasty final benediction. Then David took a shovel and dropped clods of frozen soil on his wife's coffin.

As two young men began to shovel the frozen clods into the grave, friends gathered around the family to offer words of comfort, support, and assistance. Some were neighbors; others lived in Belleville or in Mansfield and knew the Beatys as customers at their mills or stores, or at the courthouse where David's land transactions were recorded. Even Nancy Stewart, the milliner, stepped forward to express her sympathy to David and his children. "Maria was one of the nicest women I ever made hats for. I hope you folks get on all right. Let me know if I can help."

"Thank you, Miss Stewart. We'll get along, best we can ..."

David's low words drifted off into the winter air, and he wiped his eyes. He had no idea how he was going to care for his family alone.

But together, they inched through the winter, and little by little, they adapted to their loss. Ted, Guy, and their three sisters learned to cook, wash clothes, and keep the house clean. David devoted almost every waking minute to caring for his youngest son. The next spring, David relinquished some of the care of the baby to his three daughters and taught Ted and Guy more about how to plant oats, wheat, and corn. He taught them how to trap rabbits and squirrels and reminded them to avoid the few remaining rattlesnakes that lived in the rocks at the top of the hill. He resumed his land dealings, and gradually he reduced his holdings year by year as opportunities to make profitable sales arose.

1857 From David Beaty to Elijah White, 2 acres and 70 rods, $400

1857 From David Beaty to Thos. Dickerson, 50 acres 1 rood and 70 rods, $2,000

1857 From David Beaty to Geo. Johnson, 28 acres, $1,500

1857 From David Beaty to Luther Carey, 16 acres

1858 From David Beaty to Steel Thrush, 1 1/2 acres, $102

1858 From David Beaty to Elijah White, 5 3/4 acres, $300

1858 From David Beaty to H. C. Newlon, 10 acres, $800

1858 From David Beaty to Rebecca Barnes, 8 acres, $620

1858 From D. Beaty to Wm. R. Newlon, 24 1/4 acres, $1,200

1859 From David Beaty to M. W. Worden, ~1/2 acre, $595

1859 From David Beaty to John Booth, 25 acres, $1,625

1859 From David Beaty to John Seaver, 12 acres, $510

—Deeds recorded in the Richland County Courthouse, Ohio

David's involvement in the debate over abolition increased as debate over this divisive issue took on a sharper and more heated tone. At a meeting of the proponents of abolition in Mansfield, he was surprised and pleased to encounter Miss Nancy Stewart, the milliner who'd made Maria's hat and the sister of one of his partners for the trip to California. His visits to Mansfield became more frequent and were no longer just to buy or sell land. Late in 1859, when presidential candidate Abraham Lincoln came to Mansfield to exhort the assembled listeners to oppose the Fugitive Slave Law, David and Miss Nancy Stewart stood side by side near the front of the boisterous crowd, holding hands and cheering his speech.

David's children had become used to their father's frequent trips to Mansfield, and to Miss Stewart's frequent visits to their home. They came to appreciate her positive outlook on life and to like her.

I do hereby certify that on the 9th day of February A.D. 1860 I joined in matrimony Mr. David Beaty and Miss N.J. Stewart

David Paul M G

—Return filed March 2, 1860 in the Richland County Courthouse, Ohio

The presidential election of 1860 was the most contentious in years. Everyone sensed that its outcome might guide the direction of the country for decades to come. The newlyweds David and Nancy were thrilled by Lincoln's victory and the prospect of his presidency. Nancy began to fit into a vibrant household that included seven children who ranged in age from four to fifteen and a husband who radiated exuberance about the country's prospects with Lincoln at the helm.

David had sold parcels of land in earlier years, usually for more than he paid, and kept the money in the bank because he was uncertain about the future prospects of the United States. But with his favorite politician headed for the White House, his confidence in the country was renewed, and the urge to reinvest in land fueled his actions. The stories he heard at the feed mill and the arrival of letters from a cousin in Iowa that gave glowing reports about the black soil and great opportunities in that state excited him about moving there and buying a farm. He stepped up his efforts to sell his property and move west. But first he had to let his family know of his dream.

After they'd eaten supper and the girls had finished washing and drying dishes, David called everyone back to the dinner table. "We're about to do some traveling and see some new country." The older children sat up, and everyone began to pay close attention. "Our cousin Reynolds Beaty wrote me again from Iowa about how good things are there, and I'm thinkin' we're gonna sell out and move out and join him and his family."

Annetta's questions were those all of her siblings had. "Where's Iowa? Is it a long ways away? An' how will we get there?"

David's response only partly answered what was on the family's minds. "It's a ways out west from here, across a big river. We'll go out there on the railroad. An' that should be exciting. Then we'll likely have to build a new house and barn after we get there. A lot of that country is just bein' settled, not like around here, where it got settled about fifty years ago."

Nancy was surprised and unsettled by the prospect of such a big move. "How do you know what you're getting us all into? What if things turn out not to be good there? Can we come back here? Do you think you can sell our land here at a decent price before you go?

And how do we know if we'll like the people? Maybe they're still Indians way out there."

David did his best to reassure his new wife about the prospects in Iowa. "We're just goin' to the very east edge of the state, not out where the Indians are still roamin' around. And my cousin and his family are already there, so we'll have some relatives and friends right away when we get there. An' from what I know, people are pretty decent everywhere, so I wouldn't worry about makin' new friends."

Nancy was quiet, but she remained apprehensive about the prospect of a big move. Life for her had undergone a tumultuous change when she married this widower with seven lively children, but she hadn't counted on him insisting that the whole family move west, away from her friends and family, to a place where she didn't know a soul. "Well, I'm not sure about how this will all work out. I'd like to just stay here, where we got family and friends."

But David went ahead with his plans and finished selling the farm, making a substantial profit as he did so.

1860 From D. Beaty to James Thrush, 5 acres, $150

1860 From David Beaty and wife to Wm. Shade, 32 acres, $2,000

1860 From David Beaty and Nancy J. Beaty to Alex. M. Barnes, 3 1/2 acres, $170

1860 From David Beaty and Nancy J. Beaty to Alex Braines, 6 acres, $350

1860 From David Beaty and Nancy J. Beaty to John Zaaker, 5 3/4 acres, $250

1860 From David Beaty and Nancy J. Beaty, to [no purchaser or acreage listed], $900

—*Deeds recorded in the Richland County Courthouse, Ohio*

Chapter 18
Across the Mississippi

Something momentous was happening; Walker, who was six, felt it more than he understood it. He hung around the house and farmyard, keeping out of the way but within earshot, as a parade of neighbors and strangers came to the farm. His father and stepmother showed them the Beaty family's livestock, farm machinery, and household possessions. He watched these visitors leave with teams of horses, cows and calves, a flock of sheep, dishes, and farm machinery. It was exciting and a little baffling. How were they going to live without the cows for milk, and the churn to make butter? How would his older brothers and father plow without horses and oxen? Walker finally asked his father during a free moment when there were no prospective buyers around, looking and asking questions.

"We've sold the farm, and we're going to move west—all the way to Iowa. Remember, I told you all about it one night after supper." David's explanation of his plans still wasn't clear to Walker. Was Iowa so far away that they couldn't drive their livestock there, as he'd seen some of their neighbors do every spring when they moved to a new farm they'd rented?

"How far away is Iowa, Pa?" Walker looked at his father as they watched their last team of horses being led away, harnesses and all.

"Son, it's way far away. Out beyond a great big river they call the Mississippi. We'll go there on the train, but it'll take us a few days."

Walker wondered why they were going so far away, but he didn't ask. Instead, he went into the house, where Nancy and his sisters were making jam and jelly sandwiches and packing them alongside slabs of ham and roast beef and jars of pickles in the big, new wicker baskets they'd bought in Mansfield the day they'd bought new clothes and shoes for everyone in the family. It was all hustle, bustle, and excitement, and he was in the way. So he woke up his four-year-old brother Davey from his nap and took him outside to look for the family of young kittens he'd seen under the woodshed.

David was excited by the big change that he and his family were about to experience. Ever since Lincoln had won last fall's election, he'd talked to Nancy and his older children about his dream of moving to new land in the west and buying a larger farm near the edge of the developing frontier, where opportunities were likely to appear. Now that his candidate was in office, he couldn't wait to get going.

Nancy's feelings alternated between excitement about David's dream and dread about being far away from her family and friends in a place she'd never seen. Life for her had undergone a tumultuous change when she married this widower with seven lively children, but she hadn't counted on him insisting the whole family move west, away from her friends and family, to a place where she didn't know a soul. But all the work of getting ready for travel kept her so busy that she seldom had time to mourn her impending losses.

When everything was either sold or packed, David's brother-in-law Joe Kearn drove the family to Mansfield behind his high-stepping bay horses on a warm day in early May 1861. While they waited for the train, Walker darted around the platform outside the depot but kept his father and stepmother in sight. This was the first time he'd been to a train station. He'd never seen so much hustle and bustle. Men were backing wagons up to the platform and unloading all manner of things—tubs of butter, cases of eggs, boxes of cheese, trunks, bags, crates of chickens. People were milling about, talking, carrying bags and trunks, and staring at a steam locomotive sitting idle on a side track. He had trouble watching everything.

A man in a uniform yelled, "Train's comin'! Watch your horses!" The men scurried to finish unloading, drove their teams to a stout hitching rail, and tied them securely.

David motioned for Walker to come and join the family and relatives. "Listen real good. Hear that humming? That's the rails talking ... sayin' the train's getting close."

Walker listened. At first he didn't hear anything. Then he detected a low, steady hum, and over the hum a chuff, chuff, chuffing sound coming from the south. He waited for the whistle. He'd heard that sound before, very faint, way off in the distance on cold, still nights when he was about to go to sleep. The sound was lonesome, mysterious, and captivating.

He leaned toward the tracks, looking toward the sound. The rest of his family was beside him on the platform, surrounded by relatives and friends who'd come to see them off. At the far end, where piles of luggage were stacked, his two older brothers, Ted and Guy, proud of their new brown pants and jackets and their responsibility, stood guarding the family's six trunks. A few feet away, his three sisters were talking, giggling, and looking prim in new dresses and bonnets.

His stepmother, Nancy, stood beside her husband, holding four-year-old Davey by the hand and wiping her eyes. The little boy was whining, wiggling, and twisting against her new blue dress, trying to get loose. Walker wondered why Nancy was crying. He thought she looked angry and uncertain about what to do. He was too young to realize that when she'd married David a little over a year ago, she'd suddenly become mother to seven children, and that they sometimes intimidated her. And she hadn't bargained on leaving her own family and friends and moving 450 miles west. Now that the moment had arrived, it overwhelmed her.

David put his arm on Nancy's shoulder, then reached down and lifted his son into a tight embrace. "Stop your fussin' right now. An' after this, do what Nancy says." Little Davey hung quiet and still.

Nancy patted his head. "I know you want to run around, but it's not safe now, Davey." She marveled at the way the children obeyed their father, and she admired her husband's energy and knowledge of the world.

The whistle shrilled, and Walker felt a prickle as the hair on his neck stood up. Davey's eyes opened wide as he wrapped small arms around his father's neck. Walker looked toward the sound and was the first to see the moving tower of smoke above the trees where the tracks curved to the right.

"Here she comes!" His small voice was lost in the crowd.

The engine and six cars clanged and squealed to a stop in front of the platform. Steam squirted out of the side of the engine, and the crowd closest to it surged back. Horses whinnied in terror and jerked against the ropes that tied them to the hitching rail. Three men began to load cordwood from a pile on the platform onto the flatcar just behind the engine. A man stepped from the engine's cab to the flatcar, took one of the logs, and shoved it into the locomotive's firebox. Walker saw the flames lap around it before the fireman closed the iron door. Two men in uniform heaved open the door of the second car and began to unload trunks and crates. A few people got off the cars behind it.

David walked to the men in uniform. "Be real sure you load all six of those trunks." He pointed to the family's luggage and handed each man a coin. They smiled and nodded enthusiastically. When all the baggage had been offloaded, they lifted the Beatys' trunks on first. Guy and Ted moved closer to the rest of the family.

When the logs and baggage was almost all loaded, another man in uniform stepped out of the last car, put his hands around his mouth, and bellowed, "Board! Everybody on board!" Walker covered his ears.

He felt his grandfather Gault's hands lift him from behind. "Good-bye, young man. I'll miss you a lot. Be sure to always do what your father and stepmother tell you." He passed Walker to his wife, Ruth, who planted a big kiss on his cheek as she hugged him. Walker thought she felt as soft as a featherbed. He kissed her timidly on the cheek and then watched the eruption of tear-moistened hugs and good-byes that the rest of his family were sharing with the two dozen or so relatives who had come to see them off for Iowa. Nancy stifled a sob and blew her nose as she hugged her father and mother.

"Board, all aboard!" The conductor waved his arms.

David picked up a wicker basket covered with a dishtowel,

motioned for his family to follow him, and stepped up into the train. Nancy, holding Davey by the hand and still crying softly, came next. Alice stepped behind Walker and pushed him up into the train. The four older children followed, carrying carpetbags, baskets, pillows, and blankets. They sat on the low-backed wooden seats and looked out the open windows at the relatives they were leaving. Walker's uncle Joe Kearn stood tall and reserved, but his grandmother Ruth Gault was crying, and Adam Gault was blowing his nose. The rest of their relatives were waving, some as they dabbed handkerchiefs at their eyes. Walker noticed that his stepmother was still crying as she waved to her parents and brother.

The whistle blasted twice. A sharp jerk snapped their heads back. There was just time to lean out the windows and wave one last good-bye as the train lurched and clanked around the curve, whistling and billowing smoke.

The world began to rush by. Walker reached for his father's hand and felt reassured as its callused, bony expanse surrounded his small hand. Nancy pulled a handkerchief from the ample bosom of her dress and dabbed at her eyes. His sisters were very quiet, looking straight ahead. But Ted and Guy were laughing, thrilled by the speed, the noise, the jolts, and the smoke that curled around their coach. Even with his father beside him, Walker felt a little frightened. Why were they leaving? Where were they going? When would they get there? And why was Nancy crying? The whistle assaulted his ears again, and he covered them with his hands. Soon he felt sleepy as the chuff-chuff-chuff of the locomotive and the rocking of the rail car replaced the hubbub of the train station, and he fell asleep with his father's arm around him.

As Walker dozed under his arm, David looked at his family spread out on the seats beside him. His thoughts turned to the huge change they were making. He'd put his faith in stories of travelers and in his cousin Reynolds's letters that gave glowing reports of conditions in Iowa. What if his cousin was not a reliable judge of the land and people there? What if Nancy didn't get over leaving her family and home? Would she come to like Iowa? What if he got sick—could his sons take over? Oh, well, they were committed now, no turning back. Just as there was no turning back now from Lincoln's firm defense of the Union, even in the face of civil war..

As they bounced and jerked on the wooden seats, the train ride seemed like an eternity to the Beaty children. The blankets they'd brought for padding didn't help much. Ted and Guy lost interest in the passing sights and turned their attention to the food that Nancy and the girls had packed.

"How long did you say we're going to be on this smoky, bouncy thing?" Nettie glared at her father as she brushed cinders off the top of a ham sandwich and handed it to Ted.

He glared back and answered, "Three, four days if everything goes right." Nettie gave a typical teenager's groan and rolled her eyes.

Her father was having none of such behavior. "Don't be carryin' on so. We're goin' to stop in Chicago. An' stay in a nice hotel. Then we'll take a different train to Iowa. But first we'll look 'round Chicago some. It's a chance to see a bigger town than Mansfield."

Nettie looked unimpressed. "I don't see why we have to move at all. Nobody but you wants to. Our farm was nice. I loved going down to Toby Creek and catching frogs and fish. Even the rattlesnakes didn't scare me."

Her father mounted a rousing defense of his decision to move. "The land we're leavin' was gettin' worn out. Where we're going hasn't been farmed at all. My cousin Reynolds, who moved there two years ago, wrote that the soil's black down two feet or so. An' it's got no hardpan. Grows corn and wheat so big you can't believe it. And the land's real cheap."

The ringing enthusiasm of her father's voice made little impression on Nettie. Still looking put out, she dug into the basket of food, came up with a sandwich of blackberry jelly, and bit off a chunk. As she and her siblings ate, David began to recount his boyhood travels. "You kids don't know how good you've got it. When I was just three years older than Ted, we moved from Millersburg to the farm on Toby Creek in a covered wagon. Rained all of the way. Took us 'most a week to go thirty-five miles. We're going almost that far in an hour today! An' our wagon just about upset fording Toby Creek in a flood.

Water was chest high. We had to jump in and hold it from tippin' over."

Nettie stopped eating. "I'm sorry, Pa. It's just I'm real sad about leaving my friends. An' there's so many cinders blowing in. They're going to ruin my new dress." She brushed her sleeve and frowned at the black streaks.

Nancy put her hand on Nettie's arm. "We all miss everything we're leaving behind, honey. Lord knows *I* sure do." She frowned at David. "But there'll be new things and people to get to know in Fairfield. And we can wash out all that black when we get there." Nancy tried to smile and failed.

Nettie looked straight ahead, eyes down, and began eating again. The family settled into a sullen silence as the sun arced overhead and finally slanted in from the west. David felt glad not to have to hear any more of their complaints. When it got dark, they all wrapped up in the blankets they'd brought and tried to sleep.

Dawn light slanting off Lake Michigan roused David, Nancy, and the sleeping children, one by one. They pulled off the blankets they'd slept under and gawked at the expanse of water and all the buildings. As their train snaked slowly into Chicago, whistling and clanging trains on other tracks converged from both sides. Smoke and haze thickened until the lake was only a dim shimmer in the haze. The air smelled putrid. Then they were at the station amid half a dozen trains, unloading everything and bundling it into a wagon bound for a hotel.

"Will there be some food soon? I'm so hungry, I could eat a cow." Ted rubbed his stomach.

"There'll be plenty. Help load this trunk, an' we'll get there sooner." David pointed to the other end of a trunk he had started to lift, and Ted grabbed it. The family was soon devouring breakfast in a hotel dining room and then catching up on the sleep they'd missed the previous night.

After they'd eaten dinner at noon, Nancy told David, "I'd like to take the girls to the Palmer dry goods store. They say it's quite the place. Why don't you and the boys go look at some of the rest of town?" All the children looked expectantly toward their father.

He nodded. "Guess that's fine. Just don't buy much. The trunks are already full."

David and the boys walked east toward the lake on the plank walk beside the dirt street. Ahead, they saw a row of tall, windowless structures on the lakeshore.

Guy asked, "Pa, what are those tall buildings?"

"Don't exactly know, Son. Let's go look." He picked up Davey, who was sleepy, and lifted him onto his shoulders. Wagons piled with bulging sacks were bouncing down the rutted street in the same direction. "Maybe they're for storin' grain."

When they reached the lake, they saw lines of wagons full of sacked grain waiting beside the tall structures. Men were lifting the sacks off the front wagon and piling them on a wooden platform with a metal grate in the middle. A man standing beside a metal frame put iron weights on it until the horizontal arm stopped swinging up and down and balanced level. He called, "Twenty-four hundred and sixty pounds. Dump it." Men swarmed around and began pouring the wheat down the grate. Another wrote down the number on a piece of paper.

David pointed toward the top of the building, "That's where they store the grain before it gets loaded on ships to go down the lakes to Buffalo and the Erie Canal."

Guy looked up and then at his father with wonder in his eyes. "Do men carry the wheat all the way up that thing?" David laughed.

"No, Son, I reckon they have a steam engine in there, and it must pull up buckets of grain and dump them into the big bins from the top. Let's look on the other side." They walked to the lakeshore side of the building, where a ship was tied up, its hatches open. A wooden chute angled down from the building toward one of the hatches. Wheat streamed out of its low end and made a dusty, golden cascade as it fell into the hold.

David nodded. "Yep, that's sure a lot easier than loadin' it by hand a sack at a time, like I saw in Buffalo when I was comin' home from California. In Iowa, we're gonna raise wheat. Maybe it will come right through here." Ted and Guy stood rooted in place, watching first the ship, then the grain elevator that was feeding it. "Let's go see more of the town." Their father had to tug their sleeves to get them to leave.

They walked toward the smell of fresh-cut wood that came from acres of lumber stacked along the lakeshore. Three ships were tied up at docks, and cranes powered by steam engines were swinging slings full of boards off their decks to waiting wagons. Men swarmed everywhere, yelling, swearing, untying the slings, and straightening boards. Back from the shore, more swarms of men were lifting boards off wagons and piling them neatly on logs laid parallel several feet apart on the ground.

"Just look at that." Guy's voice matched his look of incredulity. "Where's all them boards come from? What do they do with 'em all?"

"I'm not sure, Son. But they must come from farther north. Maybe Michigan or Wisconsin. I've heard there's lots of pine trees up there."

Ted looked at the sea of piled boards and shook his head. "How could anybody use it all? It's not cut for burnin'. They could build more'n a hundred houses from this." They stood quiet, watching the beehive of activity for several minutes, then turned back toward downtown. After they'd walked a few blocks, the hurly-burly of the lakefront gave way to rows of stores in buildings taller than the boys had ever seen until that morning.

"There's that Palmer store where Nancy and my sisters were going." Ted pointed to a sign above the most prominent building they'd seen. "Suppose they're still there?"

David looked where Ted was pointing. "Well, it won't hurt to take a look."

A man in a suit and tie bowed and opened the door as they approached. Inside, they stared wide-eyed at a sea of dry goods and a phalanx of men in suits, each standing beside a counter.

"May I be of assistance, sir?"

"We're looking for my wife and my three daughters. My wife's kind of pretty—plump, brown hair, blue eyes. Girls are eight, ten, and thirteen. Giggle a lot. Way too much."

"Oh, yes, sir. They're over in the corner, trying on hats. This is their first visit, I expect." He bowed.

217

"Pa, do you like this hat?" Nettie tilted her head so her father could get a better look. "I think it's beautiful. Nancy says it's real well made." Nettie looked excited and anxious.

David looked first at Nettie, then at Mel and Alice, each wearing a new hat, and then at Nancy. She nodded an affirmation. "Well, if Nancy thinks they're good ones, I s'pose you can have 'em."

The girls' relieved "Thank you, Pa" came almost in unison. As the family walked back toward the hotel in the wind, chattering about their grand new adventure, each girl held onto her new hat with one hand.

David, Ted, and Guy left the rest of the family there and kept walking. They soon found the Cyrus McCormick reaper factory and marveled at its size. A guard kept them out. Then they walked toward a river that ran through the city and encountered the smell of manure and the sound of pigs squealing. Two buildings hugged the riverbank, with pens for hogs and cattle between them. Railroad tracks ran along the street, bordering the pens. They crossed the tracks and peeked into an open door.

Squealing pigs were jammed into a narrow chute at the edge of a huge room crowded with men. As they watched, a man looped a chain around the hind leg of the pig at the front of the chute. Another man opened the gate, and the pig dashed forward. The first man quickly fastened the chain to a hook on a tall, slowly rotating wheel on the wall, jerking the fleeing pig to a stop.

As the wheel lifted it off its feet, head down, a third man grabbed its front leg, made a quick stab to its throat with his knife, and stepped back before the stream of blood reached his leather apron. The pig squealed and writhed as the moving wheel lowered it slowly a couple yards from where it had started its death-journey. A second man guided the still-twitching carcass to a metal table. Then it was pushed in front of a line of men with knives and cleavers, who disemboweled and dismembered the carcass like a pack of wolves devouring a lamb. Even before they'd made the first cut, another pig was being lifted by its hind leg on the inexorably moving wheel. A third waited, unknowing, in the chute.

David, Ted, and Guy looked at each other and stepped back. As they walked toward the hotel beside the red-tinted river with its parade of floating pig heads, Guy shared his impressions. "They've sure got that down pat, haven't they?" His father nodded.

Ted pinched his nose and coughed. "Yeah, but it stinks so bad, I can't hardly breathe."

* * *

The next morning, the Beatys savored the clear May air of the prairie west of Chicago as the train chuffed toward the Mississippi River. They marveled at the endless ocean of grass, interrupted only by infrequent little, angular islands where it had been plowed. Children waved from the yards of new, bare-wood buildings perched tentatively along the edges of the fields. A gust of air blew the train smoke to the north and replaced it with the aroma of blooming prairie roses. Everyone but young Walker savored the smell. He felt it constrict his throat, and he coughed as he tried to breathe.

The day dragged by slowly. As the sun settled toward the horizon, the train snaked into a wide valley and stopped on a side track.

Ted turned from the window. "Where are we, Pa?"

"This must be the west edge of Illinois. We'll get off just across the Mississippi, at Burlington in Iowa. Tomorrow we'll take a train to Fairfield."

The platform beside their train was filled with men. Most were carrying knapsacks and blanket rolls. Ted leaned out and hailed one. "What are all you fellas doin'?"

The man turned and raised his cap to Nancy and the three girls. "We're jus' waitin' to go to the fort to get sworn in as Illinois Volunteers. Then we're goin' to go teach those damn rebels what's what. Oh, beggin' your pardon. I don't mean to swear in front of ladies." He blushed above a scraggly red beard, then addressed Ted and Guy. "You two look like you're almost old enough to join us."

Ted and Guy exchanged surprised looks. After two short blasts of the whistle, their train lurched into motion. Ted looked back and waved.

The sun hung huge and red just above the horizon as the train inched toward the bridge over the Mississippi. David shaded his eyes. "Look real good, everybody. In a minute we'll be in the west, in Iowa." Everyone but Davey and his father crowded to the window. As the train snaked out over the river, Nettie and Mel gasped and jumped back, stepping on Alice's foot. Alice hit Mel and began to cry. Nancy lifted Alice into her lap and wiped away her tears.

"Ooh, it's so big. What if the train falls off? I don't want to look." Nettie hid her eyes as she sat down. Ted and Guy stood shoulder to shoulder as they looked downriver in the dimming light.

David stood behind them. "It looks big, but you should see it down south, below Kayro an' Vicksburg an' New Orlins. A man can't hardly see the far shore down there." They watched until the river was out of sight and the buildings of Burlington surrounded them. Everyone was eager to get off the train and head for a hotel. After supper, the tired travelers turned in and slept like logs.

The next morning, they were on their way again, headed west. Around noon, their train approached Fairfield across the flat plain to the east and stopped in the middle of the village. The little town glistened as the sun erased the remnants of a spring shower. The Beaty girls burst off, pulling Davey by the hand, and looked around. David, Ted, and Guy gathered the trunks and baggage. Walker stood close to Nancy, who looked unimpressed by the little burg.

Nettie looked at Mel and frowned. "Sure is small. Smaller than Belleville, even."

Mel nodded. "Yeah, why'd Pa have to drag us way out here?"

"Well, it may be small, but it's where your father says we're gonna live." Nancy's voice and her face showed both disappointment and resolve.

David overheard them. "It's where the good land and the good prospects are. Where everything's growing. We'll work an' make it home, just like us Beatys've always done ever since my grandpa Thomas an' his family settled in the mountains in Pennsylvania 'most a hundred years ago." He hailed a man with an empty wagon and pointed toward the trunks. The man touched his cap and started loading them. David motioned the family toward the wagon. "Pick up your bags, and get in. We're here, and we've got to pull together and make something good of it, if we can."

Chapter 19
Prairie Farm

As he tugged on the curved oak handles and turned the new plow with its wide steel share and shiny moldboard upright, David wondered if he could handle this big contraption. It seemed almost twice as heavy as the one he'd sold in Ohio less than a month before. He wondered if he, Ted, and Guy could get the land prepared and seeds in the ground before it was too late—if it would rain too soon or not at all. Then there were the house and barn waiting to be built. Getting started from scratch was hard and chancy.

His sons struggled to maneuver three yoke of reluctant oxen into line in front of the huge plow and hook the chain that ran between the animals to the heavy clevis that hung from the front of the oak plow beam. They'd been in Fairfield a week. David had bought a farm, a team of horses, a wagon, a breaking plow, a brush harrow, and a grain drill. He'd bought and set up a large tent in one corner of his new land for the family to live in, and borrowed the six oxen from his cousin, who'd recommended the farm with its virgin land for purchase. Now it was time to start breaking the prairie sod. He watched his sons try to get the three ox teams positioned and wondered if they would be able to handle all six animals at once.

David bent his legs, stepped under the plow handles, and strained to lift them shoulder-high and point the plow tip downward. "Start 'em out." His voice quivered from the exertion.

Ted and Guy yelled, "Hike!" and prodded the front team with sharp sticks. The animals stepped forward, then lowered their heads and grunted when the yokes pressed hard on their necks as the chain tightened. The tip of the plow cleaved the black soil and the thick mat of roots that had multiplied in it for centuries. A sliver of young grass, cut roots, and prairie loam surged up the gleaming moldboard and inverted itself as the plow moved forward.

As the six oxen, two boys, and man strained and plodded north, a glistening black ribbon grew behind them. Walker followed the lengthening furrow. He sniffed the reassuring aroma of good, black earth, watched the wiggling earthworms as they tried to cope with a world turned upside-down, and picked up some that had been bisected by the plow. When his hand was full, he ran to show them to his father as the plowmen stopped to turn east.

"Look, Pa. The ground's full of fish worms."

David puffed and wiped his face with his sleeve. The oxen panted and drooled, their sides heaving. Ted and Guy came back to see what Walker had collected. "Son, worms mean this is real good ground. They make the dirt rich." He picked up a handful and rubbed the soil between his thumb and fingers. "See how nice it crumbles. It plows hard 'cause of all the roots, but once they're cut, it'll work up real good. We've got us some good ground here, real good." He looked around at the treeless landscape and marveled at its extent. There was not a hill, valley, or stream to interrupt its continuity. He felt like he was out on the ocean again, except without the waves. Then he gripped the plow handles and motioned for Ted and Guy to prod the oxen into motion again.

* * *

By early that afternoon, Nancy, Nettie, Mel, and Alice were planting a garden in a newly plowed corner of the field next to the site they'd selected for their house. Davey sat nearby, running the black soil through his tiny hands and watching it pile into cones and mounds. Then he knocked them down with four-year-old enthusiasm and built more.

The plowmen and straining oxen continued enlarging the black rim around the forty-acre field, furrow by slow furrow. Nancy and the girls marveled at the absence of rocks and stones in the soft, black soil and the ease with which it yielded to the hoes they were using to carve tiny trenches for the seeds of beans, squash, pumpkins, tomatoes, turnips, sweet corn, and potato seed-pieces. Walker dropped seeds into the trenches; his sisters covered them and tamped the loose soil. When Nancy and the children finished planting late in the afternoon, she imagined that the seeds were already swelling with growth and promise, and she wished it were happening to her.

After a week of arduous work, the rest of the forty-acre field had been plowed, harrowed, and planted to corn and wheat, and the garden showed tiny rows of green. They stopped on Sunday for worship and relaxation. Then David and his two older sons hitched a newly purchased team of horses to a lumber wagon and began to haul boards from Fairfield. When they paused to rest, Ted asked his father, "Do you suppose these are some of the boards we saw when we were back in Chicago?"

David shook his head. "Nope, I reckon the trees these came from were cut up north of here, in Minnesota or Wisconsin, an' floated down the Mississippi to the sawmills in Davenport or Burlington." He ran his hand gently along the straight grain of a pale amber pine board and inhaled its aroma. "Sure is nice stuff. Nary a knot in it."

Ted wiped the sweat off his face his face with his bandanna. "Why don't trees like that grow here? There was trees all over back in Ohio."

"Dunno for sure," David said, scanning the wide, flat, grassy expanse of land that surrounded Fairfield. "Some say it's too dry in summer. Others say it's because of the big fires that burned this prairie every year or two when the Indians were here."

"How come there's been so many fires here? We didn't have 'em back east."

"Lightning, maybe. Dry prairie grass burns hot as a pine knot. Let's finish this load. The womenfolk are awful anxious to get out of that tent an' into a house. Can't say as I blame 'em." He lifted a plank and slid it along the top of the lumber already on the wagon, to complete the load.

David, Ted, and Guy, along with two hired men, worked from

daylight to dark to build the house and get the family out of the tent. Nancy struggled to cook enough food for eleven hungry eaters in the makeshift kitchen with a simple stove.

* * *

In early July, they moved into the large, new house. It had five small bedrooms upstairs and a kitchen, a pantry, a dining room, and a parlor downstairs. A porch ran along the north side, off the door to the kitchen. When they got settled into their new house, everyone's resentment about the move diminished. As the season progressed and word of periodic turmoil between advocates of the Union and Rebel sides convulsed Fairfield, the Beatys' plantings grew greener and faster than any they remembered in Ohio.

David came home from a meeting of the Fairfield Temperance Society with a report of another incursion of armed rebel militia from Missouri to within a few miles of Fairfield. As he and Nancy sat on the porch, watching the sun set on the flat, treeless horizon, he said, "This war's gettin' to be serious. I reckon it's not going to be over anytime soon, like we'd hoped."

Nancy stopped darning a hole in a sock. "How long's it going to take to whip those greedy slave owners? I thought it would just last a few months."

"Guess not. I heard in town that them dirty rebels beat us bad at someplace called Bull Run, and Lincoln is calling for lots more soldiers. Those first three-month enlistments have run out, and a lot of them soldiers are goin' home. But the price of wheat's goin' up, an' the army's tryin' to buy a lot of meat to feed the troops. I'm sure glad Guy and Ted are still too young to want to go fighting." He slapped a mosquito on his arm.

Nancy resumed darning and rocking. "Looks like you got us to Fairfield at just the right time. Never saw things grow like they do here. We're gonna need lots of food to keep the kids filled up. But if it rains, we should do all right, and if prices go up, we should make a little money. This place isn't so bad after all." She waved away flies that buzzed around her face.

"Seems that way. I talked to that fellow John Simpson again. He wants to set up in business with me to pack meat an' sell it to the army. Maybe I should go in with him. I could put in some money, and Ted an' Guy an' I could work at it when there's not much to do with the crops."

This idea appealed to Nancy. She stopped rocking and looked up from her darning as she said, "Why don't you talk to him some more? Those two boys sure need somethin' to keep 'em out of mischief." She waved away a fly. "An' the way they eat! They're hungry as a pair o' young wolves. Try as I might, I can't hardly cook enough for this big crew."

"I'll talk to him again next time I'm in town. For right now, I'll keep 'em busy building the barn and putting up fence."

* * *

In the fall, David joined John Simpson in a slaughtering and meatpacking enterprise. They received a contract from the U.S. Army for forty tons of salt-packed beef and pork. Guy and Ted worked alongside their father and learned to kill, skin, cut, and pack salted meat into barrels. They watched their father dicker over prices with the farmers who drove cattle and hogs to the corrals he and Simpson had built near the railroad siding at the edge of Fairfield.

Guy began to pride himself on how accurately he could guess how many pounds of meat they would put into the barrels from each hog or steer that his father bought. He made it his personal game. On the days when his estimates were close, he rewarded himself with a furtive sip of whiskey from a bottle he kept in a box under some old knives.

After a year, he was entrusted to buy some of the cattle. Many farmers considered him too young to be an accurate judge of how much saleable meat an animal would yield, and Guy took full advantage of those who underestimated his good eye. Even before their first contract with the army was completed, the Beaty-Simpson partnership had negotiated a larger one at a higher price. Guy spent more and more time buying livestock and working in the slaughterhouse; Ted spent more time on the farm. David worked at both, usually from sunup to sundown, except on Sunday, when he went to church and then to temperance society meetings.

Nancy was busy cooking, sewing, and washing for the family, but she joined other women of Fairfield making clothing and other supplies for the Iowa troops. When they weren't in school, Nettie, Mel, and Alice helped make quilts for the soldiers. Ted and Guy were torn between enlisting, as other young men from the neighborhood were doing, and continuing to work from daylight to dark on the farm and in the slaughterhouse.

David's energy matched his enthusiasm. He had both a farm and a share of a business, and they were producing profits for him and food for the Union troops, whom he supported fervently. His big fears were that his side would lose the war. In 1864, the same year their son Charles was born, Ted decided to enlist in the army.

As David and Nancy stood by the train station in Fairfield and watched him climb aboard a trainload of young men who were part of the Third Iowa Volunteers and were headed for an army camp along the Mississippi River near Keokuk, Iowa, they shared worried looks. Nancy put her hand on David's arm and said, "He's such a nice young fellow. I sure hope he comes back alive."

David's enthusiasm for the Union cause ran head on into the thought of losing a son he cherished. "Me too! This war is getting to be an awful bloody affair." He surreptitiously wiped a tear from his eye just before Ted turned to give them one last wave good-bye.

Chapter 20
West Again

After the North won the war and Ted came limping home, the westward expansion of the United States accelerated, David heard of emerging opportunities around Iowa's capital city of Des Moines, and he grew restless to move again. In January 1868, as the family was finishing supper, he announced, "I'm ready to sell out here and move west—out near Des Moines, where I hear there's good land a man can buy cheap."

Nancy looked at him in surprise and then anger. "You're crazy, David. Fairfield's a nice little town. We all like it, and we're doing all right. Why on earth do you want to move again?"

David stood up and responded vigorously, "Back in the forties, I watched my father die in debt, and my brother and I had to work like sin to save his farm. An' I sure don't aim to wind up broke like him. I'm gonna go where there's cheap, new land and more money to be made, and that's out near where they're building the new state capital."

Nancy frowned and continued dishing up the apples she'd baked for dessert. The rest of the family sensed the determination in David's voice and resumed eating in silence while glancing furtively at each other, until Guy looked at his father and spoke up.

"You all can go west if you want to, but I'm stayin' right here. The farmers trust me, and I can make good money buyin' their pigs and

227

steers and takin' them to Chicago to sell. Besides, Sadie Barnes an' I plan to get married come summer, an' she sure won't want to traipse off to the west somewhere."

Ted, who had come back from the war thin as a rail and suffering from the chronic diarrhea he'd contracted in the army, spoke softly in the silence that followed Guy's rebellion. "I like it here, so I'll stay put, just like Guy. You folks just go on west without me."

David, who had sat down again after responding to Nancy's objections, looked surprised by the independence of his quiet oldest son, but then he reasserted his determination. "Well, I hate to see the family split up, but if you two don't want to go, we'll just move to Des Moines without you."

Walker, now fourteen, realized that if his older brothers stayed behind, he'd be his father's main helper on a new farm. He smiled to himself as the family ate their baked apples in silence.

Talk didn't resume until the three daughters cleared the table and moved to the kitchen to wash dishes. Nettie spoke in a conspiratorial whisper as she ran the dishcloth over the top plate in the tall stack in the dishpan. "I think Pa's idea's exciting. I'd love to get to a bigger town."

Mel whispered back, "So would I, but don't ever tell Nancy. She loves Fairfield." Alice dried the plate that Mel fished out of the scalding rinse water and nodded.

When David finally accepted the fact that Guy and Ted weren't about to move, he worked out a deal that suited both him and his sons: he sold the farm to Guy on favorable terms and made sure that Ted would have the opportunity to farm it, since Guy was busy most of the time buying livestock and shipping them to the Chicago stockyards and slaughterhouses. Then the rest of the Beatys loaded the unsold household goods, machinery, and livestock into rail cars, said their good-byes—tearful in the case of Nancy and the girls—and headed west.

LEAVING.—Our friend and universally esteemed fellow citizen, Mr. David Beaty, has disposed of his property in this county, and is

**about removing to Des Moines, where he has
purchased both town and country property ...**

—*Fairfield Ledger, March 26, 1868, page 3, column 1*

Corn stubble in winter on farm purchased by David
Beaty northeast of Altoona, Iowa, in 1868

**To David Beaty from Thomas H. Perkins, Exrsg,
Dated May 1, 1868, Filed June 21 1868; 160 acres,
$2,000.**

—*General Index of Land Records, Polk County, Iowa*

In late April, meadowlarks were singing as the Beatys got off the
train at Altoona, a village northeast of Des Moines. When all the
passengers were off, the train crew backed two freight cars onto a
siding beside a corral. Walker pointed to them.

"Those cars have all our things in 'em. I remember the numbers.
I'll go see how the cows and horses are." He ran to a slat-sided cattle
car and tried to open the door, but he couldn't move the latch. His

sisters looked at each other, rolled their eyes, and laughed. They were excited by their new surroundings and hoped to visit Des Moines soon. Nancy felt dubious about the prospects of reestablishing a household in a new location.

David spoke to a heavyset, youngish man with a walrus mustache who stood beside a team hitched to a green and gold spring wagon with the words ELIJAH REAMES HOTEL, FREIGHT AND DRAYAGE lettered in black on the sides, then motioned everyone to come. "This is Mr. Reames. He's going to take us to his hotel for tonight and then haul our furniture to the house tomorrow."

The stocky man appraised the Beatys and noticed that everyone except Nancy seemed excited. "Glad to meet all of ya. Just call me Lije." He smiled at Nancy and looked down at Charlie, who was holding his mother's hand. "You look about the same age as one o' my girls. How old are ya, sonny?" Charlie, prompted by his mother, held up four tentative fingers. Lije laughed and scooped him up into the wagon. "My little Ella's five. I'll bring her over to meet you all when I haul your furniture."

Walker ran up just as Lije was climbing to the driver's high seat. "Come sit up front by me, young feller. You like to drive horses?" Walker nodded with enthusiasm and jumped up beside Mr. Reames.

"Here, you start 'em out." He unwrapped the reins and handed them to the teenager.

Walker took them proudly and said, "Giddup!" The family and baggage rode behind him to the hotel, with Elijah Reames sitting calmly on his left.

That evening after supper, the five older children explored the village that was to be their new home. They were especially curious about the big house and adjoining barn that their father had bought on the edge of the village. When they returned, eager to share news of their new discoveries, they found Nancy sitting alone in the hotel room, crying softly.

The five children stood quiet for a moment, their excitement dissipated by their stepmother's tears. Nettie spoke for her siblings. "Nancy, what's the matter? Altoona's a nice place. And the house Pa bought is even bigger than the one back in Fairfield."

Nancy dabbed at her eyes and tried unsuccessfully to look cheerful. "It's just I feel so uprooted and don't know anybody. And I'm even farther away from my family back in Ohio." The five siblings looked at each other uneasily and tiptoed down to the hotel lobby, where they watched hotel guests arrive until it got dark outside and they went to bed.

* * *

At sunrise the next morning, David and Walker were at the rail siding. Their livestock had been unloaded into a corral beside the tracks. After they'd fed and watered all the animals and milked the cows, David said, "First unload the harness for Belle and Blaze and use them to roll the wagon out. After that we can begin to unload the rest of the stuff for the farm right onto the wagon."

Walker scrambled into the boxcar and hunted for the harness. He'd never felt so grown up. Back in Fairfield, Ted and Guy had partnered with their father on the main farm work, and he'd been relegated to gathering eggs, splitting and carrying wood to the house, and feeding the calves. This was more like it. He found Belle's collar and harness, lifted them carefully to avoid tangling them with the set below, and carried them to his father, staggering a little from the weight.

"Here's Belle's harness. Can I put it on her?"

David beamed as he tied the horses to the fence. "Sure. You're my main man now." He stepped back and watched Walker stand on tiptoe to fasten the collar at the top of Belle's neck. The old horse looked back at Walker with a wary eye, but she didn't move as the novice struggled to throw the harness on her back and fastened the snaps and buckles under her belly and at her neck. Walker ran back for the harness that he hoped he was tall enough to put on Blaze.

David and Walker moved the machinery and farm supplies, one wagonload at a time, along the road that paralleled the railroad to their new farm, a quarter section of virgin prairie with no fences or buildings on a gently rolling upland about two miles northeast of Altoona. Then they began to fence a part of their new land for

231

pasture. They were setting a row of posts along the road when a man driving a horse and buggy stopped and walked over.

"Howdy do. You the feller who bought this quarter section?"

David stuck his shovel into the ground and extended his hand to the visitor. "Yes, sir. I'm David Beaty. Just moved here from Fairfield."

"Sam Higgins," the man said as they shook. "We live down the road a piece. Welcome to the neighborhood."

They visited about the weather, other neighbors, and prices. Walker rested and eavesdropped. As he was leaving, Sam said, "Iffen I was you, I'd burn a firebreak around all that machinery an' them posts quick as I could. Them damn trains put out hot cinders and sparks every once in a while. An' this prairie grass burns like blue blazes."

David touched his hand to his hat. "Thanks for stoppin'. And much obliged for the advice." When they'd set a few more fence posts into the ground, he said to Walker, "Let's burn a strip around the outside of this pasture before it gets too hot and windy. I'd sure hate to have all these posts and the machinery burn up."

Walker looked skeptical. "You think we need to? We could have the pasture fenced all the way around by noon if we keep going."

"Don't ask questions. Just get some grain sacks out of the big chest, wet 'em good in the creek, and bring 'em over to the corner."

Walker mumbled under his breath as he went for the sacks. David gathered handfuls of big bluestem and wadded them into tight bundles. When Walker returned, dragging four wet sacks, David said, "I'm gonna light these torches one at a time and then make a line of fire with them. You come right close behind and beat it out while it's real small. Be real sure it's clear out. Understand?" Walker nodded, even though he wasn't quite sure he understood. Burning the grass made no sense.

David lit a grass torch and touched it to the dry prairie grass, then walked a few steps and lit another spot. He stopped and looked back. The spots grew outward and merged. "All right, beat it out." Walker hesitated, then raised a wet sack above his head and brought it down on the fire, putting it out. "That's right. Stay close behind, and just keep doin' that." David dipped his torch to the grass and continued creating a line of flame. Walker came a few steps behind, beating as he walked and thinking that this was a waste of time.

When they had burned a narrow strip around the machinery and the prospective pasture, they started again, broadening the fire line. By the time it was about thirty feet wide, they were black with soot, sweaty, and tired. They washed their hands and faces in the creek and started building fence again. When they finished the fence a day later, they drove the livestock from the stockyards to the new enclosure.

* * *

On a warm, windy morning two days later, Walker was driving the ox teams, and David was wrestling the handles of the heavy plow along the north edge of the farm beside the railroad track. They were opening the first furrow when they heard a train whistling off to the east. The oxen's heads went up, and their nostrils flared.

"Quick—stop em' so we can unhook!" David's voice was urgent.

They unfastened the oxen from the plow and led them away from the track. David stood in front of the lead team and talked to them softly and slowly. Walker stood beside the second team and rubbed the neck of the near ox. "Easy, boy. Just a train. Won't hurt you a'tall. Easy, boy. Easy."

The train whistled for the road crossing, and an ox in the third team started forward. David laid his long pole directly across the faces of the lead team. "Whoa, easy now, easy, easy." The leaders looked startled but didn't bolt. The train passed to the west, a tower of smoke blowing east behind it. David and Walker led the oxen back to the plow and continued plowing.

As they finished their round, a flock of prairie chickens flew from west to east, fast and low, cackling. Another, even noisier flock followed. David stopped, looked up, and said, "Something's not right. They don't never fly cackling like that." He looked west, where the birds had come from. A curtain of smoke was rising from a field along the tracks, a mile or so away.

"It's a prairie fire. Comin' right this way! Quick, go open the gate an' drive all the stock into the road and toward the crick. Get some sacks, an' wet em' real good. Wet your socks and pant legs too. I'll look after the teams." He tipped the plow on its side and goaded the oxen toward the machinery and posts in the corner of pasture, at a trot.

Walker rushed to open the gate. A fox ran in front of him, so close that he could have grabbed its tail. As he herded the cows, horses, and sheep toward the gate, he smelled the first whiff of smoke. His father was pulling the yokes off the oxen and shouting and slapping at them until they joined the other stock Walker was herding toward the woods and the creek.

David grabbed a handful of grain sacks and sprinted to the creek, passing the oxen and sheep. He plunged in, frantically pushing the sacks under the water. When Walker caught up, his father yelled, "Jump in. It ain't deep. Then come with me. We gotta be ready to save the machinery and posts in case the fire jumps the break." Walker stepped into the creek gingerly, and he stepped out again and ran, pant legs dripping and shoes sloshing, behind his father up the hill. The smoke was thick now. It burned his nostrils. He heard the fire crackling as it advanced.

The machinery, fence posts, and wire stood in one corner of the newly fenced pasture, just inside the firebreak they'd burned two days earlier. His father took the bandanna from his pocket and handed it to Walker. "Here, tie this around your face, so you don't eat so much smoke. Run and get next to the firebreak, and be ready to beat an' stomp out any embers that jump it. Stay close enough so's you can see me. If the whole pasture starts to burn, get upwind onto the burned ground right quick, wrap a wet sack around you, and lie down!" David was yelling now, in order to be heard above the roar of the wall of fire bearing down on them. He handed Walker two wet sacks and kept two.

The fire bore down on the outer edge of the break, coming faster than a person could run. Walker stood in its path, transfixed. A pair of rabbits ran toward him, so close that he thought they would hit his feet. He saw terror in their eyes as he coughed from the smoke, and he felt a moist warmth in his pants.

Then his father yelled, "Look behind you. There's an ember. Beat it out!" Walker turned to see a circle of fire, no bigger than his hand, growing in the dry bluestem. He smothered it with one blow of a wet sack. His father was running from one new spot of fire to another, beating and stomping. A shower of smoking grass dropped beside Walker. He was on it almost before it hit the ground. Then more blew in—so many that he lost count. He was an automaton now, flailing and stomping. His father was a dim, frantic outline in the smoke, flailing the wet sacks and stomping on tiny new burns. Walker felt the fire's heat burning exposed skin on his forehead and hands, and he turned his back to it as he sought out and extinguished tiny tufts of flaming grass that the flying embers had ignited. It was so hot; he imagined that hell might be like this.

Then it was gone. They stood panting and coughing in the unburned island of pasture, streams of sweat pouring down their red, sooty faces, and watched the retreating wall of fire jump the road and build again, the flames leaping and spiraling thirty feet into the air, racing east, away from their land.

David put his arm on Walker's shoulder. "You did great, Son. I never coulda saved it alone. Now let's round up the stock, before they get clear to Altoona, and put 'em back in the pasture. Then we'll call it a day, go home an' clean up. You smell like you need to." Walker nodded, wiped the sweat from his face, and stared at the black streaks on the damp bandanna as he felt his heart pounding.

The next morning, they were up at 4:30 and resumed plowing at daylight. The corn, oats, and wheat they planted grew rapidly in the fertile, black ground, and the Beatys, like their neighbors, dreamed of a bountiful harvest as summer approached.

* * *

At noon on a warm day in June, Walker came from the field where he had been cultivating corn, carrying some huge grasshoppers in his hand. "Look, everybody. A few of these things started flying in from the west this morning. They don't look anything like the hoppers we usually have." He opened his fist slightly so the family could see the large, brownish-green insects struggling to get free, then closed his hand quickly, went to the door, tossed them out, and washed off the brown liquid they'd spit on his hand.

During dinner, Nettie stopped eating and asked, "What's that noise on the roof? Sounds like something scrapin' the shingles."

Nancy looked through the screen door toward the clothesline and shrieked, "My sheets! They're all over my clean sheets!" She leaped up and rushed out so fast that her chair tipped over.

David shouted after her, "Locusts! Come back, Nancy!" but she didn't stop. The second she was off the porch, grasshoppers settled on her hair, face, and apron. She ran through them toward the clothesline, waving her hands in front of her face. There were half a dozen locusts on the nearest clothespin. She brushed them off, loosened the pin, and grabbed the end of the sheet beneath it. The cloth fragmented like tissue paper. The hoppers kept chewing as the pieces fell. Nancy stood transfixed for a second or two, horror all over her face, watching thousands of brown jaws devour the sheets she'd just washed. Then she ran for the house, screaming.

Food sat uneaten as the Beatys gathered at the windows and gaped. Their bright green landscape had morphed into a greenish brown sea of undulating motion. The shade trees turned from summer's lush greenery to fall's stark limbs and branches as the family stared. The horde ate almost everything: crops, gardens, laundry drying on the line, grain sacks, a leather horse halter that hung on a peg outside the barn door. Even the smooth, wooden peg was roughened by their gnawing teeth.

By evening, they were gone from the countryside they'd ruined, flying east in a cloud that obscured the sun for those awestruck Iowans who watched them appear from the west.

The Beatys and their neighbors surveyed a devastated landscape. Every green plant had been eaten. The sheep and cattle that had been in the lush grass of the pasture stood by the barn, bleating and bellowing from hunger. David listened to their mournful calls and wondered if there was enough hay in the barn to feed them. He, Nancy, and their children had a somber family discussion. "How'll we get along with no garden, no crops, and no pasture? We don't have any canned food at all." Nancy wiped her eyes.

"I don't know anything to do but buy some hay from the neighbors to feed the livestock, replant quick as we can, and hope for a good rain soon. We have to have faith in the Almighty and ask him to be merciful. I sure hope the neighbors will sell us enough seed to replant everything." David's words were more optimistic than he really felt.

They fed the livestock the hay that David bought from Sam Higgins, and they replanted their corn, wheat, and oats, working from before daylight through the long twilight. Everyone anticipated a late, lean harvest—or maybe no harvest at all, if the insect horde came again that season.

To replace the sheets that the locusts ate, Nancy patched old ones she'd already consigned to the rag basket. David and Walker repaired their old grain drill instead of buying a new one as David had planned. Timely rains nourished the replanted crops, the hayfields, and the pastures. The trees grew new leaves. And the fall frost held off long enough for most of the late-planted corn to mature enough to be safe from the frost, when it came. But the voracious horde appeared again the next summer to ravage the landscape and leave a lot of farmers struggling to feed their families and livestock and pay their mortgages.

As repeated attacks of grasshoppers and low prices strained the resources of the farmers around Altoona, David used money from the farms he sold in Ohio to buy land from some who couldn't pay their mortgages. Over the next two years, he bought four farms—most at fire-sale prices and all within a few miles of Altoona—and rented them to other farmers.

Cropland in winter on a farm north of Des Moines, Iowa, once owned by David Beaty

To David Beaty from Armstrong Taylor, Dated Sept. 22 1868, Filed Feb. 12 1869, 80 acres

To David Beaty from Andrew Jack, Dated March 28, Filed April 2 1869, 120 acres, $1,600

To David Beaty from [illegible], Dated Nov. 27 1869, 80 acres, $500

To David Beaty from Foster, Dated Dec 20 1870, 40 acres, $400

—General Index of Land Records, Polk County, Iowa

David's purchases gave him the dual roles of farmer and landlord. After decades of hard farm work, he enjoyed the change, especially since Walker, now seventeen, was taking over most of the work on the home farm.

Nancy and her three stepdaughters took advantage of the frequent train service between Altoona and Des Moines to enjoy life in the state's biggest city and center of government. As the 1870s unfolded, the three sisters were courted by and married to men they'd met in Des Moines. David tried to interest his sons-in-law in farming, but with no success. One became a teacher, another became a banker, and the third operated a butcher shop.

With his father away a good deal supervising the renters on his other farms, Walker developed an intense interest in the cattle, especially after his father bought a bull and two cows that had been imported from Herefordshire, England. The muscular, beefy conformation and the distinctive pattern of white hair on their heads and necks and dark red hair over the rest of their bodies contrasted with the boney shapes and haphazard color patterns of their other cattle. He watched with pride as the small herd of purebred Herefords he helped care for increased in number year by year.

Chapter 21
New Ventures

The periodic grasshopper attacks aided David in his search for good land to buy at bargain prices. By 1880, he had extended his landholdings into Dallas County, which adjoined Polk County on the west. He, Nancy, Walker, and Charlie moved from Altoona to a new house on a 160-acre farm that he'd bought near the tiny town of Waukee, northwest of Des Moines.

After they'd moved, David spearheaded the local temperance movement there and bought the only tavern in Waukee.

America Shearer and Samuel Shearer to David Beatty

Lot Twenty three Block Ten First Addition Town of Waukee Iowa

Filed for Record the 23rd day of April A.D. 1881 at 10 o'clock A.M.

—*Village Record of Deeds, Dallas County, Iowa*

As soon as he had the deed and the key, David, with Charlie along for company, drove his horse and buggy, mostly at a trot, the six miles from the tree-shaded Dallas County courthouse in the small village of Adel east toward Waukee. His first stop was Jed Jacobson's general store beside the railroad tracks on Waukee's Main Street.

David smiled and greeted the tall, blue-eyed proprietor who stood behind the counter, "Mornin', Jed. I need two good, strong hasps, some screws, and two padlocks." Jed moved quickly to fill the order.

"What you aim to lock up, David, your new barn?"

"No, a building I just bought here in Waukee."

Jed looked perplexed, but something in David's demeanor warned him not to ask more questions. He hustled to gather the hardware and take the money.

David and Charlie drove south a couple of blocks, stopped behind the building he'd just purchased, and tied the sweating horse to the rail. Charlie was mystified. Here was his father, the vociferous enemy of demon rum, buying a tavern and rushing to open it. Charlie stood, hands in his pockets, and watched.

"All right, Charlie. I need you to help me." David unlocked the back door and then the front door and pulled it open. "Do just like I do." He grabbed two bottles of whiskey off the back bar and walked briskly out the front door to the edge of the board sidewalk. A farmer and his wife who were driving a team and buggy along the street glanced toward him and waved. He waved back, and with hardly a pause, he opened the bottles and inverted them to drain into the gutter. Charlie stood stock-still, uncomprehending.

"Come on, Charlie. Grab some bottles an' dump 'em."

Charlie read his father's face, grabbed two bottles, and ran out the door. He paused for an instant to inhale, not for the first time, the aroma of the trickling whiskey, and shook his head. As he helped empty the tavern's stock, he took a long breath each time he was alone on the sidewalk. When there was an opportunity, he slipped a pint inside his shirt and rebuttoned it quickly.

Passersby began to stop. At first, they watched in silent amazement. Then a tall man with a red handlebar mustache said, "Seein' as how you don't want that whiskey, why don't you give it to me an' my friends, 'stead o' wastin' it like that?"

David didn't even look up and continued emptying bottles. A

tall, thin woman with two small, barefoot children broke the silence. "Thank you, Mr. Beaty! I been wantin' somebody to do something about this awful place. Now maybe my husband will come home sober once in a while. An' maybe he'll bring home enough money to buy shoes for the kids."

David nodded and smiled as he worked. "You're more'n welcome, ma'am. My father squandered his money on whiskey too. Left his family in debt when he died."

As the crowd of onlookers grew, David gathered empty bottles, carried them behind the building, and broke them. While Charlie finished that job, David screwed the hasps on the doors, closed them, and snapped the padlocks.

"You aren't gonna just close it up fer good, are ya?" the man with the red mustache asked, overtones of incredulity in his voice.

David thrust the key into his pocket and looked the questioner straight in the eye. "You bet your boots I am." Then he strode around the building to join Charlie, who was kneeling behind the buggy, attempting to be invisible. The crowd began to leave, some shaking their heads and muttering, others voicing quiet approval.

David and Charlie were the focus of everyone's attention as they drove north through Waukee and across the railroad tracks on their way home. The train for Des Moines was at the station just off Main Street, and the platform was crowded with freight and passengers. People looked their way, then lowered their eyes and whispered to those nearby. Charlie felt a flush of heat rise up his neck and across his face. He looked down between his feet and then stole a glance at his father. David sat straight and tall, holding the reins of the tired and docile mare as tightly as a stagecoach driver with six wild horses in front of him. His cheeks were a steely red that made the pockmarks as vivid as boils. Charlie squeezed his right arm close to his side to keep the bottle of whiskey from bouncing and wished he could jump out of the buggy and onto the departing train. When they got home, he hid the bottle under the corncrib floor; he threw it away, empty, two days later.

As he worked around the farm that summer, Charlie listened for the whistles of passing trains and felt a longing rise in his chest as the sound faded away. In the fall, he came home at suppertime after a visit to Des Moines and announced, "I've got a job and rented a room in Des Moines." His parents and the hired men looked up, startled.

"Startin' next week, I'll be working in the Wabash car shops, but they're gonna put on more trains, and they say I might get to be a conductor by spring."

David and Nancy looked at each other.

"Good for you, Charlie." Nancy's voice mixed pride with sadness. "Is it a nice room, I hope?"

David, who still harbored hopes that his youngest son would be a farmer, frowned and asked, "How's it pay?"

"Kinda low at first, but I talked to three or four conductors, an' they say they get paid good and get some tips from the passengers. Do you think Uncle Rob Crawford and Aunt Melissa would put in a good word for me about a conductor job with the Wabash's head man at Valley Junction after I get started?"

Nancy looked hopeful. "First you'll have to prove you're a good, dependable worker. Then they might. Now that Rob's got his own bank, he's helping lots of folks. I just wish he and Mel could have some children."

David studied his broad-shouldered, chunky, eighteen-year-old son and noted how young he appeared and how much he looked like Nancy. "You sure you don't want to stay right here and farm? We got a whole lot more land than Walker can handle. When one of the renters leaves, you could move right in and be on your own."

Charlie shook his head. "Farming's not for me, even though you got a lot of good land. Too much hard work and too chancy. Bugs always eat the crops. Or it doesn't rain when we need it, or it hails the crops into the ground. I'm goin' into something that's new and growin'." David's face showed disappointment, even though he tried to hide it.

* * *

Monday morning, as he walked toward the rooming house in Des Moines, Charlie surveyed the roundhouses, tracks, depots, coal tipples, water towers, stockyards, and warehouses that filled the low plain on the north side of the Raccoon River. Arrayed around the edges were rooming and boarding houses, cheek by jowl with the small homes of families who worked for the railroads. On a hill a few blocks to the north, the ornate Iowa State Capitol building exuded prosperity and growth, much of it based on the products of the rich land around Des Moines and the commerce the railroads carried. Charlie sensed that he'd entered a flourishing world of the future.

The unpainted, three-story house at 120 Sixth Street was sooty gray. When Charlie walked in, leaning to the left to counter the weight of the heavy bag in his right hand, the whistling, chuffing, and clanging at the Wabash Railroad roundhouse across the dirt street were drowned out by a host of loud voices around the dining room.

A short, fleshy woman with gray hair pinned into a bun at her neck looked up and addressed him. "You're Charlie, the new kid, right?"

Charlie nodded to his new landlady.

"Your bed's in the corner of the last bedroom, third floor." She shouted to be heard above the din of voices. "Lug your stuff up, and get back down here right quick before these hogs eat everything. I swear I lose money on every one of 'em, they eat so much."

When Charlie came hustling down the worn wooden stairs, Mrs. Pacowsky was putting a chipped plate and worn silverware in front of a battered chair. "Set here, kid! Joe, shoot them spuds and beans down here, ya hear me? An' don't none o' youse guys steal any on the way."

Joe, a stocky man with olive skin, looked Charlie up and down, glanced toward a tall man with red hair and a bushy mustache, and winked as he picked up the nearly empty bowl of potatoes with an elaborate gesture and handed it to the man on his left. The man with the mustache winked back. Joe smiled an ingratiating smile at the landlady and bowed his head in her direction. "Anything you say, Mother Pacowsky. Anything you say."

Mrs. Pacowsky put her large, red hands on the tops of her wide hips, glared at Joe, snorted with disgust, and stomped toward the kitchen. Charlie slipped into the chair and was ready when the dented tin bowl with two small boiled potatoes reached him. He took one and glanced hesitantly at the man next to him. The man nodded, and Charlie took the other.

"What line ya workin' for, kid?" the man named Joe asked.

Charlie stopped mashing a potato with his fork. "I'm startin' at the Wabash tomorrow. In the car shop."

Joe winked at the man with the mustache again. "Real good. We'll start ya off right. Won't we, Red?" Red grinned and nodded as he gulped a big spoonful of tapioca pudding.

The next morning, when Charlie walked into the Wabash Railroad's maintenance shop and reported to the foreman, he saw Joe and Red working on a caboose that was up on blocks with its wheels off. The foreman, a short, burly man with a curved scar on his right cheek, eyed Charlie carefully, then stepped close and shouted above the din, "All right, start by helpin' Joe, that fella over there." The foreman waved a beefy arm toward Charlie's new acquaintance. "He'll learn ya what ta do an' how ta do it. An' don't let me catch you standin' round. If I do, I'll fire ya on the spot."

"Yes, sir. I'll work real hard." Charlie nodded, bowed ever so slightly, pulled the left strap of his new overalls tighter, and hustled toward the caboose where Joe and Red were packing grease around an axle with wooden paddles. A wheel swung slowly back and forth on a chain hoist beside Red's right elbow.

"I'm supposed to help you guys." Charlie's voice was loud but a little tentative.

Joe glanced up, a grease-covered paddle in his hand. "Way you can help is to go find us a left-handed skyhook. Somebody stole ours, an' we gotta have it to put these wheels back on." He paused, appraised Charlie's face, and liked the look of innocent eagerness he saw. "You'll prob'ly find one way in the back of the shop, or maybe out in the yards somewheres. Now step lively, kid. An' don't come back without it."

Charlie looked puzzled, but after a moment, he set off at a trot. Joe jabbed his elbow into Red's ribs. "We're gonna have us some fun until that kid wises up." They laughed and continued to pack grease onto the axle as Charlie ran around the shop and yard, asking everyone he encountered if they had seen a left-handed skyhook. Most of the men he asked laughed out loud, and Charlie finally realized that he was the butt of a huge joke. It was not the last time he was a victim, but his pride made him persevere amid the hazing, noise, danger, and dust of the shop, even as he planned and arranged for a better job.

Early the next spring, Charlie walked into Mrs. Pacowsky's house, carrying a new railroad conductor's uniform and two white shirts. Four men who were playing euchre looked up. One whistled in surprise.

"You get promoted, Charlie? How'd ya do that so quick? Know some big shot?" Charlie smiled, shrugged, and walked upstairs. He didn't really know a big shot, but he'd borrowed one thousand dollars from his father to put into the project that the head conductor for the Wabash and some of the other men who lived with Mrs. Pacowsky had organized to finance, at exorbitant rates, immigrants from Italy and Germany. If he got the two thousand they'd promised him in a year, so much the better. At least the head conductor had seen to it that he got the next conductor job that came open. The loan had gotten him out of the dirt, noise, and heavy lifting of the car shops, and that was what mattered. He hung the blue wool coat and pants in the wardrobe that Mrs. Pacowsky had added to his room, tried the cap on for size, and unfolded the white shirts and tried to smooth out the wrinkles. Maybe if he paid her, she'd iron them for him, like she did for some of the other conductors.

The next morning, he was following the head conductor of the Wabash line's passenger train from Des Moines to Chicago through the cars, watching everything the man did. As the train passed his father's original farmland northeast of Altoona, he stole a quick look out the south window. Walker and his younger brother, Davey, were planting corn, their heads bent and collars turned up against the cold wind. Charlie was elated to have a job that took him out of the hard work and uncertainty of farming, and he paid rapt attention to everything his boss said and did. This was a job with glamour, adventure, and romance. Who knew where it might take him?

After Charlie got to be a conductor, he turned into a real hell-raiser. He and some of his fellow conductors became such regulars at the pool halls and bars around the railroad district that the proprietors kept a close eye on them and never, ever extended them credit. That wariness did not extend to some local young women. They flitted around the young men like hummingbirds dueling for hollyhock blossoms. Charlie had to move to a room at the Masonic Temple after Mrs. Pacowsky caught him sneaking one of the women up the back stairs late one night. He was delighted to find that the Masons weren't as strict.

The scheme to finance immigrants and then collect exorbitant repayments from them actually paid off. The enterprise didn't double Charlie's investment as he'd been promised, but the organizers did pay him $1,627. He repaid the thousand-dollar loan from David with interest and spent the rest within a week. His hangover lasted almost another week. The Wabash railroad fired him for his unplanned absence. He eventually got a job as conductor for the Waterloo, St. Louis & Pacific.

After a few months on the new line, Charlie had accumulated a group of new buddies. He'd also acquired enough gambling debts to consume two months' wages. Most of it he owed to Alex McVicar, a dark, big-boned Scot who spent his free hours in the back of the Arcade saloon in the railroad district of Des Moines, playing poker and sipping whiskey. McVicar claimed that he made more money there than he did on the railroad. Part of it came from Charlie, who never learned to keep a poker face when playing cards.

One night, after Charlie had lost twenty dollars to Alex, his old friend Joe from Mrs. Pacowsky's rooming house got him aside.

"That damn Scotchman sure wins a lot at poker, don't he?" He put his arm on Charlie's shoulder. "Can I buy ya a beer?"

"Yeah, he seems to always get the right cards." Charlie nodded and looked glumly back to the table, where Alex was dealing to a new set of victims.

Joe came back with two beers. "Ya remember the good deal we let you in on last year? Well, I just got a letter from my Uncle Reuben, an' he's got something startin' up that sounds even better." Charlie's looks brightened. Joe lifted his glass, drank a swallow, and continued.

"He's in real estate. Lives in Florida. An' he's got a chance to buy a thousand acres of land on the ocean right near Palm Beach. You prob'ly never heard of that town, but it's a real up an' coming place, from what Uncle Reuben writes. Lots of rich folks from the North wantin' to build there, then come down an' stay fer the winter. Anyhow, if he can get $100,000 together and buy this thousand acres, he says he'll be able to make 2,500 lots that'll sell for as much as a thousand dollars each. So if you could put in some money like you done before, I'll see that you get to be a partner, an' before long, you won't have to be ridin' trains. What do ya say to that?" Joe took a breath and drained his glass. It was the longest speech he'd ever made.

Charlie studied his glass, and then he gave Joe a long look. "I'm kind of short right now, but I'll let you know come Monday." He drank his beer and started to walk away. "Oh, by the way, Joe, thanks for the beer, and for the offer." He went out into the hot night and watched the fireflies as he walked toward his room at the Masonic Temple, thinking about how he could get his father to loan him a lot of money.

Early the next morning, Charlie walked into David and Nancy's house.

"Charlie, what a surprise! What brings you home today, and so early, too?" Nancy stopped washing dishes, dried her hands, and gave her son a smile and a hug. "Have you had breakfast? I can make you some real easy."

"Thanks, but I ate before I came." Charlie sat down at the kitchen table as his mother resumed washing dishes. He looked around for David. "Where's Pa? I need to talk to him."

"He and the hired man are moving the cattle to the north pasture. He should be back in a half hour or so. How's the job, and how's Des Moines? I haven't been there in quite a while."

"Job's fine. The railroad is putting on another train to Omaha next month. And I got a five-dollar tip from some really rich man the other day. A whole five dollars! Couldn't believe it."

Nancy scrubbed the black iron skillet and then poured the dishwater around the hollyhocks outside the back door. "You must be saving money, what with the railroad growing and the tips and all. It's always good to have some put aside for rainy days."

Charlie sneaked a cookie out of the jar and ate it while her back was turned. "I see Pa walking up the lane. Guess I'll go meet him. Cook some extra dinner for me." He let the screen door slam behind him as he walked toward his father. "Morning, Pa. I need to talk to you."

"Hello, Charlie. Surprised to see you here so early." David noticed how excited his son appeared and wondered if Charlie had been fired again. "That railroad job still suit you?"

"Oh, it's just fine. What I came to talk to you about is a land deal—looks like we could both make a whole lot of money if we bought in. I'd be the partner in the company, but I'd share the profits fifty-fifty with you if you'll make me a loan. Like you did last year."

Charlie and David had reached the barn. David gathered two milking stools for them to sit on as they talked. "Let me sit down. My knees hurt after I walk a long ways. Now, tell me exactly what you have in mind."

As his father listened Charlie laid out the scheme as he had heard it from Joe. He closed by asking for a loan of $15,000. He could see from his father's expression that the proposition astounded him.

Finally David responded, "Land prices are way down. That'd mean I'd have to mortgage every farm I own, and use up all my savings besides." He shook his head at Charlie's audacity.

"But Pa, it would bring you at least ten to one for every dollar you put in ... maybe more. Think what you and Nancy could do then—stop farming, even sail around the world if you wanted."

"Back in '49, when I went to California, I got enough sailing to last me a couple o' lifetimes. I'll have to talk to Nancy about your notion and think about it a lot." David stood up and tossed the milking stool into the corner.

Charlie sensed that there was nothing to be gained by more talk. Looking crestfallen, he walked toward the hired man, who was coming from the pasture.

When David returned to the kitchen, Nancy stopped kneading bread dough and smiled. "Isn't it wonderful Charlie came home today?"

"Sure is a surprise. After he got that railroad job, we almost never see him. He's home because he wants a big favor." David poured a cup of coffee from the pot at the back of the cookstove and sat down. "He wants us to loan him $15,000 to invest in a land development down in Florida. Says it will pay off ten to one. I'd like to be part of it and help him out, but I'd sure hate to mortgage all our land to do it." David drank a swallow of coffee and shook his head. "Don't know just what to do."

Nancy put down the dough to rise on the breadboard and wiped the flour off her hands as she faced David. "You've helped Guilon, and Ted and Walker, and they're mostly on their feet financially now, so maybe you should help Charlie. He's a nice boy, even if he doesn't want to farm."

David drank more coffee. "I don't know. I helped Ted and Guilon with loans for things I knew about, and that were close to home. When I tried to help Walker with that deal in Colorado, we both lost out. This deal sounds chancy. And it's a long ways away." He shook his head and tossed the remaining coffee in his cup out onto the grass. "I'm goin' to see if the corn in the back forty needs cultivating while I think this over.

At noon, when the family was gathering for dinner, Nancy gave Charlie another hug and asked, "What's this land development you want us to be part of?"

Charlie described it once again and emphasized how profitably the last project he'd borrowed money for had worked out. Then David arrived, washed his hands and face, and sat down at the table, which was laden with freshly baked bread, mashed potatoes, gravy, roast pork, peas that Nancy had just picked and shelled, and lettuce fresh from the garden. For dessert, she served freshly picked strawberries with cream.

David slid back his chair after dinner and faced his youngest son. "Well, Charlie, I've thought about your proposition all morning, but I'm still skeptical. It's so far away, and how do we know everybody in it's on the up-and-up?"

"Joe is the guy who told me about it. He's the one who let me in on the immigrant deal last year. Remember how well that paid off? I've known him ever since I went to work for the railroad, and he's a straight shooter, even though he teased me some when I first started."

Nancy put her hand on David's arm. "It sounds like something that would be good for all of us. Why don't you talk to the banker about getting mortgages on the farms? You could pay them off real quick after the money comes back in, and have a lot left over."

There was a long silence. Then David said, "Well, Charlie, I'll see what I can do."

On Monday night, Charlie went back to Mrs. Pacowsky's and sought out Joe. As they walked beside the Raccoon River, listening to the crickets and cicadas, Charlie said, "I talked to my father about this Florida land deal. He's been buyin' and sellin' land for nearly forty years. Owns four or five farms. Bought another sixty acres or so just five years ago. He's interested, and if he can borrow against them, I think you an' your Uncle Reuben could count on something from me."

Joe nodded and slapped Charlie on the back. "It'll be absolutely the best land deal you ever made, believe me!"

Two weeks later, Charlie hid the certificate for $10,000 of stock and the letter naming him as a partner in the Empire Land and Development Company, Inc. in his trunk, inside the album of pictures of his favorite female friends. He looked forward to the huge windfall, and his work as a train conductor seemed like an ephemeral episode as he dreamed of the future.

* * *

David and Nancy always held a family picnic on the Fourth of July. Each Fourth at sunrise, David would hoist the oversized American flag he'd had made in 1860 to symbolize his support of President Lincoln and the Union. By the early 1890s, it was several stars short of being up to date, but he wouldn't hear of replacing it.

Then he'd catch as many young chickens as Nancy thought they needed to feed the guests, chop off their heads, scald them, and pick off the feathers. They expected a big crowd this year, so he killed and picked feathers off ten. Ted and his wife, Anne, who had moved west from Fairfield and lived just a couple of miles away, came early to help with the preparations. David's sister Melissa and her husband, Rob Crawford, who owned one bank and managed another, would come from Des Moines as usual. So would David's sister Alice and her husband, John Schooley, who owned a meat market. This year, David and Nancy had invited Lije and Julia Reames. David and

Nancy hoped Charlie would show up, but they weren't sure, given his schedule and his priorities.

But Charlie strolled in a little late as the gathered family sat at tables under the big oaks in the front yard, feasting on the fried chicken, mashed potatoes and gravy, ham, peas, green beans, and an abundance of other food that the women had laid out. Melissa made a place for him on the bench between herself and her husband, Rob. She had a special fondness for her half-brother. He was fourteen years younger, and as the years passed with no children of her own, she thought of him more and more as a son, even though their paths in Des Moines never crossed.

Melissa smiled at her half-brother as she welcomed him. "I'm so glad you got the day off so you could come, Charlie. The railroad doesn't usually give you the day off on a holiday."

"I'm getting a little more seniority, so I was able to get off this year. First time since I switched from the Wabash. It's tough startin' at the bottom twice." Charlie speared another chicken leg off the plate, spooned more mashed potatoes and gravy beside it, and took huge bites of both. "Ma's fried chicken sure does taste good."

"Are you going to work for the railroad all your life? I'd think you'd like to do something where you'd be your own boss." Melissa wiped her hands primly on a white cloth napkin and waited while Charlie chewed the big bite of chicken.

"Don't plan to. I'm a partner in a land development in Florida, an' when it pays off, I won't have to work at all." He started to wipe his mouth with his sleeve but remembered in time and used a napkin. Rob Crawford, seated on his left, overheard Charlie's reply, and his eyes widened.

"Did you say you were a partnah in a Florida land company?" He leaned toward Charlie with a frown. His surprise accentuated his English accent as he continued, "A numbah of men have come to my banks, wanting me to invest in them, but I'm rawtha skeptical of them all. I have reliable reports that several land companies there buy swampland and sell it, sight unseen, to rich folks in New Yawk and Philadelphia. So I nevah invest any of the banks' money, or mine." He paused, and then he looked directly at Charlie. "How'd you get the money to invest, if I may ask?"

Charlie took a bite of beans and replied casually. "Borrowed it from Pa. He mortgaged his farms to get it. I'm sure it'll pay off real big."

Rob shook his head in disbelief and looked away.

A baby's wail erupted at the other end of the table. Melissa turned her attention toward her sister Nettie's newest daughter, three-month-old Grace. "I'll be glad to take her, Nettie, while you finish eating." She put out her arms. Nettie handed the girl to her sister, and Melissa soon had her lying quietly over her shoulder as she walked back and forth, humming softly.

The growing clan of children from the Schooley and Madden families chased each other around the lawn and among the lilac bushes. Lije Reames joined them in the tag game, laughing as they caught him, and pretending he couldn't catch any of them when he was "It."

Julia watched her husband, a look of disgust growing on her round face. "Lije Reames, stop acting like a kid, and come sit down, right now!" Lije ignored his wife, as he habitually did, and played more tag, then gathered two laughing children in his arms and carried them, squirming, back to the table for more ice cream and pie. Julia snorted in disgust and started helping Nancy gather dirty dishes.

While the women cleared the tables and washed dishes, the men gathered under an elm. Cigars and pipes kept most of the bugs at a distance. The talk was of cattle, horses, crops, weather, and finally, prices. When that last topic was broached, everyone turned to the banker, Rob Crawford.

He spoke deliberately, as always. "As best I can discern, this country is headed towahd a panic as bad as the one in the 1840s, perhaps worse. I believe farm prices are going to plunge in a year or so. Therefoah, I'm not writing any new farm mortgages at all, and being extremely conservative when I invest our depositahs' funds."

Lije Reames took a deep pull on his cigar. "If you're right, Rob, it's a good thing I just sold the farm. Got my money out just in time." He exhaled a plume of smoke and looked pleased.

As Melissa and Rob Crawford were driving away in their new buggy, Rob flicked the reins on the backs of his matched pair of driving horses and shook his head, "I'm worried about David and

Nancy. That greedy fool Charlie has, in all likelihood, put his parents in a very precarious financial situation."

Melissa smoothed her skirt as she replied. "Pa's always done real well buying and selling land. I expect he will this time too." Rob shook his head in vigorous disagreement. They rode home in silence.

* * *

A few weeks after the picnic, Charlie strolled toward the Masonic Temple, whistling. He'd just arrived from his trip as a conductor on a run from St. Louis, and he was looking forward to joining his friends at the Arcade saloon for some beers. When he saw Joe pacing up and down the sidewalk, looking over his shoulder, Charlie waved and yelled, "Howdy, Joe. How's things?"

Joe put a finger to his lips. "Not so loud. We gotta be quiet. And move fast."

"Why? What's the matter?" He spoke softly as he set down his bag.

"The postal inspector's on our tail, an' we gotta get out of sight right quick!"

Charlie's jaw dropped. "How come? Some problem with the Florida land deal?"

"You bet! Uncle Reuben mailed a bunch of letters and flyers about that land. Some folks bought lots that turned out to be in a swamp, and they're hopping mad. The postal inspector's got him in jail for mail fraud, an' now they're comin' after all his partners. We gotta get out of the country real fast, or we'll be in jail just like him!"

Charlie's face and voice announced his panic. "We do! Where'll we go?"

Chapter 22
Walker, Ella, and the West

On a cold March morning in 1881, Walker woke up coughing. His throat felt tighter than usual. It was the way he woke up many mornings, but he had hoped that it wouldn't happen today. He wanted to be fresh and rested when he met Ella and the rest of the Reames family at their house in Altoona for the wedding.

For as long as he could remember, asthma had been a curse on his life. After a vicious spell of coughing, he rolled out of bed, pulled wool socks and heavy work clothes over his long underwear, and went out to milk the cows and feed the pigs, sheep, horses, and chickens on one of his father's farms near Altoona. Getting outside in the cold dawn let him breathe easier, or at least he thought so.

When he finished the chores, Walker went inside, made himself some breakfast, and ate it quickly. By a quarter to eleven, he was dressed in his best and approaching the Reames's big two-story house in Altoona. His father and stepmother, David and Nancy, and his sister Melissa and her husband, Rob Crawford, were already there. His other sisters and two younger brothers, David, Jr. (twenty-five) and Charlie (seventeen), came later.

When Walker arrived, Nancy looked at her stepson and nodded approval. The six-year-old who had welcomed her into the family when she married David in 1860 had endeared himself to her then, and she had never forgotten. She'd come to love him as she tended him on nights when his asthma left him gasping and almost unable to breathe. Today, he was grown up and dressed in high style in the clothes she'd helped him select: dark gray wool pants with narrow, lighter gray stripes; a dark gray single-breasted jacket that was buttoned high across his chest; and a high-collared white shirt that reached well up on his neck. She smiled as she realized that he looked just like David must have at age twenty-five. The dark hair and mustache, hazel eyes, wide ears, and oval face—he was a reincarnation of his father, with the heavy black eyebrows of his mother added for emphasis. And he was nice, to boot. She gave him a warm, welcoming smile.

David remembered how nervous he had been at his own wedding thirty-seven years earlier, back in Ohio. And he wondered if Ella had picked up her mother's scolding, criticizing traits. *Sure hope Ella treats Walker better than Julia treats Lije,* he thought. *Doesn't seem to bother him any, though.*

There was a knock at the front door. David watched Julia Reames bustle to open it and welcome the minister. Then she motioned for David and Nancy to come and greet the Reverend Howe.

Exactly at eleven o'clock, a beaming Lije Reames emerged from an upstairs bedroom with Ella on his arm and two of her sisters who were serving as bridesmaids beside her. She was a glowing eighteen in the tight-bodiced linen gown and white veil. Her heart, already beating fast, quickened when she saw Walker. He looked handsome in that new suit. And the blue cravat with the pin made from gold that his father had mined in California set it off wonderfully. She knew he was a steady, hard worker who pleased her father. He didn't satisfy her mother, but nobody could. That was one reason that she was eager to marry—to get out of her mother's household. She admired Walker's parents: David, the stoic, hardworking adventurer, investor, and patriot; and quiet Nancy, who was as accepting as her own mother was demanding. And she loved Walker. The future thrilled her.

CERTIFICATE OF MARRIAGE

STATE OF IOWA, POLK COUNTY. March 9th 1881

This Certifies That on the Ninth day of March
A.D. 1881 at Altoona, Iowa in said County,
according to law, and by authority, I duly Joined
in Marriage Walker Beaty and Ella M. Reames,
Given under my hand the ninth day of March,
A.D. 1881.

W. E. Howe, Minister of the Gospel

IN THE PRESENCE OF David Cree, R. A. Crawford

While the wedding ceremony had been small, the reception was not. Julia Reames saw the reception as an opportunity to invite everyone who knew them or the Beatys, plus any other important people in or around Altoona whom she thought might be able to further her husband's hotel and drayage businesses. The sizeable hotel dining room was full, the wait staff attentive, the food and drink—non-alcoholic, in deference to David—abundant. Lije was in his element—expansive and generous with the cigars for the men and gracious to the women. Julia kept a worried eye on the entire operation and scolded her husband whenever something did not seem completely perfect to her. He listened impassively and then went on mingling and talking to everyone who was there.

After they had opened the gifts and the afternoon and party had waned, Walker and Ella slipped out and took the train to Des Moines. The next morning, Walker was ready to get back to the farm and the livestock he loved. Farming and family went well for the newlyweds the next three years as a daughter and then a son arrived. But Walker's asthma became more severe.

* * *

Early in 1884, David read an advertisement in the newspaper seeking investors in a foundry in Colorado. He cut it out and showed it to Nancy. "Here's what looks like a good opportunity for Walker and Ella, out west, where his asthma might clear up."

Nancy read it and looked surprised. "Why in the world would you want them to move way out there? I love having those two grandkids close by."

"But it looks like a real good chance to help Walker get over his asthma and to make some money at the same time. We ought to at least show this ad to him and Ella."

Nancy put down the ad with a frown. "I'd give anything if somebody could cure his asthma, but this sounds pretty risky. He doesn't know the first thing about a foundry. And why would somebody want to sell it, anyway, if it's making money?"

David's enthusiasm was not deterred. He'd gone west and done well. Men who'd been to Colorado had given him enthusiastic reports on the prospects there. Why not help Walker and Ella go to a place where the air was dry, and where Walker's asthma might go away, or at least abate? He went to see Lije Reames and found him receptive, to the point of agreeing to put up some of the money and talking to Walker and Ella about the idea. The two men went together to see their children. After they had listened as two-year-old Blanche jabbered, and admired two-month-old Bob as he cooed and gurgled, David shared their proposal.

"Lije and I have been talking about how to get you someplace where the asthma doesn't plague you all the time, and where you and we could make some money. We'll put up the money so you folks can move to Fort Collins in Colorado and buy into a foundry business I've been reading about. It looks like a goin' proposition, and from all I'm told, Colorado's booming. There's gold an' silver mines in the mountains. And not the little placer diggins like I worked years ago in California. These mines go right down into the rock, so they need machinery—the kind they have to make in a foundry that's close by."

Walker looked completely surprised. He'd never considered moving west, even though he'd heard his father talk about his hardships and adventures in the California goldfields many times.

"We'd have to think hard about a big move like that. I'd sure like to be in a place where the asthma don't give me fits, but I don't know the first thing about the foundry business. Besides, I'd hate to leave the farm an' all our relatives." He glanced at Ella, who looked just as surprised as her husband.

She handed the baby to Walker and looked her father in the eye. "That's a big decision. Let us have a few days to talk it over and think about it. We'll let you know."

David wasn't in a mood to wait. "It'd be a big change, all right, so think it over. But don't take too long. When I was certain of the big news from California years ago, I only waited two days before I told your mother I was goin'. Mining in Colorado looks like it's booming too."

* * *

Walker and Ella watched the shining white mountains out the train windows for two hours as the train huffed and rattled across the sparsely vegetated plain and coasted into the little town strung out along the Cache la Poudre River. The sky was bluer than any they'd ever seen. When they got off at Fort Collins, the wind pushed unfamiliar scents of pine and sage into their nostrils. They both felt far from home.

Ella took a deep breath of the exotic aromas. "Well, looks like we're here, safe and sound. Blanche, you hold tight to my hand, do ya hear?" She shifted Bob to her left hip and took another deep breath. Walker breathed the dry western air and felt his nose and throat opening up. He hustled to get their baggage.

Fort Collins had a slapdash look, like it had been hammered together by men who were in such a rush to get to the mines that they couldn't spare the time to build the town right. Ella felt a little dizzy and queasy, but she couldn't decide if it was from the long train ride or the altitude, or if maybe there was another baby on the way. She hoped it wasn't that. Another mouth to feed was something they didn't need right now.

She smelled the dry air with its hints of nearby sage and pine, looked at the dust the wind was pushing down the street, watched the river roaring by faster than she'd ever seen water move before, and felt like she was in a foreign country. The interval before Walker came with their trunks gave her an opportunity to reflect on her situation. *Shoulda known when I married Walker that he came from a restless family, always looking to move somewhere new. Well, whatever comes, we'll just make the best of it.*

As soon as he got the family settled in a hotel near the train station, Walker went to look over the foundry that he was about to buy into. Even though the foundry business was completely new to him, Walker decided that this one looked like a going concern. And Mr. and Mrs. Silcott, whose interests he was about to buy, the major owner, and the workers seemed honest and friendly. A few days later, after he and Ella had rented a house, Walker and the Silcotts went to the courthouse to complete the sale.

> **This Deed, made the Twenty Ninth day of May in the year of our Lord one thousand eight hundred and eighty four between William G. Silcott and Elga Silcott of the County of Larimer and State of Colorado, of the first part, and Walker Beaty of the County of Larimer and State of Colorado of the second part: WITNESSETH, that the said parties of the first part, for and in consideration of the sum of Twenty three hundred and fifty Dollars, to the said parties of the first part in hand paid by the said party of the second part, the receipt whereof is hereby confessed and acknowledged, have granted, bargained, sold and conveyed, and by these presents do grant, bargain, sell, convey and confirm unto the said party of the second part, his heirs and assigns, forever all of the following described lot or parcel of land situate, lying and being in the County of Larimer and State of Colorado, to wit: The undivided half of three-fourths of Lot one (1) in Block G in the Town of Fort Collins according to a plat of the sub-divisions of Block E and F made by**

F. C. Avery surveyor March 18, 1874. The above described lot contains the buildings known as the Fort Collins Foundry and Machine Shops and this deed is intended to convey the undivided one half of three fourths of all machinery used in said buildings including one twelve horsepower engine and seventeen horsepower boiler, one engine lathe and other tools including patterns and stock used and kept about said premises ...

Signed, Sealed and Delivered in Presence of I. W. Thomas

William G. Silcott, Elga Silcott

> —*Warrantee Deed K 16556 filed in the Larimer County Courthouse, Colorado*

Walker started working at the foundry and learning the business the next day. Much to his dismay, there was a deep drop in orders that summer as the mining industry entered a drastic slump. He missed the farm, especially the horses and cattle, more than he'd expected. Ella grieved for her family and friends back in Iowa and longed to go home. But Walker hadn't had an asthma attack since they arrived.

Foundry business for the fall and winter looked even more dismal than the disappointing summer. Walker wanted to get involved in something he knew, so he and John Brown, another shareholder, decided to sell out. It was November before they finally found a buyer and sold at a steep loss. As he walked out of the courthouse, Walker felt like a horse had kicked him in the stomach. When he got home, Ella looked at his long face, hugged him, and asked, "How much did we lose altogether?"

"A little over a thousand dollars. It's goin' to be real tough writin' our fathers about what happened to their money." Walker groaned as he sat down and put his head in his hands. "And I've got to ask for some more money to get started in ranching, too."

"Maybe we should just go back home and start over there. I'm sure they'd pay our train fares." Ella's suggestion was larded with hope.

Walker's head came up instantly. "We'd be quitters if we went back now, and I'm no quitter. I'm sure I can make a living raising horses and cattle. If I have to, I'll go shoot elk in the mountains and sell the meat in Denver."

"I'm no quitter either, but I'd love to get back home, where the wind doesn't blow every single day of the year."

"Wind or no wind, we're staying, and that's that." Walker stood up, slapped his cap onto his head, and walked out the door. When he came back an hour later, he started writing to his father and Lije Reames to tell them of their loss and ask for more money to start ranching.

When the reply came with a thousand-dollar check, he bought livestock to feed on the section of rangeland he'd already rented and moved his family to southeast of Fort Collins.

Bill of Sale

Know all men by these presents.

That H. T. Miller of St. Cloud, in the County of Larimer, and state of Colorado of the first part for and in consideration of the sum of Twenty One hundred and twenty five Dollars to him in hand paid at or before the unsealing or delivery of these products by Walker Beatty, of Ft. Collins, in the County of Larimer and state of Colorado, of the second part, the receipt whereof is hereby acknowledged, has bargained and sold, and by these present does grant and convey into the said party of the second part, his executors, administrators and assigns: -

One grey horse 3 years old, branded IV on left shoulder.

One grey horse 3 years old, branded OT on left shoulder.

One grey horse 3 years old, branded A/T on left shoulder.

One grey horse 3 years old, branded TU on left shoulder.

One brown horse 3 years old white front foot, branded A/T on left shoulder.

One sorrel horse 3 years old, branded A/T on left shoulder.

One brown horse 3 years old, branded >O on left shoulder.

One steel grey stud colt 2 yrs. old, branded A on left shoulder.

One Gray stud colt 2 yrs. old, branded A on left shoulder.

One black horse 2 white feet and spot on his face 2 yrs. old, branded 25 on left hip

One sorrel colt hind foot white and in face 1 year old, branded 25 on left hip.

One bay brown 1 year old, branded 25 on left hip.

One bright bay horse 3 yr old branded 22 & 25 on left hip and shoulder.

One bay colt 1 year old (white points) branded
25 on left hip.

Nine (9) yearling steers branded H over T on
left side

Three (3) coming yearling steers branded H
over T on left side

In witness whereof I have hereunto set my hand
and seal this 9th day of January 1885.

H. T. Miller

Signed, sealed and delivered in the presence of C.
C. Emigh J.C. Brown

—Bill of Sale filed in the Larimer County Courthouse,
Colorado

Walker started gentling the three-year-old horses as soon he'd
bought them. Two of the four grays were wild and unruly. One
kicked him on the hip and left him limping for two weeks. The other
two gentled down quickly, and he had them in harnesses and pulling
a wagon within a week. The unruly pair slowly accepted his firm
but understanding ways and were in the harness in a month. But
he didn't trust them in emergencies, so he sold both teams to a man
who wanted matched pairs of grays, and he continued gentling the
other horses.

The Beatys were always short of money, and Walker wanted to
pay off the loan from David and Lije. So in the winters, he and John
Brown, his partner at the foundry, hunted elk from the herds that
grazed near the base of the mountains, where the wind blew the
snow off the south slopes. As soon as they each had a wagonload of
dressed meat and hides, they drove to Denver to sell their harvest and
garner some much-needed cash. The round trip usually took a week,
but it brought in money when there was no other source. Hunting

and selling elk became a winter occupation for the pair. Ella cared for their growing family, now augmented by a second son, Frank, and fed the livestock when Walker was gone.

On a sunny day in January, as the pair of hunters was preparing to go to Denver to sell their loads of meat and hides, Walker kissed Ella and the older children good-bye and looked west. "Those clouds on the mountains look ugly. Never saw 'em like that before. An' somehow, the air feels different. Hope we don't have a blizzard."

Ella gave Walker a quick kiss and said, "Take your sheepskin coat and a scarf, just in case."

John Brown, anxious to get on the trail, waited with his team and loaded wagon beside the barn. He glanced to the mountains that stood like a wall about ten miles west, where a tumult of dark clouds was churning over the tops of the peaks. "Looks like it's storming up there for sure. But it's nice and sunny down here, so let's head south."

They started toward Denver, their loaded wagons rattling over the frozen trail. Walker kept glancing up to the mountains, where the roiling clouds grew darker and closer. Then the wind shifted from south to west and got stronger. The temperature plummeted, and a few snowflakes appeared.

By noon, when they were halfway between home and the small town of Longmont, the fury of the blizzard caught them. Snow flew by in a moving horizontal blanket, lodging as hard drifts behind every protected spot. They could no longer see the trail from the wagons, and they tied the second team to the back of the lead wagon and walked beside the front horses to find the track. Brown walked a few feet ahead, searching; Walker took the halter ropes of the horses and led them through the drifts. The trail disappeared repeatedly, and they had to hunt for it between bursts of swirling snow. Once, when they were standing side by side, searching, Walker looked at his partner's face. "Your nose and cheeks are white, John. Better rub 'em to thaw them out." Brown rubbed his snowy leather mitten on his face.

"Can't feel a thing. Good you told me. You better rub your nose too. It's white on the tip." Walker pulled the collar of his sheepskin coat tighter around his neck and shivered as he rubbed his nose. Their search was cut short by another burst of whirling snow, and they huddled together, backs to the storm, holding the halter ropes of the horses to keep them from turning east and drifting with the wind. A pack of wolves howled nearby.

"S'pose we'll ever make it to Longmont?" Walker had to shout above the wind.

"Hope so. We'll freeze to death if we don't. One thing's for sure—we don't have to worry about the meat gettin' too warm and spoiling." Brown gave a half-frozen laugh as he stamped his feet and swung his arms, slapping his mittens together in rhythm.

An especially fierce gust blew the ground beside the wagons clear of snow momentarily and revealed the trail. They stumbled south along it. The wind was so fierce at times that they had to walk in the lee of the horses to keep from being blown down. The snowdrifts hardened. The lead wagon began to tip as the straining horses inched forward, and the wheels on one side would ride up on the frozen snow while the others broke through. Brown hung on the high side to keep it from tipping, then went back to hunting for the trail. The light began to fade. Walker heard faint howls from the pack of wolves, remembered his premonition when he'd seen the clouds boiling above the mountaintops while he was still at home, and wished they'd never started this trip.

As it got darker, they led the horses south in the intervals between the fiercest gusts of wind, when they could find the trail of ruts that they were following. Walker's hands and feet were numb, but he didn't notice the loss of feeling. Suddenly one of the big bay geldings he was leading put his nose forward and neighed; then he tugged to the right and walked faster. In minutes, he led them to the entrance of Longmont, the town that they hadn't seen; with a few more neighs that received faint answers, the horse led them to a livery stable. They pounded on the door until a boy opened it a crack and peeked out. He stepped out reluctantly and opened the corral gate so they could park their wagons beyond the reach of wolves and bring their spent bodies and those of their horses into the barn.

The storm lasted two more days. When it broke, they started south again, opening the trail through the drifts. When they were halfway to Denver, a chinook wind blew down from the mountains;

it was so strong that the men were afraid that it would tip over the wagons. The temperature shot from fifteen below zero to sixty above in an hour. They shoveled snow over the meat and covered it with hides, then slogged on through viscous mud and across creeks, some of which were flooding deep enough to float the wagons.

They finally struggled into Denver in their shirtsleeves and eventually sold their meat, just now beginning to thaw, for three cents a pound, and the elk hides for a quarter each. Then they turned their patient teams north toward home. The wolves didn't follow them this time, as they'd done all the way south. Walker felt that it was a miracle he was alive.

Ella had been so busy during the storm that she'd hardly had time to think or feel. She left five-year-old Blanche in charge of her two young brothers and tried to tend the livestock to keep them alive. The hay she pitched off the stacks to feed the horses and steers was buried by blowing snow or blown toward Kansas before the famished animals could snatch more than a few bites, so she opened the fence and let them huddle around the haystacks and pull the frozen hay out as best they could. The creek froze and drifted over. She spent hours chopping watering holes for the livestock, only to have to repeat the chore a few hours later. The storm reburied the woodpile a few minutes after she dug away the drift and pried out a few armloads of wood. Snow sifted under the cabin door and between the logs where the chinking had shrunk. It didn't melt, except near the stove, until the chinook wind burst down from the mountains under a cerulean sky and transformed the weather in an instant. Only then did the fear that Ella had held at bay burst forth in a torrent of weeping.

Each day, she scanned the trail to the south, looking for her husband. Each night, she cried herself to sleep. When Walker and his exhausted team struggled in, a week late, she hugged him for ten minutes as tears streamed down her face.

"You don't have any idea how I worried about you. I know you don't have asthma here, but can't we just go back home before this weather kills us all?" She brushed strands of hair from her face and searched his eyes.

Walker's fears and longing for home matched Ella's, but reality tore his heart as he told her, "We can't just up and leave now. We don't have near enough money for train tickets. Maybe we'll be able to scrape enough together to make it by next summer."

Chapter 23
Collapsed Dreams

On the sidewalk in front of the Masonic Temple, Joe's impatience and fear burst like an erupting volcano as he yelled at Charlie, "You can go wherever you want, but I got a cousin working on a railroad in Brazil. If we can get on a ship goin' south quick enough, they probably won't catch us. There's a train to Chicago and on to New York in an hour, and we can sail from there. Get a move on, if you're comin' with me."

Charlie stood stock-still for what seemed like an eternity to Joe. Then he sighed. "An' I was all set to propose to Amelia Hubbard tonight. I'll have to hock the engagement ring to get money to travel."

Joe watched as Charlie walked heavily up the steps. "I'm headin' to the station. Will I see you there?" Charlie nodded almost imperceptibly and went in. Ten minutes later, he came out and started toward the station, walking slowly with his large suitcase. He looked back once and wiped his eyes with a handkerchief.

* * *

A few weeks later, David stood at the mailbox and looked perplexed as he held the official envelope. Why would the U.S. postal inspector be writing him? When he read the contents, the answer came quickly, and it solved the mystery of why no one had seen Charlie recently. The postal inspector's office was contacting relatives of all the partners in the Empire Land and Development Company, attempting to locate them for arrest and trial.

David felt like he'd been gored by a raging bull. He'd have to tell Nancy the awful news: she might never see her only son again, and with crop and cattle prices so low, they'd likely lose all the farms. He sighed and plodded toward the house, his heart breaking.

"Nancy, why don't you sit down? I've got bad news." His voice broke, and he wiped his eyes.

"What's bad enough to make you cry?" Nancy put her arms around David.

"We've lost a son, and we're probably gonna be stone broke." David handed her the letter and stood holding the table with one hand and wiping his eyes with the other as she read it.

"This is terrible! How could Charlie have done this to us?" She groaned, then began to sob as she ran to the bedroom and slammed the door.

David looked after her for a minute, then went to the toolshed and searched for his rifle. After he found it, he hunted high and low for shells but found only an empty shell box. He threw it on the floor and stomped it flat as he muttered, "That damned Charlie must have used the last ones when he was hunting rabbits ... and didn't tell me."

He slammed the rifle down on the tool bench, then went out and caught the driving horse, threw on its harness, hooked the leggy bay to the buggy, and whipped it toward town at a gallop. The startled animal kept turning its head to look back at its tormenter, but each pause to look brought another lash of the whip.

When David tired of whipping the horse and let it ease back to a brisk trot, he began to reflect on what he was doing. Much as he wanted to buy some shells, put one in the rifle, and blow off his head, he began to have second thoughts. What would his wife think? What about his children, his grandchildren, his neighbors? Slowly David's thoughts turned to how he and Nancy could support themselves. He knew how to cut and sell meat, and Nancy had been a milliner. Maybe they could eke out subsistence that way.

At the edge of the village, he stopped the sweating bay, turned him around, and drove back home at a walk. He rubbed the sweat off the horse, swore at Charlie under his breath, and went inside, walking slowly and feeling old. He heard Nancy sobbing in the bedroom.

As word of the disaster that Charlie had caused David and Nancy spread among the family, there were endless conversations among their other children about what a bum Charlie had turned out to be, and what could be done to help their almost-destitute parents. Melissa and Rob Crawford invited her parents to live with them in their mansion on Grand Avenue, but David and Nancy wouldn't hear of accepting charity. John Schooley, husband of David's daughter Alice, offered to take in his father-in-law as a partner in his meat market that served an upscale neighborhood near the Capitol building. That appealed to David, who insisted on earning his own way, and who'd liked working with meat ever since he and Guilon had been partners in a packing house and meat market during the Civil War. Nancy searched the downtown stores in Des Moines for weeks until she found a millinery shop that needed a part-time worker. She took the job, even though her hands were getting stiff and the pay was pitifully small. They rented one room at a boarding house a few blocks from the Capitol, and they began new lives as workers without a home of their own.

They had little left of their former lives except their pride. No one ever heard from Charlie again. The partnership between John Schooley and David Beaty didn't last. David was used to being in charge, and he didn't fit in as a junior partner to his son-in-law. Within a year, Schooley had a new partner, and David was operating his own small meat market back in Altoona. He and Nancy continued to live at the boarding house, and David commuted to Altoona each day by train to operate his tiny enterprise. He kept at it until late in 1901 when his health failed, and his son Ted had to care for him until he died late in January 1902.

1891 Schooley and Beaty (J. F. Schooley and David Beaty) meat market, 1452 e Walnut

1892 Schooley and Mitchell (J. F. Schooley and F. J. Mitchell) meat market 1452 e Walnut

1895 Beaty, David, butcher, boards, 824 Lyon

—Listings in the City Directories, Des Moines, Iowa

Obituary

Died—in Des Moines, January 27, 1902 Mr. D. Beaty, aged 81 years and 3 months.... Deceased was born in Harrison County Ohio, October 26, 1821, removing from Ohio to Jefferson county Iowa in the fall of 1860, in the spring of 1868 he came to Des Moines. He was an excellent man and is kindly remembered by those friends who knew him. He was upright in all his dealings, a man of excellent character. He leaves a wife, five sons and three daughters to mourn his loss. [Eldest son] Theodore was with his father at his death and had been at his bedside a good part of the time during the past six weeks. Funeral services were conducted in Des Moines Wednesday afternoon, interment taking place in that city.

As they watched the procession file solemnly down the aisle of the Presbyterian church, two old women pulled black shawls tighter around their heads and necks. The tall one bent her long neck and whispered to her stooped seatmate, whose hands shook with palsy, "Such a cheap coffin. You'd think the family would have pride enough to bury him in a better one."

"They may have pride, but they don't have the means anymore. Not after that youngest son of theirs lost all of David's money in some crooked land deal in Florida." The stooped lady shook her head in disapproval. "An' that boy's not even got the gumption to come back and face the music." She sniffed in disgust.

Her companion whispered, "Or to see his poor old father buried in a cheap pine box." Then they watched in stiff and disapproving silence as David's three oldest sons and three sons-in-law carried his remains out of the sanctuary and into the gray cold of a January afternoon as snow swept around the faded black hearse and two thin horses waiting at the curb.

"I hear he died in debt way over his head. It's a shame, that poor old man having to work every day when he's up in his eighties. They say all the widow got was a stove, an ice cream freezer, a table, and two chairs. You know, she still tries to work at the millinery shop, even though her hands are so stiff, she can't hardly bend 'em." The two women stood together, backs to the wind, and watched the pallbearers load the coffin into the hearse. Other mourners untied their horses and lined up their buggies behind the undertaker.

The tall woman shivered and bent toward her companion. "If it weren't so cold, I'd go to the cemetery. Sarah, you going or not?"

"They're good folks, but it's just too cold for me." The two walked away as the funeral procession began to move toward the cemetery.

* * *

"Oyez, oyez. All rise. The District Court of Polk County is now in session." The slight, blond clerk wheezed and coughed as he spoke.

The lone petitioner in the room, J. M. St. John, administrator of the estate of David Beaty, stood, fingering his report as the old judge limped to the bench and sat down heavily. The judge eyed the lawyer quizzically and asked, "What have you brought for business, Mr. St. John?"

"The final report of the probate of the estate of the late David Beaty, your honor."

"How'd it finally come out?"

"His assets amounted to $545.25, but the expenses used up a good bit of that, so we had to prorate the payments to his creditors at just over twenty-eight cents on the dollar."

Mr. St. John handed the report to the judge, who gave it a quick glance and passed it back to his clerk.

"Maher, take this and get it sworn to, then get the next case in

273

here. I don't want to waste all day on old man Beaty's stuff. He was so poor, he doesn't merit any more of my time."

The clerk hastened to call the next case.

> **After paying costs and expenses of administration there remained in my hands $116.56 which being insufficient to pay all the claims in full was pro rated to all the creditors as per order of the court at the rate of 28.2 per cent.**
>
> **Dated this 9th day of May 1903**
>
> **J. M. St. John**
>
> **Subscribed and sworn to by J. M. St. John before me on May 9th 1903**
>
> **J.P. Maher Deputy Clerk of Court**
>
> *—Final Report of Administrator, Probate 4538, Polk*
> *County, Iowa*

After David died, Nancy accepted the offer of Melissa and Rob Crawford and moved from her one rented room into their baronial home on Grand Avenue. The hardest thing for her to accept was being waited on hand and foot by the cook and housekeepers that Melissa and Rob employed. She died there in 1905.

In a corner of Woodlawn Cemetery in Des Moines, two granite gravestones stand close together. The smaller one bears the names John Schooley and Alice Schooley. The larger stone, about five feet high, is engraved along the eight-foot length with the names David Beaty and Nancy Beaty, with David Beaty Junior's name on the six-foot side.

Chapter 24
Starting Over

Whenever Walker went out of the cabin east of Fort Collins to feed and water his livestock, gusts of wind almost blew him over. As winter turned to spring in 1890, he came to feel that the wind he hated was blowing every morning, every noon, and every night. In early summer, he managed to sell all of his livestock to neighbors, and then he ended his lease on the land and paid his debts. With all of this finally accomplished, they had just enough money for tickets to Iowa.

Ella rejoiced as she packed their trunks for the trip, even though she and Walker weren't certain where they'd live or what they'd do when they got there. Walker dreaded the return to country that gave him asthma, and he felt that going back to Iowa was admitting defeat.

Once back in Iowa, the family stayed with Ella's parents in Altoona while Walker searched for a job. The day he got one, he broke the news to Ella. She was not pleased.

"You mean to tell me you took a job on a big farm, where I'll have to cook for a bunch of hungry hired men every day of the year?" Ella glared at Walker and stamped her foot.

"It'll only be three men most of the time—a few more during haying and threshing. Beggars can't be choosers, and we're close to bein' beggars. And don't forget, it's the only job I've heard of where we get a share of the calf and colt crop every year." Walker glared back at his pregnant wife. "So get packed up and ready. We're moving to the Bayliss place near Guthrie Center on Thursday."

Ella went downstairs and sought out her mother, who was entertaining her four grandchildren. "Would you believe, we're going to move way up to Guthrie Center, and I'll have to cook for hired men all the time!"

Mrs. Reames slid a doll that she and Grace were playing with off her lap, stood up, and took Ella's hand. "At least he's got a job. And the trains run back and forth every day. It'll not be like Colorado." Ella still looked dubious, so Julia made an offer, "I don't really want to, but I'll come up and help you cook when you have the new baby."

Ella looked relieved. "Thank you, Mother. That would be a big help. You're a saint to offer to help me out." Then she turned her attention to her two older children.

"Blanche, Bob, we're going to move—to a farm up near Guthrie Center. You gotta help me pack up our things again."

As one of Mr. Bayliss's hired men drove Walker, Ella, and their four children into the farmstead, the Beattys marveled at the size of the white frame house and the array of red barns that surrounded it.

Blanche asked, "Father, are we really going to live there? It's so big."

"Yup, it's our new home. Room enough for you to run all you want to."

Blanche turned excitedly to her sister and brothers. "Let's go look everything over." They scrambled out of the wagon as soon as it stopped.

As Walker and Ella began to unload trunks, Blanche, Bob, Grace, and Frank rushed off to explore the big, white house, peek into the tall, dimly lit barns, and make friends with the livestock.

"Grace, did you ever see such a big house in your life?" Blanche and her little sister stood on tiptoes, whispering at the head of the stairs and surveyed the echoing, voluminous second floor with its long hall and multitude of doors to bedrooms. Blanche led Grace down the hall to peer into an empty room or two. Then they retreated down the stairs.

Bob and Frank ran to the biggest barn and peeked in the open door. The interior seemed like a huge, dim, mysterious cavern. They inhaled the fragrances of hay and grain mingled with the pungent aromas of horse and cattle manure and sweaty harnesses. A team of horses was tied in the first stall. The gray gelding nearest the door turned to look at the newcomers and nickered softly. Bob climbed on the manger, leaned over, and stroked the horse's nose. Frank watched, and then he tried to imitate his brother, but he couldn't reach across the manger.

"Horsey nice," he said as he watched. The gray gelding stuck out its nose toward him and nickered again. "He likes me." Frank's announcement carried overtones of surprise.

The children adapted quickly to the new surroundings. Walker enjoyed managing the large farm and accumulating some livestock of his own, but Ella always resented having to cook and wash dishes for the hired men. In spite of this tension, Walker and his family lived and worked at the Bayliss farm for the next twenty years, some of which were among the most consistently profitable for American farmers.

Chapter 25
Getting Prizes, Gaining and Losing Sons

As the years passed and the century changed, Walker and Ella's family grew in size and number; Walker decided to add a second *T* to his last name; four more sons were born. They all came to regard the Bayliss farm as home, but they kept in touch with the family who lived nearer Des Moines. Both Walker and Ella made the train trip to the state's capital city for the funerals of David and Nancy, and on rare occasions they took the whole family and visited the Crawfords, Schooleys, and Maddens. The Beatty children loved exploring the Crawfords' huge mansion on Grand Avenue in Des Moines, with its long curved stairway and myriad of elegantly furnished rooms.

By 1908, Blanche had married a dentist, moved away, and had children of her own. Grace was being courted by a local farm boy. Bob and Frank were restless young men, still home, working on the farm. It was August, hot, humid, and almost time for the Iowa State Fair.

Steam swirled from the kettle of peaches that Ella was canning on the black Monarch range, and it filled the kitchen. Walker wiped his forehead as he and his two oldest sons sat at the table after dinner and he laid out the plans for the week.

"Now that the second-cutting hay's all in the barns, we've got to get the cattle ready for the fair. And we'll have to pick only the best, because we can only take one railroad car this year."

"I want at least half the space for my horses!" Frank, age twenty and pushing the limits, glowered at his father like a dog defending his turf.

"I've told you for the last time, you can't take all of your dratted horses to the fair! We're only takin' one rail car to Des Moines, and I'm going to need most of it for the Herefords." Walker wanted to hit Frank, but instead he slammed his big palm on the table and scowled at his two older sons. Bob and Frank glared back, looked at each other, and stalked out of the house, letting the screen door slam behind them.

Ella turned from skinning peaches and wiped her brow with her apron. "You may not have them two around to do part of the farm work very long. Frank had that sullen, mad look he gets, and Bob's been drinkin' and running around, from what I hear. You ready to get the farm work done without 'em?" She stood with her hands dripping, then wiped them on a dish towel and picked up one-year-old Theodore, called Teddy, who'd begun to cry after the banging door woke him.

"I don't care, woman. I've got to run my own show without trying to please all the family. We've got hired men, and Myron and Harlan are coming along. They'll be able to do a man's work soon, and they don't talk back like those two wild upstarts. It'll do those two good to work for somebody else for a while. Maybe that'll knock some sense into their heads." He tucked a chew of tobacco inside his lip, stood up abruptly, stuck his straw hat on hard, and went outside, grabbing the screen door at the last second so that it didn't bang as it closed.

Ella sighed, handed baby Teddy to Grace, who stood beside her drying dishes, and went back to washing the mountain of plates, glasses, and cups from the thirteen noon diners. Walker went to a fence by the well, where his two teenage sons were washing a bull. He was eager to get involved in a new project and forget his ongoing fight with Bob and Frank.

"Wash him real good, especially his legs and tail. He's a great one, and we want him to look his best at the fair." Walker watched closely as Myron and Harlan, his two middle sons, washed his favorite young

Hereford bull, Beau Bolivar, in preparation for the Iowa State Fair. "He's got a good body and lots of style. Might win the championship if we comb, fit, and show him right."

Myron nodded, dipped the bull's tail into the bucket of sudsy water again, and began to scrub it with a brush, then dodged the soapy spray as the bull pulled his tail loose and switched it vigorously. "You really think he could win? That would be a real boost for us, wouldn't it? Could I lead him in the show ring for judging?"

Walker considered the request. "If you work real hard to get him in tip-top shape, then maybe you could. We'll see."

Myron wiped soap out of his eyes with the back of his hand, grabbed the bull's switching tail, and began to brush it briskly before rinsing it with fresh water. He was thrilled by the prospect of being entrusted with showing the bull. Unlike his older brothers, who grumbled about traipsing all over with the cattle, Myron loved this annual outing. He savored the sociability of the gathering, the chance to see the other breeders' cattle, and the break from the routine of farming. Their cattle usually placed high in the judging, since Mr. Bayliss bought high-priced and high-quality animals to build their herds.

The next day, the din and clangor of the fair filled their ears as the Beattys led their animals from the railroad siding toward the barns on a hot, humid afternoon. Walker encountered friends he'd made at previous fairs and livestock shows. He paused to visit and appraise their string of show stock while his four oldest sons tied the eighteen animals they'd brought to the fair in the barns and returned to the rail siding for their supplies.

Bob and Frank came from the siding, carrying a rectangular wooden box about five feet long and three feet high. It was filled with brushes, combs, buckets, and feed. Stenciled in black on the front, the name "F. A. Bayliss" stood out from the gray paint and matched the black metal handles on either end. Harlan and Myron carried an array of halters and ropes that wouldn't fit in the box. Bob and Frank left for the horse barn with part of their gear as soon as they'd deposited the equipment for the cattle. After their string of show animals was bedded in fresh straw, fed, brushed, and watered, Myron and Harlan saw an opportunity to explore the fair.

They emerged from the subdued sounds of the cattle barn into a cacophony of noise and a mass of people. Most of the men and boys wore overalls and straw hats. The women and girls wore homemade dresses and carried parasols to keep off the sun. The smell of dust, hay, and manure mixed with the fumes from a few cars that were putt-putting around the grounds. Everyone stopped to gawk as the cars came nearby. A steam whistle shrilled from the midway as an engine chuffed smoke and the Ferris wheel began to turn. A mule brayed from the entrance of one of the barns, and a peacock screamed inside another building. Myron and Harlan were transfixed.

"There's so much to see! Where do we start?" It was Harlan's first time at the fair.

"Let's look at the chickens in the barn across the road. I always like to see the different breeds, especially those with strange looks and funny calls." Myron, who had been at the fair twice before, guided his younger but larger brother toward the open-sided barn filled with cages of poultry of every size, color, and shape. They wandered the aisle among a throng of spectators and stopped beside the rows of cages. A peacock strode back and forth in his large enclosure, alternately spreading and retracting his multi-hued tail and calling loudly. The sound filled the barn and reverberated across the open spaces beyond.

"Isn't he something? I'd love to have one back on the farm, so we could see and hear him every day." Myron stood admiring the bird.

Harlan tugged at his brother's sleeve. "He's way too loud to suit me. Let's go see something else." Myron followed, looking back at the peacock until he couldn't see it past the people in the aisle. Harlan was going out the barn door. Myron ran to catch up. They explored the livestock barns until it was time to tend their own show string again.

When it got dark, Walker and his sons spread blankets and pillows on fresh straw near their cattle and lay down to sleep. For Myron and Harlan, sleep was slow to come. There was just too much going on around them. They woke up early and tired and began to prepare their show animals for the judging events scheduled for later that morning and all afternoon.

As he led Beau Bolivar into the show ring to be judged against the other young breeding bulls, Myron felt exhilarated. The bull's dark red hair glistened; his head and legs were as white as fresh snow. Myron held the leather show halter high to keep the bull's head up, while always keeping one eye on the judge and the other on Beau Bolivar as the other fifteen competitors and their handlers circled the ring and lined up for the judge's close inspection. To Myron, the wait seemed interminable. Why didn't the judge just pick Beau Bolivar for first place right now? He made his thoughts go back to simultaneously watching the bull he was showing, watching the judge as he'd seen his father do, and, when necessary, maneuvering the bull to stand four-square on his feet when the judge was looking their way. The process seemed to take forever, even though he was busy every second.

Finally, after observing the array of animals for confirmation and markings, feeling their backs and sides, then watching how they walked, the judge picked Beau Bolivar to head the class. Myron beamed as he took the blue ribbon from the judge's assistant and led the bull toward the barn where his father and Mr. Bayliss waited, smiling broadly.

His father patted Myron on the shoulder. "You showed him real nice, Son. He was the cleanest and best-fitted bull in the ring for sure, and the judge knew it."

"I loved showing him, Father. Fairs and cattle shows are just great."

Walker glanced at a pocket watch he'd pulled from the front of his overalls. "There's two hours till the judging for the championship, so tie Beau Bolivar in his stall and go look around for a bit, if you want."

"Okay, I'll be back in an hour to get him all brushed and spiffed up again."

Myron replaced the bull's leather halter with one of rope, tied the bull in his stall, and hurried toward the midway and grandstand. A barker called, "Right this way, folks. Come see the fabulous two-headed calf and the world's only man with three legs! Only two cents to see two of the great wonders of the world! Step right up, folks!" Myron ignored him.

He wiped sweat from his face and stopped to watch a car race that was taking place on a recently created oval dirt track in the grass in front of the grandstand. A Stanley Steamer whizzed away from an Oldsmobile, an Apperson Jackrabbit, and a Model T Ford as they rounded the second turn. Then it blew a tire and veered to a stop in the grass beside the track, steam and smoke billowing, while the other three sputtered and sped around the dusty oval, neck and neck.

Then the Ford backfired with a sound like a cannon, and a team of terrified horses bolted across the fairgrounds, dragging their fallen driver. He skidded and rolled behind them until he lost the reins. People screamed and scattered from the path of the rampaging pair. Finally, a tall, young man stepped up, grabbed the bit of one of the terrified horses, and held on until the runaways stopped, panting, stamping, and looking back toward the car race with fear in their eyes. Myron edged closer and saw that it was his brother Frank holding the bridle and talking softly to the frightened pair. As Myron and the other onlookers watched and listened, Frank's low, soft voice and gentle caresses eased the anxiety of the big animals until the teamster, now upright and dusted off, was able to drive them away at a walk. Myron edged up to his brother.

"You're really good with horses, Frank. Where'd you learn how to calm 'em down like that?"

"Oh, just comes natural to me, I guess. But I sure wish Father'd give me some credit for bein' good with 'em. He always favors the cattle over the horses, and I hate it something awful."

He glanced around, then slipped a pint bottle out of his back pocket and offered it to Myron. "Here, try a sip. It's real good-tasting." Myron shook his head and backed away. Frank tipped the bottle to his lips, took a long drink, and wiped his mouth. "This makes me feel real good. You won't tell Father and Mother you seen me drinkin' whiskey, will you?"

He looked apprehensive until Myron nodded and said, "No, I'll never tell. But you know it's wrong to drink whiskey. Grandpa David told me so a whole lot of times before he died."

"I know. He used to tell me 'most every time I saw him. But it tastes so good, I gotta have a sip every now an' then, or I'll go crazy." He leaned toward Myron and said in a conspiratorial whisper, "Can I can trust you with something really secret?" Myron nodded, thrilled by the confidence that his older brother placed in him.

"Don't breathe a word of this to anybody, but I'm goin' to hop a train and head west tonight. It's too stifling round here with everybody tellin' me what I can't do. I've sold the three horses I brought to the fair, an' that money will get me a start out west. You just feed an' water them for me till Emmett Jones comes an' gets 'em tomorrow. He'll have the bill of sale in case Father asks. Bob's leavin' too. Just not with me."

Myron was all attention. "Feeding and watering your horses is easy, but what'll I tell Mother and Father about where you and Bob have gone and why?" He scanned Frank's face for answers, for meaning.

"Don't know about Bob, but just tell 'em I went west like Grandpa David. Gotta stretch my legs, see some new country. I'll write when I get situated. Or they can ask Nellie Reed, from over by Panora. She'll know where I am before anybody else." He turned and was gone, lost in the crowd. Myron searched among the fairgoers until it was time to get the bull ready to show for the championship, but he never saw his brother again.

When Myron came back to the cattle barn, he could barely concentrate. Frank's secret kept intruding as he fed, watered, and brushed Beau Bolivar, changed to the leather halter, and led the bull toward the show ring. He wondered what would happen to his brothers, and why Frank and Bob felt they had to leave.

"Pay attention! You act like your mind's somewhere else." His father's admonition brought Myron back to the present. He was responsible for showing the family's prize bull for the Iowa State Hereford Championship. If he won, it could mean a boost in prestige and income. If he didn't ... Myron didn't even want to think about that.

In the earlier competition with the other Hereford bulls, Beau Bolivar had been easy to handle. This time, it was different. Just ahead of them in the parade of animals was a heifer. And the pheromones that she emitted turned on the bull's mating instincts, full force. Beau Bolivar sniffed the air, then lunged forward to explore the enticing prospect at closer range. Myron dug in his heels and leaned back, slowing the bull's advance; then he managed to turn the bull's head and drag him out from behind the heifer in heat. His father jumped to help, and together they hauled the bull by the halter strap out of the line of competing animals and their handlers, and slipped a spring-loaded steel ring into Beau Bolivar's nose. Myron got him back into the parade of competitors just as it was time to pass in front of the judge. The bull was still aroused, but Myron managed to control him with strong tugs on the halter strap and the rope attached to the nose ring.

"Easy, boy, just take it easy. You'll get lots of other chances. Just simmer down. Simmer down, now." He continued to talk low and slowly to the bull as they walked, and the judge scrutinized the 1,500 pounds of testosterone-fueled muscle and bone. Beau Bolivar regained some of his calm demeanor, and by the time the animals were standing in a line as per the judge's instructions, his lust was reduced to near normal.

Myron took a chance and slipped the ring out of the bull's nose and tucked it into his pocket. When the judge made his personal inspection, the bull stood squarely on his feet and didn't flinch as the judge's hands slid across his back and ribs. As he finished, the judge looked at Myron and whispered, "Nice job of handling him. That heifer shouldn't have been allowed in the show ring in her condition." Myron nodded almost imperceptibly. The judge moved on to the next animal and didn't hear Myron's sigh of relief.

The wait while the judge appraised the competing animals and their handlers two more times seemed endless. Beau Bolivar fidgeted and tried to look toward the heifer. Myron tugged him back into a square stance that made his legs look straight, and he watched the judge out of the corner of his eye. When the judge motioned for him to bring Beau Bolivar forward to the head of the line, Myron's breath came fast. He scarcely dared to hope. Was he really going to award them the championship, or was this just another exercise? When would they know?

The judge motioned for another animal, a younger bull, to be brought into position beside them, then another and another. Only when all the animals were in line based on how the judge considered their relative merit, with the offending heifer by herself at the far end, did he motion for his assistant who carried the ribbons to come forward. He came first to Beau Bolivar and Myron.

Word of the new champion Hereford bull spread throughout the fairgrounds, and a parade of other breeders came to look over the Bayliss-Beatty show string. Mr. Bayliss and Walker were busy talking to one or another visitor all afternoon and evening while Harlan and Myron eavesdropped. Walker did not ask about the absence of Frank and Bob.

As darkness fell, the boys fed and watered the cattle and horses, cleared away the manure, ate supper, and then smoothed the pile of straw beside the animals, unrolled their blankets and pillows, and lay down to sleep. But sleep was slow in coming for Myron. The sounds of the animals breathing and moving in their stalls floated through the warm, dark air. His head buzzed from the day's happenings. Frank and Bob's secret departure circled in his mind, competing with the residual tension of the championship show. Was his family coming apart, just when it was beginning to get ahead in stock raising? Why couldn't Frank and Bob and his father get along? Why was Frank drinking whiskey after hearing the horror stories from his grandfather David about how it had ruined his own father's life and health? Myron fell into a restless sleep, with questions chasing one another around his head.

At the auction the day after the championship show, four of the Bayliss-Beatty heifers that had been bred to Beau Bolivar sold for almost twice what other bred Hereford heifers did. Their young bulls sold equally well. The rail car for their show string was less than half full for the return trip to Guthrie Center. Frank's three horses were turned over to Emmett Jones, and about half of the cattle they had brought to the fair, all that they wished to sell, had been sold to other breeders at high prices.

Before the fair was over, Walker and Mr. Bayliss turned down several private offers to buy Beau Bolivar, because they wanted to use him as a breeding bull. Walker felt elated. But Myron felt drained as he tied the last animal of the diminished show string into the half-empty rail car. His two older brothers weren't coming back home with them. Who knew where they might wind up?

Myron never saw Frank again, and more than fifty years passed before Bob and his second wife visited him.

Chapter 26
School Days

Myron was reviewing his Latin grammar when Mr. Gilchrest's voice boomed across the room. "Senior class, please stand." He closed his Latin book and stood up quickly.

The principal waited until they were on their feet—all fifteen of them—then ordered, "Senior class, come forward." They marched to the front of the room in line, just as they'd done for four years in response to various teachers' orders, and sat down on the benches that faced the principal's desk, exchanging questioning glances as they did so. Everyone looked at him expectantly.

It was June 1, 1909, almost their last day of high school, and it was unusual for them to be called forward as a group by the principal. Mr. Gilchrest cleared his throat and spoke solemnly. "This is the end of your high school studies. Some of your classmates have already dropped out. After the commencement next week, we will not have you as students again. I would like to have each of you share what your plans are for the future." He looked at the tall, lean boy at the end of the line. "James, you start."

James Grover stood up awkwardly, shuffled his big shoes, looked at the floor, and said softly, "I reckon I'll be working on the farm with my pa. He's bought some more land and wants me to help with farmin' it." Then he sat down quickly and sighed.

The principal nodded to the girl next to James. "Helen, please tell us your plans."

Helen Thompson tossed her head so that her brown pigtails swished across her homemade pinafore and stood up. "I plan to stay home and help my mother with the housework and garden. She needs me, what with seven other kids to take care of and one more on the way. Then, in a year or two, I'll prob'ly get married, I hope." As she sat down, she beamed a smile toward James that would melt a block of ice. A cherry red blush crept up James's face, and he looked even more directly at the floor. The rest of the class watched and tried not to titter.

The principal intervened quickly. "Myron, tell us your plans."

The black-haired, bony senior next to Helen stood quickly. "I like cattle and really like school. If I could get the money, I'd like to go on and study some more. But I don't know. My father's hoping to buy a farm, and he'll have a big mortgage if he does. So he can't help pay for it."

The principal smiled as Myron sat down. "Come talk to me after school." Myron looked completely surprised, and some of his classmates glanced questioningly at him as he sat down. Then the principal asked the next student in line to share his plans, and he continued the questioning until all twelve remaining students had responded. Most planned to farm or, like Helen, to become housewives and mothers.

When school was dismissed, Myron did not walk home with his brothers but instead went to the principal's office and knocked timidly. "You wanted to talk to me, sir?" When Mr. Gilchrest opened the door, Myron looked quickly around the high-ceilinged, sparsely furnished room.

"Yes, Myron. Come right in." The principal pushed up his shirtsleeves and leaned back. "I asked you to come see me because you are the best pupil in the school. And I want you to go on to college. You've got the potential to be a great teacher, or a preacher, or a lawyer. College opens the way." He paused and waited while Myron considered the career avenues that the principal had mentioned. "You said you liked to study but didn't have the money to go on to college. If I could get you a scholarship, would you consider applying?"

Myron thought about how the rest of the family would feel about him leaving. Could Harlan, Albert, the hired men, and his father do all the farm work? Maybe they'd get along if he came back each summer to help out. "Yes, I guess so. I hadn't thought I could possibly go to college. I just like learning new things." His voice sounded hopeful.

The principal beamed. "I'm really glad to hear you say that. I think I can get someone to donate money for a scholarship for the class valedictorian. You did know that will be you, didn't you?"

"Well, no, sir, I didn't. I just know my grades are good, except in mathematics. And they're only fair." Myron's look of dawning recognition pleased the principal. It was one of his rewards for administering a small-town high school in a rural county.

"Very good. I'll see what I can do. If I'm successful, I can get it set up for next year for you. Thanks for coming to see me. You can catch up with your brothers if you run."

As he ran to catch his brothers who were walking along the dirt road toward home, Myron thought about the new possibilities opened up by the talk with the school principal. What would it be like to be a teacher or a minister?

Chapter 27
Starting on Their Own Again

Walker hurried into the house as soon as he arrived from the grain elevator in Guthrie Center. "Ella, Ella, I heard there's a good piece of ground that's just come up for sale. It's north of town a couple of miles. I think we should look into buying it."

Ella stopped rolling out a pie crust and smiled. She was, as always, tired of cooking for the large crew of men that it took to run the Bayliss farm and glad to hear his news. "Is that so? Whose place is it?"

"Amanda Camp's. I understand she wants eighty dollars an acre. As soon as you finish baking those pies, let's take Teddy and go look at it and talk to her."

"I'll get ready as quick as I can. You unload the wagon, then keep an eye on Teddy for me. It'll take an hour for the pies to bake." She put more firewood into the cookstove and resumed rolling out pie crusts, but faster than before.

> **Know all Men by these Presents: That Amanda
> Caroline Camp, Single, of Guthrie County State
> of Iowa in consideration of the sum of Twelve
> Thousand Eight Hundred DOLLARS in hand
> paid by Walker Beatty of Guthrie County state
> of Iowa do hereby SELL AND CONVEY unto**

the said Walker Beatty the following described premises ... to wit: The North West quarter of the North East Quarter of Section Thirty one (31), and the West Half of the South West Quarter of Section Twenty-nine (29), and the South East Quarter of the South West Quarter of Section 29, all in Township Eighty (80), North of Range Thirty-one West of the Fifth P.M. in Guthrie County, Iowa ...

Signed the 25th day of February 1910

Amanda Caroline Camp

—Deed filed in the Guthrie County Courthouse, Iowa

Filed for record on the 8th day of Mch. A.D. 1910 ...

Walker Beatty and wife to Amanda Caroline Camp

FOR THE CONSIDERATION OF Seven Thousand and Eight Hundred DOLLARS Walker Beatty and Ella M. Beatty husband and wife of Guthrie County Iowa, hereby convey to Amanda Caroline Camp ... second party, the following real estate, situated in Guthrie County ... to wit: [legal description of the same property as above].

This mortgage is given to secure balance due for purchase money of the premises herein described and a vendor's lien is hereby reserved.

To be void upon condition that said Walker Beatty pay second party or assigns Seven Thousand

eight hundred DOLLARS March 1st 1915, with interest at five per cent per annum.

—Mortgage filed in the Guthrie County Courthouse,
Iowa

Walker and Ella were excited as they drove the buggy home from the courthouse on the muddy and rutted road. He reflected on their new venture and its antecedents. "It's a big step, what with that mortgage and all, but I'm tired of managing for somebody else. What's it been, twenty years come summer I've been doin' that? An' this looks like a good place we bought."

"Yeah, it's risky, but we've got to go out on our own sometime, and it sure will be great not to have that raft of hired men around all the time, eatin' us out of house and home. I swear I can't cook enough to fill 'em up, no matter how hard I try. I'm glad you did it."

Moving day was all hustle and confusion. Walker was up before five o'clock; everyone else arose soon after. Ella, with help from their daughter Grace, who had married and lived nearby, had already packed most of the household goods. Mr. Bayliss and Walker had arrived at a mutually agreeable division of the livestock and farm equipment, and three wagons were loaded with Walker's portion of the farm supplies, grain, and small equipment.

Harlan and his younger brother Albert got to stay out of school for the day to help move. Albert's job was to look after three-year-old Teddy so that Ella and Grace could pack the last household items and clean the house without interruption. Harlan and Myron helped move the livestock.

When morning chores and breakfast were done, Walker asked, "You women got the house things and the chickens under control? The wagons will be back for you and them around noon, I reckon."

Ella nodded as she began washing dishes. "We'll be just fine, what with Albert home to keep little Teddy out of mischief."

"All right, fellas, let's get a move on." Walker stuffed some chewing tobacco inside his lip and put on his coat. The two older boys and the hired men followed him outside. A few minutes later, he led a haltered Hereford cow into the road to serve, he hoped, as a guide for all the other cattle, pigs, and sheep. Myron and Harlan and the two dogs came behind the mixed herd, urging on the laggards and running to head off animals that turned the wrong direction at road intersections. The hired men brought up the rear, the loaded wagons they drove bouncing on the frozen ruts.

Going through the town of Guthrie Center was a real headache. It was small but had so many side roads, streets, and alleys that Harlan, Myron, and the dogs were running constantly to head off animals that didn't follow the herd. They could only relax after they finally they got all of the animals headed north beyond the cross streets that separated the rows of two-story wooden houses.

Cropland and pond on farm owned by Walker and Ella Beatty north of Guthrie Center, Iowa

The mixed entourage arrived at the Camp place tired, muddy, and hungry. Walker remained to feed and water the animals, to make sure that none of them got out and returned to the farm they'd just left, and to supervise unloading the equipment, supplies, and grain. Harlan and Myron started walking back along the rutted and now-muddy roads to help Ella and Grace assemble the boxes of household goods and finish cleaning and tidying up the house they were leaving.

"Kind of exciting to be moving to our own place, don't you think?" Myron looked toward his tall younger brother as they walked along the muddy road, eating sandwiches.

Harlan thought first about what he'd miss. "Yeah, kind of. But I'll miss climbing up to the tops of those big barns at the Bayliss place to fix the hayforks. That was exciting. The barn at this new place is so much smaller, it won't be any challenge at all." He ate a big bite of a beef sandwich, and Myron remembered how agile his brother was as he climbed up under the peaks of the barn roofs and worked on the balky hayfork mechanisms.

"Maybe you can hire out to help with the haying there next summer, if Father doesn't need you. Then you can climb the barn loft whenever the fork needs fixing." Harlan nodded dubiously, and they walked on through the mud in silence.

By evening, the Beattys were in their own home, with only some large farm equipment and hay left at the Bayliss place. For the next couple of weeks, Walker and Myron drove a team of horses pulling an empty wagon from their new farm to the old one early every day except Sunday. They returned with a load of hay and towed a mower, a corn binder, or a plow behind the wagon. When the road was particularly muddy, they had to use two teams of horses. By the time the grass was green and field work could begin, they had moved everything they owned.

* * *

Walker felt elated. The transition to being his own boss was complete, and all of the newborn calves, lambs, and pigs were his.

One evening after supper, he shared his plans to pay off the mortgage. "I'm going to plant about eighty acres of corn this spring. This farm is kind of steep, but it has a lot of good corn ground, and I think the price for corn will be up come fall."

Ella stopped darning a hole in a sock. "Eighty acres of corn will be a lot of work. Think you and the boys can handle it?"

"Oh, I think so. We've got six good horses, and I just bought a two-bottom plow. Myron's here full time now that he's done high school, and that makes a big difference. And don't forget, Albert's big enough to do a lot of chores, so Myron, Harlan, and I can work in the fields longer."

Walker's optimism was contagious. Everyone pitched in to get the land ready and the crops planted on time. They finished planting the oats and corn before the late rains, and both crops grew luxuriantly. The hay grew thick and tall on the steeper ground, and they got most of it into the barn without damage from rain.

The Hereford cows and calves gained weight in the new pastures. Albert was deemed big enough to drive the horse on the fork that lifted hay from the wagons into the barn, and he loved his new responsibility. Harlan and Myron did the hard work of spreading the hay in the mow, since Walker's asthma made it difficult for him to breathe in the hot, dusty confines of the barn loft.

They pulled the last wagonload in front of the big mow door just ahead of a black rain cloud. "Let's hustle and get this load in before it rains." Walker's voice was urgent. Rather than climbing down from the top of the load as he usually did, Myron jumped to the ground. One foot lit on a round rock, and his knee gave way, his leg twisted sideways.

His scream of pain echoed across the barnyard. "Oh, God, my knee's broken!" He lay on the ground, rubbing the throbbing joint, then trying to realign his leg. "It hurts like sin. I can't walk."

Walker and Harlan lifted him, and Harlan lent a shoulder for support as Myron hopped toward the house, his injured leg dangling. The storm hit with lightning, thunder, and a sheet of rain as they reached the porch. Walker ran back and drove the team and the load of hay into the machine shed before much of the hay got wet.

When the storm cleared, Harlan was the only one in the mow spreading the hay that dropped from the fork. Myron didn't walk unaided for a week, and he limped for several months.

Harlan and his father started building corncribs as soon as the hay was in the mow. Myron watched at first, then hobbled about and handed boards and nails to his brother and father. From time to time, his knee turned in strange directions and left him on the ground.

But day by day it mended, and soon he could walk without pain for an hour or so at a time.

As they harvested crops on the new farm, Myron was full of anticipation. His aunt and uncle, Melissa and Rob Crawford, had given a scholarship to the valedictorian of the Guthrie Center High School class of 1909, and he'd won it. He'd discussed college with his parents and applied to Coe College in Cedar Rapids, Iowa. A letter of acceptance had arrived from Coe College in response to his application. He began to dream of being on his own.

The night before Myron was to leave, the family again discussed the upcoming changes. Ella looked across at her lean, black-haired son and said, "You'll be the first one in the family to tackle college. Be sure to tend to business and work hard. Both your grandfathers started with nothing and made something of themselves. We expect you to do that too."

"Your mother's right." Walker nodded for emphasis. "If it hadn't been for that double-crossin' half-brother of mine, we'd have a whole lot of really good land right now. Instead, we got to start from scratch here in the hills and try to build back what he lost for us. But hard work will do it, I'm sure of that."

The next morning at the train station, as Walker tied up the team, Myron unloaded a suitcase and started toward the station. His father noticed the limp. "You probably couldn't have walked all day pickin' corn anyway, and I'd've had to hire a man to help me. Write us once in a while, and tell us what it's like up there at Coe. None of the rest of us knows anything about this college stuff." He smiled as he shook hands with his son.

"All right. And I'd like to hear how the farm is going while I'm gone, especially the Herefords, so be sure to write back."

The conductor yelled, "All aboard!" and Myron hustled into the train to Des Moines. Walker untied the horses and started home to the long, grueling harvest.

The eighty acres of corn yielded abundantly that fall. From mid-October until the first week of December, Walker and his hired man picked corn every day it didn't rain. Walker was up before daylight and into the field as soon as they'd eaten breakfast. When he came in from the field at dark, he ate supper, put Cornhusker's Liniment on his hands, and fell directly into bed. Before and after school, Albert and Harlan milked the cows and cared for all the other animals. Harlan picked corn with his father every Saturday. After the corn was all in the crib, Walker hauled two wagonloads to the elevator at Guthrie Center every day but Sunday. The price made the drudgery seem more than worthwhile. He banked most of what he received in preparation for paying off the mortgage, and he began to look at other land he could buy.

Release Record, No. 159, Guthrie County, Iowa.

Satisfaction of Mortgage.

I, Amanda Caroline Camp of the County of Guthrie State of Iowa, do hereby acknowledge that a certain indenture of Mortgage bearing date of the 26 day of February 1910, made and executed by Walker Beatty and Ella M. Beatty his wife, to Amanda Caroline Camp … is redeemed, paid off, satisfied and discharged in full.

signed Amanda Caroline Camp

On this 12 day of March A.D. 1912

—Record of Mortgage Satisfaction filed in the Guthrie
County Courthouse, Iowa

* * *

When Myron arrived in Des Moines on his way to Coe College, his Aunt Melissa and Uncle Rob Crawford stood at the station, waving to him. They got on and rode the ten miles with him to Altoona, where his grandparents, Elijah and Julia Reames, were waiting at the depot to chat during the train's stop there. Melissa admired Myron's new suit and shirt, which she had helped pick out and had paid for a few weeks earlier.

Rob was the first to spot Elijah and Julia on the platform, and he waved to them as the train stopped. "Hello, Lije. Hello, Julia. Nice of you to come see your grandson off to college. Mind if Mel stays with you folks a few hours? I've got to catch the next train back to Des Moines and get to work."

Lije smiled beneath his walrus mustache and extended a broad hand to the banker. "Always glad to have you fine folks pay us a visit. Sure am sorry you can't do more than say hello and good-bye, Rob. But business is business—I understand that." Then he turned to Myron, who was standing beside his aunt and uncle, and noted how his new suit changed his appearance.

"So, young fella, you're off to college to get all smartened up with book learning." Myron nodded and smiled at his grandparents. Lije slapped him on the back and said, "Now I'll be able to win the footraces when we go see you Beattys at Guthrie Center. I never could outrun you, but it'll be easy to outrun those brothers of yours. You're the fastest runner of the whole bunch."

Myron shifted from foot to foot. "I can run pretty fast, but it's hard to beat you, Grandpa."

The train whistled once, and passengers began to board. Julia stopped talking to Melissa and turned to Myron. "You do your best up there at Coe, young man. Make us proud of you, just like you did in high school. And be sure to write us a letter as soon as you get there."

"Yes, Grandmother. I'll work hard, and I'll write." He turned to shake hands with his grandfather. Lije slipped a ten-dollar bill into Myron's hand as they shook, then put his finger to his lips.

"Have fun up there at college, and don't take any wooden nickels." He grinned conspiratorially and glanced toward his wife to be sure she hadn't noticed the secret exchange of money. Myron slid the bill into his pocket, shook hands with the Crawfords, thanked them for their generosity, and got back on the train.

As it pulled out of the station, he was thrilled to be on his own and apprehensive at the same time.

The apprehension increased as the train arrived in Cedar Rapids.

Where would he find a place to live? Where would he eat? Would he be smart enough to keep up in his classes? He followed several people his age who got off the train carrying suitcases and began walking along the elm-shaded street toward the campus. One young woman smiled and said hello, but he was too shy to say anything in return, so he just smiled and nodded. At the admissions office, he showed his letter of acceptance to a middle-aged woman at the desk and inquired about economical places to rent a room and get meals, then about registering for classes.

The lady in charge looked Myron up and down before saying, "You have your priorities mixed up, I see. First you want to find a place to eat and sleep, and only then do you care about learning."

Three students in line behind him laughed, but they stopped abruptly when the lady gave them a stern frown. She handed Myron a sheet listing rooming and boarding houses near the campus. "I'd recommend Mrs. Tetzvold or Mrs. Reuter. They both run good, clean places and don't put up with any nonsense, and they're both good cooks. The prices are mostly all the same." Myron memorized the addresses and thanked her as he left.

At Mrs. Tetzvold's large brick house, students were unpacking, chatting, or lounging about by twos and threes. She looked at Myron with an appraising eye and took him to the third-floor dormitory, where a bed remained unoccupied. "How's this for ya, young man? It's the last space I got. If you'd'a brought your own bedding, it woulda been twenty-five cents a week cheaper."

"I'll take it, and I'll send home for some bedding right away, ma'am. Is that all right?" He was acutely aware that the cost of room and board was going to strain his finances. And he still had to buy books. Maybe he could get some used ones, and maybe he could get a part-time job helping in the kitchen. "Do you need anybody to work for part of their room and board?"

Mrs. Tetzvold looked him over carefully again before asking, "Where do you come from? Grow up on a farm or in town? Know how to get up early and work?"

His answers seemed to satisfy her, and she smiled as she said, "Right now I'm in good shape for help, but my kitchen assistant will be graduating at the end of this term. I'll keep you in mind for his place."

Myron woke up at 5:30 the first day of classes. It seemed late to him, but then he'd stayed up late the night before, talking with roommates. After breakfast, he was one of the first to arrive for the morning service in the dimly illuminated gothic chapel, but he sat in a pew near the back.

At exactly 7:30, President Marquis marched in, wearing his black academic robe, looked over the sparse array of mostly sleepy students, and announced that chapel attendance was mandatory, timely arrival was imperative, and that hereafter faculty members would be at the chapel door to check names. As President Marquis droned on, Myron's thoughts drifted back to the farm. He remembered how often and how loudly he and his brothers had protested when their father made them get up at 5:00 AM to help with farm chores. Now he was glad that he hadn't been raised in town, where sleeping in until 6:30 or even later was permitted.

After the chapel service ended, Myron joined the group of students filing into the classroom of George W. Bryant, professor of Latin. Professor Bryant called the name of each enrollee and told them which seat they had been assigned. A brief period of shuffling and rearrangement ensued, and Myron wound up in the second seat of the front row with Phaen Barron on his left and Fred Bowersox on his right. Both had new textbooks. Myron's had a torn cover.

When Professor Bryant began to probe the background in Latin of his new class, he discovered that for about half, this was their first venture into the language, and that for the other half, knowledge of the ancient language varied from rudimentary to fair. Myron left the first session of the class feeling more confident of succeeding in college.

As the first week of classes unfolded, the freshmen students began to start friendships, upperclassmen to renew old ones. Plans for group activities were brought forward by upperclassmen. The first was the tug-of-war between the men of the four classes.

On a Saturday morning near the end of September, members of the classes assembled along a marshy creek that bordered the campus. Five seniors arrived with a coil of heavy rope and proceeded to unroll it across the creek, taking care not to let it get wet. Then one of them blew a whistle and announced grandly, "The annual tug-of-war between the esteemed members of the sophomore class of Coe College and the lowly new freshmen is set to commence. Men, take your places. Sophomores, defend your class honor. Freshmen, this is your opportunity to show whether or not you are worthy to be enrolled at Coe College. Get over to the other side of the marsh and line up! Ladies, please stand back and cheer on your favorite class."

He bowed and doffed his cap. Then he handed one end of the rope to a burly sophomore from the football team, who motioned his classmates forward and showed them how to stand and grip the rope. Across the creek, the freshmen, who outnumbered the sophomores about two to one, were milling about and arranging themselves in a line, grasping the rope. Myron was near the middle of the line. When both sides appeared ready, the senior blew a whistle. The sophomores gave a concerted heave and pulled the rope several feet toward their side. Two freshmen were pulled into the mucky blackness of the marsh. Then the freshmen began to pull as a team, and slowly, foot by foot, they retrieved the rope and pulled several sophomores into the other side of the marsh.

The sophomore women cheered on their men with a yell, led by a long-haired and long-limbed brunette. "Soph-mores! Soph-mores! Nine-teen, thir-teen! Rah! Rah! Rah! Pull, boys, *pull!*"

The cheer invigorated their male classmates, who reversed the momentum of the contest briefly and retrieved enough wet rope for their colleagues who had been pulled into the marsh to climb out, wipe their hands quickly, and rejoin their heaving classmates. But the outnumbered sophomores didn't gain the advantage for long. The more numerous freshmen, now getting the hang of the game, pulled in unison as the freshmen girls yelled, "Skin-em-alive, skin-em-alive! Nine-teen four-teen! Go! Go! Go!"

Suddenly the line of sophomore pullers buckled, and the rope, with a few unlucky sophomores still holding it, surged swiftly toward the freshmen's side of the creek. Several men near the front of the line tumbled into the soupy muck and emerged sputtering and attempting to wipe the black goop off their hands, shoes, and clothes. The senior blew the whistle to end the contest, then called for a pull between the just-defeated sophomores and the cocky but outnumbered juniors. Someone produced a pile of rags, and the senior ordered the frosh team to wipe the rope clean and dry it as best they could.

As they were wiping the wet, black rope, a big freshman beside Myron said to him, "You're not very heavy, but you sure can pull that rope. My hands are all blistered. How come yours aren't?"

Myron looked up in surprise and ran a hand through his dark hair, "I don't know. Guess I just got tough hands and strong arms from workin' on the farm, but I have to be careful of my game knee. I'm glad it didn't go out while I was pulling."

* * *

After six weeks of class, Professor M. Hubert Scott eyed the freshman English class angrily. He rubbed his hand across his bald head and began to hand back the first exam papers of the term. When he was done, he announced, "I am sadly disappointed with most of you. Coe College is an institution of intellectual rigor, and it appears that all but a few are not up to its high standards." He paused to let his pronouncement sink in. Students shifted around in their seats. Many of the class looked toward the floor. "Out of this class, there are only five whom I consider worthy to be called true students of English at Coe. I am inviting them to join the distinguished literary society Alpha Nu. The invitations have been written on their examination sheets. For the rest of you, I suggest a thorough review the fundamentals of English grammar and literary style at each and every opportunity, and that you commit the rules of grammar and composition to memory at once. Those five students who received invitations should stay briefly after class to get details of the prestigious group which you are eligible to join. Any questions?" After an awkward silence, Professor Scott announced, "Very well, we will proceed with today's lesson."

Myron looked at his exam paper with an invitation lettered neatly along the top. He was surprised and found it hard to concentrate on Professor Scott's lecture. The five men with invitations lingered after class to learn more about Alpha Nu. When Professor Scott dismissed them, Myron hustled to his class in Old Testament history. As he slipped into his seat, Professor Evans scowled and interrupted his lecture on the meanings of the Book of Job with a question. "Mr. Beatty, why are you late? You know what time this class starts." Myron stood and responded quietly, "Sir, I'm late because Professor Scott asked a few of us who've been selected to join Alpha Nu to stay after his class. It's quite an honor."

As he sat down, there was a buzz of whispered talk. He heard a muted comment or two among the low voices: "Good for you, for standing up to the old buzzard." "Congratulations, Myron."

Then Professor Evans commanded, "Quiet down. There's no need for all this noise." Myron noticed the admiring glances directed his way as the lecture resumed. But his thoughts strayed from the travails of Job to his own money-related worries. If only he had enough money to stay here all four years. But he didn't.

After he finished the first semester of his sophomore year at Coe College, Myron came home reluctantly and resumed working on the farm. The occasional newspapers he saw had stories about President Woodrow Wilson, the war in Europe, and Progressivism. His father was delighted that prices for crops and livestock were up. Everyone else was optimistic, but he was broke. Walker and Ella were preparing to buy another eighty-acre parcel of land east of their farm and couldn't help him much with college expenses.

Know all Men by these Presents: That W. G. Savery and Hazel A. Savery husband and wife of Guthrie County and the State of Iowa in consideration of the sum of Seventy six Hundred DOLLARS in hand paid by Walker Beatty of Guthrie county and the State of Iowa do hereby SELL AND CONVEY ... the following described premises, situated in the county of Guthrie, and State of Iowa, to wit: The West half of the Southeast quarter of Section Thirty (30)in Township 80 North Range Thirty one (31) West of the 5th P.M. in Guthrie County Iowa, containing 80 acres more or less according to government survey. Subject to $5500.00 of a mortgage of

$7500.00 on this and other land which said Walker Beatty assumes and agrees to pay said $5500.00 with interest on same from and after March 1-1913 at the rate of 5 1/2% ...

Signed the 28 day of February 1913 ...

W. G. Savery, Hazel A. Savery

—Warranty Deed Record No. 167 filed at the Guthrie County Courthouse, Iowa

The next fall, Myron enrolled at Des Moines College and assisted his newly widowed grandmother, Julia Reames, in return for board, room, and train fare between Altoona and Des Moines. His father advanced him enough money for books and tuition, and in return Myron worked for his father during the summers.

Life with his grandmother was a total contrast to life at Coe College. She was mourning the loss of her husband, and it made her more peevish and critical than ever. Myron was so busy commuting, attending classes, studying, and taking care of his grandmother's house, yard, garden, milk cow, and team of carriage horses that he was almost entirely cut off from student life. He missed the friends he'd made at Coe, the Alpha Nu literary society with its dramatic recitations and formal dinners, and the lively banter of the rooming house. But semester by semester, he was making progress toward a college degree.

* * *

When the interurban train from Des Moines reached the station at Altoona, Myron closed his German textbook, hopped off, and trotted along the shady street to his grandmother's house, book bag bouncing at his side. "Hello, Grandmother. I'm home early to clean out the barn and haul in a load of fresh hay for the cow and horses, like you told me to."

Julia Reames, overweight, arthritic, and in a bad mood, snapped,

"It's about time you got here and did something useful. I've been expecting you all afternoon, so get a move on. And before you go out, bring me those pills on my dresser upstairs." Myron tried not to look intimidated as he stood briefly beside his grandmother, who sat in her overstuffed chair with her feet on a footstool. Then he nodded, changed into his work clothes, grabbed the pills as he came downstairs, and was out the door before his grandmother could think of any other chores. He wondered what she'd do for help when he graduated. That day couldn't come too soon. Why couldn't she be more like Lije, his fun-loving grandfather? Why had God taken Lije to heaven and left his crotchety wife for the family to contend with? He mulled that question over as he forked the pile of manure behind the barn onto the wagon and rode the bouncing load toward his grandmother's farm at the edge of the village. No good answers came to him. Oh, well, he'd graduate soon. His grandmother would have to find someone else to dump her complaints on.

He scattered the manure on a field of corn stubble, forked hay from the barn to the wagon, and returned in time to cook supper for himself and his grandmother. After he'd washed and dried the dishes, it was back to the books. Graduation was getting close, and he had to study for the German exam. His grandmother was grumbling about having to move, now that he would be leaving and she could not care for her house and animals alone.

THE TRUSTEES OF DES MOINES COLLEGE

at Des Moines, Iowa

Upon the recommendation of the Faculty, have conferred upon

Myron W. Beatty

the degree of BACHELOR OF DIDACTICS and by this Diploma make known that he is entitled to all the HONORS, RIGHTS and

PRIVILEGES to that degree appertaining.

Given this second day of June, in the year of our Lord one thousand nine hundred and fifteen ...

After the commencement ceremony, Myron visited briefly with his Aunt Melissa and Uncle Rob Crawford, then went directly to Altoona to pick up his clothes and say good-bye to his grandmother. He found her packing and fussing about the house.

"Hello, Grandma. I'm back to get my clothes before I go home to Guthrie Center. Can I help you with anything else?"

"You could help by making this dratted rheumatism go away. Every time I try to move, it hurts like all get-out and just keeps on hurting. Mrs. Dean is coming to get me and my stuff in about an hour, and I'm not halfway ready. Otherwise, don't bother me."

"Grandmother, I can't do anything to help your rheumatism, but I can carry these boxes to the front porch."

"All right. As long as you're here, make yourself useful." Myron watched his grandmother move slowly and heavily toward the dining room, then picked up the boxes in the kitchen and carried them to a pile on the front porch. She was still packing tablecloths when he came downstairs, carrying his suitcase.

"Good-bye, Grandmother. I hope you like it at Mrs. Dean's house. She'll treat you real well, I think."

Mrs. Reames stopped folding a tablecloth. "You've given me a big boost. I couldn't have stayed here so long without your help. The best of luck to you. Now move along, and don't bother me." She turned back to the tablecloths she was sorting, then thought of something, paused, and yelled at her grandson, "When you get home, tell your mother to come and get some of the stuff I won't be needing anymore."

"I'll tell her, Grandma. Good-bye!" Myron waved and hustled toward the train station.

On the train west from Altoona, Myron thought about his future. With a college degree, he could teach school or work in a business, but what he really looked forward to was getting back to the farm and being around the Herefords. He loved those gentle animals: the way they liked being brushed, the way the calves frolicked around the fields in the evenings, the way they crowded around to be fed. He pondered his options and wondered if the best one would be possible. *Maybe there'll be a teaching job right near home,* he thought, *so that I can work on the farm mornings, evenings, and all summer. Then maybe I could buy some Herefords of my own with what I earn teaching and what Father pays me.* The idea sounded wonderful but maybe impossible.

Chapter 28
Coming Home

Myron was coming back to a changed household and neighborhood, wondering if he would fit in. His brother Harlan had graduated from Guthrie Center High School and left to join his uncle Will Reames, who was farming in Minnesota. Albert was a husky, round-faced boy of fifteen who loved working with the livestock. Teddy, age eight, had just finished second grade. Prices for farm products were going up. European nations were at war and importing more food from the United States. All the news was about that war and whether or not the United States should get involved.

When the train pulled into the station, his father was standing beside a new black Model T Ford with side curtains. Myron was amazed to see his conservative father with it. "Hello, Father. This car's a surprise. When'd you buy it?"

"Just last week. Bought it after we sold four young bulls last month. Got near a thousand dollars for 'em. This jitney only cost four hundred. I'm plumb tired of always having to hitch up a team to go anywhere. This thing's tricky to start, but after you once get it moving, it's real good, 'cept on real steep hills. For those, you've gotta turn it around and back up."

Myron put his suitcase on the back seat of the new Ford and watched his father. Walker adjusted the throttle lever and the spark-timing lever on the steering column, then stood in front of the car and spun the crank. The engine kicked back once, but he got his hand out of the way in time to avoid getting hurt. It finally started, and they both hustled onto the front seat. Walker reached below the steering wheel and pushed the spark lever up and the throttle down. The engine ran smoother and faster. Then he pushed down the low-gear pedal with his foot and released the handbrake. The car jerked, then chugged forward and gained speed. Walker took his foot off the low-gear pedal and pushed up the throttle lever. The engine slowed a little, but the car went faster.

As they drove through the town, Walker waved to several acquaintances, who looked surprised, then waved back. He steered awkwardly but managed to keep his new purchase on the road as they drove north, up and down the hills toward home, and parked in the machine shed. Myron was amazed at how quickly they arrived.

"This thing is really nice for going to town and back, isn't it?"

His father beamed. "That's for sure. It prob'ly saved me an hour over using the horses." Walker ran his hand slowly along a dusty fender to reveal the shiny black paint. "Now I can get back to plowing corn quicker. As soon as you get into your work clothes, you can hook up the sorrel team and start cultivating the corn in the east field. The quack grass is already pretty thick in it."

Myron took the hint and hustled into his overalls and farm boots. He curried and harnessed the sorrels, talking to them as he worked. "It's great to be back here with you guys." The horses shifted in their stall and looked at the newcomer warily. In a few minutes, he, the sorrels, and the cultivator were starting down the first row. The cultivator shovels lifted and overturned the carpet of young weeds growing between the corn hills as the team settled into a slow, steady pace. He could tell they'd done this before.

Myron looked down from his seat to be sure that the cultivator shovels weren't throwing dirt over the young corn plants, adjusted a lever on the cultivator two notches, then looked around the greening fields of corn and grain that stretched in all directions. The sun was warm on his back. The aroma of the newly turned soil rose to complement the soft smell of the growing corn and offset the occasional bursts of intestinal gas that the horses emitted as they settled into the work of pulling the cultivator. At the end of the row, the team stopped while he lifted the cultivator shovels, then turned like automatons into the next row, ready to start the return pull. It felt good to be back on the land.

A week after he'd returned home, on the first rainy day, when he couldn't work in the field, Myron walked to town. At the Guthrie County superintendent of schools office, he inquired about teaching opportunities and learned that a school district about two miles north of the farm was looking for a teacher. That was close enough that he could live at home and walk to it. He went to visit the school board chairman, and after a short conversation, he left with the job and the key to the schoolhouse. The pay would be sixty-one dollars per month—enough to let him save to buy some Herefords.

At supper, he shared the news. "I've got a job starting in September." Everyone looked up, waiting for details. "I'll be teaching at District School 19. It's close enough that I'll be able to live here, help with the farm work, and walk back and forth."

Walker spooned mashed potatoes to his plate and looked pleased. "That's good. What does it pay?"

"Sixty-one a month."

"That's darn good for teaching school. I heard they paid the woman who taught there last year forty-seven."

"Well, they always pay a woman less than a man. Besides I've got a college degree, so they pay me more."

"It's good you've got a job close to home, but how will all that walking be on your bad knee?" His mother leaned across the table and put her hand on his arm.

"It may be good for it, if I don't twist it. I'll pay attention to where I'm going and pick up my feet, so don't worry." Myron's response seemed to reassure his mother, even though he had a few doubts himself.

Walker was pleased at the prospect of having Myron home again, and he wanted to be sure he stayed. "Since you'll be working here all summer, and then mornings, evenings, and Saturdays once school starts, I'll give you two heifer calves next spring. You can pick out the ones you want after they're born."

"Thanks, Father. They'll be better than money, because they'll help me start a herd of my own." Myron's warm smile told Walker that he'd made a good offer.

But as the summer passed, Myron's doubts grew. Teaching would be something totally new for him. At least he had the benefit of having four years of college behind him, and of being a man and better able to enforce discipline. He wondered how young women who had just graduated from high school and then started teaching managed, and how well he would do in this new profession.

But the classes went much better than he'd expected. By Christmas, he knew that he could do a good job of teaching, but that it would grow boring after a year or two. What he really loved was being with cattle. The times before and after school when he was tending the cattle were what he loved. So he kept teaching to earn money to buy more Herefords.

Chapter 29
The War Years

Walker drove the wagonload of corn up the ramp and onto the scale at the elevator that stood beside the railroad tracks in Guthrie Center. The horses shied at the metal grating over the scale, but finally they walked warily along either side of it. The operator came out of the office alongside the scale. "Got another load of corn to sell ya, Jake," Walker said. "How's the price today?"

"It's up again, just like it's been goin' all fall." Jake adjusted the weights on the scale beam.

Walker climbed off the wagon and stood alongside the scale, holding the reins. "Good. How much you paying?"

"It's up to one dollar and one cent for number two dent like you got." Jake jiggled the weight on the balance beam to his left until the free end of the beam lifted off its base and floated between the upper and lower supports; then he wrote down the weight of the load and wagon. "How's that suit you?"

"Just great. This time last year, it was only sixty-nine cents. Maybe I'll quit hauling for a while and let the price go up some more."

"Ya could, but don't wait too long if you've got a lot yet to haul. Price could go back down."

Walker nodded, then opened the tailgate and began shoveling ears of corn out the back. When he had finished, he called, "Jake, come and weigh my empty wagon and figure what you owe me.

It's goin' to be a pretty penny, an' I've still got twenty or so loads to haul."

He waited while Jake wrote a check for $61.25, then drove to Main Street, tied the team to the hitching post behind the bank, and went inside, whistling.

By the time he'd finished hauling all of his corn to the elevator a month later, the price was up to $1.29 per bushel. The next year, as the demand for food was augmented by the Great War, the price averaged $1.43, and Walker paid off the entire mortgage on the eighty-acre addition to the farm.

He and his neighbors marveled at how prices for cattle, hogs, corn, and oats went up month by month as the war in Europe dragged on and Great Britain and France bought more and more feed and foodstuffs from the United States and Canada. It appeared that their bonanza would never end.

When he'd finished paying off the mortgage, Walker began to look at farms for sale closer to Des Moines. He and Ella felt isolated from their families because they lived sixty miles away. His three sisters and their husbands all lived in and around Des Moines. Ella disliked the long train trips to Altoona to see her mother.

After he'd finished all of the preparations for winter on the farm, Walker took the train to Des Moines to visit his relatives and to hunt for a new farm. He had looked for several days when the one that Julius Kratzer had for sale caught his eye. Its 180 acres were nearly level, its soils were deep, it was only eight miles west of Des Moines, and it had two houses, one large and one small, and two large barns. But the price was steep—two hundred dollars per acre.

Walker was staying with his sister Melissa and her banker husband, Rob Crawford, so as they finished dinner in the ornate home on Des Moines' Grand Avenue, he asked Rob for his view on buying Kratzer's place.

Crawford considered Walker's question as the maid cleared the dining table and brought a pot of tea. His measured response surprised Walker. "The prospects all indicate there'll be a major drop in farm prices when the war ends—which it might do rathah soon. I'd be extremely cautious about taking on any debt at this time. Extremely cautious indeed."

"Even if I can sell our place at Guthrie for a good price and pay mostly cash for Kratzer's place?" Walker's question and his expression betrayed his eagerness to make the purchase.

"Remembah that your present farm doesn't have the fancy buildings and level land of the one you're proposing to buy, even though yours is bigger. I'd estimate you'll get $22,000 or maybe $24,000 for it, if you're lucky."

Walker's confidence was undeterred by his brother in law's conservative advice. "That's probably about right. But I've paid off the mortgages on our home place and the new eighty in short order, way ahead of schedule. I don't think paying off a $12,000 or $14,000 debt on a land contract would be any problem at all."

Crawford flicked a crumb off his tie and sipped his tea. "I know you're a hard, thrifty worker, and I wish you the best, but it seems cleah that farming won't be as profitable the next few yeahs as it has been during the war. And if you get into trouble, I probably won't be able to help you out."

"Well, thanks for your advice, Rob. I'll think on it. But now it's about my bedtime." Walker walked up the spiral staircase to the third floor and spent a restless night.

All the way back to Guthrie Center, he pondered how to pay for Kratzer's farm. As the train rocked and clicked westward, he wrote numbers on a sheet of paper. *I can't sell our hilly farm for anywhere near what his place will cost*, he thought, *but maybe I can get enough to buy that place on a land contract and get him to carry me for the difference if I pay a good rate of interest.* He kept studying the numbers intently, erasing a few and replacing them with others. His thoughts returned to his recent experiences buying land. Paying some cash down and getting a loan for the rest had worked great when he bought land from Miss Camp and the Saverys. He'd paid off both mortgages way early. By the time the train stopped in Guthrie Center, Walker was looking out the window and humming to himself.

The move to the new farm was by far the biggest the Beattys had ever made. Walker, Myron, and Albert spent almost a week moving machinery to the railroad siding and wrestling it into boxcars. Then they hauled the household goods in the Model T, paying special attention not to break the glass jars of canned fruits, vegetables, and meats that Ella had brought up from the cellar and wrapped in newspapers.

On the last morning, they drove all the livestock to the stockyards by the rail siding. Walker walked in front, leading a team of horses for the cattle and pigs to follow. The procession was much longer than when they'd come along the same road in the opposite direction five years earlier. Ella and Teddy came behind, driving a team and light wagon with the remainder their household goods—bedding, a few dishes, an iron griddle, and a frying pan, all wrapped and packed in boxes. The men had barely closed the door on the last rail car when a switch engine and crew chugged up, moved the cars with all their possessions to the main line, and hooked them to the waiting freight train. At the depot, Ella unwrapped jelly sandwiches, which they ate as they waited for the eastbound passenger train to take them to their new home.

"I just hope we're making the right move. We had the place here all paid for free and clear, and now we're in debt again." Ella frowned and looked at her husband.

Her words caught Walker by surprise. "It'll be a good move for us, Ella. I figure with prices the way they are, we'll be able to pay off the contract to Kratzer in three, maybe four years at the most. And you'll like the house, an' being nearer your mother." Ella looked tired but reassured as she rewrapped the remaining sandwiches and put them in a canvas bag.

The cars on the eastbound train were nearly full of soldiers traveling east on their way to France. The Beattys and other new passengers took what few seats remained open, even though they had to spread out into different cars. Myron and Albert sat among several of the young men.

After a few miles, one of them looked at Myron and said, "How come you're not in the army and wearing a uniform like us?"

"I've got a bad knee. It goes out once in a while. When I went to be inducted last year, the doctor said it wasn't good enough for me to get in."

The soldier remained curious. "What do you two fellas do, if you don't mind my asking?"

Albert spoke up quickly. "We're farmers. And we're moving to a new farm near Des Moines. I'm still in high school, but my big brother's already finished college. He's been a teacher, too. After we get the crops planted on the new farm, he's taking a trainload of Herefords out west for a man we know. Sure wish I could go along."

The soldiers in nearby seats stopped playing cards and began to eavesdrop. A tall, blond man with blue eyes volunteered, "I been west oncst. Them mountains are real purty. How far ya gonna go?"

Myron said, "I'm going to a ranch near Harlowtown, Montana. Ever heard of that town? It's on the Milwaukee Railroad's new line to Seattle."

"Cain't say as I have, but I been to Montana. Rode the Northern Pacific all the way to Seattle. The east part's dry and kinda boring to ride through. But them mountains on the west side are real steep and purty." His vigorous nod reinforced his declaration.

Myron thanked him, then turned to look out the window as he pondered his upcoming trip. He wondered what it would be like to be in country that was dry and full of mountains. *Sure must be different from here,* he thought. He tried to picture it from the descriptions of Colorado that his parents had shared with him and his siblings around the stove on winter evenings. Blizzards and chinook winds came to his mind immediately. As the train slowed to enter the rail yards at Valley Junction, his thoughts came back from the imagined West to central Iowa and the tasks ahead.

* * *

The new farm was in stark contrast to the one they'd left. The one they'd sold was all hills and valleys; this one was broad and level. The big white frame house and its smaller companion at the end of a long driveway were dazzling in contrast to the small, unpainted one tucked beside a hill on the farm north of Guthrie Center.

The Beattys admired the buildings as they drove their livestock from the railroad yards to the pasture behind their new farmstead. Myron made sure that all the livestock were in pastures or pens and that the gates were securely shut. He and his father looked over the new farm before he walked back to the railroad siding to start unloading the Model T, farm machinery, and household goods. "Looks like a nice place, Father."

Walker spat out his tobacco juice and ran his hand across his forehead out of habit, even though it wasn't warm enough for any sweat to have formed. "It's good land with real fine buildings. And it's big enough for either you or Albert to farm with me if you want. And one of you can live in that little house when you get married. At my age, a fella's got to plan ahead for the next generation." He looked proud.

The level fields were easier to work than the hilly ones they'd left, but they stayed wet longer in the spring, so the crops were planted late—but not too late for the cutworms that hatched in abundance and ate most of the young corn. Walker and Myron worked from daylight to dark replanting the decimated fields. As he replanted corn with the new corn planter, Walker wondered if this was a portent of trouble ahead for the new farm. When the price of corn plummeted that fall, he worried even more about the debt he had assumed when he bought this new farm.

Chapter 30
Myron's Trip West

Myron's heart had done somersaults when John Shoesmith, a local Hereford breeder, large land owner, and acquaintance from several fairs and livestock shows, asked him to take responsibility for a trainload of cattle being shipped west. He'd always had his father looking over his shoulder on anything related to farming and the cattle. This was like a gust of fresh air in a hot and dusty haymow. He worked early and late to finish replanting corn so that his father's new farm would be in good shape when the time came for him to go west.

As he walked toward the stockyards by the Valley Junction rail siding on a day in mid-May, he heard the continuous, undulating sound of discontented cattle bawling. It arose from inside the pens where three hundred yearling steers and heifers plus seventy-five cows with young calves milled about. The cows were looking for their offspring among the multitude of calves, and the calves gave high-pitched bleats as they tried to find their mothers and suckle milk from a welcoming udder.

As Myron arrived, carrying a cardboard suitcase, a locomotive pulling a string of rail cars with slatted sides chuffed up. It stopped so that the first four cars were in front of the chutes that sloped up from each of the cattle pens to the level of the train floor. Six men who had been sitting on the top plank of the fence jumped down and opened the doors of the front cars, pulled back the gates that had blocked the ends of the chutes, and began to force cattle up into the cars.

The bellowing and bleating grew louder. Myron climbed over the fence and joined the work crew. As soon as the first four cars were filled and the doors shut, the engineer pulled the train forward until the next four cars were in line with the chutes, and the loading process was repeated. In less than an hour, all the animals were on board.

John Shoesmith, who had been watching, motioned Myron aside. Myron hustled over to where Shoesmith, a tall, red-faced man of about fifty, was standing, and he listened to his new boss's instructions. "I want you to keep close track of how often they unload my stock for feed and water. The railroad promised me it would be every thirty-six hours, no more. If there's any problem, or if the guys at the stockyards injure any of my cattle unloading or loading them, send me a telegram right away. Understand?"

Myron nodded, "Yes, sir. I'll keep a close watch and let you know if there's any problem. I hate to see cattle hurt or mistreated."

Shoesmith held out his hand with a check between his thumb and forefinger. "I'm sure you'll do a good job. Here's a month's pay. By the way, you can stay and work on the ranch after you get there, if you want."

Myron took the check and then grasped Mr. Shoesmith's hand, "That sounds good. I'll consider it. Now I better get on board, or they'll leave without me. I'll keep in touch." He grabbed his suitcase and ran to the loaded cattle train, and after wiping the cow manure off his shoes, he climbed into the caboose.

After two short whistle blasts, the train began to move through the rail yards, slowly at first, but then faster and faster as it reached the open countryside and headed west toward Omaha, then north on the broad floodplain of the Missouri River. From time to time, its mournful, penetrating whistle drowned out the steady clickety-clack, clickety-clack of the wheels. To Myron, it spoke of adventure and trust; it was the first time he'd had anywhere near this much responsibility. He was elated. There was nothing to do now that all the animals were safely on board, so he relaxed, letting the sway of the train guide his thoughts. Soon he fell asleep.

As he dozed, Myron dreamed of mountains with steep white peaks that dominated the plains below them, like the ones his parents had talked about from their days in Colorado. He dreamed of herds of white-faced cattle grazing on the plains in front of the mountains. He imagined that they were his and that men on horseback were rounding them up and driving them toward a large corral. The clickety-clack of the train wheels slowed and then stopped. Myron awoke with a start.

"How far have we come?" he asked, looking up at the conductor.

"'Bout a hundred fifty miles. We're just at the edge of Sioux City, goin' up along the Missouri. Want some coffee? Cups are there in the cupboard."

"Sure, that would help me wake up. Thanks." He poured a cup of the hot liquid and tasted it, then puckered his face. It burned his lips, and the taste made him want to spit it out. "You make a real potent brew here."

The conductor got down from his high seat and buttoned his vest. "It's been boilin' for quite a spell. If it's too strong for ya, just toss it out the window."

Myron let it cool for a few minutes and then drank it down. By then, the conductor was climbing down from the caboose, and his replacement was coming aboard. Myron moved alongside the train, peering into each car, looking for any animals that were down and unable to get up or any that looked sick or distressed.

All of them were on their feet and seemed to have adjusted to their cramped accommodations. The cows and calves appeared to have been paired up as they were being loaded. That was good, because it would be another twelve hours before they were unloaded to be fed and watered. He said hello to the new engineer and fireman and told them that the cattle were traveling well. Just to be sure, he looked into each car again on his way back to the caboose. They sat on the side track for several hours while three troop trains went by, going east.

When the cattle train finally got to Aberdeen, South Dakota, the Milwaukee Road's stockyards were bustling and bawling with activity and sound. The wind carried these sounds of anxious animals and moving locomotives to Myron's ears even before the train eased to a stop. He pulled his hat down firmly to keep it from being blown off and walked to the front of the train.

The engineer leaned out of his high window with a paper in his hand and said, "Better get back on board. They're not goin' to unload your cattle here. Goin' to take 'em on another three hundred fifty miles or so to Miles City before they unload 'em. So get right back on. We're pullin' out as soon as we get more coal and water."

"You can't do that! They'll have been in those cars for two days by then. No, sir, I won't stand for it." Myron jumped up the steps of the locomotive and confronted the engineer. "Let me read that piece of paper." He took the order sheet from the surprised man and scanned it. "I want to see the chief dispatcher. You wait right here till I get back."

The dispatcher looked up in surprise when Myron burst through the door, waving the piece of paper. "Something I can do for ya?"

"There sure is. You can get that trainload of cattle that's scheduled to go right on through to Miles City unloaded here for feed and water. This shipping order is just plain wrong. It'll keep the cattle on the train way too long at one stretch." Myron put his finger on the offending sentences for emphasis. "This doesn't take into account that we sat on sidings for five or six hours as we came from Valley Junction."

The dispatcher studied the paper that Myron had thrust at him. "You sure you know what you're hollerin' about, young fella?"

"I sure do. We left Valley Junction at 9:30 in the morning, an' that's almost twenty-eight hours ago. It will be another twenty hours to Miles City—way too long for cattle to be without water and feed."

The dispatcher looked at the clock, then wrote some numbers on the order and studied them. "Kinda looks like you got a point. But I don't know if we got space fer that many cattle right now. Let me call the yard boss an' see how many open pens he can scare up."

He cranked a black telephone and waited. "Millie, get me Joe on the line right away." There was a long wait. Myron watched the trains moving back and forth in the freight yard, all the while making sure his train didn't leave. "Joe, where you been? Sleepin' again? Say,

I got a big trainload of cattle sittin' in the yard, and they need feed an' water and a twenty-four-hour rest. How many pens ya got open?" He listened for what seemed like an eternity.

"Joe, I know you hadn't planned on 'em, but can you handle a trainload right now?" He listened again, drumming his fingers on the table. "Then start gettin' ready. I'll get 'em to back the train in." Myron left the dispatcher's office alongside a railroad employee who was holding a new set of orders for the engineer and conductor. He felt a sense of accomplishment.

When all the cars had been unloaded and the cattle were crowding and jostling around the watering troughs and hay mangers in the pens, he studied the animals to see if any showed signs of having been injured during the ride. They all appeared to be in good condition, eating and drinking hungrily. He hustled to the restaurant and hotel across the street.

As far as Myron could tell from their dress and conversation, most of the men in the restaurant were railroad workers. They wore red bandannas around their necks and narrow-striped bib overalls and matching caps. The morning wind carried the sounds of trains and livestock and the pungent smells of manure and coal smoke from the stockyards into the open windows, but no one noticed. He slid onto a seat near the end of the counter and lifted the stained menu from the rack behind the salt and pepper shakers.

"What'll ya have, fella?" A buxom waitress with a stained white apron over her dress appeared from out of nowhere before he'd even had time to look at the menu. She tapped her pencil on the counter and shifted from foot to foot. "If you don't know what you want, I'm not goin' to wait all morning."

Myron looked up quickly, "Sorry to not be ready. Just bring me a big order of bacon and eggs and potatoes."

"How ya like yer eggs? Any coffee?"

"Yes, please. And cook the bacon and eggs real well." She made a few strokes with her pencil on a small pad.

Then she yelled to the cook, "Big order of hen berries n' bacon an' spuds. Burn 'em some for this new guy."

Everyone looked at him as echoes of her smoky alto voice reverberated over the quiet talk. "Here's some coffee for ya." The cup clanked against the counter, and some coffee slopped onto its worn linoleum surface. She wiped it up with the end of her apron and moved on. Myron ate quickly, listening to snatches of conversation about train schedules, switches that needed repair, and other details of railroading. After he finished breakfast, he found a room at the hotel.

The noise and smell from the stockyards were like an aromatic lullaby after the big meal. He went to sleep in broad daylight and slept until dawn the next day, when he awoke with a start, grabbed his suitcase, and rushed downstairs.

By the time he'd gulped down breakfast and hustled to the stockyards, the Shoesmith cattle were being reloaded. They all looked healthy but were audibly unhappy at being moved again. Myron resumed his place in the caboose, with a different conductor for a companion.

As the train rumbled west across the plains, Myron studied the horizon across the treeless landscape. Some of it was covered with grass, but most had been fenced, plowed, and planted to wheat. Small houses, some made of sod, others with unpainted board walls, sat on the edges of the cultivated fields. At most of those close to the track, a bevy of plainly dressed, barefoot children shaded their eyes against the sun and waved as the train passed. He and the conductor waved back.

"So this is what the high plains country looks like. Not near as pretty as Iowa." Myron's opinion brought a rejoinder from the conductor.

"Yer seein' honyokers who took up homesteads an' think they can make a go of it on a half section out here in dry country. Most of 'em came when the price of wheat went through the roof. Not many of 'em are gonna last." Myron nodded agreement, even though he had only the faintest inkling of how brutally bad the situation would become for most of these new settlers.

West of the Missouri River, their route traversed hilly landscapes with dark gray shale exposed on hilltops and the edges of gullies. The sparse grassland seemed to go on forever until they came down into a broad river valley, and the track curved southwest. On the right, he saw a river nearly bank-full, running faster than any water he'd ever seen. On the left was another train, with NORTHERN PACIFIC lettered on the coal car, heading east on a nearby track.

Myron looked perplexed as he tried to understand the new scene. *That's funny. There wasn't another railroad anywhere in sight just a minute ago.* He motioned to the conductor. "How come this country's got no people but two railroads?"

"That there's the Northern Pacific. They come through here along the Yellowstone back in the eighties an' got the good route with all the towns. Besides that, the government gave 'em every other section o' land on both sides for about ten miles back from the tracks. They been sellin' it for a big price these last few years. We came along thirty years later with no land grant an' had to take a route up across the driest country—what they call the Big Open."

"How come it's called that?"

"Cuz it's real big an' it's wide open. No fences, almost no towns, just some sheepherders, lots of sheep, sagebrush, an' grass. But the sheep love it. In the fall, we haul out millions of 'em, an' a lot of cattle." The conductor waved toward the west, where steep, bare cliffs of pale yellowish shale towered above the far side of the river. The train began to slow.

They turned to look ahead, over the tops of the cars. "Miles City's comin' up. We're scheduled to stop to unload yer cattle for feed and water. If you're lucky, there might be a horse auction goin' on. It's really somethin' to see!"

As the train coasted and squealed to a stop, Myron scanned the scene. There were small houses along both sides of the track, and a few dirt streets that extended back two or three blocks. Wind was driving swirls of dust along them, among the ruts and potholes. He pulled his hat down tighter as he got off, checked the cattle in the pens as they ate and drank, and found that they'd all traveled well. Then he headed toward the sound of the fast, intermittent chant of an auctioneer and joined a nearby crowd sitting on bleachers made from rough planks for his first experience of the West.

"Ride 'em, cowboy! An' don't go pullin' leather!" The admonitions came from a tall, lean man near where Myron had found a seat. The speaker wore a black leather hat with a wide brim, a denim shirt, and faded denim jeans that were tucked into his boots. His face was young, bronzed, and leathery, and his gaze followed another tanned young man who was trying to stay atop a bucking horse inside a round, wood-fenced corral alongside the bleachers.

The horse was snorting as he crow-hopped in a tight circle while trying to reach back to bite the cowboy's leg. All he could reach were the rider's leather chaps. He abandoned that effort, humped his back, and began to buck with all his strength, turning from end to end as he did so. The cowboy's head snapped from side to side, and his free arm waved as he tried to keep his balance. His hat came off and blew to the edge of the corral. An onlooker climbed the fence and retrieved it, then hastily scrambled out as the bucking horse ran for him, mouth open and foaming.

A gate opened, and two horsemen entered. They maneuvered their mounts along each side of the bucking horse, crowding up close. The rider on the bucking horse pulled his foot out of the left stirrup and put his arm across the shoulder of the rider on his right, then rose from the saddle suddenly, swung free of it, and hung alongside his rescuer until they reached the corral fence. Then he let go and climbed out of the corral, just ahead of the teeth of the bucking horse he'd been riding.

The voice of the auctioneer rose above the crowd. "All right, all you folks who need rodeo stock, here's your last chance to buy a real mean bronc. You seen him buck, so ya know he'll give your audiences a thrill and your cowboys a ride and a half for their money. Who'll open for a hundred dollars?" There was silence among the onlookers. "He's big, he's mean, he's young—he's just what you need for yer rodeo string. Who'll give me eighty?" A man wearing a high-crowned hat with a wide brim raised his hand a few inches without looking up.

"All right. I've got eighty, now who'll make it ninety? Ninety, ninety, ninety, who'll give me ninety for this mean piece of horseflesh?" Across the arena, a hand moved a few inches. "Now a hundred. Who'll give me a hundred? Yes! I've got a hundred, now a hundred ten. This is the last bucking bronc we'll sell today, so get him if you want him. Who'll give me a hundred ten?"

As the auctioneer sold the bronc for a hundred and five dollars and the mounted attendants hazed the animal out of the ring, Myron studied the men around him on the bleachers. Predominantly they were dressed in Levis, boots, and large, black felt hats. The minority, wearing bib overalls, modest-sized hats, and work shoes like his, sat in small clusters throughout the crowd. They studied the six large, lively horses now running loose in the arena and leaned back and forth as they exchanged comments in low voices.

"Folks, we're ready to start selling work horses, and we've got some real good ones. Look 'em over, and buy the ones you need." The auctioneer's voice boomed over the wind and above the low murmur of the crowd. "We'll sell one, two, three, four, or all six together—your choice. What am I bid on these fine young horses?" A man leaned in and spoke with the auctioneer's assistant, who signaled the auctioneer. "I've got a hundred twenty a head to open, an' he'll take all six. Who'll give a hundred thirty? Yes, one thirty. Now one forty. Who'll bid one forty?"

Myron overheard an onlooker say to the man next to him, "It's real tough to outbid the army this year. They buy whatever they want, even if the price is out of sight."

The price went up rapidly and finally stalled at two hundred fifteen dollars. He was amazed by how much the work horses sold for compared to the bucking horse. *The army must need lots of horses in France to pull artillery pieces and wagons,* he thought. He thought of his brother Harlan, who had been drafted and shipped off to basic training a few months before Myron came west. He worried about his brother's welfare and felt fortunate to be here instead of overseas, wearing khaki. It made the nights when his injured knee kept him from sleeping seem less onerous.

Myron hadn't eaten since Aberdeen, so after a short time, he headed for the Branding Iron Cafe across the street from the auction ring and had a well-done steak before going back to check the cattle in the pens again. It was dusk when the train pulled out of Miles City, headed for Harlowtown. He pulled on his jacket, buttoned it all the way up, and went to sleep on a bench in the caboose.

When he woke up, the sky in the east was beginning to glow purple. The train was traveling along the valley of a very small river. He could see a few deciduous trees silhouetted on the banks, but they didn't look like any he'd seen before. Farther back from the river, on the tops of low hills, he could see a few small evergreens growing in irregular patches. The engine was laboring hard. As he watched the landscape, the sky lightened ahead of the sunrise. He climbed to one of the high seats, where he could look above the train to the west. The view made him gasp. In front of them was a jagged wall of mountains, the white tops of its distant peaks shimmering in the sun's first rays, the lower slopes still shadowed. He sat mesmerized, watching the sunlight creep down the snow, enlarging the area of brilliant white above the blue-green trees below.

"Real purty, ain't they?" The conductor's remark broke into his reverie.

Myron gave a start. "Oh, yes. They're really pretty. I hadn't even realized you were awake. How far to Harlowtown?"

"We're 'most there. Hear how hard the engine's workin'? Harlow's where the Milwaukee stops using steam and hooks onto electric engines for the pull through the mountains. Otherwise we'd have to put on pusher engines to get up the grades, an' they're a big bother. Nice thing with electric—on the downgrades into the valleys, the engines put juice back into the lines. Understand?"

Myron thought he vaguely understood, and he nodded but didn't say anything, because the train was moving onto a side track and approaching a stockyard so newly built that its lumber was still pale tan. He took a quick look at the mountains, then picked up his suitcase and stood by the steps. The train journey was over. It was time to check on the cattle one last time as they were unloaded, and then to decide if he wanted to stay and work on Shoesmith's ranch or go home immediately.

He walked into each pen as the cattle came down from the cars, looking for any animals that were lame or appeared to have been bruised or hurt. In the third pen, he saw a cow that limped badly, and he maneuvered to get up close. He saw an area of raw flesh on her right rear leg, just above the blood-covered hoof. He shook his head and went to retrieve a bottle of iodine from his suitcase.

When he returned, he called to the head yardsman. "One of these cows has a bad scrape on her leg. Could you help me put some iodine on it?"

"Aw, that happens all the time. Don't worry yourself about it."

The bearded man was burly and olive-skinned. He looked unhappy about the request.

"I want to disinfect it, and I need help to keep the cow in the corner while I do."

"Oh, I s'pose, if you feel you gotta." The bearded man turned and joined Myron as he climbed the fence into the pen of milling and bawling cows and calves. The lame cow was easy to spot but hard to get close to. She was spooked by the experience of having been herded in and out of railroad cars and having her leg scraped in the process. Finally they got her isolated in one corner of the corral. Then she lunged, head down, toward Myron, who dodged out of her path at the last instant.

"Let's get out of here. She's pretty mad, and she would just as soon kill us as not," the railroad man yelled.

"Not so fast. I'm responsible for these cattle, and I aim to get her leg treated." Myron looked around for an implement to protect himself with, and he spotted a piece of two-by-four lying just outside the corral. He scrambled over the fence, picked up the piece of lumber, and climbed back in.

The two men isolated the injured cow in another corner, and when she made a lunge to gore him, Myron brought the two-by-four down hard directly on top of her head. The cow stopped, snorted, and shook her head as if to make the sudden headache disappear. Myron uncapped the iodine one-handed with his teeth and moved warily toward her injured foot, the club raised in his right hand. The cow snorted and shook her head menacingly, but she didn't charge him. Myron brandished the club in her face; then, in a lightning-fast move, he splashed the iodine on the wounded leg. The cow bellowed and kicked, just missing his hand as he jerked it back.

"Now we can get out and let her alone." He stepped back, keeping an eye on the angry cow, and recapped the iodine bottle as he moved toward the far edge of the corral.

The railroad man followed. "You're good with cattle, aren't ya?" He nodded in approval.

"I'm responsible for this whole trainload, and I don't like to see injured cattle not treated." Myron looked at the railroad worker earnestly and put down the piece of two-by-four. "Much obliged for your help."

Then he walked north up the hill to a massive, stone hotel that dominated the tiny town, took a seat by the window of its restaurant where he could see the rail yards, and ordered breakfast. He kept a lookout for cowboys from John Shoesmith's ranch, who were supposed to come for the cattle. As he ate, he tried to decide whether to get on the next train east and go home as he had planned, or to stay here to work for Mr. Shoesmith and see more of the mountains and the vibrant, young western culture he'd only glimpsed. When a group of men came riding over the hill from the south, he noticed that one of them was leading a saddled horse with no rider. *Maybe that's a horse they're bringing for me,* he thought. He poured more syrup on his pancakes, ate them quickly, and hurried back to the stockyards, still wondering whether he should stay or go. Then he looked up at the mountains and decided.

Chapter 31
Hoeing a Tough Row

Life on Mr. Shoesmith's ranch was rigorous, but Myron found it exciting. He loved being out on the open range among the cattle, even when the wind was blowing. And he found the task of hauling hay to feed them during snowy intervals of winter bracing but rewarding. The sight of lines of cows devouring the hay he'd forked from the bobsled onto the snowy ground along the creek was beautiful. Even the job of chopping holes in the ice of the creek so the cattle could drink didn't bother him.

But after World War I ended, the price of cattle plummeted every year, and when drought set in during 1920 and the cattle failed to gain weight, ranchers were in big trouble—John Shoesmith among them. After Shoesmith's money-losing dispersal sale in 1921, Myron stood on the railroad platform in Harlowtown, ticket in hand, waiting for the eastbound train to take him back to Iowa.

He took a last look westward toward the Big Belt Mountains, then southwest toward the Crazy Mountains, and sighed. He'd come to love the vivid way those mountains punctuated the sky and brought drama to the landscape and to his life on the dry and windswept rangeland to the east. As he contemplated the changes ahead, his thoughts were a tumult, but one goal was clear. "If there's any way I can, I'm going to come back someday and live where I can wake up and see mountains."

The man next to him overheard the muttered comment, gave him a sharp look, and then stepped away. The whistle shrilled on the passenger train that coasted east from Twodot along the Musselshell River. Myron, still looking west, stepped back from the tracks as it approached.

After the train crew had switched engines from electric to steam and Myron was on board, he pulled out a recent letter from his mother and reread it.

Dear Son,

I'm glad to hear you're thinking about coming home. We've all missed you. Harlan came back from France after the Krauts got beat, and has gone to farm next to your uncle Will up in Minnesota. Teddy's in high school. He's the only boy left at home to cook for, since Albert and Glenn Boston got married last year. They live in the little house near the road. I don't hardly know how to cook so little.

Your father is working hard as ever. His asthma is bothering him a lot. He and Albert have more than they can do, what with all the farm work and the livestock. We can sure use you if you come back.

Albert and Glenn's baby girl, Evelyn, is real sickly. And that's a big worry to them, and a big expense too. They've hired a RN to take care of her. She's a real nice farm girl from Vermont and a real good worker. Takes right hold and does whatever needs to be done. It takes a lot off Glenn and Albert's mind to have her nursing little Evelyn. I hope we can get enough for our corn and hogs to be able to keep paying her, but it will be a miracle if we can. Prices just seem to keep going down.

Well, I got to stop and go hoe the weeds out of the garden. Your father and Albert are too busy with the field work to do it ,and Teddy is gone to school.

Your Mother

Myron put away the letter. Times seemed to be tough everywhere. He looked north out the window at the Big Snowy Mountains while the train cruised down the Musselshell Valley. As the snow-capped peaks disappeared from view behind the speeding train, he looked back toward them and sighed.

When his parents and Teddy met him at the train in Valley Junction, Myron thought Ella looked just like she had when he left, but Walker looked older: his beard was grayer, and he seemed stooped. Teddy had grown to be a lot taller than either of his parents. That evening, while they were milking the cows, Albert asked Myron to come meet his wife and baby daughter.

After supper, Myron appeared at the door of the small house. A young, black-haired woman answered his knock. She wore a starched, white uniform and was holding a whimpering baby on her hip.

He gave her a shy smile and asked, "Are Albert and Glenn home? I've come to meet Glenn and Evelyn."

"Oh, you must be Albert's brother from out west. I've heard them talk about you. They had to go and get some new medicine for Evelyn from the doctor. But they'll be back soon. Won't you come in and wait?" She smiled as she opened the screen door, held it open with her hip, and waved the flies away with her free hand.

Myron stepped in quickly before too many of the flies found the opening. Evelyn's whimpers grew into wails. Mary Pierce, RN, put her tiny charge over her shoulder and hummed softly as she walked back and forth across the kitchen. Myron sat down by the wooden table and waited, watching the scene and noting that the nurse was quiet, attractive, and self-assured as she attempted to comfort the crying child. At the sound of a car, he went to the door, and he opened it when Albert and Glenn arrived.

"Sorry not to have been here, Myron, but little Evelyn's got to have some new medicine." Albert looked worried and apologetic as he walked in past his brother. Glenn, as young as Albert at twenty-one, walked in next, carrying a bottle.

"So you're Myron. Good to meet you. Excuse us while we give little Evelyn this medicine." She uncapped the bottle and took her daughter in her arms.

Myron said, "I'll come back another time." Then he excused himself and left. Mary smiled at him warmly as he went out the door.

He made sure to return to check on Evelyn's health every day. His niece's chronic illness provided a splendid excuse to visit Glenn and Albert's home, and in the process, become close friends with the nurse they employed to care for her. When Albert and Glenn's money ran out and Mary accepted a job in Massachusetts as a public health nurse, Myron felt as if a pillar of his life had been cut away.

The wartime euphoria associated with high crop and livestock prices had degenerated into grim determination mixed with despair and anger for every farmer with debts and every banker with farm loans in his portfolio. The cattle that Myron had left in the care of his father had doubled in number, but they were worth a lot less than when he'd gone west. He joined in the Beattys' farm work, just as he'd done before his trip, and he worked for neighbors to earn extra money whenever the opportunity arose. During the cold, arduous days of corn picking, he always worked at home until their corn was all in the crib. Then he picked for neighbors.

* * *

On a fall evening, after a long day of picking corn, Walker sat in the dining room close to the kerosene lamp and added up what he'd received for the year's crops and livestock, then shook his head. His gray hair and beard accentuated the strained lines around his eyes and across his forehead. "We've got just a little more than enough saved up to pay the interest on Kratzer's loan. We're not going to be able to pay down much at all on the principal. I sure hope next year's better." His voice sounded tired.

Ella, Myron, and Teddy came to look over his shoulders at the numbers as Walker continued to talk about their situation. "We had good crops and sold quite a few cattle, but the prices aren't even half what they were when we bought the place. Guess we'll just have to keep farmin' and hope for better prices."

Ella put her hand gently on Walker's shoulder. "I'm sure things will be better next year and we can pay off some more then." She rubbed the part of his shoulder that she thought hurt most from throwing corn into the wagon all day. Walker sighed, smiled, and leaned back, enjoying the massage.

Myron looked at the numbers and decided that there wouldn't be money to pay down the loan next year unless prices rose dramatically. He wondered how Albert would react when he learned the news tomorrow. Not well, he guessed.

He tried to say something supportive but still honest. "I'm sorry about the low prices, but everybody's in the same boat if they're a farmer and in debt. Anyhow, I'm going to bed, so I can get up early and finish picking corn before it snows." As he walked toward the stairway, his parents noticed that his limp had returned. Before Myron went to bed, he wrote a postcard to Mary Pierce.

Dear Friend Mary,

I write a few lines to tell you that I was very glad to get your letter and learn that you like your new job. I hope that your patients are all doing well.

We are getting along, but with the low prices, it's a tough row to hoe. Tomorrow we plan to finish picking corn, and none too soon, as it feels like snow is coming. The Herefords you admired are doing well, and my herd is a little larger than when you were here. Since prices are low, I intend to keep most of the increase, and I hope things improve in the years ahead.

What a fine little verse you sent in your letter.

Thank you. I would like to see Whittier's birthplace myself. Please think of me when you go.

Sincerely,

MWB

The next morning, he was up an hour before daylight, feeding and currying the horses and hauling a wagonload of hay to the Herefords. When Walker arrived at the barn, Myron was milking a Guernsey cow.

"Morning, Son. Looks like you really want to get that last corn out of the field, given how early you've started chores." Walker picked up a milking stool, sat down beside a black and white cow, and put a milk pail between his knees.

"Well, we've got to get every ear we can, if you're going to be able to pay off that loan to Mr. Kratzer." Myron turned one of the cow's teats sideways as he squeezed and sent a stream of milk into the mouth of a tawny yellow cat that sat a dozen feet away, waiting for her treat. Albert, who usually joined in the farm chores, hadn't arrived by the time they finished milking, so Walker and Myron started walking toward the house, each carrying buckets of milk..

Walker looked toward the small house as he carried two full buckets of milk toward the big house. "I wonder if little Evelyn's worse again. Her being sick all the time must wear out Glenn and Albert. Sure hope not. They have enough heartache for two or three families already."

He slowed his pace momentarily before speeding up along the path. At the house, Myron cranked the De Laval cream separator while his mother replaced the buckets as they filled with skim milk. She set the can of cream outside to cool, while Myron and Walker carried the skim milk to the pigs before sitting down to breakfast with Ella and Teddy.

As they were finishing the meal, Albert came into the kitchen, looking distraught.

"We've been up all night with Evelyn. Dr. Shotwell just got here.

He's with her and Glenn. So I came to tell you he says she isn't goin' to make it." A muffled sob erupted from deep in his chest.

Walker and Ella were on their feet instantly, and they put their arms around their son. Myron stood in front of his brother and took both of Albert's hands in his. Teddy stood by, looking uneasy and restless, then got his books and rushed out the door, headed for school. Walker, Ella, and Myron followed Albert to the small house next door and tiptoed in. Glenn and Dr. Shotwell were standing beside the crib, peering intently at the tiny girl under the blanket.

Myron's thoughts turned back to summer, to when Mary Pierce had nursed his now-dying niece for several months. He put his hand in the pocket that held the postcard that he'd written her the night before. He remembered her smile and how sunlight brought out the auburn tint in her long, black hair; he recalled how sharply it contrasted with her starched, white uniform. He wished his family had had enough money to keep paying her for the skilled care that Evelyn required, and that Mary had not gone back east to take a new job.

Evelyn moved and gave a faint moan. Her mother began to run her hand back and forth slowly along the girl's tiny body. Dr. Shotwell shook his head. Walker, Ella, and Myron all stepped closer to the crib, and Ella put her arm across Glenn's shoulder.

"We're all so sorry for little Evelyn, and for you and Albert." She squeezed Glenn in a one-armed hug as she spoke. Glenn kept rubbing Evelyn softly and muffled a sob.

Walker put his hand on the crib railing and bent forward as he looked at the flushed face and watched the irregular, labored breathing of his granddaughter. "I'm real sorry, little girl. The good Lord wants you in heaven more than he wants you to stay with us, I guess. And he's in charge." He paused for a long time and then wiped his eyes. "Good-bye, sweet one. We'll all miss you." He spoke so softly that his family could barely hear the words.

Ella, Myron, and Dr. Shotwell murmured amen softly and tentatively when he finished. Glenn began to sob. Albert put his arms around her and held her as Evelyn's breathing became more irregular and finally stopped altogether.

Two days later, friends and family gathered at the rural church a few miles east of the Beatty farm. Walker's three sisters and their husbands came from Des Moines. Glenn's parents, Mr. and Mrs. Boston, Glenn's twin brother and his wife, and several of the Boston family filled the two front rows of pews. Even though the Beattys were rather new to the neighborhood, enough neighbors and friends came to fill all but a few pews in the small church.

Myron looked at the plain white walls and simple architecture and furnishings he'd seen on Sunday mornings since he returned. The casket he and Teddy had made, surreal in its smallness as it rested in front of the pulpit on a stand large enough to hold the coffins of adults, added a radically new dimension to the familiar surroundings. The gray sky framed by gothic windows of clear glass portended a storm. His thoughts drifted briefly to how blue the sky in Montana had been, then to how much corn they still had to pick before it snowed.

The minister, wearing a black robe, entered as the last of the family sat down. When Mrs. Woods stopped pumping the organ and the final chords of the hymn "Abide With Me" died away, he rose to speak.

"Dearly beloved, this is a day when it is hard to see the glory of God through our tears and sadness. But we have come here believing in the promise of the resurrection through our Lord Jesus Christ."

Albert put his arm around Glenn's shoulder as she dabbed at her eyes with a handkerchief. Mrs. Boston held her daughter's other hand. Albert's round face was redder than ever, especially around his eyes. Ella looked like she might cry at any time.

The minister continued, "God, in his wisdom, has elected to take little Evelyn Beatty from among us and leave us bereft of her presence. Yet he has also left us with a message of hope. The words of the Psalmist state that message well for our ears. 'The Lord is my shepherd. I shall not want ...'"

The service was short, and at its conclusion, Myron, Teddy, and two young men of the Boston family carried the small casket slowly to the waiting hearse mounted on the chassis of a Model T truck. The congregants, after considerable cranking of their cars, followed the hearse a few miles to the small cemetery south of the village of

Waukee and stopped beside a newly dug grave on the east side of the road.

The northwest wind blew a scattering of snow across the flat landscape. Everyone turned up the collars of their coats and wrapped scarves around their necks. The four pallbearers laid the casket on a pair of ropes that spanned the open grave, then lowered it slowly as the minister intoned, "Ashes to ashes, dust to dust. The Lord giveth, and the Lord taketh away. In your mercy, receive Evelyn, this young and innocent child, into the joys of your kingdom, we beseech you. And grant us your peace in her absence. Amen."

As soon as he stepped back and the people began to walk to their cars, the undertaker and his assistant pulled out the ropes and began to shovel dirt into the hole. Glenn glanced back and began to sob as she got into their Model T. Albert tried to comfort her. Myron walked over and cranked Albert's car furiously until it started. Albert leaned out the window as he drove away, "Many thanks, Myron. We want to get away from here."

As Myron joined his family in the car, Walker said, "Well, I guess we better get to pickin' corn before there's any more snow. Glenn's folks are goin' to stay with her. An' Ella, I suppose you'll be busy renderin' lard." Ella sighed and nodded.

By early afternoon, Walker, Albert, and Myron were walking side by side through four inches of snow in the field of standing corn. As they walked, each grasped the ear of corn on the plant closest to him, and in one fluid motion, stripped off the husk with a steel peg strapped to his thumb, wrenched the ear free from the stalk, and threw it against the wide board that extended vertically about three feet above the opposite side of the steel-wheeled farm wagon with an enclosed wooden box. The work of picking and husking and the steady bang-bang-bang of corn ears hitting the board before they fell into the growing pile in the wagon created a rhythm that soothed a little of the hurt from their loss.

When they reached the end of the field, the horses turned the wagon around and started back with a little help from Walker, pausing only to be sure that the pickers were abreast of the wagon; the bang of corn ears on the board started again. By dusk, they had picked two wagonloads.

As the three men stood in the loaded wagon returning to the corncrib, Walker looked down at the ears of corn beneath his feet. "There's at least sixty bushels in this load, an' it ain't worth barely forty dollars. Four years ago, it woulda been worth ninety, maybe a hundred. An' what it costs to grow it hasn't gone down one penny." He shook his head and shrugged. "Oh, well. Guess we just have to keep on farmin' and hope things get better."

His sons nodded and looked away. Albert's thoughts were about what he would say to Glenn and how empty and quiet it would be in their childless house tonight. Myron thought about how much he would like to have a place of his own out west, a place he could share with Mary Pierce, the black-haired nurse he'd fallen in love with. And how unlikely that prospect appeared to be.

Chapter 32
Striking Out on His Own

"Listen to this. A man named Daniel Plowman at Salesville, Montana, wants to sell a two-hundred-acre ranch for $2,500. That's in my price range. Guess I'll write him." Myron looked up from the Spring 1925 issue of *Western Farm and Ranch Exchange* and looked at his mother, father, and brother Teddy. His enthusiasm brightened the mood of the household a little. He reached for a pen and paper.

But Walker was skeptical. "Does that ad say anything about the house and barn, or how much of the land is cultivated?" His father's questions made Myron pause.

"It says there's a log house, log barn, and other buildings, but it doesn't say anything about how much is cultivated. I'll ask in the letter."

When Myron came in from shocking oats ten days later, there was letter to him from Mr. Plowman. He tore it open and read as he drank from the dipper that hung on the galvanized water pail in the kitchen. "Look, Mother, he sent a long letter and even some pictures of the place. Isn't that a pretty spot? Right beside some mountains."

Ella stopped peeling potatoes for supper, wiped her hands on her apron, and looked at the pictures. "It is kinda pretty. But isn't it awful dry? You kept telling us about how dry it was on that ranch Mr. Shoesmith had out there—so dry nothing would grow. Is this place dry like that?" She put down the pictures, resumed peeling potatoes and dropping them into a pan of boiling water, then turned the meat that was frying in the black iron skillet. Myron read through the letter.

"He says there's about forty acres of crop land. Most of the rest is pasture with trees for shade for the cattle, and there's a creek runs right through the place. He irrigates crops from it. Being able to irrigate in dry years would be a godsend. He says he's harvested eighty bushels of oats an acre. That's more than we get here."

Ella looked up from the stove and said, "That sounds pretty good."

At supper, Walker was still skeptical. "If it's so pretty and grows such good crops, why's he want to sell it?"

Myron looked at the letter again. "He's seventy, and he and his wife want to stop ranching and move to town. And the place has made them a good living. He says there's about fifty acres of pine trees that a man can cut in the winter and sell for some extra money. He's already cut trees on about a hundred acres and converted the land into pasture."

His father picked up and studied the pictures that Mr. Plowman had sent with the letter. "That pasture land looks kinda steep, but the crop fields look to be pretty smooth. Maybe it'd be all right for you as a place to start. How much money you got saved up?"

Myron did some quick mental addition. "From what I've earned and what I've made from the cattle, almost three thousand dollars. That'll be just about enough for me buy the place, pay the railroad to haul my cattle, machinery, and horses out there, and leave me with enough to pay for a ticket to Vermont."

"Oh, so you're goin' to Vermont, are you?" Walker grinned slyly at Myron.

"As soon as we get the oats threshed, I'm planning to go meet Mary Pierce and her family. They live way up in the north end of the state. She's coming up from Massachusetts to be home when I'm there."

"That's no surprise. I've seen a lot of letters coming and going between you two lately." Walker smiled as he spoke. "She's a good woman. Not one of those flapper types. Sure was a great nurse to poor little Evelyn. Albert an' Glenn said she was nice to have in the house. Took hold and helped with whatever needed doing, when she wasn't taking care of that sick little babe. Hard to believe that was 'most four years ago already." He stepped to the back door and spit a stream of tobacco juice outside. "Well, good luck. You'll need it these days, what with the low prices and all."

Myron was elated as he picked up a pen and addressed a letter to Mr. Daniel H. Plowman at Route 2, Salesville, Montana. He enclosed a check, as earnest money on the land, and suggested a date of early September to complete the transaction in Montana. As soon as the oats on his father's farm were threshed, he bought a round-trip ticket from Des Moines to St. Albans, Vermont, and started east.

The thought of seeing Mary again was thrilling. It had been almost four years since she had left Iowa, leaving behind only a promise to answer his letters. He whistled as he stood at the station, a lean, muscular, black-haired man of average height, from whom happiness bubbled like steam from a boiling kettle. As the train approached, he broke into a baritone rendition of "Carry Me Back to Old Virginny" until the hiss of steam and clatter of train cars drowned out his words. A couple nearby looked at him and smiled.

In Chicago, when he boarded the Canadian National train that would take him through southern Canada to Montreal, he felt like an adventurer leaving for a safari into the heart of Africa. His excitement intensified when he arrived at the station in Montreal and was surrounded by French-speaking Québécois. The short train ride south to St. Albans passed in what seemed like an instant. But he was apprehensive that Mary's parents would not approve of him as a son-in-law when they learned that he planned to move to the West.

As the train pulled into the station, he looked out the window and saw Mary. She looked excited as she scanned the train for a familiar face and waved when she spotted him through the train window. Standing next to her were a short man with light brown hair and a gray-haired older man with a mustache and beard. *Must be her brother and father*, he thought. *They look like farmers*. Myron got his bag from the conductor and hurried off to meet the Pierces for the drive to their farm.

Mary beamed as Myron walked down the train steps. She took

his hand and said, "Father, Leon, this is Myron Beatty, the man who's come all the way from Iowa to see me."

John Pierce put out his hand and said, "A'yeah, it's good to meet you," in an accent that Myron had never heard before. Leon's accent sounded just like his father's.

Myron couldn't believe the size of the Pierces' two-story white house along the road northwest of the village of Franklin. It stood regally under large maple trees, across the road from a long barn, also painted white. "Your house is huge. Did you say all the lumber for it came from this farm?"

"A'yeah, that's right. We cut the trees the fall and winter of '95, right after the old house burned down." John Pierce turned and spoke with pride as his son, Leon, slowed the car and turned into the driveway. "By the summer of '96, we had them all sawed into lumber and the house pretty well built when Mary arrived the last of June. Used a lot of men, but they were lookin' for work all over the place back in those days, an' worked cheap. Had to pay the finish carpenters 'most a dollar a day, but the others worked for less. The biggest cost for the whole shebang was for nails and shingles." He paused as Leon parked the car.

Then it was a flurry of meeting people: Mary's mother, Myra; Leon's wife, Mabel, and their five young boys, who were scooting about, peeking at their aunt's boyfriend from behind their mother's skirt; and finally, Wilbur Murgatroi, the French Canadian hired man, who had managed to find something that needed fixing at the house just then. Myron was a little overwhelmed by all of Mary's relatives and retreated with his bag to the upstairs bedroom to which Myra Pierce directed him. As soon as Myron had left his bag in one of the numerous bedrooms upstairs and returned to the capacious dining room, John took him to see the cows and the barn. He'd never seen a herd of Jerseys before. With their big, dark eyes and dished, feminine faces, they looked like living toys as they congregated by the barn door, anticipating the evening milking. He reached through the fence and rubbed the heads of the closest ones.

"A'yeah, they're all real gentle, but keep away from the bull in that pen over there. He'd sooner kill you than look at you." John Pierce's admonition caught Myron by surprise. He glanced toward a nearby wood-fenced pen where a Jersey bull was pacing back and forth and pawing the ground with his front feet.

"That bull's sure different than the Hereford bulls I raise. They wouldn't hurt a flea, but some of my cows are a little feisty, especially when they have young calves."

"Oh, so you raise cattle, do you?" John looked surprised. "I thought they only raised corn and hogs in Iowa. Think I've seen pictures of them Herefords, but I've never seen a live one. How many you got?"

Myron did a quick calculation. He knew his cattle by name, not by number. "Counting all the cows and this year's calves and the bull, I've got about thirty right now." John Pierce seemed to be impressed.

Leon and Wilbur appeared, each carrying two galvanized milk pails, and John's attention turned to milking. "A'yeah, it's milkin' time, Myron. You can stay and watch us milk, or you can go back to the house and rest. Whatever suits you."

Myron looked at the long line of waiting Jerseys and made an offer. "Would it disrupt things too much if I milked a few? I'm sure I'm not as fast as you folks, but I'd be glad to help out a little."

"A'yeah, if you want to help, we'll be done that much sooner for supper." John Pierce looked toward his son, Leon, who pulled a dust-covered milking stool out of a pile of straw and handed it to Myron along with a milk pail. "An' we'll be much obliged to ya. That third cow there is pretty quiet—why don't you start on her?"

The milking proceeded with little conversation as the four men filled their pails, then emptied then into covered galvanized cans. Myron couldn't milk a fourth of the cows, but he was able to come fairly close to it, even though his hands ached long before he was done. John and Leon Pierce thanked him for his work when the last cow was milked.

The next morning, Mary took him to see the spring that supplied water to the farmstead through a quarter-mile-long line of hollowed-out logs laid end to end. Myron marveled when he saw the line of what the Pierces called pump logs snaking along the ground and the stream of cold water they delivered to a huge, circular, concrete tank in the cellar. These Yankees were ingenious and thrifty. Why pay cash for metal pipe when a homemade substitute could be created from a tree by some work with a long-handled wood auger?

Then she led him across her father's newly harvested hay fields to the grove of sugar maple trees that covered the entire north side of the farm and reached all the way to the boundary between the United States and Canada. As they walked through the maple woods, holding hands, they came upon a large, unpainted building with a huge chimney. "This is the sugar house," said Mary. "Want to see inside?"

Myron nodded. He was curious. She opened the door and led him in. Directly in front of the big door, Myron saw a large, rectangular, metal pan that covered the entire top of a stove with a firebox large enough to hold several four-foot logs at the same time.

"Just how does this maple sugaring work?"

Mary was eager to explain. "In the fall, the men cut wood enough to fire the stove when we're boiling sap. It takes a lot. They stack it right there beside the door. Late in winter, when the days begin to get warm but the nights stay frosty, they drive the metal spiles you see on that table over there into the tree trunks and hang a bucket to catch the sap on each one. They put out about a thousand or so."

She pointed toward a huge pile of inverted metal buckets stacked along one wall. "Then the real works starts. Every day, as soon as milking and breakfast are done, some of the men hook a team of horses to that sled with the big tub on it, the one sitting along that wall. Then they go to from tree to tree and empty the sap from the buckets into the tub. While they're doing that, the rest of the family comes to the sugar house and starts the fire. I used to work in here too, until I went off to nursing school. As soon as the first sledload of sap gets here, they fill this big pan and start boiling it. Boiling's real tricky. If you get the fire too hot, you scorch the syrup and ruin the whole panful. But you can't stop boiling too soon, or the syrup'll be watery, and nobody will buy it. You have to know exactly what you're doing. When you think it's thick enough, you test it and then drain it out into those gallon cans you see over there in the corner." She paused to let him look around.

Myron could see that this was a complex operation that took a lot of teamwork. "How much syrup do you make in a day?"

"It depends. Some days the sap runs real well—other days, hardly at all. An' it takes about forty gallons of sap to make a gallon of syrup. So maybe on a good day, we'd make twenty-five gallons of syrup. Sometimes we have to keep boiling until after dark to be ready for the next day. It's hot, hard, sticky work. And so's tramping through knee-deep snow all day, going from tree to tree, carrying buckets of sap to the gathering tub. Then the men have to feed and milk the cows before they can go in for supper. Everybody works together. It's just like in the operating room at a hospital." Mary's eyes sparkled as she recalled the exciting but strenuous teamwork of her family at sugaring time.

But Myron's mind was elsewhere. "Mary, there's something I've been wanting to ask you." He took a small box out of his pocket and opened it. "Would you marry me, and come all the way to Montana to live in a log cabin?"

Mary took the ring that gleamed in the dim light and slipped it on. "Of course I would. I'd follow you to the end of the earth." She gave him an enthusiastic hug as they shared a long kiss. The dim light of the big shed, the earthy smell of the maple woods outside, and the eager warmth of the woman he loved left Myron overwhelmed. He hoped the moment would never end.

They sat a long time, holding hands and talking about the future. Myron told her of his plan to buy the place on the edge of the Montana mountains and move west with his cattle. He showed her the pictures that Mr. Plowman had sent. "It's not much of a house, but it looks warm and cozy for the two of us. Nothing like the big house you grew up in. But I can buy the whole place without going into debt."

"The house doesn't matter. If I'd wanted to marry somebody with a big house, I'd have married one of the doctors at the nursing hospital where I went to school. There were a lot of them around who were interested. But I wasn't, and I'm so glad." She gave him another hug and a kiss. They strolled back to the farmhouse for dinner at noon, both radiant with happiness, and told her family of their plans.

When they shared their news, John Pierce smiled and said, "Congratulations. Can't say as I'm surprised. All Mary's been able to talk about lately is this wonderful fellow from Iowa an' how she hopes he'll want to marry her."

The rest of his visit passed in a rush. Before he knew it, Myron was on the train again, headed for Iowa. It seemed like he was living in a different world. His worries about whether Mary would want to be his wife were behind him. Now his concerns were about getting his Herefords and his machinery to Montana and buying the Plowmans' ranch. Then he and Mary could set a date for her to come west for good. Doing all of that before winter would be a tall order. He wasn't sure it was possible.

Chapter 33
Montana Again

Myron was excited as he made plans for his big move. It had been eight years since he'd gone west the first time. And for that trip, he hadn't had to worry about any of his own possessions, only someone else's cattle.

This time, he enlisted his father and his brothers, Albert and Teddy, to help him move his machinery and cattle to the stockyards and rail siding. They were intrigued by his venture and pitched in eagerly. The entourage was very modest. The machinery included some that his father had sold him, because it was extra, and a few items he'd bought at farm auctions. He'd bought a team of horses from his father, who needed every penny he could get to pay down the loan to Julius Kratzer.

The small herd of docile Herefords walked to the stockyards without major problems. Myron stayed to supervise their feeding while his father and brothers returned home for his car and his bags. His mother and his sister-in-law also came to see him off to the West. The family drove up just before the train crew pulled a pair of cattle cars in front of the loading chute.

Myron checked to see that the rail cars were clean, and then he urged his cattle up the chute and into the first car, making sure that each cow had her calf beside her as she entered. When more than half of the herd had been loaded, he motioned to the stationmaster to close the door and signal the engineer to move the train ahead one car length. Then he led his bull up the chute with a halter and tied him at the end of the car, where he'd put some hay and a half-barrel filled with water. He nailed a pair of wooden panels across the car to make a small enclosure for his prize possession; then the rest of the cattle were loaded. The team of horses was coaxed into one end of the boxcar that held his Model T and farm machinery, and the door was shut. Everything was ready to go.

"Well, good luck out in them mountains, Myron. Write us when you get there." His father extended a large callused hand as he spoke, remembering his years beside the Rockies in Colorado.

Ella put out both hands for a double shake. "Take good care, Myron. We'll miss you and all you did for us." Myron grasped and squeezed his mother's hands for a second, then shook hands with Albert, Glenn, and Teddy.

"Thank you all for everything. I'll get along fine, and I'll send a card as soon as I can, after I get settled." The engineer blew two short blasts on the whistle, and Myron hustled to get on board the caboose.

The train took the same route he'd traveled eight years earlier. Myron slept as best he could in the caboose. When they reached South Dakota, with its low humidity and blue skies, he began to watch the countryside. Most of what he saw was abandoned fields full of tumbleweed and Russian thistles, and empty homesteaders' shacks that outnumbered the occasional bedraggled ones that were still occupied.

Main Street in Harlowtown, Montana, looked down-at-the-heels. Vacant storefronts and houses were as common as occupied buildings, a striking change from the thriving town he'd seen eight years earlier, when new buildings had seemed to sprout everywhere from the sagebrush. While the train was stopped to change engines, he checked the cars with his cattle and horses to be sure they were all right. He looked to the west once again, searching for snow on the mountains, but since it was September, it had all melted.

The engine whistled, and the train began to move. This would be new country for him, all the way. He climbed to the cupola of the caboose so that he could look to both sides as well as directly over the train. The absence of smoke and noise from a steam locomotive was a welcome change. In front of him, the train seemed like a quiet, red snake as it moved up the grade through dry grasslands amid hills and mountains, curving first left, then right according to the dictates of the rails and the electric line overhead. They passed an occasional tiny hamlet with its stockyard by the siding, and then, without warning, they were going down a gradual grade. As they moved westward, a creek appeared alongside, and the rails followed its sinuous descent toward the Missouri River. After many miles of emptiness, he noticed a wooden sign proclaiming the tiny hamlet they were passing to be Sixteen.

Myron looked to the brakeman and asked, "Sixteen what?"

"We've been following Sixteen Mile Crick all the way down from the top of the grade. Guess the little town musta been named after the crick."

"How'd the creek get named Sixteen Mile?"

"Dunno. It's just Sixteen Mile Crick. That's all I know 'bout it."

That ended the discussion, and they continued in rocking silence, broken only by clickety-clacks of the wheels as the train curved to the south and traveled up the valley beside the Missouri River. This country looked just as dry as that around Harlowtown but a lot steeper. They were in the heart of the mountains now. After a while, Myron could see a wide valley ahead; its features, and those of the mountains to the south and east, were emphasized by the low angle of the western sun. The train pulled onto a side track at a little town named Three Forks, and the brakeman prepared to leave the caboose.

"Here's where we're gonna unhook you and your stuff, and a few other boxcars besides. The train up to Bozeman will take you the rest of the way tomorrow. Good luck up there." The brakeman smiled as he departed.

The engineer and brakeman eased the cars with Myron's livestock in front of chutes that angled up from wood-fenced corrals and unhooked. Myron watched his cattle and horses come down cautiously and then make a beeline for the water troughs and mangers full of hay. When he had assured himself that all of the animals were in good shape and had ample hay and water, he took his cardboard suitcase and walked across the tracks to a two-story, white, wooden building with a sign in front proclaiming it to be the Hotel Sacajawea.

Myron gave the man tending the desk a quarter and got a room key. After he ate supper, he lay down and was asleep almost the minute his head was on the pillow. The dry, cool air was a refreshing relief from the heat and humidity of Iowa. He slept deeply.

At dawn, he was up, breakfasted, and across the road at the stockyards, waiting for the local train crew. When they arrived, he helped them load his animals back into their rail cars, then climbed into the caboose.

As the short train chugged out of Three Forks toward his final destination, Myron's excitement built with each clickety-clack of the wheels. He studied the landscape from the high, narrow seat. The two cars with his livestock and the boxcar with his farm machinery were directly in front of him. Far up ahead, beyond the rest of the short train and the laboring steam engine, he studied a range of mountains that stood like a wall in their path. Bare rock near the tops of the peaks contrasted with the blue-green of the trees below. To his left, a river had cut vertical cliffs along the base of steep hills that had a thin cover of dry grass and sagebrush. To his right, hills covered in grass and sagebrush bordered the tracks. He'd never seen such a variety of topography or such natural beauty. His reverie was interrupted by the brakeman by his side.

"That's the real Three Forks of the Missouri right over there." The brakeman pointed north to a lone promontory a mile or so away. "They say that hill's where Captain Clark spent two days, back in 1805, making a map of how them rivers come together. The Jefferson joins the Madison from the west, right over there. Then the Gallatin comes in downstream a little ways." Myron looked north, trying to fix the scene in his mind, as the garrulous brakeman continued.

"We're goin' up alongside the Gallatin. First stop's Manhattan, right by the Holland Settlement. Lotta Dutchmen all round there. Strange folks. They don't do a lick of field work on Sunday, just milk their cows an' go to church and listen to a preacher harangue all day. Ya sure wouldn't catch me doin' that."

The route gradually left the river, and as the valley widened, Myron saw fields of shocked grain on both sides of the tracks, waiting to be threshed. The tan stubble between the rows of shocks was divided by long, widely spaced thin strips of bare soil.

"Are those irrigation ditches? Guess I'll have to learn how it's done. I'm buying a place in Cottonwood Canyon, south of Bozeman."

The brakeman nodded. "Yep, you'll find out soon enough that irrigating's no picnic. Just hard, dirty work, wadin' through mud daylight to dark. Not something I want to do a'tall. Cottonwood Canyon, huh? Then we'll be puttin' you and yer stuff off at Patterson siding. Closest one to Cottonwood. Be about five miles to drive your cows and move your machinery. Pretty country, but lotsa snow in the winter. You'll need a lot of hay." The brakeman basked in his opportunity to orient a neophyte to the mountain west.

Myron thought he'd never seen such beautiful country. As the train chugged up the valley, he studied the encircling mountains. The steep ones he'd seen first were closer now. Others had come into view on the south, anchored by a jumble of high, rocky crags to the southwest. Closer in, the valley looked like a huge garden. Green and tan cultivated fields, green pastures with ditches filled with irrigation water. Cottonwood trees along the creeks. Acres and acres of shocked wheat and barley on all sides; fields of oats still waiting to be cut and shocked. Houses, barns, roads. Lots of cattle and sheep in the pastures. Green fields with stacks of hay shaped like large loaves of bread. Mountains around three sides of this verdant valley, hills on the fourth. Myron studied it all as the train crossed the Gallatin River. He was so excited and happy that his thoughts went back to his Coe College days and how happy he'd been there.

"This place reminds me of the stadium at Coe College where I went to school back in Iowa. Used to run track there a little, when my knee didn't bother me. The mountains are like the bleachers, the valley floor's the running field. Running was fun. And these folks could sure use some purebred Hereford bulls to improve their cattle. Feels like the right place. Sure hope my fiancée likes it too."

The brakeman looked perplexed but nodded politely and then began to wave his lantern out the window to signal to the engineer to stop. "We're comin' to Patterson siding. Hope it goes good for you here in the valley. Some folks last, a lot don't."

As Myron unloaded his cattle into the corral at the rural siding, a man in a Model T Ford drove up and stopped. The driver, who had white hair and wrinkles in his face around his mustache, appeared to be in his seventies. He came to the corral and said, "You must be Myron Beatty. I'm Dan Plowman. My wife and I figured you might get here today. She's home, cooking up a big dinner in case you came." He put his hand between the planks of the corral fence. Myron shook it vigorously.

"It's awful nice of you to come, Mr. Plowman. I wasn't sure just how to get to your place." Myron beamed at his good luck to have been met by the man whose farm he was buying.

"Right up the road that way." Daniel Plowman pointed straight south, toward the mountains. "I've sold all my cattle, so we can trail yours up there right now, if you're ready."

The cattle were eager to get out of the confines of the corral. Myron herded them toward the road, where Mr. Plowman had parked his car and stood beside it to turn them south. Myron came behind, riding one of the work horses and leading the other. Mr. Plowman expertly eased his car through the walking animals and used it to block each open gate and side road when the cattle passed. When they finally reached a lane that intersected the main road near the mouth of a mountain canyon, he parked across the road and forced the animals to turn east, toward a bridge over a fast-flowing creek.

The cattle were afraid to step on the bridge at first, but finally, after many shouts by Myron and Mr. Plowman, one cow and her calf skittered across. The rest followed, and Myron led the horses across behind them. By then, Mr. Plowman had driven across, circled around ahead of the animals, and was herding them into a pasture behind a log barn.

"Well, you're here all safe and sound. Bet you're glad the trip's over. Come on in, an' meet the missus." He started toward a log cabin that sat on a smooth terrace above the creek and beckoned for Myron to follow.

Small hayfield in mountain valley on farm in
Cottonwood Canyon owned by Myron Beatty,
1925–1930

Myron lingered for a few moments to take in the surroundings. To
the southeast, an open field with two stacks of hay in it extended to
the base of a mountain slope about a half mile away. The mountain
crest sloped downward all along the east side of the ranch. Three of
his cows were walking toward the top of the slope, exploring the
limits of their new domain. He imagined how far they might go if
they got out of the pasture. *Sure hope Mr. Plowman has good fences.*

West of the buildings, the creek sluiced and churned through
its bed of large rocks as it descended to the northwest, creating a
constant babble of sound. Across the creek, a long, narrow field with
another haystack occupied the space between the creek and the road
at the end of the lane. Beyond them, another mountain rose to the
west. It looked beautiful and exotic—nothing like the flat expanses
of Iowa. He inhaled the aroma of pine drifting down the valley from
the mountains to the south. *What a great place to live,* he thought. He
rushed in to meet Mrs. Plowman, eat a hearty dinner, and set the
date to compete the land purchase.

This Indenture, Made this 18 day of September A.D. in the year of our Lord one thousand nine hundred and 25 between Daniel H. Plowman and H. A. Plowman, husband and wife, Salesville, Gallatin County, Montana, the parties of the first part, and Myron W. Beatty, a single man of Bozeman, Montana the party of the second part; WITNESSETH, That the said parties of the first part in and for the consideration of Twenty Five Hundred ($2500.00) Dollars in hand paid, the receipt whereof is hereby acknowledged, have GRANTED, BARGAINED AND SOLD and by these presents do hereby GRANT, BARGAIN, AND SELL, CONVEY AND CONFIRM unto the said party of the second part, and to his heirs and assigns, forever, the following described real estate, situate in the County of Gallatin, in the state of Montana, to wit: The South Half (S1/2) of the Southwest Quarter (SW1/4) and the West half (W1/2) of the Southeast Quarter (SE1/4) of Section Twenty-Two (22), and the Northwest Quarter (NW1/4) of Northwest Quarter (NW1/4) of Section Twenty-Seven, all in Township three (3) South of Range Five (5) East of Montana Meridian, Montana together with all the tenements, hereditaments, appurtenances, water rights, water ditches to the same belonging and all estate title, interest claim and demand of the said party of the first part therein. TO HAVE AND TO HOLD the above described premises, with the appurtenances and privileges unto the said party of second part, and to his heirs and assigns forever ...

Daniel H. Plowman, H. A. Plowman

—Deed filed at the Gallatin County Courthouse,
Montana

The fall days flew by for Myron. He moved his machinery and supplies from the rail car to his new ranch and simultaneously helped the Plowmans move to a little house on the west edge of Bozeman. He met the neighbors family by family, let them know he had purebred Herefords for sale, and arranged to buy twenty tons of hay to supplement that which Mr. Plowman had sold him with the ranch. Before the first snow fell, he'd weaned the calves, inspected and fixed all the fences, cut enough firewood for the winter, and repaired the chinking between the logs of the house. He also bought a flock of chickens and a milk cow.

By the second of December, it had snowed several times. Since he knew he might not return that day, Myron arranged for Jesse Bradley, his neighbor down the valley, to feed the cattle and chickens, gather the eggs, and milk the cow. Then he did chores extra early and drove his Model T to Bozeman, allowing some extra time because of the snow on the road. At the Presbyterian church, he made sure that all of his prior arrangements were confirmed. Then he drove to the north edge of town and paced back and forth at the train station for a half hour before the North Coast Limited arrived from the east. It was a momentous day. Mary would be on the train, and they would be married as soon as she arrived.

As the train coasted into the station, she was at the window, waving. He saw her and waved back, then scurried to a spot right beside the Pullman attendant as soon as the train stopped. She looked radiant but a little tired from the three-day journey as she stepped down from the rail car. After a hearty embrace and a long kiss, they retrieved her bags and drove the Model T sedan straight to the courthouse. A few minutes later, Mary held the marriage license tightly while Myron drove to the Presbyterian church in the heart of downtown Bozeman.

As they went up the side steps, Mary said, "Myron, I'd like to change into my wedding dress before we do the ceremony."

"You look beautiful just as you are, but I'm sure there's a room in the church where you can change."

Two women were standing beside the pastor's study as they came in. One stepped forward, smiling confidently. "Hello, and welcome. You must be the bride and groom. I'm Lena Conkling, and Reverend

Klemme has asked Mrs. Welch and me to be witnesses to your marriage." Both exuded the self-confidence of middle-aged women married to successful men.

Myron responded to her welcome. "Hello. It's nice of you both to take time to help us out. I'm Myron Beatty, and this is my fiancée, Mary Pierce. She came from Vermont on the morning train, and she's wondering if there's a room where she could change into her wedding dress."

The two women looked at each other, then Mrs. Welch replied. "Certainly. There's the choir room right around the corner." Mrs. Welch put her hand on Mary's arm. "Just come with me, and I'll help you get ready." Mary handed the marriage license to Myron.

Myron knocked softly on the door marked PASTOR'S STUDY. The Reverend Klemme, a tall man, bald as a billiard ball, opened it. "Pastor Klemme, my fiancée has arrived from Vermont, and we're just about ready to get married. She and Mrs. Welch will be here in just a minute."

Pastor Klemme was used to dealing with nervous bridegrooms, so he got right to the point. "Come right in, Mr. Beatty. Do you have the marriage license?" Myron reached into the pocket of his suit and removed a long sheet of paper.

"The top part's all done. All you have to fill out is the bottom, below where it says Certificate of Marriage." He handed the sheet to Pastor Klemme, who scanned the top portion briefly and began to write in the spaces near the bottom.

When Mary and Mrs. Welch appeared, he stood up and said, "You must be Mary Pierce. It's a pleasure to meet you. We've all been anxious for you to arrive, especially Myron. And now you're here."

"It's a thrill to be here and to meet you, sir." Mary smiled at Myron as she spoke.

The ceremony was brief, simple, and, for Mary and Myron, memorable. Reverend Klemme spoke briefly about the attitudes that made for a happy and enduring marriage, then asked, "Mary, do you take this man to be your wedded husband, to have and to hold from this day forth, for better or for worse, in sickness and in health, till death do you part?"

Mary's soft "I do" carried an undercurrent of certainty that thrilled Myron through and through. He hoped his answer would sound equally certain. In a moment, they were man and wife, and they were signing the bottom of the marriage certificate.

> **Certificate of Marriage**
> **State of Montana,**
> **County of Gallatin**
>
> **I HEREBY CERTIFY, That on the 2nd day of December in the year of our Lord one thousand nine hundred and twenty five at Bozeman in the said county, I the undersigned, a Presbyterian Minister did join in the HOLY BONDS OF MATRIMONY, with their mutual consent, according to the laws of Montana, Myron W. Beatty of the County of Gallatin State of Montana and Mary P. Pierce of the State of Vermont**
>
> **Rev. H. G. Klemme**
> **516 So. Willson Ave. Bozeman**
> **In the Presence of Mrs. Leon D. Conkling, Mrs. Howard Welch, Witnesses**
>
> **Signed Myron W. Beatty, Groom, Mary P. Pierce, Bride**

As they walked out of the church arm in arm, Myron tucked the certificate into his coat pocket.

"Well, I planned for us stay here in Bozeman until tomorrow morning. The neighbors are going to look after things at the ranch for me."

"I've been looking forward to seeing this cabin in the mountains for so long, I'm ready to go there right now. All the things I brought with me are in the car. Do you need to buy some groceries while we're still in town?" Mary sounded so eager to see the ranch that Myron changed his mind instantly.

"All right. We'll go to Sawyer's store and get some groceries and then drive home." They drove east along Main Street, dodging a couple of trolley cars until they reached the principal grocery in town. After buying groceries and gasoline for the Model T, they headed south along snow-covered roads toward Cottonwood Canyon. There were about four inches on the ground in Bozeman, but by the time they reached the mouth of the canyon, there was a foot of snow on the road. Myron shifted to low gear and gave his full attention to keeping the Ford in the tracks he'd made coming out early in the morning.

Mary watched, fascinated, as the car chugged across the glistening white landscape set off by pine trees on the steep slopes. She recalled the letters that Myron had written and thought, *This country's so pretty, it's easy to see why Myron wrote me such glowing letters about it.*

When the car tracks they were following turned from the main road down a short lane toward the creek, she spotted the set of log buildings on the flat beyond it. "So this is where we'll live. It's absolutely beautiful. And this is the bluest sky I've ever seen."

Myron's full attention was devoted to guiding the car as it strained to get up the snowy slope beyond the bridge, so he didn't respond right away. When they were finally at the top, he looked across at his bride and said, "I'm so glad you think it's pretty, because I hope we can live here together for a long time." He paused and looked at the array of log buildings that were vividly outlined by the afternoon sun, and at the cattle lying down nearby and chewing their cuds or eating hay he'd spread on the snow that morning. "It's nothing fancy, but I own it and the livestock free and clear. Not like my father and mother, who've been struggling for the last eight years to pay off their land contract."

As she started toward the cabin through snow that came almost to the tops of her four-buckle overshoes, Mary said with a laugh, "Good thing I was raised on a farm in northern Vermont, where it snows a whole lot in the winter. Otherwise this would be a big shock."

While Myron drained the water from the radiator in the Model T, she carried her suitcases into the cabin, lit a fire in the stove, and looked around. It was small but solid. With a fire in the stove, it would soon be cozy. Her new and exotic adventures had started. Who knew what those adventures might be? But whatever they would be, she was ready.

Chapter 34
Life in the Mountains

As December morphed into January, then February and March, the newlyweds set about building a life together. Myron got up at about 5:00 AM, even though sunlight didn't arrive in their narrow canyon until 7:00 or 8:00. He built a fire in the cookstove, then went outside to feed hay to his Herefords, milk the mixed-breed cow, and bring the brimming pail into the cabin to sit by the cabin door while the cream rose.

Mary was up and busy before Myron finished his outside chores. She lit a fire in the stove that heated the living room and bedroom, put oatmeal on to cook, and set two places at the table beside the south window with a view of the white bulk of the mountain and its protruding green trees. Then she added wood to the fire that Myron had started in the cookstove, put the cast-iron skillet on the left front corner, directly over the firebox, sliced bread from the loaf she'd baked the day before, and dropped a dollop of bacon grease into the skillet to fry the eggs in.

In the intervals when their work was done, Myron introduced Mary to the neighbors: the Jesse Bradleys who lived just down the canyon, the Frank Doneys who lived a mile or so farther to the east beyond the mouth of the canyon, the Harold Mickelberrys who lived northwest along Cottonwood Creek, the Seymour Kents who lived a little farther down the creek, and the Arch Plums who lived a mile or so up the canyon at the end of the road.

Then there was the most intriguing neighbor of all, "Daddy Van" VanAusdale and his quiet, friendly wife. Daddy Van was an old, stove-up cowboy who had settled down to a quiet life in a log cabin on a rocky tract of land along Cottonwood Creek after many years of riding, roping, and trailing longhorn cattle from Texas to Montana. He smoked a pipe every waking minute and looked at the world through rheumy, red-rimmed blue eyes that were much the worse for wear from their many years of being wreathed in tobacco smoke. The many years he had slept on the ground had given him rheumatism, so Daddy Van spent most of his days sitting. And if there was a visitor who would listen, he told stories of his early life along the cattle trails, with marauding Indians, harrowing stampedes, violent thunderstorms, mean horses, and demanding trail bosses as the feature attractions. He rarely spoke of the days of dusty boredom between those dangerous episodes, even though they probably occupied the vast majority of his time as a cowboy.

Myron and Mary were equally intrigued by Arch Plum, their neighbor up the creek. Arch was a transplanted Kentucky hillbilly who owned a few acres of land as far from civilization as he could get. He, his wife, and a whole flock of kids lived at the end of the road with their backs to the mountains. They existed hand-to-mouth from the garden they raised, the cow they milked, the deer Arch shot whenever the opportunity presented itself, the meager cash he earned from the timber he cut and sold, and the occasional work he did for neighbors at harvest time. There were rumors that he made and sold bootleg whiskey, but none of the neighbors were ever quite sure.

The members of this little community depended on each other for help in emergencies, for sociability, and for the shared information that flowed from farm to farm as neighbor visited neighbor. Their contacts with the rest of the world consisted of occasional visits to Bozeman and whatever the mailman who drove Rural Route 2 delivered to their mailboxes—nothing more. And in winter, the mailman couldn't always make his rounds, even when he left his car at home and drove a team of horses and bobsled over the drifted roads.

Mary's training as a nurse made her a welcome addition to the community. She would be summoned from time to time by one neighbor or another to help with delivery of a baby, repair of a wound from an accident, or the occasional serious respiratory illness that had laid someone low. Most of what she could do was offer comforting words and lead the family in simple actions to ensure sanitary conditions, good nutrition, and rest for the ailing or injured neighbor. But the fact that this new neighbor had been trained in a hospital and was a registered nurse gave her both respect and authority in her role as caregiver. News of her ability and her training spread by word of mouth, and she was asked to help families in trouble with increasing frequency. Often she returned at the end of a stint of nursing happy that her patient had recovered, but sometimes she returned mourning the loss of a neighbor and new friend.

After a year and a half of married life, Mary found herself pregnant. Her medical training led her to visit Dr. Foster in Bozeman as her pregnancy progressed. Dr. Foster's advice, after he learned where Mary and her husband lived and calculating that the baby would arrive in mid-March, was for her to come to Bozeman before her labor began, so she would be certain to be at the hospital and not stuck in a snowdrift when the critical moment arrived.

As the time for the baby's arrival approached, Myron and Mary, who had been snowbound for a couple of weeks, picked a day when the sun had softened the snowdrifts and started for Bozeman in the Model T. They were able to follow the tracks made by teams of horses pulling bobsleds loaded with hay along the road, until they came to a steep hill just beyond the mouth of the canyon. The Model T just couldn't overcome the deep snowdrifts and steep upgrade. They were stranded.

While Mary waited in the car, Myron hiked over the hill to the Doney farm and explained his predicament. Frank Doney quickly unhitched the team of horses from the bobsled he was using to haul hay, hooked a log chain to the doubletree, and followed Myron up the drifted road to the stuck Model T. With the team pulling on the front bumper and the Model T doing its best, they bobbed and bounced over and through the snowdrifts to the hilltop. It would be downhill from there to Bozeman; Myron thanked Frank Doney for his help, and he and Mary set out again on the snowy and drifted road.

After they'd gone about a mile, they were able to follow the set of car tracks that Frank Doney had made a few days earlier and arrived at the modest home of their friends the MacDonalds in an hour. Myron returned home, took care of the livestock, and then drove a team and bobsled to his neighbor Frank Doney's place every day and telephoned Mary at the MacDonalds'. Mary stayed with them three days until her labor pains started, and Howard MacDonald drove her to the hospital.

After a long labor, a dark-haired baby boy arrived on March 13. Myron had come to Bozeman, whenever he could get through the snowy road, to keep in touch with Mary, but on the early morning when his son arrived, he was once again snowbound in Cottonwood Canyon. He got to Bozeman and learned the news two days later, after spending nearly all day shoveling drifted snow and enlisting the help of Jesse Bradley and his team of horses to pull the Model T through the worst drifts. It was a week before he felt confident that the road was passable enough to bring his wife and newborn son home to the log cabin.

As time passed, Myron and Mary became more and more a part of the Cottonwood Canyon community. But they had a problem. The farm that Myron had bought could not produce enough feed and forage for his Herefords. The need to buy hay and haul it as much as three miles drained his pocketbook and burdened his days. He began to keep his ears and eyes open for a more productive farm. But he didn't want to borrow a lot of money, as his father had done, to get one.

Chapter 35
Losing Out

On a crisp day at the beginning of winter in 1928, Myron parked
the Model T in a log shed, drained the water from the radiator,
looked at the cattle lying down and chewing their cuds in the nearby
corral, and went into the cabin. All was quiet. He'd left Mary and
their eight-month-old son to visit the Jesse Bradleys when he went
to pick up the mail—the weekly *Bozeman Courier* newspaper and
a letter from his father. He slit the envelope carefully and began
to read the single page inside. His father's news seemed ordinary
enough at first, but then came the thunderbolt.

Valley Jct Nov 16–28

Dear Myron and all the family:

I have thought every day for a long time would
write you but put it off from day to day and have
started finally. We are having lots of rain since
Oct 15 and the fields are so wet cant get out with
a load of corn: we are getting along slowly: We
have the best yield and quality we have ever raised:
will yield at 60 bu and had in 65a besides Albert
had 12a on the piece of timber ground we sold to

Conrad Johnson: it is making 90 bu. Corn is hard
and dry and lots of new corn is being shelled and
sold at about 70 cts: There is no old corn in the
cribs and I think it will bring a fair price. We have
finally lost the farm after paying the amount on the
enclosed slip. [$29,421.90 on a $36,000 contract
plus $4,552.14 interest] Kratzer deceaved me as he
told me not to worry as he would not sell without
getting a good amount for us and then came back
and took the bottom price: for land values are surely
at the bottom: lot selling at 100 to 125 per a. Jess
Compton offered 36 dollars an a more 18 months
ago than now. He offered 175 per a then and 139
now: He is in debt on the farm as much as we were
and is spending 1000.00 on the barns now.... I don't
know what we will do: Think we will move to Valley
[Junction]: It is a tragidy for old people to get out
with practicaly nothing. Alberts have not found a
farm yet and there are not many that are any good.
Farm rents have fallen and are mostly from 10 to 12
per a cash

Love to you and all, Your Father
Walker Beatty

When Myron finished reading, he pulled the scrap of worn cloth
that served as a handkerchief out of his overalls and wiped his eyes.
Then he folded the letter and carefully put it back into the envelope.
He knew it was one he'd want to share with Mary and then keep.
Maybe he'd even give it to his son someday far in the future, after
the baby grew to be a man and could deal with sad messages. He
pondered what to put into the letter that he knew he'd write back
to his parents in a day or two, after he could better organize his
thoughts.

Then he sharpened his ax and walked up the hill to cut trees that
he'd sell to get money to buy hay. Come what may, he and his wife
were not going to lose their farm or their Herefords.

His father's next letter came more than four years later, after Myron and Mary had moved twelve miles from Cottonwood Canyon to a farm with better soil about eight miles west of Bozeman.

Des Moines IA 1-20-32

Dear Myron and all the family,

After a long time will write you a few lines: I have almost quit writing letters. Are having very warm for January. Mercury rose to 50. I notice by papers that you have it mild in the west. it is needed here for there are so many out of work. I havent been out to Alberts this winter for I am staying in close and their house is cold. he is getting along fairly well but it is a hard row to hoe. Business is not picking up any here and doesn't look bright for the future. I see by the paper they are forclosing on the land of Billy Newman he bought all of the land south of the R.R at $200. per acre and has lost all.

Myron put the letter beside the one he'd gotten more than four years earlier. He sensed defeat and impending death in his father's words and decided to sit down in the battered rocking chair he'd brought from Iowa before he pumped water for the cattle.

As he looked out the window across his own snowy and mortgaged acres, toward the Spanish Peaks, stories he'd heard from his grandfather David floated through his mind like the mist that floated off Dry Creek on cold mornings. Stories about land. About his great-great-grandfather Thomas Beaty, who came to America for it in the 1700s. About how he got land and then almost lost it. About Thomas's son John and his family moving west across Ohio for better land on the frontier. About David's own life: how he'd sailed around the Horn to California as a forty-niner, gotten smallpox, and come home with his skin scarred for life. Rumors that David had once owned four big farms but had been reduced to poverty by some immense tragedy. Bits and pieces of his heritage. Things he hadn't thought about in years.

Those stories he'd heard from his grandfather merged with his own memories and worries—of how hard he'd worked to help his father try to pay that land contract to Mr. Kratzer, of how he and Mary were struggling to pay the interest on the mortgage Nick Aajker held on their land and not have it foreclosed as had happened to his father and mother. Things he'd tried to put behind him by moving west to Montana. It was strange how sad and foreboding news from someone he loved triggered deep memories.

The cows and calves had been bawling and milling around the empty water tubs for most of the afternoon when Myron finally walked to the pump and began the heavy pulling on its handle that lifted water ninety feet to the thirsty herd. When he finished an hour later, his arms and shoulders aching, the sun was dipping behind the wooded sides of Pine Butte four miles to the west, but the family stories were still running through his head. He knew deep in his bones that come what may, he was going to hang onto his land.

Chapter 36
The Great Depression

The spring weather of 1933 was ominously dry, with just enough rain to germinate the wheat and let the alfalfa green up before the water was turned into the Farmers Canal. As soon as the canal filled, Myron and the other farmers it served began to irrigate everything—pastures, hayfields, gardens, and grain. They knew that water would soon be in short supply, because the snow pack in the mountains that fed the river and the canal was way below normal.

In late June, the court-appointed water commissioner cut back the water flow in the canal to just enough to meet the needs of those lucky and relatively well-off farmers who owned early water rights. Everyone else waited for their crops to begin to wither and compound the austerity that they were experiencing from the Great Depression.

House on Myron and Mary Beatty's farm near
Bozeman, Montana, circa 1935

Myron knew that his crops would never survive without more water,
and he was determined to save them. So he asked his neighbors and
the ditch rider who supervised the canal if they knew of anyone
with old water rights who would rent the use of their water at night.
He knew that it would be brutally hard, but he'd irrigate all night
using a flashlight if it would save his crops and his farm. Finally he
heard of a possibility and set out in the Model T on a forty-mile
trip to the far end of the valley to negotiate. He left Mary at home
to pick raspberries and care for their five-year-old son, who just that
morning had begun to throw up his food and run a fever.

As the morning progressed, Mary took her son's temperature
every couple of hours and became alarmed when it climbed quickly
past 103. She phoned the office of Dr. Heetderks and spoke first to
a nurse, then to Dr. Heetderks himself.

"Hello, Doctor Heetderks. This is Mary Beatty, and I'm calling
because my son is getting sicker by the minute." Then she listened to
the doctor's questions.

"He started getting sick early this morning and began throwing
up. I'm a registered nurse, so I took his temperature. It was 99.5
when I first took it. Now it's 103.5. When I felt his abdomen, it was
inflamed and real tender."

"Can you bring him to my office right away?"

"I'm sorry, doctor, but my husband is gone all day, trying to rent some old water to save our grain crop. So we're stranded until he gets back."

"Don't worry. I'll call my wife, and we'll drive right out to take a look. How do we get there?"

Mary described where they lived, and later she began to scan the road for a car. In about a half hour, the doctor and his wife arrived. After a few more questions and a brief examination, Dr. Heetderks said, "I think it's his appendix. We've got to get him to the hospital and operate as fast as we can. Leave a note for your husband, and get ready to go."

In less than an hour, the boy was in the operating room, where strangers strapped his arms and legs to the operating table and put a mask that spewed a noxious-smelling gas over his face, and he passed from terror into unconsciousness.

When he woke up, he was in a hospital bed with a nurse standing on one side of it and his mother on the other. His father arrived in a little while, but he didn't stay long. Of course his mother stayed by his side, and his father came to the hospital for a few minutes every day. When the boy asked, his mother said that his father had to return home and do everything at the farm, including irrigating all night long, then milking the cows, feeding the chickens, and gathering the eggs before he could make himself a meal and fall into bed.

After a week of brutal work, Myron's opportunity to rent the irrigating water at night ran out, but he'd saved most of his grain crop, and his son was making slow but steady progress toward recovery.

It was a grateful but somber couple who climbed into the Model T with their son for the trip from the hospital to home, ten days after the emergency appendectomy had saved the boy's life. Their only child was alive and getting stronger, even though a tube was still draining pus from his abdomen. And they had some prospects for a grain crop, but they had no idea how they'd pay the hospital and doctor's bills, with the abysmal prices for grain and livestock they saw in prospect. And then there was the mortgage.

As soon as they were home, Mary and Myron began picking and selling raspberries from the large planting in their garden. Neighbors came to pick for a share of the crop. When the harvest was over three weeks later, they'd netted forty-one dollars and eaten a lot of raspberry pies. They put the money toward interest on the mortgage. Dr. Heetderks said that there was no hurry at all about paying his bill, and the hospital gave the Beattys time to pay off what they were owed.

When grain harvest time arrived, Myron joined a round-robin threshing team of neighbors who worked with the owners of a steam engine and grain separator as it went from farm to farm. Myron worked for days, getting the grain bins ready for the harvest. He and Mary killed, cleaned, and cut up fifteen year-old hens that Mary would stew for chicken and dumplings to feed the threshing crew. She enlisted the help of two neighbor women to help her on threshing day. Their son, who still had a tube draining pus out of his abdomen, was admonished to keep out of everyone's way and not cause any trouble.

* * *

Early on a hot September morning, the boy heard the chuff-chuff-chuffing of the approaching steam engine and stood in the road at the top of the hill that divided the farm into a high, nearly level terrace and a lower gravelly flood plain along Dry Creek. He could see the huge, black engine and the grain separator it was pulling coming toward him along the road, and he expected it to slow down or puff harder as it climbed the hill to the farmstead. But the black giant kept its slow, steady pace all the way to the top.

The boy retreated to the dry grass of the front lawn and watched as the behemoth made a wide turn and clattered through their farmyard toward the edge of the grain field. Then he sneaked out where he could see the two men on the engine get off and dig shallow trenches for the wheels of the grain separator and pull the big, metal contraption forward into them. He stood transfixed as the operator unhooked the engine from the separator, turned the black behemoth around, and backed it away from the separator while his partner unrolled a long, heavy belt. The man on the ground with the belt climbed on the wheel of the grain separator and lifted one end of the belt over a wide pulley near the front of the machine. The man on the steam engine climbed down, picked up the other end of the heavy belt, and climbed slowly up beside the huge flywheel that protruded from the side of the engine's boiler about eight feet off the ground.

He strained as he slowly slipped the belt over the flywheel. When he felt that it was properly centered, he climbed back down to the controls and slowly backed the engine to tighten the belt until it hung snugly between the engine and the separator. Then he pulled a lever that started the big flywheel rotating very slowly. He and his partner squinted from several angles to see if the belt was centered on the two pulleys on which it was rotating, decided that things were not quite in line, and moved the engine forward and then back until they were satisfied with the alignment.

By then, several neighbors with wagons and several men that Myron had hired as field pitchers had arrived and were busy loading bundles of the shocked grain onto the wagons. A neighbor called Grandpa Richardson had also arrived with the water wagon that served the steam engine. The boy gaped at its cylindrical stave tank, from which water seeped along the joints. Grandpa Richardson pulled the wagon alongside the steam engine, draped a hose between the wagon and a large metal water barrel on the back platform of the engine, climbed atop the round water wagon, and began to pull a long, wooden lever back and forth to pump water from his wagon into the reservoir on the engine. The engine operator spoke to Grandpa Richardson, who took the reins of his horses and drove away from the engine, then got off and held his horses by the bridle. The engine operator pulled a cord, and an ear-splitting whistle signaled that all was in readiness to start threshing.

As the first wagon loaded high with bundles of wheat was driven alongside the rumbling and clattering grain separator, the engine operator slowly increased the speed of the flywheel, and the separator responded by rotating, clanking, and clattering faster and faster. The man atop the wagonload of bundles made sure that his team was not alarmed by standing next to the noisy apparatus, looped the reins tightly around the notched two-by-four board that protruded above the load, picked up his fork, and began to throw bundles onto the long, open-topped conveyor at the front of the grain separator. He watched the moving crossbars that rotated on its flat floor carry the bundles up and into the yawning maw of the machine, heard the deep-throated hum as the spinning cylinder below caught the bundles, knocked the grain from the straw, and sent the two components on their separate paths. He began to pitch bundles from his load even faster, and he was joined by another man with a loaded wagon, who parked on the other side of the separator and began to throw bundles from his load onto the conveyor. The engine's steady chuff-chuff-chuffing deepened a little in pitch but didn't slow down.

An amber arc of straw and dust began to shoot from the long pipe at the rear of the separator and settle into a tiny, conical pile about fifty feet away. Grain began to trickle from a small chute high on the side of the separator into a wood-sided wagon that Myron had parked below it. Grandpa Richardson drove his water wagon alongside the steam engine again and finished filling the water reservoir. The engine operator shoveled coal into the firebox. Everything chugged, shook, rotated, or blew straw and dust. Threshing was under way. The boy was fascinated by the organized bustle and noise of it all. But he remembered his parents' stern admonition and watched from a distance.

Exactly at noon, the engine man looked at the watch in the pocket of his bib overalls and blew a piercing blast on the engine's whistle. Then he pulled a lever that turned off the power to the big flywheel that powered the threshing machine, and it rattled to a stop. Everyone changed what they were doing, and the boy retreated to the yard beside the house. The men with horses unhooked them from their wagons and headed for the barnyard. The men who didn't have horses to care for headed directly to the farmhouse, stopping outside to splash water from the enamel washbasin on their faces and hands, then wipe them on the grain-sack towels that Mary had hung on nails above the rough box that held the basin.

Then they trooped inside and attacked the bowls of potatoes and gravy, chicken and dumplings, and green beans, and slices of apple pie that Mary and her neighbor Lilly Bradley had rushed to the table. They filled all of the chairs and other, improvised seats in both the dining room and the kitchen. When the men who had to care for their horses before they ate arrived, they found the towels soggy and all of the places to eat in the house filled. So they heaped their plates with food, sat down on the dry grass in the shade of the house, and ate heartily.

As Mary and Lilly rushed about, collecting a heterogeneous array of plates and silverware, some men pulled sacks of Bull Durham tobacco and Rizla-X cigarette papers from their overalls, rolled rough cylinders of tobacco, licked the edges of the papers, stuck them to the dry edges, and pushed gently to seal the seams they'd created. After a match was passed from hand to hand, they smoked in silence. One nonconformist pulled out his pipe and lit it. The boy stood off to the side and watched in silence.

His father came to eat, sweating and red-faced, after everyone else had been fed. He'd been scurrying about, helping the teamsters find a place to tie their horses, forking hay to the twenty hungry animals, and straining on the handle of the pump for nearly half an hour to refill the water barrels they'd emptied. At five minutes to one, the engine man walked to his somnolent black engine with the lazy column of smoke wafting from the stack, shoveled in some coal, and, exactly at one o'clock, blew the whistle and engaged the engine's big flywheel that powered the threshing machine.

As Myron hurried to eat a little of the dinner on his plate, the teamsters had anticipated the engineer's signal, and some had already untied their teams and hooked them to loaded wagons and were ready to start pitching bundles into the threshing machine when it started to rumble and vibrate. Others were driving their horses back across the half-empty grain field to the partly loaded wagons they'd left for the noonday break. The men who pitched the grain bundles from the shocks of grain on the ground up to the wagons walked behind them.

One-armed Walter Jones was among them. The boy stood at the edge of the field and marveled at how Jones was able to control the pitchfork and lift a bundle of grain with only one arm. Jones managed to pitch as many bundles up to the waiting wagoneers as his two-handed compatriots, by wedging the end of the fork handle under his sternum, then guiding the fork with his one arm to spear a bundle of grain and toss it in an upward arc to the man waiting above.

By late afternoon, the wagon with last load of grain bundles clattered in from the very back of the farm. When its load had been threshed, the engine operator and his partner shut down the grain separator, turned the big engine around, and backed it until the tongue of the grain separator could be hooked on, then chuffed slowly from the field into the farmyard and stopped.

The men driving wagons had all left before them. The boy stood beside the house and watched them heading up the road to the next farm on the threshing route to reload their wagons and be ready when the engine and grain separator arrived.

Myron and the engine operator conferred briefly, then Myron wrote a check to pay the threshing fee. It was among the numerous checks, most very small, that he'd written that afternoon to pay the day laborers who had worked in the field, pitching bundles onto the wagons. He was glad that the bank had reopened after the New Deal's bank holiday earlier in the year had tied up the modest sum he had in his checking account. When the last of the threshing crew had gone, he and Mary did the minimum necessary to care for their animals and fell into bed deeply tired but glad that their grain was not in the field and vulnerable to a hailstorm.

The prospects for selling that grain at anything above rock-bottom prices were dismal. Later in the fall, as they sat by the kerosene lamp, calculating how to allocate their meager funds among the mortgage holder, the hospital, the doctor, and property taxes, they decided that the interest on the mortgage had to come first, then the property taxes, a few dollars on the hospital bill, and the doctor's bill last. It was five years before they finished paying Dr. Heetderks all that they owed him for saving their son's life. He didn't seem to mind the delay. A few years later, he came to the farm again, this time to buy some Herefords to stock the farm he had just bought. That and other livestock sales gave Myron and Mary enough cash to replace the worn-out Model T Myron that had brought from Iowa with a used Model A Ford.

Even though he was a diehard Republican and criticized every New Deal initiative and program as wasteful, Myron realized by 1939 that he finally had enough assets to become a candidate for the New Deal's Federal Land Bank loan program to replace the private mortgage that had kept them in abject poverty for nine years. He swallowed his prejudice and asked for one. The new loan allowed them to pay off the expensive mortgage they had assumed when they bought the farm, and the lower interest payments left a few dollars for modest improvements.

House on Myron and Mary Beatty's farm near
Bozeman, Montana, circa 1960

First they scraped together enough money to paint the house, which had last been painted just after it was built in 1903. They also bought storm windows to cut down the winter winds that used to blow the curtains almost horizontal during a blizzard, even with the windows shut. The best place to be on windy winter days was still right beside the stove, but the storm windows provided at least psychological improvement, since the curtains didn't blow anymore.

In 1941, they bought their first radio, a small, battery-powered device that opened the world to them. On December 7, as they were sitting down to dinner after church, Myron turned on the radio, as had become his habit. Some routine news was interrupted by a breathless announcer who reported that the Japanese air force had attacked and devastated the American fleet at Pearl Harbor.

Harvested hayfield on farm Myron and Mary
Beatty purchased in 1930

After that, lots of things changed as the United States went to war and the Great Depression disappeared. Myron and Mary had survived, still owning their farm and still working hard side by side. During the war, they were able sell their Herefords for excellent prices and pay down the mortgage until, in 1947, they made the last payment.

When the hard-working couple drove home after making that last payment, Myron parked their nearly new Oldsmobile, looked at their farm with freshly painted buildings, newly installed electric poles and wires, and a barnyard full of cattle, and said, "Well, Mary, we've done it. These few good acres in the prettiest place in the country are ours, free and clear."

Author's Note

The events of this book are fictional but based on real people.

About the Author

Marvin T. Beatty has been studying soils and land since he was about eight years old. His earliest explorations were digging in the soils in road banks beside his parents' farm in Montana. He majored in soils at Montana State University and then analyzed and mapped soil patterns on landscapes for use by conservationists. While a faculty member of the University of Wisconsin, he carried out research on soils and interpreted soil maps for farmers, foresters, land-use planners, developers, homeowners, sanitarians, and engineers. During retirement, he volunteered his expertise as a soil scientist with archaeological teams that were searching in the West for the First Americans—the earliest inhabitants of the Americas.